OWEN LACH

Founder's Mercy

Book One of the Neskan Chronicles

First published by Jetspace Studio 2021

Copyright © 2021 by Owen Lach

All rights reserved. No part of this publication may be reproduced, stored or transmitted in any form or by any means, electronic, mechanical, photocopying, recording, scanning, or otherwise without written permission from the publisher. It is illegal to copy this book, post it to a website, or distribute it by any other means without permission.

This novel is entirely a work of fiction. The names, characters and incidents portrayed in it are the work of the author's imagination. Any resemblance to actual persons, living or dead, events or localities is entirely coincidental.

Owen Lach has no responsibility for the persistence or accuracy of URLs for external or third-party Internet Websites referred to in this publication and does not guarantee that any content on such Websites is, or will remain, accurate or appropriate.

First edition

ISBN: 979-8-9855022-1-3

Contents

Advance Praise

"A tightly-plotted queer sci-fi adventure with complex world building, urgent political themes, and nuanced characters that are easy to root for."
  –Ryan Douglass, New York Times bestselling author of *The Taking of Jake Livingston*

"Lach breathes some new life into the genre with a likable cast of characters, an engaging romance, and a well thought out premise."
  -Publisher's Weekly BookLife

"Owen Lach's debut YA sci-fi novel, Founder's Mercy, feels like a well-oiled machine. This is an unpretentiously accomplished debut and a cracking, fun read."
  -The Queer Review

Content Advisory

While this book is written for younger audiences, some content may still make readers uncomfortable. This includes: descriptions of violence and death, death and/or loss of loved ones/family members, scenes of betrayal and loss of trust, scenes where characters are held against their will.

Official Log of Captain Chander Sanyal

CSF Samuel Jennix, 27 June 2451

After a long, three-year punch through the wilds of voidspace, we've emerged into realspace at the beacon orbiting CST86318. The Colony Bureau named it Pamu. I'm not sure how much I like that name, but it is what it is. And now First Officer Marta Kanerva is reminding me that these logs are a historical record, so I've just committed Pamu's very first faux pas. At any rate, we've verified the tracking data of the Colony Fleet, and Navigation Officer Clarinda Osoria has launched the final Nav Beacon for the Fleet's tracking system. We have an estimated ninety-day deceleration cruise into the Pamu system ahead of us. So I've ordered Kanerva to begin reviving the rest of the crew members from cryo-sleep. On a more personal note, I've just seen the first telescope images of CST86318-B. No, Neska. I should say Neska. It's a lovely blue and green gem orbiting in the black. And it fills me with a strange sense of hope that I haven't felt since we first launched more than three years ago.

Chapter 1

The steam whistle finally blew out its shrill screech, marking the end of another long, boring laundry shift. That annoying sound couldn't have come soon enough for Adan. He'd just finished folding and stacking the last of the thin, starched bed sheets into the rolling hamper. His back hurt so much that his already heavy canvas apron felt like it was made of lead. And the foul-smelling fumes from the cleaning fluids had given him a pounding headache. For the past hour, he'd hungered to be back outside, drinking in the cool, damp air. More often than not, that last hour was always the toughest part of his shift.

Adan reached up to wipe the sweat from his forehead. Then he caught a glimpse of his reflection in the window of a nearby washer. He frowned. His shaggy, black hair was matted down to his skull with sweat. His normally warm, olive-brown skin looked ashy and dull. The whites of his dark brown eyes were more red than pale. And he was definitely still too skinny, even after a season of hauling around heavy bundles of linen.

"Get that cart over to the docks, Testa!"

Startled, Adan turned to see Ulla, his shift foreperson, looming over him like a storm cloud. He sighed and grabbed the edges of the hamper. "Right away, boss."

Ulla growled. "Don't 'right away' me, Testa. Just do it."

"Sure thing, boss."

Thankfully, Ulla didn't stick around to see his order carried out. Adan had never worked for someone as unpleasant as him before. Nothing seemed to bring his foreperson any joy, not even the end of the shift. If anything, that seemed to make Ulla even crankier. But Adan was stuck with him. He couldn't even go to the Labor Bureau and request a different work assignment. He was only sixteen and unqualified for anything beyond manual labor. Working the laundry plant was the best he would get compared to his few other options.

So Adan hustled the heavy cart along as fast as he could safely manage, cutting a path through the other workers as they left their own hampers behind. Only one or two had to angrily jump out of the way to keep from being rolled over. As Adan shoved his cart into the nearest open space, he heard the unmistakable sound of his best friend Bo calling out behind him.

"Incoming!"

Adan looked back to see Bo charging along behind his runaway cart with an almost feral grin. Even after a long day in the laundry, Bo somehow still managed to look good. His chunky black hair had a spring to it that refused to let it lay down no matter how much he sweated. His golden-brown skin never looked pale or dull. His deep brown eyes always sparkled. Add in the fact that Bo was taller and more muscular than Adan, and it was clear which of them was the pretty one. He shook his head and stepped back as Bo, carefully judging the basket's angle of approach, piloted his hamper into the space next to Adan's.

Adan heard the raspy growl of someone clearing their throat behind him. He turned to see Jurda, another first shift worker, spit a generous glob of mucus onto the floor. "Another hard day's work for the good of the Union, eh, Testa?" Jurda asked before lifting his heavy, sweat-stained apron over his head. The old citizen was a lifer. He'd been working in the Union laundry plant since before Adan had been born. But Jurda was ideally suited for it, with a strong back and an easy-going temperament. Sometimes the Union job office was a little too on the nose.

Adan smiled at the old-fashioned refrain. "All work is worthy, Jurda."

"Yeah," Jurda replied, nodding, "that's what they say. Big plans for yourself this evening?"

Adan pulled his own apron off, then shook his head. "Not really. Just house chores, and maybe a few games of Tik-Tix."

"Don't listen to him, Jurda," Bo advised. "Adan will be out dancing the night away like he does after every shift."

Jurda barked out a hearty laugh, which quickly turned into a heavy, wet, coughing fit. Bo frowned out of concern and glanced at his friend, but Adan shook his head. Jurda had already made it clear that his chronic lung condition was a forbidden topic of discussion. But it was also an excellent opportunity to break away.

"I'll see you tomorrow, Jurda," Adan called out, then grabbed Bo by the arm and pulled him away. Jurda, hunched

4

over with his hands on his knees, still managed a meager wave.

"That cough sounds really awful," Bo whispered as the pair walked past the stark rows of giant industrial washers and dryers toward the workers' locker rooms.

Adan sighed. "Yeah, it probably is, but he doesn't like people talking about it."

Stories like Jurda's were all too familiar among the workers. Despite the Bolvar Union's promise of guaranteed healthcare, a lifetime of working around the toxic chemicals in an industrial laundry had its price. Just like everything in Bolvar did. The Union provided its citizens with food, shelter, education, and protection. And all it asked for in return was a total devotion to the State.

Bo nodded. "That's alright. We've already got plenty to talk about."

Adan smiled. "We sure do. Like, the way you almost killed me with that damn cart of yours."

Bo scoffed, then put his arm around Adan's shoulder. "As if you were in any danger. That part is yet to come."

Adan forced himself to grin. He'd been putting on a brave face ever since Bo had proposed his big idea. Then he made a sour face and ducked out from under Bo's arm. "Right now, the only danger I'm in is passing out from your stench."

Bo frowned and lifted his arm to smell underneath it. Then he made the same sour face. "Damn, you're not kidding. Okay, first, showers. Then danger."

Adan's stomach growled loudly enough to be heard over the noise from the shift change. "First, showers, then food," Adan suggested with an embarrassed grin. Then he laughed.

Bo laughed along with him as the pair ducked into one

of the locker rooms. It was brighter than the dreary surroundings of the main plant, even if the muddy yellow wall tiles sucked most of the life from the room. The showers were a big perk of the work assignment. Few jobs had them available, but the laundry plant's chemicals made it a must. Since the group home where Adan and Bo lived had frequent and seemingly random water shutoffs, the end of their shift was sometimes their only chance to shower for the day.

The showers were also a good place to talk. The high humidity levels made it less likely that there'd be any listening devices. And the constant sound of running water would confuse any that might be there.

The two of them quickly found their lockers, stripped out of their coveralls and underclothes, then tossed the dirty uniforms and aprons into the laundry bin. After grabbing clean towels, they walked over to the crowded showers and found a pair of empty nozzles.

Adan slapped the push valve and stuck a hand under the stinging spray. But after a few moments, the water still only came out lukewarm.

"Boiler's down again," he muttered as he stepped into the water flow. It felt positively frigid on his overheated body, but at least it cooled him down right away.

Bo grimaced, then stepped under his own spraying nozzle. "Balda's great brassy ass! How can they run a damn laundry and have no hot water?"

Adan grinned. "The Union provides."

Bo rolled his eyes. "All hail the Union." He grabbed for the bar of soap perched on a nearby ledge and started lathering himself up. "So, we're still on for tonight, yeah? I'm sensing some uneasiness from you." Then he handed the soap to

6

Adan.

"I mean, I can't think of any way around it. So, yeah." Adan soaped himself up, too.

"Around what? We're just scouting tonight. That's no big deal."

"I know, but it puts us one step closer to the real thing. It's one thing to plan something like this. It's another to pull it off."

"You know why we're doing it, right? It's this or a lifetime of blissful servitude to the glorious Bolvar Union. You can't tell me you're okay with that. We'll be serving our five before we know it."

Their five. As in their five years of mandatory service in the Bolvar Union Defense Force, which every able-bodied Bolvaran served as soon as they turned eighteen. And it was less than two years away. Adan sighed, then forced himself to smile. "Yeah, I know. But what if we get caught?"

"We're not gonna get caught. I mean, we won't even be out after curfew. For all intents and purposes, we're not doing anything wrong."

Adan laughed and set the soap back on the ledge. "Intents and purposes? Are you a Magistrate now?" He pushed the shower valve to restart the water flow then rinsed himself off.

Of course, Bo was right. He was always right. Bo was the most cut out for service of the two. Adan wasn't sure he'd even survive one year in the Gray Coats, let alone five. Part of him suspected that was the real reason Bo had insisted on their joint escape plan. To protect his friend. But that was only paranoia. Just because Bo was more physically capable didn't mean he was any more cut out for service than Adan was. And the two of them had discussed their plan at length and worked out as many angles as they could think of. After all, they'd been at it for a year.

Adan finished rinsing himself off just as the water cut out again. He immediately started shivering. The icy water had done its part to cool him off a little too well. He reached for his towel and started drying himself off before he froze.

"So," Bo said as he reached for his towel, "we're good?

Adan nodded. "Yeah, we're good. Sorry."

Bo flashed him a sunny smile. "No worries, friend. Now, let's get dressed and get out of here."

The pair of them hustled back into the locker room to retrieve their clothes. For Adan, that included a pair of thick, dark, denim trousers and a sweater that one of his former housemates had knitted. On top of that, he wore an old Utility Bureau jacket that he'd had to patch up at the elbows. And he had his boots, of course. Since his feet had finally stopped growing, it was the first pair he had that he'd really been able to break in instead of bust through. Once he slipped them on, Adan stood back up and grabbed his jacket from the locker.

"You know," Adan said as he stuck an arm into a sleeve, "you're—"

A klaxon suddenly blared, and Adan froze. Unlike the shrieking steam whistle, this was a rarely used alarm. Adan hadn't heard it since they'd done drills back at the Instruction Center. And, unless it was another drill, it could only mean one thing. A flux storm was coming.

Everyone in the locker room stood there, dumbfounded, for a moment. Then their years of drilling kicked in, and their stillness quickly transitioned into smooth-flowing chaos.

Bo looked at Adan in a near panic. "Do you think that's real?" he called out, struggling to be heard above the commotion.

Adan shrugged his other arm into his jacket. "I don't know. Let's just get to the shelter. If this really is a flux storm, I don't wanna get fried."

"Yeah, yeah. You're right."

Adan grabbed Bo's jacket, handed it to him, and then grabbed his arm. "Come on."

Adan led his friend out to the corridor to join the flood of people hurrying off the plant floor. They had two minutes after the alarm started before the shelter doors were sealed. If you were caught outside the shelter after that, you took your chances. But no one ran, shouted, or shoved. Every one of them had been drilled and drilled on what to do in the event of a flux storm, a rare but dangerous fluctuation in the planet Neska's already strong magnetic field. Normally harmless to people, the field's strength was still troublesome for unshielded electronics and wireless transmitters. But, during a flux storm, the local disturbances in the Neskan magnetic field could be seriously harmful or even fatal. Or not. You never knew until it happened, and it was better to be safer than sorry, right?

There were flux shelters all over Bolvar. A big plant like the Union Laundry had two, each large enough to hold at least half the staff on duty. Adan and Bo were assigned to the Number Two shelter, so Adan directed his friend into the opening on the right side of the corridor. They filed in behind the people before them and took their seats on one of the long benches lining the chamber walls. Then a bell started clamoring. That was the final warning before the door closed. The door had to be closed and the chamber entirely sealed when the flux storm hit it. That was the only way to deal with magnetic radiation. It penetrated even the tiniest opening and, if it was a harmful level, everyone inside would feel it.

Adan felt the pressure change inside the shelter as the door swung closed. Then there was a dull, loud thud. The bell stopped ringing, and the lights all went out. After a moment, battery-powered emergency lights flickered on. Everyone sat calmly and quietly, controlling their breathing as best they could. The chambers weren't ventilated, so the air inside was all they had until the door opened again. Everyone had heard stories about shelter doors failing, turning the chambers into giant tombs. Adan knew that's what Bo was most worried about. He'd struggled with a fear of enclosed spaces for as long as they'd been friends. It was one of the few times Adan was the more confident of the two.

Bo's breathing was already swift and erratic, and there was no telling how long the flux storm would last. So, Adan reached over without looking and took his friend's hand. Bo immediately squeezed his grip, almost to the point where it hurt Adan's knuckles. But Bo's breathing slowed down and became more regular. And everyone sat there, in silence, waiting.

They were lucky to be in there at all. If you found yourself too far from a shelter during a warning or, worse, if there was no warning, you took your chances. Most of the time, there were no issues beyond damage to any poorly shielded electronics or unsecured magnetic metals. That was the thing with magnetism. Most of the time, it was harmless. Until it wasn't. But it was why things were the way they were on

Neska.

Stories of the First Explorers would have you believe that the tech they possessed was wondrous. At least some of them had to be true. After all, the First Explorers had journeyed all the way to Neska from a distant star. And Adan had taken the well-guarded tour of the Union's Old Tech Museum. It displayed recovered, nonfunctional items with lengthy, printed signs describing what those items had once done. But devices that literally took apart the tiniest pieces of matter and knitted them back together to turn one thing into another just didn't seem believable to Adan. They'd called that one a Printer. But Adan had also seen an actual printing press, a giant machine that didn't take anything apart or put it back together.

Bo's hand had grown uncomfortably warm, and Adan could feel his palm start to sweat. He kept holding on, though. That's what you did for your best friend, no matter how bothersome it got. It was strange, being irritated by holding Bo's hand. There was a time when Adan had longed for a chance at physical contact like that. But that was before they'd really grown close at all. Bo was like a brother to Adan now. And Bo would never be interested in anything more than that, anyhow.

The bell eventually sounded again, startling the quietly waiting crowd. Then the door unlocked with a loud clunk and began to swing open. Adan had no idea how long they'd been in there. Several minutes, at least. But it could've been longer. Time passed differently in a sealed space like the flux shelter, as if shutting the doors somehow blocked the proper flow of time, too. As the door slowly opened, Adan felt the incoming flood of cool, fresh air right away. He quietly chuckled at the sensation. Only spending time stuck in a flux shelter could make the laundry plant air seem fresh. Adan was glad they'd had time to shower before the storm alert. The person sitting to his left clearly hadn't.

Bo gave Adan's hand a final squeeze, then let go. "What's so funny?" he asked as he stood up.

Adan shook his head as he stood. "Nothing, just some stupid thoughts in my head. Come on, let's get out of here."

Since they were already dressed and ready, they could head straight for the exit back out onto the street. The talk Adan heard on the way out of the plant was that the flux storm had only been a minor one. At least in their district. The news broadcasts on the wireless the next day would praise the city's orderly response to the storm alarms. Sadly, there was one fatality, but it was due to negligence and not the storm itself. A citizen who'd been asleep when the alarm sounded tried to slip past the closing door of their shelter and got crushed. Thankfully, the citizens already inside that shelter were unharmed during the storm. More thankfully, the door still opened afterward. But Adan didn't want to imagine stepping over the dead citizen's mangled corpse to get out.

By the time Adan and Bo were outside, Bo seemed to have gotten his spirit back. He was smiling, which made Adan smile. The chilly autumn air was crisp and fresher than usual in the Lowers, the Bolvaran district that was home to the laundry plant and many other Union industrial facilities. Shutting the whole city down, even briefly, had given the night air a short reprieve from all the belching smokestacks.

Their walk took them up busy Bartok Street. It was the main road through the Lowers, so traffic was a mess.

Between shift changes and the flux alert, the streets were jammed with delivery vans, and the Union Transit trams were packed full. But Adan enjoyed the walk anyhow. The sidewalks were lined with licensed goods outlets, Guildhalls, and public houses where Bolvarans could gather for food and drink. Neither was usually very good, at least not in their district. But it was nice to come together with friends and neighbors for a little while anyway, swapping stories, singing songs, and catching up on the latest gossip. And the street was well lit, unlike some of the smaller roads and lanes in the district. So, it was crowded and lively, especially with all of Bolvar recently emerging from their storm shelters.

If you went far enough up Bartok, you'd reach the Public Square where Bartok crossed Daigur Avenue. The Square was closed for public festivals twice a year—in the summer on Landfall Day and in the winter on Founder's Day. Otherwise, it was a confusing confluence of tram tracks, traffic, and the giant bronze statue of Balda Tomari, the first Chairperson of the Bolvaran Union Committee. It was well known amongst citizens in the Lowers because some quirk of its orientation meant that Balda's rear end had been windblown shiny and smooth. It was rumored that a citizen could be blinded on particularly sunny days if they looked right into the glare of Balda's ass.

Adan's favorite part of the Square was the spectacular view he got of the grand government houses and stately mansions up the hill in Gallur Heights. The dark, snow-capped eastern peaks of the Osbaks rising in the distance perfectly framed the scene. Adan sometimes imagined what it would be like to live up there, where the air was always fresh and the views unobstructed. To never worry about the power going out or the water shutting off. To have someone making delicious meals for you every day and ensuring your clothes were always mended, clean, and pressed.

Most people, Adan included, just took it as a fact of life that the powerful and prestigious government officials, industry leaders, and Union Committee members were given better treatment than the average Bolvaran was. The Union may have promised everyone a place to live. But they never guaranteed that it would be nice. Most people thought the Union placed the Public Square where it was to offer that particular view. Some would say it was meant to remind the citizens in the Lowers about the rewards of hard work. But most people, like Adan, figured it was meant to remind citizens like him of his place.

As they approached the turnoff for the group home, Bo abruptly halted. "How about we stay out and get food somewhere? I'm not sure I feel like going home yet."

That was an excellent suggestion, even if it was out of the blue. "Sure, why not? Is everything alright?"

Bo nodded, then reached into his pocket and pulled out his old timepiece. He'd found it as a child, broken and discarded in the street. Then he spent literal years figuring out how it worked and how to get it working again. Adan had been seriously impressed with his dedication. "Sure, everything's fine. It's just, we've still got a few hours before our little project, and I'd like to stay out for a while."

Maybe Bo was still shaken up from the storm shelter. That would explain things. "I think Mother Agra is serving tonight," Adan shared.

Bo smiled and nodded. "Yeah, that's perfect! Let's go there."

Adan laughed and looked up at the street signs on the

corner to orient himself. Then Bo put a hand on Adan's shoulder and started to lead him back the way they'd come from. They only had to backtrack a couple blocks, then cut across Bartok and head down toward the river. Mother Agra's was a public house squeezed between an old warehouse and the hydroelectric plant at the Lower Falls. It was an odd location, off the more well-traveled paths, but it had an unbeatable view of the Daralsha River. And Mother Agra was one of the best cooks in the Lowers. She could work magic with leftovers and scraps, which was a good thing since that was what she usually ended up serving.

The pair of them wandered down the brick-paved laneway leading off Bartok, then crossed over Renming and continued until Adan spotted Mother Agra's. All the lights were on, and the front door was wide open, which meant she was serving. Best of all, there was no line to get it. The flux storm must've sent many people running home, cutting into the crowds that usually gathered there.

After climbing the front steps, Adan and Bo went inside. The main dining room was warm and homey. Its old-fashioned gas lamps cast a flickering, golden glow on the dozen or so tables and the diners sitting at them. Mother Agra was setting some mugs of beer on a table when she spotted Adan and Bo. The older citizen had aged to the point where it was near impossible to pin down how old she really was. Her long, patterned skirt and thick, cable knit sweater didn't offer any clues. Neither did her long, silver hair, artfully braided and bundled up under a red kerchief.

"Come on in, citizens," she called out, then waved at the empty tables, "and grab a seat anywhere you like."

"Thanks, Mother," Bo offered in reply. He looked toward

the table in the back with a window facing the river. "How's that, Adan?"

"That's perfect."

Adan slid between a pair of occupied tables and took one of the empty seats at the table Bo had chosen. The sun had already fallen well past the western Osbak peaks, blanketing the city in dusky rose shadow. But the lights from the hydroelectric plant shined brightly, dancing off the rough surface of the river as it gathered at the Lower Falls.

Mother Agra shuffled over to stand next to them. "Welcome again, citizens. I've got a lovely Marsh Pig Stew with roasted vegetables, dark bread, and beer."

Bo smiled and batted his long eyelashes at the older citizen. "Only beer? Got any bashki?"

The curtains of Mother Agra's wrinkles spread wide across her russet face as she smiled. Then she smacked him on the back of the head. "As if I'd serve bashki to a child! You'll be lucky if I don't bring you dishwater."

Bo bowed his head respectfully. "Sorry, Mother."

She shook her head, then turned to Adan and smiled. "Nice to see you as always, Adan."

"Thank you, Mother." Then his stomach growled loudly. "If that's the stew I smell, I can hardly wait."

She smiled even more broadly. "I'll bring you an extra-large helping." Then she looked back at Bo and scowled before wandering off toward the kitchen muttering about bashki and children.

Bo chuckled as soon as she was out of earshot. "I thought it was worth a try."

Adan shook his head but smiled. "You should've known better. She'll have us washing dishes if you're not careful.

Besides, if you really want to get your hands on some bashki, you just have to wait until tomorrow."

"That's true. Assuming everything goes according to plan."

"Assuming?"

Bo chuckled again. "I mean, of course, everything will go according to plan."

Adan still wasn't convinced. "Maybe we should go over the plan again. Starting with tonight."

Bo nodded. That was another reason the pair liked Mother Agra's. She had no love for the Union and made sure the wireless was always playing loudly. That, plus the loud conversations from the other diners, made it safer from listening devices and eavesdroppers than most public places they could go.

Later that night, Bo explained, they would meet up with Min Silta, a friend from his childhood that he'd recently reconnected with. Min had agreed to lend them their delivery van the following night. They would show the two where they parked it overnight and where they kept the keys. When they took it, it was important that Min wasn't directly involved. If Adan and Bo got caught with it, Min could claim that it had been stolen. As long as they returned it before dawn with a bashki barrel in the back, everything should be fine.

"They get a barrel?" Adan asked. "So, then how many do we need to get?"

"One for Min. Calin doesn't want one."

"Calin? Who's that?"

Bo sighed, frustrated at the interruption. "Calin Dambolen. She's the forger."

"Oh, yeah."

"So, one for Min and six for the Thatcher."

Thatcher, as in thatch rat. The notorious, six-legged vermin had once infested the thatched roofs of early Bolvaran houses before the days of the Union. They'd long ago migrated to the sewers and were a constant nuisance to any Bolvaran with a basement. But Bo wasn't referring to the small, scaly pests. He meant the person who smuggled Bolvarans past the wall. That was another condition of living in the Bolvaran Union. You could only leave with permission, which required an approved reason. Scouting for resources was the most common reason for leaving the city. And scouts were always accompanied by Gray Coats from the Defense Force to protect them from raiders who lived past the mountains. There was no way Bo and Adan could pass themselves off as scouts, and the whole reason they'd come up with their plan was to avoid their mandatory five years of service as Gray Coats in the first place.

Still, seven barrels was a lot for just the two of them. Bashki, the Bolvaran liquor distilled from sorghum, was stored in great, heavy barrels that needed at least two people to lift. They only had a short window to make their stop at the distillery, so they'd be cutting things close under even the best of circumstances.

Mother Agra soon reappeared with a tray in one hand. She scooped off the bowls of steaming stew and set them down on the table between Bo and Adan. Then she added a basket with rough, dark buns, a pair of spoons, and two mugs of beer.

"There you go, citizens," she said proudly.

"Thank you, Mother," Bo replied respectfully.

She glanced at him, then nodded. "Just so you're aware, we

won't be serving any food tomorrow during the Glories. But I'll have the beer taps open for anyone that wants to come by and listen on the wireless."

Adan picked up his spoon. "That's good to know." Then he dipped it into the stew and took a careful bite. It was so delicious his eyes nearly rolled back into his head. "Founder's grace."

Mother Agra smiled proudly, and the gas lamps caught the rosy glow in her cheeks. "I'll leave you both to eat." Then she turned to greet another set of newcomers that had just walked in.

Bo took a bite of his stew and closed his eyes with pleasure. Adan smiled and took another bite. It was basic fare, but it was warm and hearty in a way that suggested it was made with love. He got a chunk of marsh pig in his next bite and savored the way it almost melted on his tongue. Aside from several local varieties of fungi, marsh pig and ridge fowl were the primary protein sources in the Bolvar Valley. Once native to the marshes around the banks of the Daralsha, most of the marsh pigs in the city were now raised in giant Union facilities. They were easy to care for and grew fast, so their meat was an everyday staple at Bolvaran tables.

"See," Bo said between bites, "even Mother Agra is taking the night off of cooking for the Gories."

The Glories, or the Gories, as Bo put it, were the Duels of Glory. Those were heavily hyped, monthly arena contests where people convicted of crimes against the State were paired off to fight to the death for the right to have their citizenship restored. Civilized folks like Mother Agra usually referred to them as the Glories. Adan didn't know many civilized folks. Most of the people he knew called them

19

the Gories. But they were also the key to any chance of success with their plan. Most of the city shut down for the Gories, either to listen to them on the wireless or, if you were lucky enough to have tickets, actually watch them. That left Adan and Bo with a window of opportunity where the bashki distillery upriver from the Lowers would be almost totally unstaffed. There would be a minimal staff on hand to watch the place, but they would almost certainly be listening to the Gories on the wireless. Hopefully, that meant they wouldn't waste any time verifying the forged order forms Bo and Adan would present to them.

"Where are we supposed to be delivering all this bashki anyway?" Adan asked.

Bo smiled mischievously. "Here."

Adan nearly choked on the sip of beer he'd just taken. Then he laughed. "That's why you asked about the bashki before? You're such an ass."

Bo smiled and made a slight bow. "You've got to admit, it's a brilliant plan."

Adan didn't know if he'd use the word brilliant to describe it, but he was willing to admit that it was a pretty good plan. The forged papers meant that they even had a chance to talk their way out of trouble if they were stopped and questioned. A small chance. Maybe.

Once they'd loaded up the van, the pair would deliver six barrels to the Thatcher then return the van with the remaining barrel to Min before the clock struck thirteen. And after they brought the barrels to the Thatcher, they'd find out how long they had to prepare for their journey west.

"Okay," Adan said after he took the last swallow of his beer, "so, then tonight we just go see Min."

Bo nodded. "Yeah. They want us to wait until their partner is asleep. Their partner works an early shift, and they're usually asleep by ten."

Adan glanced over at the large clock hanging on the wall by the door. It was almost nine, so they had another hour before they had to be there. That was plenty of time for another beer if Mother Agra had enough. Adan was about to ask Bo if he wanted more when he caught some movement outside the open door. Several dark figures were striding up the front steps. Then Adan noticed the shape of their silhouettes.

"Bo," Adan murmured. "Clubbers."

Bo turned toward the door just as the black-uniformed group stepped inside, their ever-present clubs in their hands. Adan's heart sank as the possibility that they'd been snitched on came to mind. He shifted restlessly in his seat, but Bo turned to him and put a hand on his, then smiled and shook his head.

"Relax," he whispered.

Adan inhaled slowly, then nodded.

"Your attention, citizens," announced a large Clubber with an ochre complexion. They were muscular to the point of nearly bursting through their uniform. Probably the Squad Chief. There were four of them in total. So, not an entire squad, unless the others were waiting outside. "We're here for Luca Nellan. As long as Citizen Nellan comes along without any fuss, there won't be any trouble."

Adan, like the other diners, started looking nervously around the room. Whoever Nellan was, they were in for a world of trouble. If they were even there. Getting picked up the night before the Gories could only mean that the planners hoped to pad the bill.

21

The Clubbers stood uneasily, tightly gripping their long, thick clubs. Then one of them shifted slightly, and chaos broke loose. Someone on the other side of the dining room jumped up from their chair, violently knocking the table back and sending bowls and mugs crashing to the floor. Diners shouted and screamed as the runner–probably Citizen Nellan–lunged toward the door to the kitchen. But the Clubbers didn't give chase, standing firm where they were. Then Adan realized where the rest of the squad probably was. Sure enough, just as Nellan reached the kitchen door, it swung open to reveal the looming hulk of a hidden Clubber. Nellan quickly backpedaled but couldn't stop in time. The Clubber lashed out and smashed their club hard against the side of Nellan's head. They dropped almost immediately to the floor.

The Squad Chief let out a deep sigh and reached into their long black cloak to pull out a folded-up piece of paper. Then they walked over to the fallen runner, their heavy boots crunching on the shattered pieces of ceramic scattered on the floor. They looked at the paper, printed with a black and white photo of someone's face, then down at the citizen lying on the floor, then at the other Clubber, nodding. "Yes," Adan heard them say. "This is him."

The other Clubber nodded, then reached down and hauled Nellan to his feet by one of his arms. The Squad Chief grabbed Nellan's other arm, and the pair of them carried the unconscious citizen back to the front of the dining room. The Chief handed Nellan over to a squad member, then turned back to face the dining room again and sought out Mother Agra. "Our apologies for the mess, Mother." They sounded surprisingly sincere. Then they turned and followed the others out into the night.

Adan let out the breath he'd been holding. "Founder's mercy."

Then, just like that, everyone went back to talking and eating as if nothing had happened. The people who'd been sitting with Nellan knelt down to help Mother Agra clean up the mess near their table. Adan looked at Bo, who frowned and shook his head.

"See," Bo said quietly. "Nobody cares. It's like they're all marsh pigs floating in their damn river vats. As long as they get fed and entertained, the Union can do whatever it wants."

"I know," Adan replied.

"That's why we gotta get outta here, Adan. Seriously. Or we'll turn into one of them."

"I know."

Bo huffed, then shook his head again. "Come on. Let's get out of here. We've got an appointment to keep."

Official Log of Captain Chander Sanyal

CSF Samuel Jennix, 14 September 2451

The Jennix has completed its final deceleration burn and is now three days out from Neska. My compliments to Nav Officer Osoria on her flawless calculations. Planetary Science Officer Jun Zhao has been pouring over scans and data from the planet. Several of the satellite units in the Orbital Net have malfunctioned and are inoperable. But, we're still well within our mission tolerances.

Neska is a fascinating place. It's nearly identical to home in so many ways. Our former home, I mean. The planet's size and mass are within five percent of standard. A Neskan day is just over twenty-six hours long, and Neska orbits Pamu every 386 days. Even the climate and atmosphere are so close to optimal that they're far better than what we left behind. The only data point that significantly varies from baseline is the strength of Neska's magnetic field, which produces some spectacular auroras. It's too bad there's no land anywhere near the poles.

Chapter 2

Min lived on the edge of the Daralsha Flats district near the far side of the Lowers, but Adan and Bo still had plenty of time to get there. The arrest at Mother Agra's had left Adan pretty shaken up, and the public house had lost some of its homey charm for him. Not that there was much to be done about it, beyond what they were already doing. Citizen Nellan's fate was probably one of his own making. If you acted against the Union, then they reacted accordingly. Except it wasn't always certain when you were acting against the Union.

When he was still in school, Adan's least favorite subject was Citizenship. At the beginning of every lesson, the students were required to stand and recite the Oath of Loyalty. Then they spent the rest of the time reading directives from the Bolvaran Union Committee, listening to recordings or the occasional live broadcasts from the Committee Chairperson, or memorizing important Union directives. And, once per quarter, a Union Loyalty Officer would show up to test them on everything. If you failed the Officer's tests, you were held back from advancement and sent to remedial instruction. If you kept failing, eventually, you were sent away for Special Instruction. Adan had seen more than one of his classmates disappear after visits from the Loyalty Officer, with the only explanation being Special Instruction. Theoretically, you could return to General Instruction once you'd satisfied whatever requirements they had. But Adan had never known anyone to come back.

By some unspoken agreement, Adan and Bo stuck to the busier, better-lit streets as they made their way up to the tram. The crowds had thinned since they were last there. When Adan looked up, he saw why. Heavy clouds had gathered over the Valley while Adan and Bo were eating and would undoubtedly be dumping their rainfall onto the city at some point soon. It may have been normal autumn rain, or the flux storm may have stirred things up enough to bring about the rainfall. Either way, Adan assumed that he and Bo would be getting wet before they made it back home.

They walked to the first tram stop and waited. A small group was gathered there, which meant the last tram must've left a while ago. That was a good sign. Soon enough, Adan heard the clanging from the conductor's bell and turned to see the old coach rambling up the rails. Like all the trams on the Bartok Line, it was painted a dull, light green on the outside. But it had the same unpainted interior and deep red canvas seating as the other lines in the Valley. Union tram cars were large enough to hold fifty seated passengers, with room for at least that many standing. The late hour and the looming weather meant there was still plenty of room for Adan and Bo to grab seats next to each other when they boarded.

"Looks like it's gonna rain," Bo commented once the tram got underway.

"Yeah, I noticed. I wish I'd brought a hat."

Bo chuckled. "Me, too. Just so you know, when we get there, Min is a little strange."

"Strange, how?"

Bo shrugged. "They just have this way about them, I guess. You'll see. But they're nice enough, and they've got no problem helping us out."

Adan nodded, unsure of what to make of Bo's warning. He glanced out the window as they approached the next stop and saw the first few droplets of rain already falling. The people walking by picked up their pace, hurrying to get wherever they were headed before the coming deluge.

Then Adan spotted a pair of Clubbers across the street hassling a citizen who'd been pasting posters onto some nearby buildings. Adan couldn't see what the posters said, but it must've been something the Clubbers didn't like. One of the Clubbers grabbed the stack of posters from the citizen's hand and tossed them down onto the sidewalk while the other shoved the citizen against the wall.

Adan instinctively turned. Everyone knew it wasn't a good idea to get a Clubber's attention when they started getting aggressive. Which was most of the time, in Adan's experience. Clubbers were officially Constables of the Bolvaran State Security Force, but nobody Adan knew ever called them that. Maybe the elites up in Gallur Heights did. Adan couldn't imagine anyone from Gallur falling victim to a Clubber's angry truncheon. The State Security Force wasn't the worst thing the Union could throw at you, either. Just the most visible.

The rain was still sprinkling down when they got off at the Delan stop. There was no sign announcing the boundary between the Lowers and the Flats. But most people more or less understood Delan Street to be where one stopped, and the other began. Adan had noticed the subtle shift in the district's character as they left Mother Agra's behind, too. There were more residential buildings interspersed with the warehouses and factories. The Union Safety and Sanitation Bureau building that served the two districts sat heavily on the corner of Bartok and Delan. It was an imposing, almost brutal structure like most official Union buildings were. The State couldn't be bothered with any meaningless frills in their designs. Unless you were up in Gallur, of course.

Then Adan spotted a few of the posters that citizen from earlier had been putting up. He glanced over his shoulder to see if any Clubbers were about, then walked over to read them.

The State is a Lie, read the headline printed across the top in large, boxy letters. Beneath that was a block print showing a pod of marsh pigs floating in a bog. Adan wondered who'd originally drawn it. It was good work. *Citizens are only Fuel for the State Machine*, continued the message underneath the artwork. *Bring Down the State! Bring Freedom to Bolvar!* At the bottom of the poster was the distinctive dagger and spanner logo of the Motari, the troublesome Bolvaran underground resistance. They'd named their group after Samu Motar, the first Bolvaran publicly executed for treason.

"That's the poster?" Bo wondered as he looked over Adan's shoulder. "No wonder those Clubbers were upset."

Adan nodded. "Yeah, only the Motari would be bold

28

enough to just paste these up out in the open like that."

"I wonder if this is why that citizen got snatched back at Mother Agra's, too," Bo said.

Adan shrugged. "Who even knows? These days, it seems like sneezing too loud will get you a citation."

Bo chuckled. "I know you're kidding, but, honestly, it's not that far from the truth. Remember Maren?"

Adan shuddered at the sound of that name. "Oh. Yeah."

Maren had been a fellow resident of their group home. He was one of the many Bolvaran children raised by the State when their parents couldn't do it. But Maren was angry all the time. About everything. Adan knew it must've been because of some trauma or another that Maren had suffered when he was young. Maybe his parents had mysteriously vanished one day, too? But Maren never disclosed what it was. Instead, he took his anger out on the Union, the system, and anyone unfortunate enough to get in his way. After being dragged home past curfew by the Clubbers for graffiti or vandalism one too many times, the House Patron decided to confront him about cleaning up his act. Maren told her exactly where he thought she should shove her friendly advice. A half-hour later, the Clubbers showed back up and took Maren away.

"What do you think happened to him?"

Adan shrugged again. "I don't know. I never heard. At least he never showed up at the Gories."

"As far as we know."

"Yeah. He probably just got a couple extra years tacked onto his five and started serving early. I've heard that happened to someone at another home."

Bo nodded. "Yeah, I think I heard that, too." He glanced over at Adan with a sly grin. "You had a crush on him, didn't you?"

Adan grumbled at the reminder. But it was true. Who could blame him? Maren had lovely eyes and a friendly smile, at least when he wasn't raging out. And, of course, he had those broad shoulders, and– "Yeah, I did. I've always had a thing for troublemakers, I guess."

Bo chuckled. "Oh, really? Is that why you had a crush on me? Because I'm such a troublemaker?"

Adan rolled his eyes and smacked Bo lightly on the arm. "I'd rather kiss a marsh pig."

Bo laughed and puckered his lips. "Come on, I've got to be prettier than a marsh pig."

Adan glared and shook his head. "Stop it."

Bo frowned, then sighed. "I'm sorry. I didn't mean to make fun of it. I liked that you had a crush on me. Nobody else even seemed to like me at all."

That was true. Adan was shy and quiet back then. He'd been mostly tolerated by the other kids living in the home. Bo was a new addition, sent over from a home being torn down and replaced by something else. The others were immediately suspicious of him, even accusing him of being a Union spy. But Adan could see right away that Bo was okay. And the intervening years had been kind to Bo. He was no longer the awkward, gangly kid he'd been back then.

"Alright, fine. Apology accepted."

Bo smiled. "Good, because we need to get moving soon if we want to make it back before curfew."

After crossing over Delan and walking toward the river for a few blocks, Bo led them into a tiny cobblestone laneway wedged between a pair of brick-faced industrial buildings. As the pair navigated around stacks of crates and the occasional trash bin, Adan couldn't imagine maneuvering a delivery van through a space that clogged and narrow.

They found Min standing near the end of the laneway next to a door into an ordinary-looking three-story building. Min was tall and lean, with long, straight, black hair tied back beneath a black cap. Their complexion was so pale it was almost perfectly white. On closer inspection, Adan realized it was a white powder they'd applied to their face. It gave them an almost ghostly appearance against the thick black coat they wore over black trousers and boots. Adan had no idea how they kept all that black clothing so dark, and he worked in a laundry.

Min waved but didn't smile when they saw Bo. Then they gestured for the pair to come closer. "Your timing is perfect," they quietly announced once Adan and Bo were close by.

"Of course," Bo confirmed. "Your partner is already asleep?"

Min nodded, their thin lips set into a flat, unreadable expression. "Yes, she's upstairs." They looked Adan up and down. "Is this your friend?"

He took that as his cue to introduce himself and stuck out his hand. "I'm Adan."

Min looked down at it like he was offering them a rock eel. But they reached out and shook his hand anyway. Their fingers were bony, and their hand was ice cold. "Pleased to meet you, Adan. Come on, let's get inside before we get any wetter. Remember to keep your voices down."

They turned and opened the nearby door, then led the pair into a tall garage with three black delivery vans parked inside. All three vehicles were variations on the standard, boxy Union design. They were mostly clean, save for a few

31

scratches and dings here and there. But only one of them looked big enough to hold the bashki barrels. That was the one Min led them to.

"You'll need to take this one," they explained, "since you're hauling such a big load."

Bo nodded. He must've already explained the details of their plan to Min. Hopefully, his trust in them wasn't misplaced. "It'll hold everything?"

"Easily. But you'll want to drive carefully when it's loaded, so everything doesn't bang around too much in the back. I assume you won't be sticking around long enough to properly tie everything down."

Bo chuckled. "I mean if there's time."

Min flashed a brief smile. Apparently, Bo's charm was enough to cut through even their serious demeanor. "And you're comfortable driving a van this large?"

Bo nodded. "I am. I've been trained on the laundry trucks to fill in for the delivery drivers when needed."

That was partly true. Adan and Bo had both received that training, which included some time in the driver's seat of a delivery truck. But it hadn't involved any actual driving. Adan had wondered about that, too, when Bo mentioned using a delivery van. But Bo was confident about operating one of the vans, so Adan kept his mouth shut.

Min nodded. "Good enough. If you can handle one of those, this van won't be a problem."

Adan felt like he should try to join the conversation. "What are these vans for?"

Min looked at him in surprise. They may have forgotten he was there. "Transporting corpses to the burn centers. I manage the morgue transport for all the western districts."

Adan's eyes went wide with surprise. "Oh. Great."

Then Min actually smiled. "I know. Some people call me a ghoul, but I don't mind. I enjoy the work. And nobody I drive around has any complaints about anything."

Thinking about his work supervisor, Adan could imagine the appeal of that. "At least that's something."

"Yeah, that's great," Bo said a little impatiently. "Maybe now you can let us know how we'll get in here and borrow it tomorrow?"

Adan chuckled nervously. While Min was strange, like Bo had warned him, they were also charming. In a weird way. But Bo's impatience made Adan uncomfortable.

Min frowned. "Speaking of complaints. Alright, I can see that you're anxious, so I won't delay you. Come with me."

They led the pair over to a wall-mounted lock-box hanging near the door. After showing them how it opened, they pointed out the dual sets of keys for each van. Theirs was van number three. They claimed the steering was a little loose, and the brakes were spongy, whatever that meant.

The timing was flexible. Min and their partner would be out at a Gories gathering for the evening. They promised to leave the door from the laneway unlocked so the two of them could get in. Adan and Bo would just need to fold the sliding doors to the main road open to get the van out. Once they'd driven it onto the street, they needed to close the garage doors again. Otherwise, someone would notice that one of the vans was missing. If Min was asked about it, they'd be forced to claim it was stolen, as agreed.

"I understand," Bo confirmed. "Don't worry, we won't forget."

Min nodded. "I'll have to say the same thing if you're

caught."

"I know," Bo replied.

Min nodded again. "If something goes wrong while you're out and you need to abort your operation, just make sure you get the van back here in one piece. Even if you don't have the bashki. As long as the van gets returned, I won't have to answer for anything."

Adan was surprised to hear that. "Without the bashki?"

Min shrugged. "I have a good life here. A comfortable life. But I know that's not the case for everyone, and I've got no love for the Union. That's why I'm helping you. The bashki is just an added perk."

Adan began to look at Min in a new light. Their appearance may have been a little odd, and their manner a little off-putting, but they were still a decent person. Adan could appreciate that. "Thank you, Min."

They smiled. "Thank me when it's over. Preferably with a barrel of stolen bashki." Then Min glanced at the large wall clock mounted over the door. "Unless you have any other questions, you should probably get going."

Adan checked the time. It was nearly eleven, leaving them only two hours to get back home before the thirteen o'clock curfew.

"You're right," Bo agreed. "We should go." Then they offered their hand to Min. "Thanks again."

Min smirked, then shook Bo's hand. "You're welcome, of course. You know I could never say no to you."

Bo chuckled, and Adan suddenly saw the connection between them. Not just as an old friend. Had Bo ever explained how well they knew one another? But before Adan could say anything, Bo grabbed one of his sleeves and gave it a light tug. "Come on, Adan."

Adan nodded and followed Bo back out into the laneway. The sprinkle had turned into light rain. It was still manageable, but Adan knew it was only a matter of time before it turned into a downpour. He glanced over his shoulder and saw Min standing in the open doorway. They waved at him. Surprised, he smiled and waved back. Then they went back inside and closed the door. Adan turned back around in time to keep himself from stumbling into a trash bin.

Bo, who'd been watching him, laughed. "I take it you like your new friend?"

"They seemed nice. And they seemed very familiar with you."

Bo nodded and lowered his head. "Yeah. I thought you'd probably notice that. I know Min from the group home I lived in before I met you. But we lost touch after we got split up. It happened all in one night, with no warning, so none of us knew where the others went."

With the new context, Adan thought back to the night Bo had arrived. No wonder he'd seemed so lost and alone. He'd been sent there with no notice, no warning. He must've been scared to death. But he hid it so well that Adan never saw it. "I had no idea, Bo. I'm sorry."

Bo nodded and waved off the apology. "It's fine. It's all in the past. And you were a good friend anyway, even if you didn't know." Then he stopped and turned to face Adan. "I mean you are. You are a good friend."

Adan smiled. "Damn right I am."

Bo laughed, then started walking again. "Anyway, I ran into one of my old housemates a few months ago totally by chance. And she told me where Min was at. So, once we started talking about our plan, I thought they'd be a good person to ask for help."

The pair turned onto Delan and started walking toward the tram station. "I guess it makes sense why you trust them now," Adan confessed.

Bo chuckled. "I guess it's a good thing you trust me. But, yeah. We were really close. We basically grew up together, you know?"

Adan shook his head. "Honestly, no. I was never very good at making friends. Sometimes I feel like things worked out with you by accident."

Bo smiled. "Or fate."

When they got back to the tram stop, they huddled out of the rain under the meager overhang. Adan's hair was already starting to stick to his head again. He wiped some of the moisture off and laughed. "Two showers in one day? I wonder what I did to deserve such luxury."

Bo ran a hand through his thick hair, which refused to lay down. "The Union provides."

They heard the bell from the approaching tram as soon as they saw its single headlight shining onto the puddle-filled street. Bo stepped forward toward the curb and waved his hand to ensure the tram driver saw them and stopped. A few minutes later, they were sitting in the nearly empty carriage as it pulled away. The only other occupants were a sleeping construction worker, their hard hat pulled down over their face, and a pair of unknown citizens sitting up ahead of them. They looked like they were probably older, even if Adan could only see the backs of their heads. One of them had a head full of short, tight black curls sprinkled with bits of gray and silver. The other had twisted their thick, black hair into locs that fell past their shoulders and were spiraled through with silver and white. Adan thought it was lovely. When he looked over at Bo to comment on it, he saw that his friend had fallen asleep. Adan snorted and rolled his eyes. Of course, he had. That boy could sleep anywhere.

Adan looked out the window next to Bo, watching the streetscape roll by. The Lowers typically had a rundown, well-worn appearance. It was comforting in a way. Sure, the district was cheap and shabby compared to Gallur Heights or the Arena District. But it was his district, where he lived and worked. It was home.

The rainfall had given the street a beautiful, glossy sheen. The lights reflected back up from the puddles in the street. Their watery reflections danced across the windows beyond the sidewalk. It was enchanting to watch.

Then one of the people sitting in front of him coughed loudly enough to briefly rouse the sleeping construction worker. Hopefully, they weren't sick. That was the last thing Adan needed to deal with.

Adan settled into his seat as the tram slowed at the next stop, trying to get comfortable. They still had several stops to go before they had to get off. When the doors opened, two more citizens got on. Adan was immediately suspicious. They were both mysteriously dry despite the now heavy rain falling outside. There was nothing special about them otherwise. One was taller than average and older, with short, graying black hair and a goatee. The other was of average height and carried a little extra weight around their midsection. Their clothing was ordinary but clean. Too clean. Like it was all brand new. And when the heavier one leaned over and said something to the tram operator, Adan knew there'd be trouble. The pair were Pinchers.

Adan reached over and lightly elbowed Bo, hoping to wake him without too much of a fuss. If Min had snitched on them, the Union might not just send Clubbers. They might also send in Pinchers. A special bureau of the State Security Force, the Pinchers operated out of the Pinch, a part of the Valley only accessible through a narrow canyon. It wasn't a proper district, and nobody lived there. Not by choice. The Defense Force Training Center was located there, away from the rest of the city. Adan had visited the Pinch once when he toured the Old Tech Museum there as a child. But the Pinch was known by most as the location of Utrogg House. The infamous building served as the Pinchers' headquarters and the prison where they kept the citizens who committed crimes against the State. Most of those people sleeping in Utrogg House that night were soon destined to appear in the Gories.

Adan elbowed Bo again and finally roused him. Before Bo could say anything, he grabbed Bo's hand and squeezed it twice. It was their secret code for trouble. Bo immediately sat up and looked around, then spotted the Pinchers.

"Oh," he whispered.

"Yeah," Adan whispered back.

Then the Pincher speaking with the operator stood up. The operator closed the door and got the carriage moving again. The taller Pincher approached the other pair sitting toward the front and said something. Adan couldn't hear what it was, but he could guess. They were checking Citizen IDs.

The heavyset Pincher walked past them and stopped next to Adan. They were clean-shaven, and their sienna complexion was lightly wrinkled, especially around their eyes, as if they squinted too much. But, when they smiled, that smile didn't reach those eyes. "Good evening, citizens. I'm Agent Banog from State Security." They reached into their long coat, pulled out a black wallet, and then opened it to display their badge. "Would you mind showing me your identification cards, please?"

Adan carefully reached into his trouser pocket, mindful of the Agent's other, unseen hand hidden in their jacket pocket. Pinchers didn't carry clubs, after all. They carried firearms. He pulled out his wallet and flipped it open to display his Union Citizen card.

The Pincher reached out and took his wallet, examined his ID card, then handed it back. "Thank you, Citizen Testa." Then he took Bo's card and did the same. "Thank you, Citizen Shen. Your cooperation is appreciated."

By that time, the other Pincher had approached Agent Banog and leaned in to whisper something. Banog nodded, then turned their attention back to Adan and Bo. "Please remain seated at the next stop," they quietly instructed the two of them.

Adan gulped and nodded.

The Pinchers continued down through the carriage until they reached the remaining rider, the sleeping construction worker. Adan allowed himself a moment of relief but didn't relax. Just because they hadn't grabbed him and Bo yet didn't mean there wasn't a squad of Pinchers waiting at the next stop.

"Wake up, citizen," the taller Pincher loudly commanded the construction worker. Adan, fearing to turn around, watched the reflection in the tram window.

The worker snorted, and the snoring stopped. Then they reached up and pushed their helmet off their face. "What's going on?" They sounded confused and barely awake.

"We need to see your identification card, citizen."

"What?" The worker was still confused. But Adan was no longer sure it wasn't an act. Being asked to show your ID was a common occurrence in the Union, especially in the Lowers. "Why?"

The Pincher didn't seem to buy it, either. "I'll ask you one more time, citizen. Your ID, please."

"Dammit. Fine." The construction worker reached into their reflective vest, and Adan saw each of the Pinchers tense up. Was that citizen why they were onboard? Had then been expecting trouble?

The worker pulled something out of their vest. A wallet, maybe. Then they tossed it in the face of the closest Pincher. "Here's your damn ID," they called out and leaped from their seat. But the other Pincher, the one who'd spoken to Adan, was ready for the move. They lunged forward, pushing the worker back into their seat, then shoved a gun into their face. Adan and Bo quickly ducked down beneath their seats for whatever cover it might provide them when the shooting started.

But there was no gunfire.

"That's enough, Motari trash," the Pincher growled. "Stay in your seat, and you might not get hurt."

"Hey, what the hell is that!" the worker suddenly cried.

Adan cautiously peaked his head up far enough to see the window reflection again. Was that citizen really a member of the Motari? Or was the raid just an excuse for the Pinchers to get violent? Then Adan spotted something in the tall

CHAPTER 2

Pincher's hand. It looked like a white plastic tube. When the Pincher pressed it against the worker's neck, Adan realized what it was. A syringe. They'd just injected the citizen with something.

"Founder's mercy," Bo whispered.

Adan glanced sideways to see that Bo had caught it too. They'd heard stories about things like that but had never actually seen it done first hand. Unlike the Clubbers, the Pinchers didn't normally operate out in the open. They tended to stick to the shadows, relying on their supposedly extensive network of informants. Of course, the rumors would have you believe that nearly everyone in the Valley was an informant, which couldn't be true. So, what had forced them to come out of the shadows and drug a citizen in public like that?

Then Adan felt the tram start to slow again. They'd reached the next stop. When the doors opened, another pair of suspiciously clean but rain-soaked citizens stepped aboard. Unlike the first Pinchers, these two had their badges pinned to their overcoats.

"Please remain seated, citizens," one of the new Pinchers announced. "This is a State Security action and will be over shortly."

The pair of them walked to the back of the car and helped the first two lift and carry the construction worker to the front of the carriage and out the door. Adan hoped they were only unconscious and not dead. He sat up in his seat and peered out the front window to see the Pinchers place the worker into the back seat of a black, four-door auto. Most citizens weren't authorized to have their own autos, so Adan had only seen them a handful of times. Rarely had he been so close to one outside of the Founder's Day parade.

Then the Pinchers all got into the auto, the lights came on, and it drove off.

"Does anyone need to get off here?" the operator shouted back to their passengers.

"No," Bo called out.

Their stop was the next one. If it hadn't been raining, Adan would've been tempted to get out and walk the rest of the way. The air in the tram was uncomfortably thick with tension. But no one else got up or said anything, so the operator closed the door and started the tram moving again.

Bo leaned in close to Adan. "Can you believe we just saw that?"

Adan shook his head. Witnessing two arrests in one night, including one by the fabled Pinchers, was a lot to take in. "No. When they first came aboard, I was sure they were here for us."

"Thank the Founders they weren't."

Adan grunted in agreement. "Do you think that citizen was really part of the Motari?"

Bo shrugged. "I have no idea. But I do know one thing."

"What?"

"We've really got to get out here."

Private Log of Captain Chander Sanyal

CSF Samuel Jennix, 14 September 2451

The Colony Fleet is overdue. They were due to emerge from voidspace yesterday. Osoria and Kanerva have double and triple-checked the Nav beacons but found no issues. When Kanerva asked the standard protocol for a delayed Colony Fleet, I told her that we must continue as planned. It rarely happens, but it's not unheard of for an unknown variable to delay a voidspace jump by days or even weeks. Kanerva publicly accepted this for the benefit of the crew. But, she knows the truth as well as I do. There is no fuel for a return jump. Thus, there is no returning for us, Colony Fleet or not.

Chapter 3

Adan sat down on the edge of his skinny bed, wedged in with a small dresser and chair inside his tiny room. Although he used to have more space when he shared a bunk room with another housemate, Adan relished the privacy that even his meager bedroom offered him.

The House Patron had assigned Adan the room a few months ago when its previous occupant aged out of the home and left to serve their five. While he'd been excited about it, he had trouble sleeping at first. Adan hadn't had his own room since moving into the group home and wasn't used to sleeping alone. He eventually adjusted to it. But the best part of having his own room was when he was awake.

Adan slipped off his work boots, then crawled all the way onto his bed and lay down. It wasn't the most comfortable mattress. His old one had been better. But it worked well enough to let him stretch out his aching back and rest. Adan's body needed the break after a restless night and a long shift at the laundry plant.

He slid his hands behind his head and looked at the painting nailed to the wall across from him. It had been done by one of the room's previous occupants. Adan didn't know who. It had been in there for as long as he could remember. Maybe even since before he first moved into the group home. Unlike the dull, faded, peeling yellow wallpaper on his walls, the painting was bright and colorful.

It was a simple landscape and not even particularly well done. But Adan recognized the location from memory. It depicted a spot upriver from the city where Lanbro Falls tumbled down from the mountains into Lake Suloa. Scrubby trees and tall grass dotted the cliff sides, reflected in the impossible blue of the lake. The deceptively peaceful surface of Suloa hid the fact that it sunk almost a kilometer into the rock. His teachers had explained that it was a remnant from the long-ago meteor strike that had created Bolvar Valley in the first place. The space rock had torn open Neska's crust with fiery fury. Scientists theorized that the resulting up-flow from the planet's molten core had taken hundreds of years to solidify.

The area was a popular getaway for those that could get a pass to leave the city. Adan's parents had somehow managed that and took him there as a small child. The trip was one of the few memories he still had of them. His family had camped out on the lakeshore and fished for rock eels. Adan remembered them sitting around the roaring campfire that chased away the chill in the mountain air, eating fire-roasted eel while his parents told stories from their youth.

But the happy memory was stained with sadness. Adan had come to live in the group home not long after that. He never found out what happened to his parents. One day they'd dropped him off at the Instruction Center and gone to work. But they never came back for him. He sat on the front steps for several hours, scared and close to tears, waiting for them until someone from Union Health & Welfare came for him. They'd told him his parents were gone while they stood by as he packed up his few possessions. The State would take care of him from then on. Then they brought him to the group home.

The saddest part was that he could no longer remember their faces. Even revisiting that memory from the campfire, his parent's faces were just blurs. Adan only recalled the idea of who his parents were anymore. At least the memory no longer brought him any tears.

Then Adan heard a knock and looked up to see housemate Riela smiling as she leaned through his doorway. "I see you're well into your daily brooding," she commented.

Riela was a little older than Adan. She'd already been living in the group home when he'd first arrived. She was the closest thing Adan had to a friend in the home aside from Bo. Riela was never particularly nice to him, but she was also never mean.

"Just resting my back," Adan replied a little defensively. "It was a rough day at the laundry."

She nodded. "I'm sure your late-night out had nothing to do with that."

Adan eyed her suspiciously. "Are you keeping tabs on me? Because that's the Patron's job, not yours."

Riela huffed. "Don't be an ass. I don't care how late you were out. I happened to be awake when you and Bo came back. Not that you'd notice."

Notice? What was that supposed to mean? Lately, she'd go days without acknowledging him. "What do you want, Riela?"

"Who says I want anything?"

"Fine. Then please go away."

She huffed again and awkwardly shuffled her feet. "Alright, there is something I want. One of my workmates is having a Gories party tonight and invited me. Word has it they even scored some bashki. But tonight's my night as House Monitor."

While the group home had a live-in Patron, it was common for the older kids to take turns as the Patron's second and help mind the younger kids that lived there. Adan didn't especially enjoy it, but he didn't mind doing it, either. Riela was obviously implying that she wanted him to do it for her. Of course, Adan already had plans that evening.

"And?"

Riela rolled her eyes in frustration. "And I'm asking if you'll do it for me. I'll take your next turn in exchange."

"Why not ask your brother?"

Her brother, Tavi, was a year older than her and would soon be headed away for his five. While Riela had never been mean to him, Adan couldn't say the same about Tavi.

"You don't think Tavi was the first person I asked? He's been invited to the same party."

"Oh."

"Yeah. So I'm asking you."

Adan shook his head. "Well, I can't do it."

"Why not?"

He smiled at her sweetly. "Why is none of your business. I said no."

47

She scoffed and smacked his doorframe. "You're such an ass, Adan. I'll remember this."

"Remember what? Do you know what I remember? How about when your brother stole my towel while I was in the bath. And then locked me out of my room. Or the time when he broke the Patron's tea mug and convinced her that I'd done it."

"That was Tavi, not me."

Adan sat up and rested his weight on his elbows. "Sure. But what did you do about it? Nothing. So don't go thinking it's okay to threaten me when I don't drop everything for you."

"Fine," she announced. "I get it. I'm the ass, and now it's payback time."

Adan sighed. "I really can't do it tonight, Riela. I would if I could. You know I don't care about the Gories. But I can't."

Riela frowned. "I don't suppose I should bother asking Bo, either."

Adan smiled. "You can ask, but you'll get the same answer."

Riela sighed and let go of his door frame. "Well, I suppose it was worth a try. Whatever it is you two are up to, I hope it's fun." Then she turned and walked away.

Adan considered laying back in his bed. It was nice to be off his feet for a little while. But if he didn't get moving again, he was in danger of losing his momentum. And he needed all he could get for what was coming up that night.

So Adan stood up and walked over to his closet. Next to his small collection of street clothes hung a navy work coat he'd taken from the laundry. Adan had removed the sewn-on patch identifying it as a laundry worker's jacket. But he'd left the sewn-on name tag. It said his name was Argin. He stripped out of his sweater and tossed it on the floor. Then he looked down at his chest and noticed his muscles. His chest actually had gotten bigger since he'd started his work assignment. Adan bent an arm and flexed it, then noticed his arms were bigger, too. But he was still skinny. He pressed a hand to his side and ran it down his ribs, counting them. Definitely too skinny.

Adan shook his head, then grabbed a dark brown t-shirt from the dresser and pulled it over his head. Then he took the jacket from the closet and put it on. It was too big, but it would work for one night. Bo had also taken one from the laundry. Even if it was the wrong kind, having any sort of uniform went a long way to establishing your credibility with people in the Union. Throw some impressively forged paperwork on top of that, and almost no one would question you.

"Well, don't you just look the part?"

Adan turned to see Bo standing in the doorway, mimicking Riela's stance. Adan turned on his heel and posed, modeling the jacket like it was the latest thing worn up in the Heights. "You like it? Because, if you want one, I know somebody who's got an extra."

Bo laughed. "It just so happens that I already have one. But it looks much better on you."

Adan rolled his eyes and held his arms out to his sides. "Are you kidding? You could fit two of me in this thing."

Bo leaned in to read the name tag on Adan's jacket. "I'd offer to trade, Argin, but mine's even bigger."

Adan grinned. "Fair enough."

"Now, get that thing off before someone sees you in it."

Adan nodded and took the jacket off. "As if anyone cares what we do. Well, except Riela. She was in here earlier trying

49

to get me to take her Monitor shift tonight."

"Ah. Yeah, she just asked me, too."

Adan smiled. "I warned her that you'd say no."

Bo shrugged. "Maybe she thought she could charm me into it."

"What? She was nice to you?"

Bo laughed. "She tried to be. It must've hurt. She looked like she wanted to jump out of her skin."

Adan threw the jacket onto his bed and sat down next to it. "Like she wanted to jump your skin, you mean."

"Don't start that again."

Adan chuckled. "You're the worst when it comes to that. Half the people we know have or had crushes on you. You're the one everyone wants."

Bo sat down on the bed next to him. "If you say so. But that doesn't matter right now. We've got things to do."

Adan nodded. "Then I guess I'd better put my boots back on."

"Yeah. You'd better."

After he finished getting dressed, Adan rolled the Argin jacket into a tight wad and shoved it into Bo's backpack next to his jacket. They didn't want anyone in the house to see them, especially the House Patron. She would ask why they had them, and Adan didn't want to outright lie to her. A lie of omission was much easier for him to manage.

The pair stopped in the kitchen and grabbed some sandwiches from the cold box to eat while they were on the go. Adan didn't waste any time biting into a sandwich once they were out of the house. After Adan stuffed the first one in his mouth, Bo dug into his backpack and pulled out the jackets. It was a clear evening sky over the Valley, which meant it would be cold. At more than 1,200 meters in elevation, it got cold a lot in Bolvar.

Once he had his jacket on and buttoned up, Adan took a bite from his other sandwich while Bo put on his own jacket. "So," Adan said between mouthfuls, "what's our first stop?"

"We're going to see Calin."

"The forger?"

Bo nodded. "Yes. She's not far from here."

"Close enough to walk?" Adan was still feeling apprehensive about the tram after the night before.

Bo nodded again. "Yeah. She lives and works in the Central District, but she's meeting us at that tea house on Loribar Street."

"She's from the Central District? What does she do?"

Bo stopped suddenly and looked around to see who was nearby. Then he leaned in closer to Adan. "Don't tell her I told you this, but she's a clerk for the Union Records Bureau."

Adan almost gasped. "Are you serious? How do you even know her?"

"She's a friend of my parents, alright. Now, come on."

Bo started walking again, forcing Adan to hurry to catch up. Adan suddenly had a million questions. He knew almost nothing about Bo's parents. Bo would get irritated or upset every time he asked, so Adan eventually stopped asking. And now they were on their way to meet a friend of his parents? Adan was astounded.

The thing about Bo was that he was an open book about almost everything. It was one reason why the two of them got along so well. Adan always knew where he stood with his best friend. But there were a few topics that Bo had made clear were untouchable. His parents were one of them. Another

51

one was a scar Bo had on his lower back. When Adan first asked about it, Bo told him it was an accident and nothing more. After that, he refused to talk about it. Adan let it go. If it was important, Bo would explain it.

So finding out that Bo was in contact with a friend of his parents and was close enough to them to ask them for help with their heist was a big shock. How long had they been in touch? How well did she know Bo? For that matter, how well did Adan know Bo? Those questions would just have to wait, though. If Adan ever got answers to them at all.

"Hey," Adan called out, "slow down."

Bo slowed his pace and looked back over his shoulder. "Sorry."

"It's alright. As long as you're alright."

Bo sighed. "I am. It's just going to see Calin has got me in a weird place. Seeing her reminds me of my parents, and I don't like to think about them, you know?'

Adan nodded. "Yeah." He knew why he didn't like to think about his parents, at least.

"It'll be fine. I'll be fine. We just gotta get this over with."

Adan decided to leave things there for the time being. They both needed to be aware and alert, and things were starting to turn into distractions. So he kept quiet as they crossed over Bartok. The sidewalk was crowded with citizens already out and about in anticipation of the upcoming Gories tournament. Every public house would soon be full, and every wireless set would be tuned to the broadcast. The crowd made Adan feel a little more anonymous. The flip side, of course, was that any Pinchers in the crowd would blend in, too.

Loribar Street was one of the highest points in the Lowers,

running along a low hilltop that paralleled the river. The tea house was in an old utility building that had been repurposed after the utility grid in the Lowers was moved underground. It was a tall, narrow, brick building with rooftop seating that afforded people a view of the whole district. Adan and Bo had discovered it a year ago. When they went for the first time, they also discovered that it featured live music. The bands there played weird music that Adan wasn't sure he liked, with a strange mix of electrified guitars, drums, and horns. But it was at least a change from the marches and symphonies you always heard on the wireless.

A small, three-piece band played softly in the corner when they walked in. The main floor was about half-full, with subdued patrons murmuring among themselves. There would be no Gories broadcast there, so most people listened to it elsewhere. But not everyone liked the tournament, despite the usual push from Union newsreaders that enjoying the Gories was patriotic. Places like the tea house offered an alternative.

Adan and Bo each poured themselves a steaming mug from the giant tea urn in the back of the main room, then they hit the stairs that wound up the inside walls of the building. It was a four-story climb to the roof, so Adan was a little winded when they got there. When Bo opened the door to head out to the rooftop, a chilly gust of wind blew in and almost made Adan drop his mug.

Once he was outside, Adan was immediately taken by the view. The sky was dark enough that the street lamps had been lit, and Adan could see all the way down to the river. He found the hydroelectric plant, then looked upriver until he saw Founder's Arena. The massive, open-air stadium sat tens of thousands of citizens. It was typically used for political rallies and community celebrations. But the Arena was lit and dressed in Union flags and banners for its most popular use, the Duels of Glory. Adan could only imagine how loud it must be as thousands of people filed in and found their seats. It would be even louder later in the evening as the duels got underway. But the audience would have to endure a series of long speeches beforehand.

Bolvar House, the seat of the Bolvar Union and home to the Union Committee, sat across the Daralsha from the Arena. In between them, the Daigur Bridge spanned the river. It, too, was lit and draped with Bolvaran flags.

Then Adan noticed that someone else was already sitting on the rooftop. They were bundled up in a thick, charcoal gray overcoat and holding a steaming mug of tea with hands wrapped in shiny black gloves. Adan couldn't see their face, only their conservatively styled, short black hair streaked with silver. The wind had tousled it a bit, leaving a few wisps of black and silver hair sticking out from the rest.

"Aunt Calin!" Bo called out.

Calin turned at the sound of her name. Then she smiled and set her mug down on the table in front of her. "Bo! Come on over."

Adan and Bo walked over to Calin's small table, the only occupied table on the rooftop, and sat down. Bo sat to Calin's left while Adan took the seat across from her. Calin was older. Based on the wrinkles in her face, Adan guessed at least fifty. She had a warm, tawny face and rosy red cheeks, no doubt from the icy wind. A pair of small, narrow glasses hung from a chain around her neck. Otherwise, she wore no jewelry or accessories.

Calin noticed Adan's inspection of her appearance but silently allowed it. Then she glanced down at the name patch sewn onto Adan's jacket and smiled.

"I know Bo told me your name, but I don't remember it being Argin."

"I'm Adan," he offered. "This wasn't originally my jacket."

Calin nodded. "That explains why you're practically swimming in it. I'm Calin Dambolen. It's nice to meet you, Adan. Bo hasn't told me much, but he speaks highly of you."

It was surprising that Bo had spoken of him at all, considering Adan only just learned about her on the way to the tea house. "That's nice to hear." Adan wasn't sure what else to say.

Bo quietly cleared his throat. "Do you have the papers, Aunt Calin?"

Her gaze flickered over to Bo, then back to Adan. "Is he always this impatient with you?"

Adan couldn't help smiling. "Only when he's annoyed with me."

Calin nodded in understanding. "Yes, his mother was like that, too." Then she turned her gaze to Bo. "But he has his father's eyes."

Bo groaned. "Founder's mercy, Calin. Do we have to do this every time?"

The older woman frowned. "Do you think you're the only person who knew them, Bo? Do you believe that you're the only one who was hurt when they died?"

Bo's face showed his short struggle with something he wanted to say but didn't. Then he relaxed his scowl and bowed his head. "I'm sorry, Aunt Calin."

She reached out with a gloved hand and placed it on his

arm. "Apology accepted. Perhaps you'll forgive an old citizen for bringing up the past. I see so much of them in you. It's hard not to think about them when you're here."

Bo looked up and offered a brief smile. "Of course. Seeing you reminds me of them, too."

Calin sighed, then took her hand back and reached underneath her overcoat. She removed a set of folded papers, set them on the table, and slid them across to Bo. "Here is what you asked for. I still don't want to know why you need them. I imagine it's something that would get us all in trouble if I did."

Bo smiled, grabbed the papers, opened them, and looked them over. After a moment, he nodded, folded them, and stuffed them into his own jacket. "This is perfect. Thank you."

"Of course." She picked up her mug and took a sip, then turned her gaze over Adan's shoulder. "The damn Duels of Glory. What do you kids call them? The Gories? Such a vile event."

Adan glanced behind him to see the Arena, then turned back to Calin. "Have you ever been?"

She nodded, her focus still far away from him. "I have, of course. You can't be in my position without having to attend on occasion." Then she focused on Adan and smiled. "I'm sure young Bo told you what I do despite my asking him not to." Adan nodded. "I'm not really his Aunt," she added, "but his parents were friends of mine. And I'm glad to see he has someone like you."

Adan didn't follow. "Like me?"

Calin laughed softly. "Someone who would follow him into trouble, of course. Speaking of which, I imagine you

56

have to be going. I'll stay up here a little longer so that we aren't seen leaving together."

Bo nodded and stood. Then he leaned in and gave Calin a soft kiss on the cheek. "Thanks again, Aunt Calin."

Calin accepted the kiss and patted his arm. "Be careful," she advised, then looked at Adan. "Both of you."

Adan nodded and stood up from his chair. "We will be," he assured her, even if he didn't believe it himself. Then he turned and walked toward the stairwell door with Bo on his heels. Adan's mind raced after everything that just happened. He'd learned more about his best friend Bo's story in the last few minutes than he had all in the years they'd known each other. He desperately wanted to pry but knew better.

When they reached the main floor, they deposited their mugs in the dirty dish bin and made for the exit. The crowd hadn't changed, but the band must've taken a break. Their instruments were sitting alone on the unoccupied stage. Adan stole a quick glance at Bo as they walked to the door, but his friend's face was blank and unreadable. Adan reminded himself to leave things alone.

The night air out on the street felt warmer than it had up on the roof. The nearby buildings blocked most of the wind they'd felt up there. The street was almost empty of foot traffic. Most citizens were already wherever they planned to listen to the Gories broadcast.

A streak of movement caught Adan's attention. He turned to see a pair of thatch rats scurrying off the street into the laneway next to the building. That's when he spotted a Motari symbol painted onto the laneway's brick wall in garish red. Did that mean the tea house was a Motari meeting spot or safe house?

"Alright," Bo announced as he started walking back down the hill, "let's have it."

"Have what?"

"I know you, Adan. You have a thousand questions swirling around in your head." He stopped at a curb to wait for a truck to pass by. "So, let's get it over with."

Adan frowned. Bo was obviously in his feelings about their meeting with Calin. And it sounded like he might want to take them out on his friend. "Have I ever pressed you on something you didn't want to talk about?"

Bo sighed and shook his head. "No, you haven't. I'm sorry. Calin just stirs all this up in me. It's not your fault."

"Okay, then. Apology accepted."

"I know I've kept some things from you, and I appreciate that you accept that. So, really, let's talk about it."

Adan patted his friend's back then stepped off the curb into the street. "How about you just tell me."

Bo gulped and nodded. "How much do you remember about your parents?"

Adan had feelings about that, too, but he'd talked about it with Bo before. His friend knew his story already. "I remember how they were. My father was funny. He was a storyteller. He liked to work with his hands. My mother was sweet and kind unless you crossed her. Then even the Founders themselves couldn't hold her back." He went silent for a moment, remembering the fishing trip to Lake Suloa again. "But she was never like that to me. That's all I really remember about them. I can't even remember what they looked like."

"And you never found out what happened to them?"

Adan shook his head. "No, I never did."

"I know what you mean about remembering how they were. That's how I remember my parents, too." He paused while they passed by a group of citizens gathered outside the door of a public house. "My name isn't really Bo Shen. Or, at least, it hasn't always been. The name my parents gave me is Bo Neren. My parents were Elio and Laina Neren. My mother worked in the Records Bureau with Aunt Calin. My father was a Commander in the Gray Coats." Bo paused again, knowing the gravity of what he'd just said.

Adan was shocked and struggled to keep that from showing on his face. If that's who his parents were, how did he end up in some random group home in the Lowers? Kids like him usually went to one of the Academies. Adan searched for something to say. "Oh."

Bo nodded, smiling bitterly. "I know, believe me. You see, my parents were accused of treason. Both were publicly tried and convicted, and both were executed. But Aunt Calin did her best to protect me. Since she's in Records, she changed my name and replaced my birth certificate. She also decided it would be safer for me to stay out of the Academies in case anyone there might recognize me. So she had me placed in a group home. Bo Neren was the child of traitors and would have that hanging over his head his whole life. But Bo Shen is just an ordinary citizen, maybe without the hand up that being the son of a Gray Coat Commander would bring him, but also without the shame of being a traitor's son."

Now Adan understood why Bo was reluctant to talk about his past. In some ways, having his parents' whereabouts be a mystery was preferable to Bo's story. Then again, at least Bo had a story. Adan would almost rather know his, even if it meant they were dead. He also understood a lot more about why Bo was looking to escape from the Union.

Adan wrapped an arm around his friend's shoulders. "Well, you'll always be my friend, Bo Shen. Even if you smell bad."

Bo chuckled. "I think I smell fine."

Adan laughed. "Are you sure your nose even works right?"

Bo rolled his eyes, then sighed. "Thanks for understanding."

He obviously meant his story, not his smell. Adan smiled. "Of course. Honestly, I'm not even sure my nose works correctly."

Bo laughed and pushed Adan away. "You're such an ass. That must be why we're friends."

"Must be."

"Alright. Let's go get us a van."

Official Log of Captain Chander Sanyal

CSF Samuel Jennix, 17 September 2451

The Jennix has finally assumed orbit around Neska. Now that the entire crew complement has awakened from cryo-sleep, the ship is starting to feel crowded for the first time. The final count is 197 souls after we discovered three cryo-sleep pods that malfunctioned during the voidspace jump. But Security Officer Sander Varin's investigation turned up no evidence of foul play.

I've ordered Colony Services Officer Nestor Bowen to begin final preparations for landfall. Bowen tells me that everything will be ready to go within 52 hrs. That's how long two days are, now. We've spent the last three months living on Neskan time, and it was a surprisingly easy adjustment. For me, at least. Some of the crew have had trouble, but our Medical Officer, Dr. Marketta Palo, was able to help them with some simple hormone adjustments.

Chapter 4

Adan and Bo slowly crept down the narrow laneway as they made their way toward Min's garage. They'd gotten off the tram one stop early and walked the extra distance to keep them from arriving too soon. They also varied their route from the day before in case they were being followed. It turned out they almost needn't have bothered. The tram carriage was empty. The streets were empty. The city had become a ghost town, and any watchers would be plainly obvious.

"I've never seen the city like this," Adan commented, amazed. He'd always been stuck at the house during the Gories of previous years. If he had only known things shut down to that extent, he would've snuck out more often.

Of course, Bo, the plan's mastermind, had known all along. "It's perfect. We have the streets to ourselves."

Adan had been suspicious of that sentiment at first. Wouldn't that just make what they were doing more obvious?

But, now, during their heist, he saw the truth of it. Everything was more obvious. If there was any Clubber activity, Adan and Bo would see it coming, too. And, so far, they'd seen nothing.

They finally reached Min's door. Bo tried the handle with a gloved hand. Even if fingerprint technology was unreliable, they were still anxious to leave none behind. The door came open with no trouble, so Bo quietly stepped inside the garage with Adan right behind him.

Bo pulled an electric torch from his jacket and switched it on. The light was weaker than they would've liked, but finding one at all, especially with working batteries, had been lucky enough. Adan watched as Bo swept the light across the room but saw nothing out of order. This was one of the pinch points, as Bo put it, in their plan. If Min turned on them and informed the Clubbers, they could have a squad lying in wait as they tried to take the van. Bo didn't think Min would do that. But you never knew for sure.

Using Bo's torchlight, Adan opened the wall box that held the keys. He grabbed a set labeled number three and pulled them from their hook.

"Good," Bo whispered. "Give them here."

Adan handed them over, then followed Bo over to the largest van. Unlike the other two vans, it was backed into its space, making it easy to get out of the garage. Another favor from Min, no doubt.

Bo stood on his toes, shined the light through the front window, and moved it about. There was nothing in the van except the two seats for the driver and passenger. Satisfied, he stepped around to the driver's side door and opened it.

"It's not locked," he said. "Try the other one."

Adan did as instructed and found the other door unlocked too. "You get it started," he suggested, "and I'll get the garage door."

Bo nodded and climbed inside the van. Adan shut the door on his side then walked toward the garage door in front of the van. It was a set of hinged panels that folded together, sliding on tracks mounted above and below it. Adan found the simple twist handle, turned it, and undid the latch. Then, holding tight, he pulled it to the side until the panel started to move. Once he had it partially opened, he moved around to the other side and pushed until the panels had folded together. The opening was probably wide enough, but Adan went back and pushed the other side open anyway.

He gave a thumbs-up to Bo, who reached forward and pressed the starter button. Adan winced when the engine rumbled to life. That was their next pinch point. If, for some reason, Min and their partner had stayed home, they would definitely hear that. So might the neighbors. If it was any night other than a Gories night, they probably wouldn't even get the van out of the garage. But no lights came on above the garage, and no one came running. So, Bo put the van into gear and gently pulled it forward. Once it was all the way past the garage entrance, Adan pulled the nearest side shut. Then he went back and did the same with the other side, making sure he was inside the garage so he could latch the doors.

Standing there in the eerie darkness in a stranger's garage gave Adan a moment of pause. But he shook it off. They had the van, and Bo was waiting. He crept back toward the laneway door until his eyes adjusted. Then he exited the garage into the alley and turned toward the street. Bo had the van parked there, its headlamps still off, while Adan walked around and climbed in through the passenger door. Once he was in his seat, he pulled the door closed and fastened the lap belt around himself.

Bo looked over and smiled. His face looked almost ghostly in the partial light of the street lamps, reminding Adan of Min and their white-powdered face. "Are you ready?"

Adan nodded. "Let's get moving."

Bo put the van back in gear and gently stepped on the accelerator. The van started to move forward, slowly picking up speed as Bo gained confidence.

"I see what Min meant about sluggish steering. It feels like I have to spin the wheel farther than I'd expect to get this thing to turn."

"But you'll be okay driving?

"Yeah, it won't be a problem."

Adan nodded, settled back into his seat, and tried to get comfortable since they'd be driving for a while. Then he pulled a folded sheet of paper from his jacket and opened it up. Adan had sketched out their route map by hand with an ink marker stolen from the laundry. He looked it over in the dim lights, then looked up and tried to find a street sign to orient himself.

The distillery was on the other side of the Daralsha, upriver from the Flats. They looked at several different ways to get there when they planned their route. The most direct path would've been to cross the river on the Daigur Bridge. But the crowds at the Arena and the proximity to Bolvar House made that too dangerous. The Geraba Bridge was also an option. But it was downriver, past the hydroelectric plant, which would've taken them out of their way and put the majority of their driving on the unfamiliar east side of the city. The Meki Bridge seemed like their best bet. It was upriver from Daigur Avenue, so most of their driving would be through the Flats. The distillery was just upriver from it, too.

"We're coming up on the end of the street," Bo announced. "Is it right or left?"

Adan glanced back at the map. He had the route memorized, but he wanted to be sure. "It's left. Then, two blocks up, take a right on Dolanai."

"Got it." Bo slowed them as they approached the intersection, finally stopping them at the corner. "Okay, that must be what Min meant by spongy brakes. It almost felt like we weren't going to stop."

Adan nodded, watching as Bo spun the large steering wheel to the left and pulled them forward onto the empty street. He couldn't imagine what it must be like to deal with traffic in the big, heavy van. As he turned to look back at the map, he saw a wireless set mounted in the long dash panel next to a set of switches. "There's a wireless in here. Should we turn on the Gories broadcast?"

"Do you want to listen to it?"

"Not really, but it might be helpful to know what's going on, just in case."

Bo shrugged without taking his hands off the steering wheel. "It's up to you. It won't bother me." He slowed the van again as they approached the intersection with Dolanai, then turned them right and started to speed up again.

Adan reached over, turned on the power switch for the wireless, and heard a dull, tinny version of the Bolvaran anthem play through the dash-mounted speaker. Min had left it tuned to one of the Union broadcast frequencies. "They must be done with the speeches already."

"That's alright," Bo confirmed. "We've still got hours before the matches are over."

The Duels of Glory were organized in a classic tournament style. Each participant was paired off based on whatever qualities the organizers thought would bring the most entertainment. The fighters were given a choice of small, handheld melee weapons to use, depending on their preference. Each pair would then square off and fight to the death. The winners of each round paired off again for another go. The weapons grew in size with each successive round, too. By the end of the night, the final two fighters would duel, and the winner would receive a pardon for their crimes and have their citizenship reinstated.

It was an awful system, rewarding someone for their bloodthirstiness and knack for violence. The Union claimed that the winners demonstrated the necessary grit and drive to push through their challenges that made a good Bolvaran citizen. In some years, the winner would be even granted a commission in the Gray Coats based on their abilities. Most years, the winner was so injured they could barely work at all. Sometimes, the winner was awarded their citizenship posthumously. If they had a family, only they would benefit from that.

The most famous Gories winner was Eider Arana. He was already a hero of the Gray Coats when he was convicted of sedition. His unit had been attacked by raiders out beyond the western Osbaks. Outnumbered and outgunned, his Commander had ordered the unit to retreat. Eider and two others stayed behind to provide cover while the rest of his unit retreated to safety. The two soldiers who'd stayed behind were killed in the fighting. But Eider was still alive when a heavy motorized unit finally sped to his rescue and cleared out the raiders with cannon fire. His Commander had privately praised him for his courage and determination. But orders were orders, so Eider was publicly tried and convicted. Usually, acts of sedition in the Gray Coats were punishable by execution. But the Magistrate, recognizing the potential for trouble among the citizens who'd learned of Eider's heroism, offered him the chance to compete in the Duels of Glory instead. Of course, being a well-trained fighter, he easily won every match and was proclaimed the victor.

Eider spent the rest of his days, and many more after his passing, as the Union's showpiece for the Duels of Glory. As long as you had the heart and the drive, his story went, you could triumph over terrible odds and return as a valued citizen of the Bolvaran Union. That was the official version, at least. In truth, Eider lived out his days as a broken citizen, betrayed twice by the Union he was forced to serve. Once, on the battlefield, and again, during his tribunal. Rumor had it that, when he was asked later in life about choosing to fight in the Gories, Eider responded that he was given no such choice. It was either that, or his family would be exiled to live beyond the wall and take their chances against the very raiders he'd made a stand against. Adan didn't know if that part was true, but he wouldn't have been surprised if it was.

"–brings us to our first match-up in tonight's Duels of Glory. Luca Nellan was convicted by the Union Justice Bureau of treason against the State for collaborating with raider clans beyond the wall to divert precious Union resources–"

Adan grunted, then reached out and switched off the

wireless.

Bo let out a low whistle. "Founder's mercy."

They'd watched Nellan get picked up only a day ago, and he'd already been convicted and sent to the Gories. "The mercy of Union justice, maybe. That was fast."

Bo nodded, his mouth set in a grim line. "Too fast. With the way he tried to run from the Clubbers, I think he knew this was where he'd end up."

Adan shifted uncomfortably in his seat. The knowledge that if the two of them got caught, they could end up facing off in their own Duel of Glory made him uneasy. But, it would at least be a swift end, rather than rotting away in a Pincher prison carved into the stone peaks that encompassed the Bolvar Valley. "You're probably right." The thought amplified his desire to escape the city walls, even if his only experience beyond them was the well-protected enclave of Lake Suloa. "What do you think it's really like out there?"

Bo shrugged. "I don't know. I doubt it's the lawless badlands that the Union claims it is. People have been living out there for as long as there's been a wall. And it's where we're always looking for new resources. It can't be that bad."

"Yeah," Adan agreed, "it really can't." Union life was deceptively comfortable. Adan was housed, clothed, and fed every day. And he would be for the rest of his life. Unless he said or did the wrong thing and was snatched off a tram on his way home one night. "The thing is, at least here I know what I'm in for. Out there, I don't. I'm just scared of the unknown."

"I hear you. Except that's not really true. You think you know what you're in for inside the wall. But do you really? How much has changed since we've grown up? How much

69

more will change?"

That was a good point. The Union relied on his fear to keep him obedient—his fear of them and his fear of what they claimed to protect him against. "We should be coming up on Meki soon."

Bo nodded. "I see it." He slowed the van as they approached the intersection. He was getting better at using the spongy brakes.

Adan leaned forward as they stopped to check out the traffic on Meki Street. A few other trucks and vans were about, and an empty orange Meki Line tram rumbled along the tracks toward the bridge. Once the road was clear, Bo turned them onto Meki and accelerated to catch up to the tram carriage. The street was lined with row houses and apartment buildings, most six or seven stories high. Adan would conceivably end up in a building like one of those after serving his five, assuming he survived. Where would he live out beyond the wall? He had no idea how people did it out there. Did they have cities or towns? Did they all live in tents? Were they nomads roaming the great plains west of the Osbaks in an endless search for food and resources?

"Damn," Bo suddenly commented. "That's not good."

Adan returned his attention to the road ahead as they approached the Meki Bridge. The massive stone-faced steel structure was initially built high enough for boats and barges to pass underneath. There'd been a time when the Daralsha was more heavily used for transport. But the river could be unpredictable at the best of times. Sometimes it was downright dangerous, and whole cargoes were lost. So the city had since transitioned to trucks and rail transit for moving goods around. Then Adan noticed flashing tail lamps

70

ahead of them as drivers slowed for a security checkpoint.

Adan glanced at Bo, whose face was tight with grim determination. "Don't stress," he suggested. "We've got the paperwork and an empty van. If we have to get checked, now's the best time."

Bo grunted. "I'd rather not get checked at all. But, you're probably right."

Adan nodded and looked downriver to catch another glimpse of the Arena, with stately Bolvar House across the river. He could probably see the tea house they'd gone to earlier but couldn't pick it out from all the other buildings in view.

Then Adan felt the van slow as they approached the checkpoint. The Clubbers had lowered the gates on the eastern side of the bridge. They were checking every vehicle before they allowed them to pass. It would be Adan and Bo's turn next.

"Stay calm," Adan whispered. "We've got this."

Bo pulled the van forward until a Clubber directed him to stop. A half-dozen of the black uniforms had set up around the gate. Several of them were gathered around another, smaller van that had been moved over to the side of the bridge. Adan tried very hard not to look that way or think about what they were doing. Once the van stopped, a pair of Clubbers approached the van on the driver's side. One of them stopped near Bo's door. Bo rolled down the window to allow them to speak.

"Let's see your delivery order, Citizen," the Clubber requested.

Bo dug the forged paperwork out of his coat and handed it over. "I see we're not the only ones who have to work during the Glories."

The Clubber nodded as they unfolded the papers. "The Union provides." Adan thought he detected a note of frustration in the Clubber's voice.

"All hail the Union," Bo responded.

Meanwhile, the other Clubber had gone to the back of the van. They opened the double doors and flashed their torch into the open space. "Empty," they called out.

The first Clubber nodded, then handed the paperwork back to Bo. "Seven barrels? That's a lot of bashki."

Bo shrugged then took the papers back. "Is it? Seems like a regular order to me."

The Clubber nodded. "I suppose you'd know that better than I would. Drive safely, Citizen."

"Thank you." Bo rolled the window back up as another set of Clubbers raised the gate. Then he slowly pulled the van through the opening. "Alright, I guess the papers really work."

"See," Adan confirmed. "I told you we'd be fine."

Bo nodded. "Which turn is it again?"

Adan didn't bother consulting the map. "The first left, then the second left after that."

"Okay, I see it."

They had to stop and wait for a tram heading in the opposite direction to pass by. Then Bo turned off of Meki into another industrial area. It was one more remnant of how the city once used the river. Industrial buildings had been built up along the riverbanks to take advantage of access to transport they no longer needed. But it was still valuable to have access to water and hydroelectric power. Especially if you ran a distillery.

When Bo took the second left, the street angled downhill toward the Daralsha. Adan spotted the distillery right away. It had a painted sign fixed to the side of the building that had to be ten meters tall, lit from above and below with bright floodlights. "Premium Bolvaran Bashki," Adan read.

"Only the best for our Thatcher," Bo added with a grin.

"The delivery entrance is just on the other side of the building there."

Bo craned his neck out and looked. "Ah, yeah. There it is." He turned left into a narrow driveway with a sign that said Entrance. Then he slowly drove them alongside the massive brick structure until they could turn and pull up to a series of tall, roll-up doors set in a row along the backside facing the river. One of them was open and lit. There were no other trucks or vans parked back there.

"That must be it," Bo announced. He slowed the van to a crawl, then pointed the front away from the building so he could back them in. That turned out to be the most challenging maneuver for him, requiring creative use of the side mirrors to aim them properly. But Adan felt the dull thud as the van made contact with the great spongy stoppers at the base of the door opening.

Adan undid his seat belt, stood up, and walked to the back of the van. After opening the rear, he caught his first glimpse of the distillery. The inside of the building seemed even more enormous than it was on the outside. A mass of tubes, piping, and vats started to Adan's left and ran along the far side of the space. Stacks of wooden barrels standing two or three high were lined up before him. Adan also saw a smaller, freestanding structure that could've been the office.

Bo walked up next to him. "Do you see where to go?"

Adan nodded and pointed at the structure. "I'm thinking there."

Bo nodded. "Looks like as good a place as any to start." He reached into his jacket and pulled out the forged paperwork. "Let's go."

Adan followed him out of the truck as they walked across the distillery toward the potential office. It was a wooden structure, only a single story tall, and painted a dull shade of light green. There was a door on the left-hand side, along with a window shaded by blinds and a sign that said Distillery Transport Office.

When they got to the door, Adan could hear the muted sounds of the Gories wireless broadcast. That was good. They'd been counting on that. Bo straightened his posture and puffed out his chest. Then he reached out and knocked loudly. He waited for a few moments but got no response, so he reached out to knock again. But the door opened before he could.

"Yeah?" The uniformed distillery worker at the door was probably not much older than they were. They wore a deep blue coverall that zipped in the front and had the beginnings of a sparse, black mustache sprouting above their thin lips. Their name tag said Godan. Godan seemed irritated. "What do you want?"

Adan casually glanced over Godan's shoulder and saw that the office was otherwise empty. Talk about a skeleton crew. Plus, he could clearly hear the Gories broadcast loudly playing.

"We're here for a pick-up," Bo announced, then held out the paperwork.

Godan looked confused. Or annoyed. Maybe both. "What

pick up? There's nothing on the books for tonight."

Bo nodded toward the paperwork he was holding in front of him. "It's a last-minute order. The details are all here."

Godan grumbled and took the paperwork from Bo, carefully unfolded it, then read it over. "Seven barrels," they read aloud. "For a public house. In the Lowers? Are you sure about this?"

"Hey, we're just doing what we were told," Adan replied. "It's not like we want to be doing this tonight either."

Godan cracked a grin. "Yeah, I hear that. I have the least amount of seniority, so I got stuck here by myself." He looked down at the paperwork again, then nodded. "Okay, this all looks good. I'll sign out seven barrels for you, but you'll have to load them yourselves. Alright?"

Bo nodded. "Sure, that's fine. Just let us know which ones to take."

Godan turned and walked back into the office, then set the papers down onto a metal desk next to a giant, open ledger. They picked up a pen, used it to find a specific spot on one of the ledger pages, then licked the tip of the pen and wrote down a series of numbers on the forged order. Then they made a notation in the ledger. Once they were done, they set the pen down, picked up the paperwork, and brought it back to Bo. "These are the barrel numbers to take. They should be close to your van. There are hand trucks on the other side of the office if you need one to load up."

"Perfect," Bo commented. Then he craned an ear, pretending to listen to the broadcast. "How's it been going?"

Godan smiled. "Started slow, like they always do. Except for one duel. A convict named Nellan tore through his opponent in record time. Even the announcers were stunned."

Nellan again. Maybe he'd end up being the one to win his citizenship back. "We'll let you get back to it," Adan declared, "so we can get loaded up and out of here."

Godan nodded. "Alright. I'll be here. Knock if you need anything." Then they turned away and closed the door behind them.

Bo couldn't keep the grin off his face. "Come on. Let's go find those hand trucks."

Adan, also grinning, nodded and followed Bo around to the other side of the office structure. Several two-wheeled hand trucks and a few four-wheeled carts were parked there. Bo and Adan each grabbed a two-wheeler and walked them over to the barrel stacks. Each of the barrels was a meter tall and more than a half meter wide in the middle. And each was painted with a long serial number for tracking. Godan had indicated a set of seven of those for the pair of them to take. Bo looked over the numbers and found the sequence buried behind a few other stacks of barrels.

"That ass," Bo spat.

"Let's just take the closest ones," Adan suggested. "It's not like it matters. Considering how much the attendant is paying attention, we could probably take them all. "

Bo laughed and nodded. "That's a good point. It's too bad we don't have a bigger van." He pulled his hand truck back to the barrels closest to the trucks. Then he took hold of a barrel and tried to move it. "Balda's ass! This thing must weigh more than I do." He gestured for Adan to come over to him. "Here, help me with this. I'll pull it up, and you slide the bottom of the hand truck underneath it."

It took a few tries before they finally got the two-wheeler under the barrel. Then they tilted the hand truck back to wheel it over to the van. It took both of them to negotiate the trip, but they eventually got the barrel inside the van. Adan had expected it to be difficult, but not for it to take that long. And that was only the first one. But the second one was easier, and they each handled the last few by themselves.

The weight from the barrels strained the van's suspension. Adan saw that it was noticeably lower over the rear wheels. And they took up the whole cargo space. Adan was barely able to get the rear doors shut. The barrels also blocked the way back to their seats in the front. But Bo's parking job, effective as it was, had left a big enough gap between the van and the building to squeeze through and jump down to the pavement. Then they climbed back inside the van using the front doors.

By the time Adan was back in his seat and buckled in, he was sweating. "There'll be someone to help us unload these for the Thatcher, right?"

Bo chuckled. "Yeah, several someones, I'm sure. We won't have to touch them again." He started the van's engine, put it into gear, then started pulling forward.

"Do you know what they're even going to do with them?

Bo shrugged. "I don't, but I assume that they'll smuggle them out of the city, too."

Of course. "So we'll be just like Nellan? Collaborating with raider clans to divert valuable Union resources?"

Bo laughed. "I suppose so. Although I don't know how valuable this bashki is. It's not like it's hard to come by here."

"Here," Adan repeated. "Maybe it's hard to get out there."

Bo nodded. "Could be." He pulled up to the street that led them back to Meki and turned right. "So, back across the bridge?"

Adan nodded. "I think so. There was no checkpoint on the western side. And if they're watching for us, it might seem suspicious not to head back the same way."

"You're probably right."

"So we'll take Meki all the way to Bartok and turn left there." They planned to meet the Thatcher in the Lowers, downriver from Mother Agra's. That meant they could cut straight through the Flats and the Lowers most of the way.

"Okay, got it."

They had to wait at the intersection for another orange tram to pass by before turning right and heading back across the bridge. Adan could hear the strain in the van's engine as Bo pressed on the accelerator. It probably hadn't carried that much weight in a long time, if ever. But they were soon cruising back across the bridge. Adan saw the checkpoint they'd gone through on the other side. To his relief, there was nothing up ahead.

The lights were still ablaze at Founder's Arena. According to the van's dash panel clock, it was just past eleven-thirty. They'd been at the distillery for less than an hour. The Gories would be going on for at least another ninety minutes, which gave them plenty of time to deliver and offload the barrels then return the van before the event was over. But they could take longer than that if they needed to. The Union's thirteen o'clock curfew was suspended on Gories nights since the tournaments usually ran at least that late. Still, it was nice to have the roads all to themselves.

Adan stared out the passenger window at the different buildings as they drove by. They were in a nicer part of Bolvar than Adan typically saw. The streets seemed to be in better condition, all the lights worked, and there was even an occasional park stuffed between buildings. But, as they drove past one of those parks, Adan caught sight of something that sent chills down his spine. A black auto was parked at the intersection. It looked just like the one he'd seen from the tram the night before. Its lights were off, and he couldn't see if anyone was inside it. But it could only be one thing. Pinchers. The only other citizens who used autos were Union and Committee officials who needed to be driven around Bolvar. It was unlikely that a Committee member was out and about during the Gories. And ordinary citizens like him usually had to make do with walking and Bolvar's transit network.

Once they'd driven past the auto, Adan leaned out so he could look back in the side mirror. Everything stayed quiet for a few moments. Then the auto's lights came on, it pulled out onto Meki, and started following them.

Adan groaned. "Damn it."

Bo quickly glanced at him. "What's that?"

"Pinchers, I think. Following us in a black auto."

Bo checked the mirror on his side. "I see the lights back there. You're sure it's the Pinchers?"

Adan nodded. "I saw the auto when we passed it. It's the same kind they had last night."

Bo gulped. "Okay, they could be following us. Or it could be a coincidence. There's only one way to find out." He slowed the van as they approached the next intersection and turned left. Then Bo pressed on the accelerator hard, slowly building up speed. "Are they following us?"

Adan kept his eyes on the mirror through his window, waiting for the auto to make an appearance. After a moment, he saw it turning to follow them. "I see them."

Bo smacked the wheel. "Damn it."

Adan took a breath, trying to calm himself. "It could be anything. They may not know who we are. They may just be bored."

"I know," Bo answered, sounding strained. "But, even if they don't, I can't exactly lead them back to the Thatcher."

"Oh, yeah." Adan tried to remember all the times he'd poured over the city map. Where could they go to lose a Pincher auto in a van full of bashki barrels? The barrels! He had a dangerous idea. "How upset do you think Min will be if we show up without their barrel?"

Bo glanced at him suspiciously. "What are you thinking?"

"We could use one of the barrels to slow them down enough to get away."

Bo chuckled. "Founder's mercy, Adan! Alright, I'll slow down and let them catch up a bit, then turn uphill. You climb back there and get ready. Do you think you can knock one out the back by yourself?"

Adan was already getting out of his seat. "I will if I have to." He climbed onto the nearest barrel, then crawled across the tops of the others until he was near the back doors. The way they'd set them inside, there was just enough room for Adan to brace himself against the side and push a barrel out with his legs. Assuming his legs held up. Adan's mind started racing, wondering what they would do after that. Would they still make it to the Thatcher's? Would they have to ditch the van and run? No, he couldn't let his thoughts drift. He needed to focus.

"Are you ready?" Bo called back to him.

Adan gulped. "Yes. Just let me know." He could feel the van slowing and wished the back doors had a window to look through. But he leaned forward anyway, ready to throw the rear doors open, hopefully without falling out himself.

"I'm making the turn. Hang on and get ready!" Adan made sure he was well situated as he felt the van lean into the turn then straighten back out as they headed uphill. "Okay, now!"

Adan grunted and flipped the door latch. The doors flew open, revealing the front of the Pincher's auto and the shocked expressions on the Pinchers' faces. Adan scooted backward and braced his shoulders against the van's side wall. Then he set his boots against the barrel closest to the edge and pushed as hard as he could. It was almost too hard, and the barrel immediately tipped away from him. Adan scrambled to grab onto a piece of the van's metal framing to keep himself from sliding out. Then he watched as the barrel fell all the way out and smashed into the front of the auto with a loud bang. The surprised Pincher behind the wheel frantically tried to control the auto, but it still swerved to the side and smashed into the building there. Adan watched smoke pour from the auto's crushed front end as they pulled away.

"You did it!" Bo shouted. "Okay, hang on and get ready to grab the doors. I'm going to hit the brakes a bit."

"Alright," Adan called back as he carefully slipped into the space left by the missing barrel. "Ready." He felt the van slow, then waited while the doors swung toward him. He quickly grabbed them when they came within his reach, then slammed them shut. "Got it. Now get us out of here."

Bo let out a whoop as he pressed the accelerator, and Adan felt them speed up. They'd actually done it. They'd gotten the Pinchers off their tail. All they had left to do was get to the Thatcher's without being spotted by any others. He started climbing over the remaining barrels to get back to his seat but struggled to keep a grip on anything. He had so much adrenaline in his system that his hands were shaking. When he got close enough, he tightly grabbed the back of his seat and started pulling himself forward.

"I'm taking a corner now," Bo warned him, "so we can get back on track."

Adan kept his grip as he felt the van lean. "I like the sound of that."

"Nice work back there. I almost–damn!"

Adan barely had time to register what was happening when he heard a series of loud pops echo through the van. The window next to his seat cracked and blew out, then the van suddenly veered to the right with a loud screech. Bo was shouting as he struggled to stay in control. But the building ahead of them slammed into the front of the van. Adan was thrown forward, hitting his head on the dash panel so hard that he saw a flash. Then he slumped to the floor, dazed and in pain.

Bo let out a loud moan, his body awkwardly splayed atop the steering wheel. Adan tried to get to him, but it hurt to move, and his head throbbed with his rapid heartbeat. Then he heard a loud voice call out from outside the van.

"This is a State Security Force action! We're armed and approaching the vehicle. Do not move!"

Adan slumped back down to the floor in defeat. The Pinchers had gotten them, after all.

Official Transcript from the bridge of the CSF Samuel Jennix

19 September 2451

Captain Sanyal: Trim that burn, Koskinen. I'm seeing multiple alerts here.

Flight Officer Koskinen: Just following the atmo insertion program, Captain. Permission to manually adjust?

Captain Sanyal: Granted. Take the stick, Koskinen.

Flight Officer Koskinen: Aye, Captain.

Nav Officer Osoria: Hey, is anyone else seeing these mag field readings? My numbers are spiking here.

First Officer Kanerva: Checking it now, Osoria. Stand by. Okay, I'm–

Nav Officer Osoria: Another spike right in our flight path! Damn, it's going to fry us.

Captain Sanyal: Language, Osoria. Koskinen, abort the atmospheric insertion. We can try again after another–

ALARM SOUNDS

Flight Officer Koskinen: I've lost flight control, Captain! We're going to miss the abort window!

Captain Sanyal: Kanerva, get those flight systems back up. If we can't abort our landing, I'd prefer if we could steer this thing.

First Officer Kanerva: On it, Captain.
Captain Sanyal: And will somebody silence that damn alarm!

Chapter 5

Adan had been lying on the cold metal bench for long enough that it was starting to warm up. Either that or his back was going numb. His head still throbbed, and his ears rang from smacking the dash panel in the van. The Medic who'd examined Adan said that he'd sustained a mild concussion. Then they'd wrapped his head with a bandage tight enough to hold his skull together. But when they'd offered him a painkiller, the Pincher standing guard nearby refused on Adan's behalf. As long as he could stand for his tribunal, that would be good enough. Adan was almost surprised to see the bench when they brought him to his cell. Part of him assumed that standing meant he wouldn't be sitting down for a while.

Adan hadn't seen Bo since their auto ride to Utrogg House in the Pinch. The Pinchers who'd pulled them from the van hadn't bothered with guns or syringes once they'd determined that neither of them was in any condition to put up much of a fight. That was good. The Pinchers were a little jumpy after Adan's stunt with the bashki barrel. Well, most of them were. A few of them seemed impressed, and Adan heard a few whispered jokes about hauling their agents in for driving while drunk.

Neither Adan nor Bo said a word. That had been harder for Adan than he expected. Part of him wanted to beg for mercy. The rest of him wanted to yell and scream. But everybody knew that you never volunteered any information to the Pinchers if you didn't have to. It was when you had to that things got tricky.

Adan was desperate to know if Bo was alright. He seemed physically okay after the crash. Adan was the one who hadn't been wearing a seat belt, after all. But Bo looked defeated from the moment they pulled him out of the truck. He'd stared straight ahead for the whole auto ride across the Valley. And the Pinchers separated them as soon as they got to Utrogg.

The Pincher headquarters, Utrogg House, was a vast, imposing block of a structure. It loomed like a great, dark cube on one side of the Pinch, which was a small valley on its own. There weren't any windows, so Adan had no way to judge how tall it was. And there only seemed to be a single entrance, although that couldn't be true. It was just what the Pinchers wanted you to think, that there was only one way in or out. When you were at Utrogg, you were there to stay.

He was still dressed in the clothes from the heist. They'd taken his ID card, but they let him keep the Argin jacket, which was a small mercy. The cell was freezing. If Adan had to guess, he'd say it was actually carved into the surrounding stone. The one time he'd put his hand on the wall, the cold felt deep and penetrating in a way that even an icy winter day never did. It was an old cold.

After they verified his identification and took him to the Medic, the Pinchers dumped Adan inside the cell and left him there. The room was sparse, with nothing but the metal bench and a metal door with the small, barred window. Adan had no idea how long he'd been in there since then. He tried counting his breaths for a while, but that got boring fast. And that was the feeling he'd been left with. First was the pain of the accident. Then came the fear and worry about what would happen to him and Bo. Finally, the soul-crushing boredom of laying alone in a cold, silent prison cell set in.

Eventually, sleep came. Adan couldn't remember falling asleep, but the sudden rattle and clank at the door set him immediately upright. His bandaged head swirled in that haze of confusion you got when you woke up for the first time somewhere new. Someone was unlocking his cell door. Adan was in a Pincher prison cell. That meant his half-remembered dreams about being chased across the city in a van full of coffins were based on actual events.

Adan lightly shook off his haze, straightened his posture, and mentally prepared himself for the questioning to finally begin. He and Bo had spent many evenings coming up with what they'd say if they were caught. Hopefully, Adan would be able to keep his answers straight. When the door finally opened, a tall, thin soldier in a light gray military dress uniform walked in with a folder tucked under one arm. Their skin was pale. No, it was more than pale. It was the lightest shade of pink Adan had ever seen. And their straight, shoulder-length hair was an icy blonde. They were the first Defense Force soldier he'd seen inside Utrogg. Everyone else had either been Pinchers or their staff. And they the first blonde person Adan had seen in a long time. That was interesting.

Most people in the Bolvar Union–and most people on Neska, in fact–had varying shades of brown skin. Complexions ranged from Adan's warm, olive-brown to brown as dark as ironwood. And most Neskans had brown eyes and black hair. Light skin and hair weren't unknown on Neska. Some of the First Explorers had looked like that. But most of them hadn't, and their five centuries' worth of ancestors reflected that. So it was rare enough to be noticeable when you spotted someone with light-colored skin or hair.

Another soldier, dressed in a mottled gray and black Gray Coat combat uniform, followed the first one inside, carrying a wooden chair. They set the chair down in the middle of the cell, then turned and left. A moment later, the door closed again.

The tall, blonde soldier sat down on the chair, crossed one booted leg over the other, and opened the folder to read its contents. They must've been an officer. They had rank markings perched on their shoulders, but Adan didn't know what the symbols meant. Their name tag said Sala.

Adan tried to hide his impatience while waiting for them to say something. Their silence could've been a tactic to break him down. Leave him alone all night, then torment him with a silent, disinterested companion. Adan nearly started tapping his foot but caught himself in time. Being cool under pressure was hard work, he realized.

After a few moments of reading, the soldier closed the folder and looked at him with their piercing blue eyes. Adan rarely ever saw those either, so they seemed strange and foreign to him. Then they spoke in a clear, smooth voice. "Have you not seen blue eyes before, Adan Testa?"

It was such an unexpected question. Adan wasn't sure what to say. "Not that I can recall."

They nodded. "I recognized that stare. Sometimes it's the uniform. But I doubt you're aware of my rank."

That wasn't a question at all, but they stopped speaking and looked at him expectantly. "No," he replied, "I'm not."

They nodded again. "Very well. I am Commander Cristina Sala of the Bolvar Union Defense Force. I use she and her pronouns. You may address me as Commander Sala or simply Commander. Understand?"

Adan nodded. "Yes, Commander."

"Very good." She flashed him a thin smile, then uncrossed her legs so that she could cross the other one instead. "As I understand it, Citizen Testa, you and Citizen Shen were apprehended by the State Security Force after you used impressively forged documents to illicitly obtain seven barrels of Premium Bolvaran Bashki from the distillery. You also attempted to evade capture and used one of those barrels as a weapon to impede your pursuer. That was a remarkable attempt at problem-solving."

Impressive? Remarkable? This didn't seem like any inter-rogation he would've expected. "Thank you, Commander."

She laughed. But it was a cold sound echoing off the bare, stone walls. "Don't thank me yet, Citizen Testa. You still have to stand before the Magistrate. But I requested to see you first, and my rank means that request couldn't be refused." She stood up, set the folder down on the chair, and began to pace back and forth across the width of the chamber. "You see, I know the name Testa. I know it very well, in fact. And, seeing you, now, it's clear that I know you, too."

Knew him? How was that possible? "I don't understand. Commander."

Sala stopped, then turned to face him with a hand on her hip. "No, I don't imagine you would." She picked up the folder and opened it. "Ten years in a group home in the Lowers," she read from the file, "a basic education in one of the lesser Instruction Centers, and a brief stint at a Union laundry plant." She looked back up at him, her eyes narrowed in judgment. "And yet, somehow, you and Citizen Shen nearly pulled off a theft that would've been difficult even for an experienced grifter. And tossing the barrel out the back of the van?" The Commander chuckled. "Well, let's just say that two of the Pinchers' finest won't be doing any fieldwork for a while. That was your idea, yes?"

Adan wasn't sure what to say, whether to admit it or deny it. He suspected that she already knew the answer to that somehow. "Yes, Commander."

Sala shook her head and smiled. If he didn't know any better, he'd say she was impressed. Then she flipped the folder closed with a crisp snap. "I understand that, with the charge of attempted murder of a State Security Force officer on top of the other charges, you're likely bound for the firing squad, Citizen. But I plan to have a word with the Magistrate before your tribunal. Hopefully, we will see one another again." The Commander turned and approached the door, then pounded on it three times with her fist. As the door was unlatched from the other side, she turned back to face him. "Don't let me down, Testa." Then Sala was gone.

The other soldier returned to retrieve the chair, then slammed the door shut and locked it again from the outside.

Adan jumped to his feet and started pacing around the cell. What had all that been about? The Commander said she knew him. Had she known his parents somehow? If so, what did that mean? There were too many questions to wrap his head around. To top all that off, Sala basically admitted that his life was in her hands. A firing squad? If Adan ever needed mercy from the Founders, it was right then.

Then Adan heard the sound of someone unlocking the door again. He quickly returned to his seat on the bench. Two Clubbers came through the open door dressed in their all-black uniforms. Their clubs were still attached to their belts, which meant they were probably sent to fetch him, not beat him. Hopefully.

"Stand up, Citizen," one of them commanded, "and turn around."

Adan stood, turned, and allowed the other Clubber to pull his hands behind him and slip a set of metal shackles onto his wrists. Then they tested the chain before letting him go. "It's done."

"Excellent," the first Clubber commented. "Come with us, Citizen. It's time to stand for your tribunal."

They weren't wasting any time putting him before a Magistrate. Say what you will about Union justice. It was nothing if not swift.

The Clubbers led Adan back out into the corridor and then to another metal door. It opened on their approach, and he was taken into a central chamber with a similar door on each side. Was Bo behind one of those doors? The Clubbers stopped Adan in the middle of the room, then asked him to hold still while they searched him again. Was that because of the Commander's visit? There obviously wasn't a lot of love between the Gray Coats and the Security Force. But Adan had nothing for them to find.

Satisfied that he hadn't recently acquired any new weapons, they marched Adan forward through one of the doors into a maze of bare corridors. With all the twists and turns, Adan quickly lost track of which way they were headed. They ultimately stopped at another metal door which slid open to reveal a lift chamber. Then they all stepped inside.

The lift led to a larger, more pleasant chamber than the one they'd briefly stopped in. The room had a polished stone-tile floor and wood-paneled walls. Wooden benches lined the exterior. Adan also noticed a pair of wooden doors, one to his right and one to his left. Someone was standing in the middle of the room. They were dressed in a crisp, white shirt with black trousers, shoes, and a tie. They held a thick, hidebound folder under their arm. Evidently, they'd been waiting for him. "Citizen Adan Testa?"

"Yes," one of the Clubbers responded, "this is the Citizen in question."

"Excellent work. Thank you, Constables." They looked Adan up and down, seemingly unsure if he could possibly be the citizen in their thick file. "Citizen Testa, my name is Galba Urstin," they finally said. "I'm a Clerk with the Union Justice Bureau, and I've been assigned to your tribunal. First, you're going to take a seat on that bench." They pointed toward the one on the right side of the room. "And you'll wait there until you're called. Then you will stand before the Magistrate, who will recite the charges against you and ask you any questions they may have before passing sentence on you. It's in your best interest to be respectful and answer those questions honestly. Do you understand?" Adan nodded.

"Good. Now, please, take your seat."

Adan began to walk to the bench then stopped. "Citizen Urstin? Do you know what happened to Bo–I mean, Citizen Shen? The one I was taken in with?"

The Clerk shook their head and approached Adan until he was within arms reach. Then he smacked Adan across the cheek with an open palm. "You were not given permission to speak, Citizen." Then they looked at the Clubbers behind him. "Let's see if you perhaps can control him while I'm out of the room, shall we?"

The Clubber who'd first spoken took hold of Adan's arm. "My apologies, Clerk Urstin. It won't happen again."

"See that it doesn't," the Clerk instructed them, then left the room through the door next to Adan.

The Clubber roughly hauled him over to the bench and threw him down. "Remain seated, Citizen. And no talking."

Adan nodded, his face still stinging from the Clerk's blow. Defeated, he let out a quiet sigh. At least it was warm in the room. He could still feel the chill from his cell leeching off of him. There was nothing else in there–no clock or any way to tell what time it was. It had to be sometime in the morning by that point. Adan couldn't imagine he was important enough to wake a Magistrate in the middle of the night.

Adan felt cold, tired, and hungry. The shackles were starting to chafe at his wrists. He did his best to adjust the position of his arms and relieve the pressure. This earned him a pair of looks from the Clubbers guarding the lift doors. So, Adan stopped fidgeting and resigned himself to waiting. Adan felt small. Here he was, not even seventeen years old, still more than a year away from serving his five, and he was about to be judged on crimes that could lead him to the firing squad. He'd hardly lived his life yet, and it was potentially about to end.

But Adan didn't have to sit there for very long before the Clerk returned.

"It's time, Citizen Testa," they informed him before addressing the Clubbers. "Bring him."

Adan stood with the Clubbers' help. Then he followed Urstin through the door into the tribunal chamber with his security detail right behind him. The room was wide and tall. The walls were paneled with polished wood, and the floors covered in a soft, deep blue carpet. Two more Clubbers in black uniforms stood to his left at the back of the room, one on either side of a pair of ornately carved wooden doors. A gallery of partially filled seating took up most of the chamber. One of those seats was taken by Commander Sala, with an armed Gray Coat seated on either side of her. The gallery faced a grand, commanding structure made from the same shiny wood as the wall paneling. It could've been a giant's desk. An older citizen in red robes with starch-white hair and a deeply wrinkled, dark brown face sat behind it. They must've been the Magistrate. They looked a little like Bo's Aunt Calin except for being much older and meaner.

Urstin led Adan to a spot in the middle of the room where a small wooden railing stood about waist height. "Stand here," they instructed him, "and face the Magistrate. You may address them as Magistrate when necessary. Otherwise, you must remain quiet until you're asked to speak."

Adan nodded while the Clubbers behind him retreated to stand on opposite sides of the door they'd used to enter the room. Urstin walked around the railing and stood behind a podium to Adan's right. "May it please the Magistrate," they announced. "The Bolvar Union Justice Bureau presents Citizen Adan Testa in the matter of tribunal number 523-1115-01."

The Magistrate lifted a small wooden mallet and banged it on a wooden block on the desk in front of them. "So presented. I call this tribunal to order. The Clerk will now recite the charges."

Urstin nodded and cleared their throat before speaking. "In the matter of the State versus Citizen Testa, the citizen is hereby charged with possession of forged documents, misappropriation of State resources, willful destruction of State assets, and the willful attempt to injure, harm, or cause the death of duly deputized Agents of the State."

The Magistrate nodded. "Thank you." Then they looked over and made eye contact with Adan. "Please state your name for the record, Citizen."

"Adan Testa, Magistrate."

The Magistrate nodded. "Citizen Testa, is it correct to say that this is your first time standing before a tribunal?"

"Yes, Magistrate."

"Well, I must say that this is an impressive list of charges for a first-timer, especially one so young. How old are you?"

"Sixteen, Magistrate."

They nodded again. "Yes, very young, indeed. You participated in the theft of seven barrels of premium bashki. Tell me, Citizen Testa, what is it you intended to do with all of that bashki?"

Urstin had warned Adan to answer honestly, but he couldn't see how admitting to a plan for being smuggled out of the Valley would help him at all. Mainly because the Justice Bureau would want to know the Thatcher's identity, and Adan had no idea who they were. But he and Bo had prepared for this eventuality, too. "We intended to open an unlicensed public house, Magistrate."

The Magistrate cracked a smile as if that was the answer they'd expected. Hopefully, it would do. As far as Adan knew, no one knew about their intention to leave the Valley aside from him, Bo, and the Thatcher.

"I'll be honest with you, Citizen Testa. I don't believe that answer for a moment. I can't imagine an honest answer, but it doesn't really matter. Typically, charges such as this should send you before the firing squad, especially with that stunt you pulled with the barrel." The Magistrate paused and looked over Adan's shoulder. Were they looking at Commander Sala? "However, it's been suggested to me that a better resolution to this matter would be to have you start your mandatory service a little early. And as no one was seriously injured in that incident and you're only a little more than a year away from your term of service anyway, I'm inclined to agree."

The Magistrate fell silent, and Adan stood there anxiously, trying not to fidget, while he waited. Then they sighed and lifted their little hammer. "Citizen Testa, I hereby sentence you to commence your term of mandatory service in the Bolvar Union Defense Force immediately, with the time between today and your eighteenth birthday to be added to the required five years of service." They banged their hammer against the block again, then turned to the Clerk. "This tribunal is concluded. Clerk Urstin, please remand the custody of Citizen Testa over to Commander Sala from the Defense Force."

The Clerk remained silent for a moment, their expression

unreadable. Then they nodded, turned to face Commander Sala and the two soldiers sitting with her, and waved them forward. "Citizen Testa, the Justice Bureau relinquishes custody of you to the Bolvar Union Defense Force."

Whatever the Commander said to the Magistrate had obviously worked. Adan had avoided a trip to the firing squad. The irony of his punishment, of course, was that he'd been sentenced to do the very thing he was trying to escape from in the first place. As happy as he was to not be headed to his execution, he couldn't help but feel cheated. It felt as if everyone else was in on some big scheme that he was only then just finding out about.

Adan turned to face the seating gallery and saw Commander Sala standing in the aisle as the soldiers approached him. He was no longer the Justice Bureau's problem, so he didn't have to look at the Magistrate or the Clerk anymore. One of the soldiers had brought the Commander's chair into his cell, but he'd never seen the other one. Both were dressed in the Gray Coats' traditional, gray-patterned battle uniforms. The soldier he'd seen before was older, maybe in their forties, if the specks of silver in their black buzz cut were any indication. Their copper face was slightly wrinkled around their eyes as if they'd spent a lot of time in the sun. The other soldier looked younger, probably just a few years older than Adan. No doubt they were serving their five. They had a deep brown complexion, with eyes almost as dark. Their thick black hair was braided into rows and tied at the back of their head.

"Citizen Testa," the soldier who'd delivered the chair said to him, "I'm Third Chief Osaben. I've been ordered to bring you to the Commander. Follow me."

Osaben was polite in both words and tone, but their expression left Adan no doubt that, if he refused their request, there'd be trouble. He nodded to them, then they turned and started walking toward the Commander. The younger soldier gestured for Adan to follow, then took up their position behind him when he did. The Commander and the soldiers led Adan through the door onto a polished-stone landing with a matching stone railing separating a pair of meter-thick columns. Dual sets of stairs led down from either side of the landing. Commander Sala stopped in the middle, then turned to face the rest of them.

"Commander," Osaben announced along with the traditional Bolvaran salute, a closed fist placed over the heart. "Your orders?"

Sala nodded. "Stand by, Third Chief." Then she turned to Adan and smiled. "I'm pleased that the Magistrate accepted my suggestion, Testa. And you should be pleased to have avoided the firing squad today."

Today? He didn't like the implication that a firing squad might still lie in his future. "Yes, Commander. What happens now?"

"Now, we will bring you to the Defense Force Training Center, where you will become Provisional Trooper Testa and be assigned to a training squad. Unfortunately for you, Testa, the Security Force doesn't allow ordinary Citizens to pass through here unrestrained, so those shackles will have to stay on." She looked at Osaben and nodded. "Take his arms.

Osaben and the younger soldier each grabbed one of his arms, then walked him forward behind the Commander as she made for the nearest staircase.

"It's unpleasant," Sala said over her shoulder as she started down the stairs, "but we'll be out of this place soon enough. Then the real unpleasantness will begin."

Private Log of Captain Chander Sanyal

CSF Samuel Jennix, 22 September 2451

We found another lander this afternoon. Or what's left of it. Surprisingly, half the personnel survived. But not Bowen or his senior staff. Of all the people to lose, it's the only ones who know how to plan a damn colony. Maybe it's for the best. There's still been no sign of the Fleet, so Colony's carefully orchestrated plans are meaningless anyway.

At least we still have Zhao. He's spent the past three days going over our systems to discover the extent of the damage. The Jennix is a total loss, of course. I've recommended a commendation to Kosinen for bringing us down as skillfully as she did. And I'm meeting with my Senior Officers tomorrow to start putting together a salvage plan. We've still got 186 souls to care for, Fleet or no Fleet. And I'm not going to let this planet take them, too.

Chapter 6

The two Gray Coats removed Adan's shackles after leading him through the front and possibly only entrance to Utrogg House. Then they put him into the back of a small gray-painted, four-door Defense Force truck. Osaben and the Commander rode in front seats while the unnamed soldier sat in back next to Adan. Pale, silvery light spilled over the eastern tips of the Osbaks while most of the Pinch still lay in shadow. So it was morning. Adan was tempted to ask what time it was but decided it didn't matter. The only question he really wanted to ask was where his friend was. But Adan didn't expect that he'd get an answer for that, either.

The drive to the Defense Force Training Center was short. The DFTC was also in the Pinch, the tall, narrow valley within a valley. The high stone cliffs surrounding the cluster of buildings that made up the Pinch felt oppressive. They were a reminder that Adan's plans to escape were even less likely to happen anymore. Soon they drove through a gate into a fenced compound, stopping when they reached the front of a short, white stone building. Like Utrogg House, it had no windows.

Two Defense Force soldiers stood guard at the nearby building entrance. One of them stepped over to open the Commander's door. Osaben and the other soldier got out by themselves. The younger soldier gestured for Adan to follow them, so he slid across the seat and climbed out of the truck. The soldiers all went through a series of salutes, then the Commander, Osaben, the younger soldier, and Adan went inside.

Unlike Utrogg house, someone had made an attempt to make the DFTC seem less unpleasant. The walls in the entrance hall and corridors had been painted a light shade of blue-gray, and the floor was covered in shiny, black tile. The overhead lighting was bright. And everything was spotlessly clean.

After passing through a checkpoint where everyone had to show their IDs, Adan followed the Commander down the building's winding corridors until they reached a black door at the end of a short hallway. The slender boots she wore made a distinctive click-clack sound on the hard tile as she walked. The Commander opened the door and led Adan into an office. The walls were covered in framed awards, certificates, and photos. Sala sat in the heavy, padded office chair behind a light-gray metal desk. Then she gestured for Adan to sit in one of the wooden chairs in front of the desk. The nameplate sitting on the desk said Commander Cristina Sala. It was her office, of course.

The Troopers hadn't followed them inside, but Adan would've been surprised if they weren't standing right outside the door. Sala didn't speak as she opened a desk drawer and pulled out a set of files. The Commander's wall clock said it was almost six-thirty in the morning. It had been nearly eight hours since they'd crashed the van full of bashki. Adan was glad he'd managed to get a little sleep. But he was starving and desperately wanted something to eat.

Then the Commander cleared her throat. "I imagine that you're exhausted after your night in the cell," she suggested, "and you have a long day ahead of you, so I'll make this brief. I serve the Union as Commander of the Defense Force Training Center. You will be one of our newest Provisional Troopers. Since we already inducted this month's training squads, you'll be starting off two weeks behind the others. That means you'll have to work extra hard to catch up. Third Chief Osaben and First Trooper Mannix are my training instructors. They answer to me, and you answer to them. Understand?" Adan nodded. "Provisional Troopers should answer their superiors verbally," she added.

"Yes, Commander."

Sala looked down at the files sitting on the desk before her, then looked over Adan's shoulder. "Osaben?"

The door opened, and Third Chief Osaben stepped inside. "Yes, Commander?"

"I believe you have two squads that are each short a Provisional Trooper?"

"Yes, Commander. Training Squads Ten and Eleven."

Sala nodded. "Perfect. Let's put Testa in Squad Ten. And assign him a mentor within the squad to help him catch up."

"Understood, Commander."

Adan spoke up before he even realized it. "What about Bo?"

The Commander leveled her gaze at Adan and, for the first

time, he felt the full force behind it. He gulped but stopped himself from apologizing. "Citizen Shen shouldn't be your concern at the moment." Then she paused and seemed to consider what to say next. "But I want you focused on what's happening here," she added, "so I'll share that Shen's tribunal is happening later this morning. I've asked the Magistrate for the same sentence given to you, and I have no doubt they will do that. When Citizen Shen arrives here, he will be assigned to another training squad that is short a Trooper."

"So you're splitting us up?" Adan heard Osaben shift behind him. He'd spoken up out of turn again, and the Third Chief didn't like it. Adan knew he was pushing his luck.

The Commander pushed her chair back, stood, and walked to the front of her desk. Then she reached out and took hold of his chin, lifting Adan's head to look at it directly. She turned his head to the side, pointing his reddened cheek at her. "It looks like I'm not the first person you've spoken to out of turn today. You may want to break yourself of that habit, Testa." Then she let him go and sat down on her desk. "Of course, I'm splitting you up. While it happens to be the best way to fit you into our current ranks, I would have done it anyway. I've seen what the two of you can accomplish together, and I will have none of that here. My goal is to mold your ambition through heavy training and strict discipline into something that will benefit the Defense Force." She paused for a few moments while her words sunk in. "Make no mistake, here, Testa. You owe me your life. Therefore, I own you now." She paused and allowed a tiny smile to creep onto her face. "Furthermore, I know who you are."

Adan finally understood what she'd meant when she said that earlier. "You know what happened to them. My parents."

It wasn't a question.

Adan heard Osaben move again and saw the Commander glance at them and shake her head. Once again, he spoke without permission, but she hadn't stopped him yet. Adan suspected that it would be his last opportunity to speak up like that without getting into trouble. He needed to take advantage of it.

The Commander looked back at Adan and smiled. Maybe she was pleased that he'd worked out her meaning. "I do, Citizen Testa. Just like I also know Citizen Shen's true identity." Adan sharply inhaled before he could stop himself. "I see you do, as well. If I'm satisfied with the progress you've both made during your term of service, I'll keep the information I have about Citizen Shen to myself. And I'll share the information I have about your parents with you."

So there was the promise and the threat. Sala knew the answers Adan was looking for. And she knew the information Bo was trying to hide. All Adan and Bo had to do was fall in line for the sake of each other.

Adan heard a knock on the door just before First Trooper Mannix stepped inside. They were holding a bundle of stacked, folded clothes with a pair of black boots on top.

The Commander looked at them as they stood there. "You have Testa's uniform, Trooper?"

Mannix nodded. "Yes, Commander."

Sala nodded, then leaned back at Adan. "What about you? Do you have any more questions or outbursts?"

"No, Commander," Adan replied.

"Very well." Sala stood. "Stand up, Testa." Adan got out of his chair and stood facing her. "Place your right fist over your heart and repeat after me. I, Citizen Adan Testa."

Adan put his fist over his heart. "I, Citizen Adan Testa."

"Do solemnly swear to faithfully serve the Bolvar Union without question or complaint."

"Do solemnly swear," he repeated, "to faithfully serve the Bolvar Union without question or complaint."

"And to always place the needs of the Union, the Committee, and its Citizens above my own."

Adan took a breath before continuing. "And to always place the needs of the Union, the Committee, and its Citizens above my own."

"For the entire duration of my required service in the Bolvar Union Defense Force."

Adan paused for just a moment, then sighed. "For the entire duration of my required service in the Bolvar Union Defense Force."

The Commander smiled. "Wonderful. Then, with the power granted to me by the Bolvar Union Committee and for the Founders' glory, I hereby induct you in the Bolvar Union Defense Force. Welcome aboard, Provisional Trooper Testa."

Adan kept his face impassive and tried to ignore the bead of sweat running down his back. So that was it. Despite everything he'd done, he was now a Gray Coat for better or worse. "Thank you, Commander."

Sala nodded. "You may stand at ease, Trooper. Osaben?"

"Yes. Commander?"

"Bring Testa to the barracks so he can meet the rest of his squad. And make sure he gets cleaned up and changed."

"Right away, Commander. Come on, Testa, let's get moving. Mannix, you're with us."

Adan followed Osaben out into the corridor with Mannix

on his tail. Osaben led them to the t-intersection at the corridor's end, then stopped and turned to face them.

"Alright, Provie, stop right there and listen up. I've already introduced myself to you, but you've joined our ranks now, so I'll do it properly. I'm Third Chief Tam Osaben. I use he and him pronouns. You may address me as Chief or Third Chief Osaben. This is First Trooper Veris Mannix, who uses they and them pronouns. You should address them as First Trooper. Understand?"

"Yes, Chief," Adan responded.

"Outstanding. Now, I don't know what the Commander sees in you or why she let you talk back to her like that. But you're a Provisional Trooper now, and I can guarantee you that kind of behavior has consequences it didn't have a few minutes ago. Do I make myself clear?"

"Yes, Chief."

"Outstanding. You're joining Squad Ten. What the Commander said about playing catch-up is no joke. You're behind, so the next few weeks will be tough for you. Now, grab your things from Mannix, and let's get you to your barracks."

"Yes, Chief." Adan reached out and took the stacked clothing and boots from Mannix. Then Osaben turned and led them down the right-hand corridor. They passed a series of numbered doors lining both sides of the corridor until they reached door ten, where they stopped.

Osaben glanced at the timepiece on his wrist. "The Provies should all be awake by now. Mannix, I'll give you the honor of introducing Testa. I'll handle getting things set up with the instructors."

Mannix nodded. "Yes, Chief."

Adan watched Osaben continue down the corridor, then

107

turned back to Mannix.

"Come on, Testa," Mannix said, "let's get this over with." They opened the door and led him inside the barracks room. Adan saw eight narrow beds, four on each side facing the center, with a tall, standing locker next to each one. The bed on the right, closest to the door, was still made. All the others had clearly been slept in.

Seven people were milling around the room in various stages of undress. They must've recently woken up. Then Mannix reached under their uniform jacket and pulled out a whistle on a chain. They put it to their lips and blew out three short chirps.

"Come to attention," someone called out. Suddenly everyone dropped what they were doing and rushed to stand at the foot of their beds facing the center of the room. Some of them were still wearing their sleeping clothes, either just bleached-white undershorts or shorts and a tight, bleached-white, sleeveless undershirt. A few had already put on their gray trousers.

"You call this pathetic slouching standing at attention?" Mannix shouted. "Straighten those backs, Provies!" Everyone made a decent attempt to properly stand up straighter. Adan thought they did a good job considering they'd only been working at it for a couple of weeks. But Mannix growled and stuffed the whistle back down into their uniform. "Absolutely deplorable. You're lucky I'm not here to drill you, or we'd be at this all day." They looked over at Adan and gestured for him to step up. He took a reluctant step forward, then Mannix grabbed his arm and pulled him until he was standing in front of them. "This is Provisional Trooper Testa. Your Commander has seen fit to add him to Squad Ten. Maybe she wants to have someone in this squad who might actually pass their first round of Monthlies. Mostok!"

The Trooper standing in front of the last bed on the left stepped forward. They had a handsome face with a firm jaw and a smokey brown complexion, a muscled, athletic build, and a lightly hairy chest. Their short black hair was parted on one side. "Yes, First Trooper!"

"Who's your Second Team Leader?"

"Provisional Trooper Tabata, First Trooper."

"Step forward, Tabata."

The Trooper standing across from Mostok stepped up. In many ways, they were Mostok's opposite. They were taller, with a willowy build. Their wavy black hair fell to their shoulders and was swept to the side to reveal a narrow, golden-brown face. They were already wearing mottled gray uniform trousers with a tight, white, sleeveless undershirt. "Here, First Trooper."

Mannix grunted again. "Tabata, your team is short a Provie?"

"Yes, First Trooper."

"Not anymore, Tabata. Testa is now on your team. Mostok, you and Tabata are responsible for ensuring that Provisional Trooper Testa is brought up to squad readiness for your upcoming Monthly. Understood?"

"Yes, First Trooper," Mostok and Tabata answered in unison.

"Outstanding," Mannix shared, echoing Chief Osaben. "You're dismissed, Provies." As the others fell out of formation, Mannix grabbed Adan's arm and turned him around to face them. "Here's your Trooper ID," they said, handing over a new ID card. Adan looked at it to see that it had the same photo from his citizen ID card. "Keep it with you at all times. Understood?"

"Yes, First Trooper."

"Good luck, Testa. You're going to need it." Mannix surveyed the rest of the people in the room, then shook their head. "Founders help us," they murmured, then walked out of the room and closed the door.

Adan stood there and endured the withering judgment of the others. He could think of worse ways to be introduced to his new squad. But he still felt exactly the same as he had when he'd first been introduced to his housemates at the group home ten years ago. Add in the fact that he was more than a year younger than everyone else in the room, and Adan felt entirely out of place.

Mostok and Tabata, the two Provisional Troopers–or Provies–that Mannix had spoken with, walked over to him. Neither looked very pleased, but Mostok less so. They looked him up and down with their deep-set, rich, brown eyes, then frowned. Then they looked over their shoulder at the rest of the squad. "Alright, everyone, the party's over. We've still got a whole day of training ahead of us." Adan heard a series of moans and groans as everyone got back to making their beds. Then Mostok turned back to Adan and held out a hand. "I'm Garun Mostok. I'm the Squad Leader for this group of misfits and asses. Oh, and I'm a he."

"Adan Testa," Adan replied as he shook Garun's hand. Up close, the Squad Leader was even more handsome. "Also a he."

Tabata held out their hand next. "I'm Jenra Tabata, she and her."

Adan shook her hand, too. In contrast to Garun, Jenra's

small eyes were a striking hazel that was almost green. "It's good to meet you."

Jenra smiled. "I don't believe that for a second, but thank you."

"So," Garun said, frowning. "What's your story, Testa? Did the Commander really send you to us? And what's with the bandage on your head?"

Adan reached up and touched his head without thinking. Then he quickly lowered his hand. He wasn't sure what he should tell them. The whole truth? Partial truth? Make something up? Adan was at a total loss.

Garun's frown turned into a scowl, and he stepped up close to Adan. "Come on, Testa. If you're here to slow us down, then you can just turn around and walk right back out that door."

Jenra frowned and grabbed Garun's shoulder, pulling him away from Adan. "That's enough, Garun. Give him a break and get your team ready. I'll handle things with Adan."

Garun looked like he wanted to protest, but he just shook his head. "Fine." Then he turned and walked back to his locker.

Jenra gave Adan an apologetic smile. "Sorry about him. He's not a morning person. He'll warm up to you eventually." She looked down at the stack of clothing in his hands, then back up at him. "They really just tossed you in here, didn't they?" Adan nodded. "Well, we'll just have to do your orientation as we go along. But the first thing you need to do is get ready. Can you shower and get dressed in twenty minutes?"

Adan shrugged. "That depends on how far away the shower is. I can take a good enough shower in five."

"Then that'll leave you fifteen minutes to get dressed. The showers and other facilities are back there." Jenra pointed over her shoulder to a door on the other side of the room. "Towels and soap are in there already." Then she pointed to the locker next to his bed. "You can put your old clothes in there for now. They'll get confiscated at some point, but there's no need to worry about that now. Anything else?"

Adan's eyes opened wide with a sudden overload of questions, then he smiled and shook his head. "No. I'll go get showered."

The communal facilities included toilets, which he hadn't factored into his shower time. So, including some time in a toilet stall and removing and discarding his head bandage, it took him ten minutes before he started getting dressed. Thankfully he was plenty experienced with that already. His uniform included three pairs of clean undershorts, three sleeveless undershirts, and three pairs of socks. The trousers and jackets were covered in the same mottled gray pattern he'd seen the other Troopers wearing. Adan was surprised to see Testa name patches attached to his uniform jackets. How did anyone have the time to do that already? Adan had just finished tying his last boot when Jenra collected him for their morning meal.

On the way to the mess hall, Jenra explained how the day would go. After they ate, the squad would have several hours of classroom education. Each day was a different lesson, ranging from basic mechanics to military tactics to weapons training. Even though the squad had a head start on him, Jenra assured him that they were all still beginners. It would take a little catch-up, but he wasn't that far behind.

After their classroom lesson, the squads had physical

training. Squad Ten had been studying basic hand-to-hand combat so far that week. Once that was finished, they moved on to squad duty. The DFTC was maintained by the Training Squads. Each squad was assigned a maintenance activity for two weeks before rotating to another. Squad Ten was due to start their second duty assignment that day.

"It's not laundry, is it?" Adan asked.

Jenra shook her head. "No, we've got classroom cleanup. Why?"

"I was working in a laundry plant until yesterday."

Jenra laughed. "Well, when it's our turn, then you'll have a head start on the rest of us."

The line for the mess hall was filling up fast when they got there. There were eleven squads currently in training, with two more scheduled to start the following month. But eleven squads meant eighty-eight Provies would be getting into line. Well, eighty-seven, Adan corrected himself. Until Bo showed up. There was no sign of him yet, and Adan didn't know which squad was number eleven.

All the Provies lined up by squad in the order they arrived. While there was always enough food for everyone, getting there earlier meant you had more time to eat it. It looked like half the squads were already in line when Squad Ten arrived. Adan was glad they weren't too late on his behalf. A pair of Troopers stationed at the mess hall entrance checked everyone's ID before they were allowed to enter. A whispered question to Jenra gave Adan his first insight into the DFTC's control over the Provisional Troopers. If you didn't have your ID, you didn't eat.

After collecting his tray and a mug of tea, Adan followed Jenra over to their table. There were eight seats per table, and each squad ate together. Jenra invited Adan to take the seat next to her. Then she started introducing him to everyone. It was helpful that everyone had their surnames on their jackets because he would never remember them all otherwise. There were two teams in his squad. He was on the Blue Team, led by Jenra. The other two members were Simi Andur (he pronouns, great hair) and Wellan Ruda (he pronouns, beautiful eyes). The other team, Team Red, was led by Garun, their squad leader. The remaining members of the squad, and his team, were Uso Araga (he pronouns, tall and really muscular), Sabina Nabar (she pronouns, infectious laugh), and Fan Nuria (they pronouns, really tall and possibly even skinnier than Adan). Once the introductions were complete, they started on all the questions.

"So, where are you from?" Simi asked.

"The Lowers," Adan answered. "A group home a couple blocks off Bartok near Daigur."

"What was with that bandage?" Wellan wondered.

"I was in an accident. A delivery van I was riding in crashed into a wall."

"You look pretty young to be a delivery driver," Sabina commented. "How old are you?"

"Almost seventeen."

"Come on," Simi challenged him. "If you're only sixteen, what were you doing in a delivery van?"

Suddenly it was the moment of truth. Adan figured the real story would probably come out anyway, so he decided it wasn't worth the effort to cover it up. "My best friend Bo and I stole seven barrels of bashki from the premium distillery in a borrowed delivery van. Then some Pinchers started chasing us, so I pushed one of the barrels out the back of the van and smashed their auto. But some other Pinchers shot the tires out on our van. So we crashed, and I hit my head on the dash panel."

Wellan let out a low whistle. Everyone else at the table stared at Adan in shock. Everyone except Garun, that is, who looked at him with narrow-eyed contempt.

"That's why you're here," Garun announced. The disgust in his voice was clear. "This is your punishment? Because, if what you say is true, you should be standing in front of a firing squad instead of eating breakfast at my table. How is that possible?"

Jenra shook her hand and shot Garun an angry glare. "Your table?"

But Garun ignored her. "Answer the question, Testa."

Not Adan anymore. Now he was back to Testa. He kept his expression casual and shrugged. "You'll have to ask the Commander, I suppose. But I don't imagine she'll want to explain herself to you any more than she did to me."

Garun couldn't contain his shock. "The Commander? Are you telling me the Commander herself plucked you from a firing squad and put you in my squad? I've never heard a bigger load of marsh pig slop in my life."

Jenra leaned forward and put her face between Garun and Adan. "That's enough, Garun!"

For a moment, it looked like Garun wouldn't accept Jenra's rebuke. Then he slammed his fist on the table, stood, and stormed off. The rest of the squad sat quietly, at a loss for what just happened, until Uso finally spoke up.

"I guess that means Mostok's not gonna eat his toast, right?"

Everyone chuckled as Uso reached across the table and took Garun's toast from his tray.

Jenra frowned and shook her head. "I'd say that Garun's just being an ass, but I've never seen him act like this before."

"That's true," Wellan added, "but then we barely know each other yet. It's only been two weeks."

Adan didn't know what to make of Garun's outburst, but he was glad the rest of the squad seemed to accept him. "How did he end up as Squad Leader, anyway?"

"Oh, that's easy," Sabina answered. "His family is up in Gallur Heights. Supposedly he even has an uncle on the Committee."

"I thought it was a cousin," Fan claimed.

Sabina shrugged. "Alright, maybe it's his uncle's cousin, then."

"At any rate," Jenra added, "don't let him get to you."

Adan nodded. "My shift supervisor at the laundry plant was a lot worse. His default setting was unpleasant until shift's end when he got really mean."

"Are you talking about Ulla?" Uso asked between mouthfuls.

Adan laughed. "You were at the laundry plant?"

Uso nodded. "For a year. This is a lot better."

"Hey," Wellan cut in, "what about your friend? He got picked up too, right?"

Adan sighed. "He's supposedly on his way here, too. The Commander said that she was assigning him to another short squad."

"That'll be Eleven," Jenra shared, then glanced at the clock on the wall. "Listen up, Ten. We've got to head to our lesson, so everyone get those last bites in."

Everyone except for Adan quickly saluted her. "Yes, Trooper!"

Adan saw right away that Jenra had already earned the squad's respect, despite only being the second in command. Hopefully, that would help smooth things over with their actual Squad Leader. Adan didn't understand why, but Garun definitely didn't like him.

Garun was already in the classroom when Squad Ten arrived. He didn't acknowledge Adan at all. Until Garun got over whatever petty, childish issue was bothering him, Adan preferred the silent treatment. And he intended to give Garun whatever space he needed for that.

The squad's lesson for the day was Neskan geography. Adan remembered studying it at the Instruction Center. It was one of his favorite subjects. It also came in handy when he and Bo started planning their escape, dreaming of what life would be like on the other side of the Osbaks.

But the version of the map they displayed in that day's class was different from the one he'd seen before. It was more detailed, for a start. Bolvar was there, of course, both the city and the valley it was named for. The Bolvar Valley ran vaguely north to south, following the path of the meandering Daralsha River, and was wider in the center than at the ends. The valley was surrounded by the Osbak Mountains. The chain spanned the eastern coast of Ateri, Neska's only significant landmass. The Eastern Ocean lay along the coastline to the east of the Osbaks. To the west was the Badlands. Or, so Adan had been taught.

Adan noticed several settlements marked on the new map throughout the Eastern Osbak foothills on the edge of the Tepani Plains. The grasslands spread west toward the vast Adak Desert. Most of central Ateri was sand. According to the instructor, those settlements Adan saw were Bolvaran

117

Defense Force outposts. They staged troops and weapons there to protect resource gathering expeditions from raiders.

He was surprised to learn the Gray Coats were stationed so far outside the wall. How hard would it be to escape west if Adan were to get posted there? He'd already be outside of the city and across the mountains.

After class, Garun had the squad line up in pairs and walk in formation to the Physical Training Center. He and Jenra led the procession, with Adan and Wellan in the rear. Adan didn't know if that was what they usually did or if Garun was just asserting his authority.

First Trooper Mannix was waiting for them when they arrived. They looked to Adan like they could take most people apart without breaking a sweat. So they probably knew a thing or two about close combat. The squad started the lesson by removing their jackets and lining up in a row. Adan went through the warm-ups with the rest of the squad, then Mannix paired everyone off for sparring practice. They assigned Adan to Jenra for that part. Since the squad had been an odd number before Adan arrived, Jenra had been sparring with Mannix. That made her the ideal candidate for catching Adan up to the rest of them. But Mannix also had a warning for Jenra.

"He's barely a day into recovering from a concussion," they reminded her. "So no heavy contact. Just stick with the basics."

"Understood, First Trooper."

Mannix nodded, then moved off to check the next pair's form.

"I didn't think the Defense Force would care about me that much," Adan shared once Mannix had walked off."

Jenra looked around to make sure everyone was out of earshot, then leaned in close enough to whisper to him. "They don't. You're an asset of the State now. Damaging you would be like driving a delivery van into a wall."

Adan just managed to stop himself from laughing out loud. Jenra winked at him and then showed him the basic sparring stance. After he had that down, she led him through the offensive moves she'd been taught. Once he felt ready, she invited him to try knocking her down.

Adan suddenly wasn't sure. "For real?"

Jenra laughed. "Why? I thought you were ready. I don't want you to attack me. Just try to knock me down."

"Alright."

Adan stepped back into a grappling position, then lunged forward and tried to get his arm around Jenra's neck. But she was ready for him. She grabbed his arm, used his momentum to pull him forward, then twisted his arm back behind him. Once she put her other hand between his shoulder blades, Adan couldn't move without hurting his shoulder.

Then Jenra let go of him. "That wasn't bad, but you need to anticipate your opponent's defense. It's like chess. You have to think about your next move before you even take your first one."

Adan smiled. "I've never played chess."

Jenra laughed. "Then it's like Tik-Tix. When you know your opponent is about to play a blue counter, you play a red one to cut them off first."

Adan nodded. "Ah, strategy. That I know."

"Okay, then, Citizen Strategy. Let's try again."

Adan reset his stance and lunged again. He was ready to pull his arm away as soon as she grabbed for it. But Jenra changed things up, ducking under his lunge and grabbing him around the waist. Then she twisted while falling backward and had him on the ground underneath her.

"No fair," Adan complained as Jenra helped him back up.

"It's not going to be fair until you learn all these moves."

Then Adan noticed some commotion from the rest of the squad. He looked over to see Third Chief Osaben walking into the training area. The Chief said something to Mannix, who nodded, then grabbed their whistle. They blew a loud chirp to get the squad's attention.

"Take a ten-minute breather, everyone," Mannix announced. "I'll be right back."

Adan smiled. "Oh no. And I was having so much fun, too."

Jenra laughed and sat down, then patted the mat next to her. "Come on, Citizen Strategy. Take a seat and enjoy the downtime. It's rare."

He nodded and sat down, watching Osaben and Mannix as they left. What could that be about, he wondered. Then he realized what it had to be. "Bo," he said aloud without realizing it.

"Is that your friend?" Jenra asked.

Adan looked at her in surprise, then nodded. "Yeah. That has to be what's going on. Bo's finally here."

"You must be worried about him."

Adan sighed. Suddenly all the anxiety he'd felt that morning came rushing back. "I haven't seen him since before the Pinchers locked us up. I just want to know if he's still okay."

Jenra frowned. "Was he hurt in your accident?"

Adan shook his head. "Not really. I mean, maybe. I thought he might have cracked a rib, but the Medic looked at us

120

separately. So, I don't know."

"Can I ask you a personal question?"

Adan nodded. "Sure, why not?"

"Are you and Bo, you know, romantic?"

Adan shook his head. "Me and Bo? No, I'm not his type." He thought about the girls Bo had developed crushes on, then looked at Jenra. "You're more his type, actually."

"But he's your type," she said with a smirk.

Adan chuckled. "Is it that obvious?"

Jenra shook her head. "Yeah, to me. My brother's gay, so I know all the signs."

Adan laughed. "There are signs? I wish someone would teach them to me. That would save me a lot of heartaches."

Then Jenra laughed, too. "Okay, maybe there aren't exactly signs. I just have a sense for it. But I hope your friend is alright."

"Me, too."

Mannix still hadn't returned when their ten-minute break was up. So Garun took charge of the squad, ordering everyone to pair off and resume their hand-to-hand practice matches. But when Jenra tried to join up with Adan, Garun stepped in and took her place. Jenra immediately protested. Garun didn't like that.

"Are you questioning my orders, Tabata?"

"No, I'm questioning your judgment. Mannix already warned me to go easy on him because of his concussion. Besides, he's Team Blue, which makes him my responsibility."

"And this whole squad is my responsibility. Now, step aside. I'll go easy on him. I just want to see where he's at."

They sounded just like his parents arguing when he was young. It was eerie to watch. Adan shook his head and stepped up to Garun and Jenra. "It's fine, Jenra. He's right to test out my skills."

Jenra looked at Adan with suspicion. Truthfully, Adan hoped to win some points with Garun by taking his side. It looked like Jenra probably realized that, too. He hated to do it, but Garun could probably make his life difficult if he wanted to. So, it had to be done. Jenra shook her head and stepped away, offering Garun her spot. "If you say so. Don't let me get in your way."

Garun nodded. "Alright, Testa. You know the basic grappling position?"

"I do."

"Then let's start there." Garun crouched down slightly and put his hands out by his sides. "I'll be on defense. You try to knock me over whenever you're ready."

Adan widened his stance and got into position. He shifted his weight slightly, back and forth, as he looked over Garun's stance. Then he feinted a forward lunge to test Garun's reaction and saw his arms twitch. Adan smiled, then lunged for real, aiming for Garun's waist. Garun moved forward to close the gap and wrap his arms around Adan before he could block. But Adan was ready for that. He twisted to his side and let Garun overshoot him. Then he grabbed Garun from behind and fell forward, letting their combined weight bring them both down to the mat.

Garun started squirming, so Adan rolled off him and stood up. Garun pushed himself up and dusted off his thighs. "Not bad, Testa," he said reluctantly. "Let's see if you can do it again."

"Yes, Squad Leader."

Adan returned to his position and resumed his grappling

stance. Garun got back into his stance, and Adan could already see Garun putting more weight on his right side. He was anticipating that Adan would try the same attack again. So Adan lunged forward just like the first time, and Garun stepped up to get Adan into his reach. Then Adan twisted in the opposite direction. Garun shot right past Adan, leaving his other side totally exposed. Adan had him on the floor a moment later. Garun pushed up before Adan could roll off, throwing Adan back onto his side. His Squad Leader was obviously losing his cool.

The rest of the squad had already given up on their practice sparring. Instead, they started gathering to watch the new addition take on the Squad Leader. Garun didn't even seem to notice. His jaw was tightly clenched as he pushed himself back up to his feet. His nostrils flared as he inhaled sharply. "Looks like you may be a little more advanced than you let on, Testa."

Adan shook his head. "Jenra's a good teacher," he countered. Not to mention that he knew a thing or two about defending himself from bullies. After all, he'd spent years fending off the playful and not so playful attacks of his older housemates. And those instincts told him that it was probably time to lose.

Garun walked back to his position and got back into his stance. "Let's try it one more time, Testa."

Adan glanced over at Jenra, who just shrugged. You chose this, Citizen Strategy, her expression said. You've got to finish it. Adan nodded at Garun. "Alright." Then he got back into position.

He could already see the difference in Garun's stance. The way he flexed his thighs, Adan guessed that he was planning on charging forward the minute Adan moved. Both times before, Garun had tried to get Adan within arms reach. If Garun tried that again, then he'd let him.

Adan lunged, and, as expected, Garun charged forward. Adan kept straight on, aiming for Garun's waist. But Garun twisted at the last moment and swung his bent arm back at Adan's face. Garun's elbow struck Adan right in the eye socket with an audible smack. Adan dropped like a stone onto his side as the pain flared through his skull. His vision flashed and blurred, and, for a moment, he thought he would pass out.

Suddenly Jenra was there, kneeling down next to him. "Adan!" she called out, then helped to roll him onto his back. "Talk to me, Adan. Are you alright?"

Then Adan heard Garun burst out laughing. "Well, it looks like the new Provie isn't so good at this after all."

"Stand down, Mostok!" That was Mannix, who must've just gotten back. Or, had they been there the whole time? Adan wasn't sure. Everything was confusing.

Garun snapped to attention. "Yes, First Trooper!"

Then Mannix was kneeling over him. "Look at me, Testa."

Adan tried to focus on them, but their face was blurry and indistinct. "Everything's foggy."

Mannix reached down to hold his head still with one hand, then gently probed his brow and cheek with their other hand. "Doesn't feel like anything's broken, but you still need to get looked at. Tabata, get this Trooper to the Medic." Jenra nodded. Then Mannix stood and rounded on Garun. They struck him hard across the face with an open palm, knocking him off his feet. "My office, Mostok. Now."

Official Log of First Officer Marta Kanerva

Neskan Colony, Day 91, Year 1 (Neskan Calendar)

We just had our second monthly Officer's meeting. There was a lot of debate, but we eventually decided on the full five years. That's the longest state of emergency the Colony Bureau protocols allow for. But we agreed that we'd know by then if Neska would be a viable colony or not. Until then, the Captain remains in charge, and I remain First Officer. I'll officially inform the crew of this today. But I've already had Sander and Marketta quietly testing the waters for this, so I know they'll support the Captain's decision. Who's to say whether they'll feel the same in a year or two? As long as everyone's still alive in a year or two, I'll be happy enough.

Chapter 7

After examining him, the Medic decided that Adan probably didn't need an x-ray. But they'd still excused him from squad duty for the day and forbade him from participating in any physical training for two weeks. In the end, Garun hadn't done any permanent damage with his cheap elbow shot. But he had given Adan a serious-looking black eye.

"I think it makes you look dangerous," Jenra commented as she walked him back to their barracks.

Adan had intended to join in with squad duty instead of skipping out on it. It was only light duty. But his visit to the Medic had taken too long. "Danger prone, more like."

Jenra chuckled. "It was a cheap shot. Breaking the rules is no way to win a sparring match."

First Trooper Mannix had wholeheartedly agreed with that sentiment. Part of Adan felt sorry for Garun after Mannix had smacked him down to the floor. Not that Garun didn't deserve it. "I wonder why he hates me so much."

"He doesn't hate you, Adan. But he's obviously threatened by you for some reason. Maybe he's jealous?"

Adan scoffed. "Of me? I'm just a thatch rat from a group home in the Lowers. I haven't got a damn thing for him to be jealous of."

"I don't know. My guess is that it's all the attention you're getting. The way the Commander dropped you into the middle of the squad this morning in your street clothes and head bandage got his attention. Then you tell us that story about getting nabbed by the Pinchers after an auto chase and shoot out. I bet most of the squad thinks you're the most interesting person they've met since they got here. Or maybe ever. I know I do."

Could that really be why? It made sense. Garun was probably used to being the center of attention. Being the Squad Leader just fed that part of his ego. And here came Adan, stealing his food supply. "If that's true, then it'll just be a matter of time before he discovers that I'm probably the least interesting person in the squad."

Jenra smirked as she opened the barracks door. "I seriously doubt that's true."

The room was empty. The rest of the squad had gone to their daily cleaning duty while Jenra and Adan were with the Medic. Adan walked in and sat down on his bed. "It's always been true. I don't know why being here makes that any different."

Jenra sat down next to him, shaking her head. "You know, sometimes you really are only sixteen, Adan. No offense."

Adan furrowed his brows in confusion. "None taken. I'm not even sure what that's supposed to mean. Besides, I'll be seventeen soon. It's not like you're that much older than me."

"It wasn't an insult. I just meant that you're still figuring out who you are. And part of that job is realizing that you're not as boring and ordinary as you thought."

Maybe Jenra had a point. The Adan serving extra time in the Defense Force as a punishment for a bashki heist gone wrong was different from the Adan who worked in a laundry plant. He grinned at Jenra. "It's a good thing you're so wise. Otherwise, I'd never learn."

Jenra scoffed and rolled her eyes. "Fine, never mind, Citizen Boring." There was a knock on the door. "Come."

The door opened, and Third Chief Osaben walked in. Jenra jumped up to stand at attention, with Adan a few beats behind her.

"Stand at ease, Troopers," Osaben instructed them.

Adan relaxed his knees and put his hands behind his back. Osaben walked over and inspected Adan's black eye. "Looks like Mostok got you pretty good there, Testa."

"Yes, Chief."

"I read the Medic's report. Since you've been excused from physical training for the rest of the month, we'll have to make other arrangements for you to spend that time productively."

"Arrangements, Chief?"

Osaben nodded. "You're a valuable State asset now, Provie. And the State will squeeze that value out of you somehow."

"Yes, Chief."

"But we'll deal with that tomorrow." He turned to Jenra next. "The reason I'm here is to see you, Provisional Trooper Tabata. Effective immediately, you are hereby promoted to the role of Squad Leader for Training Squad Ten."

Jenra was so shocked she was momentarily speechless. "I, uh– Yes, Chief."

Osaben smiled. "Never thought I'd hear you stumble over your words, Tabata. The Commander has decided that Mostok is not fit to continue as Squad Leader. You were the logical replacement. You'll need to choose a Second to take over Blue Team, as well."

Adan almost blurted out his question but stopped himself in time. "Permission to speak, Chief?"

Osaben nodded. "Speak, Provie."

"What will happen with Mostok?"

"Mostok will rejoin his squad, of course."

Adan was surprised to hear that. It sounded like removing him from his Squad Leader position was only the beginning of his punishment. The rest would be returning Garun to the squad as a regular old Provie. "Outstanding, Chief."

Osaben grunted. "I'm so glad to hear you approve, Testa." He glanced at his timepiece. "It's nearly mealtime, Tabata. You may want to go collect your squad. I'll leave it to you to inform them of the change in leadership."

"Yes, Chief."

Adan and Jenra relaxed from their stance the minute the door closed behind the Chief. "Wow," Adan uttered as he sat back down on the bed.

"No kidding," Jenra agreed. "I didn't see that coming."

"How do you think Garun took the news?"

Jenra shook her head. "There's no telling. I guess I'd better keep my guard up unless I want to join you in the black eye club, Citizen Dangerous. Come on, let's get everyone and get some food before they're scraping the bottoms of the pans."

Jenra walked over to the door and opened it to reveal Adan's best friend standing there. Bo had finally arrived! He was already dressed in his Trooper gear. He had a bruise on his

129

forehead and his left arm in a sling but otherwise looked no worse for wear. And Bo was smiling, so he must have been okay.

"Adan?"

"Bo!" Adan ran up to give his friend a hug, forcing Jenra to step out of the way. But Adan stopped when he ran into the sling. "Oh, sorry."

Bo laughed, then wrapped his right arm around Adan and pulled him close. "It's okay. Just be gentle."

Adan gave him a soft hug then stepped back. "Are you alright?"

Jenra politely cleared her throat. Adan had forgotten she was there. "So, you must be the getaway driver?"

"I'm sorry, Jenra," Adan hurriedly apologized. "Bo Shen, this is Jenra Tabata. She's my Squad Leader."

Bo snapped to attention at the mention of her title and saluted. "Provisional Trooper Tabata."

Jenra shared a surprised smile. Adan imagined her new rank would take some getting used to. "Stand at ease, Provie," she ordered him. "I'm glad you're here and mostly okay. Adan's been worrying about you all day."

Bo looked down at the sling on his arm. "Yeah. It's just a sprain. And my ribs are wrapped so tightly I can hardly breathe." He looked at Adan's face. "But that's quite the shiner, Adan. I don't remember that from last night."

Adan reflexively put his hand to his cheek. "Yeah, this is more recent."

"Well," Jenra announced, "I'll go get the rest of the squad. That should give you both a few minutes to catch up before you meet us in the mess line."

"Thanks, Jenra," Adan called out as she walked out and let

the door close behind her. He looked back toward his bed. "Feel like sitting?"

Bo nodded. "Sure, why not." He followed Adan and sat next to him on Adan's bed. "So, I assume you met the Commander?"

Adan shivered at the mention of her. "I'm still not sure what to make of her."

"She knows who I am, Adan."

"I know. She told me. She also told me that she knows what really happened to my parents."

Bo stopped. "Seriously? Do you think she's telling the truth?"

Adan shrugged. "There's no way to know for sure. But I think so. She doesn't have any reason to lie about that. She basically owns us."

Bo sighed. "Yeah, she said that to me, too. She saved us from the firing squad, right? I'm still trying to figure out if that was a good thing or not. Your eye isn't filling me with confidence."

Adan chuckled and pointed to his black eye. "This? It's nothing. Just a minor disagreement with my former Squad leader."

Bo looked impressed. "Really? I see you're already making friends with important people."

Adan laughed. "I don't know about friends. But Jenra seems nice."

Bo nodded and looked over toward the door as if she was still standing there. "She does seem nice."

Adan laughed again. "I already told her she's probably your type."

Bo rolled his eyes. "Great. So, there goes my game."

"Whatever. I got you in with her. You're welcome." Adan sighed as the obvious question came to his mind. He didn't want to bring it up since it would force them to acknowledge an uncomfortable reality. But there was no use putting it off. "What do you think happened?"

Bo let out a long sigh. "I wish I knew. I mean, someone must've turned us in. That much is obvious. But who?"

"It had to be either Min or Calin, right? Who else knew?"

Bo grunted with frustration. "I've known Calin my whole life. If she wanted me in here, she could've just made it happen. And Min? They're the last person I'd expect to throw in with the Pinchers."

"Which would make them a good informant."

Bo stared ahead toward the door. Adan could see the fatigue on his face. And his skin had lost its usual glow. "I suppose that's true."

"What happened to you in the Pinch? After they separated us."

"Nothing. The Medic patched me up, then they left me in that cell. The Commander came to visit me and offered her veiled threats. Then my tribunal. Then here."

Adan glanced down at Bo's sling. "So all that's from the crash?"

Bo chuckled. "What, like they tortured me? What would I know that they'd want that badly?" He shook his head. "No, this is just me banging into the steering wheel too hard. I still can't believe the damn Pinchers shot at us."

"Yeah. I feel like I'm responsible for that. If I hadn't tossed that barrel–"

"Are you kidding?" Bo interrupted. "That was amazing. You know they'll be talking about that in the Pinch for a long

132

time."

Adan groaned. "Don't remind me. Now we've got targets on our backs."

Bo shook his head. "No. Now we've got another chance to try again. Only next time we'll plan things better." He glanced back at the door. "We should get going. I don't want my squad leader to start beating me up, too."

"Yeah, you're right." Adan grabbed Bo's arm. "I'm glad you're okay, Bo. I really was worried."

Bo smiled. "Same here. You know, that shiner makes you look kind of dangerous."

Adan laughed. "You're not the first person to tell me that."

The two friends left the barracks to join their squads. Both Ten and Eleven were just getting into the Mess Hall line. Jenra nodded to Adan as he slipped into line. Garun wasn't there. That was fine. Adan finally felt happy for the first time since he'd gotten to the DFTC. Yeah, he and Bo were stuck doing the very thing they tried to escape from. But at least they were together. And alive.

Garun finally showed up once everyone was seated and started eating. The whole squad stopped and watched him when he approached the table and looked for the empty seat. Everyone sat in a long moment of uncomfortable silence while Garun stood there. His expression was grim but otherwise unreadable. Then Jenra finally spoke up.

"Have a seat and join us, Garun."

A look of relief briefly flashed across his face. Then Garun nodded and sat. Adan struggled with how to feel about the state of things. Part of him wanted to rub it in that he'd ultimately come out on top of their confrontation. But Adan knew he had to make peace with the fact that Garun would still be part of the squad. It helped that Garun refused to look at him while they ate.

After dinner, the Provies were given an hour of what they called liberty. It was free time where they could choose between several approved activities, including visiting the DFTC Library, Physical Training Center, or Gun Range. Adan hadn't been approved for firearms yet and wasn't allowed any strenuous physical activity. That left going to the Library or sitting in their barracks room as Adan's only choices. Although he was plenty tired, Adan wasn't ready to go to bed yet, so he opted to see what the Library was about.

Jenra warned him to keep his expectations low, but Adan was surprised to see how big and well-stocked it was. The only Library he'd seen before was a small closet in the Instruction Center. Compared to that, the DFTC Library was huge. Adan counted at least two dozen pairs of shelves, all filled with books. He didn't know where to start.

"You look lost, Trooper."

Adan whirled around in surprise to see an older citizen standing behind him with a pair of books in their hands. They were dressed in plain, dark trousers and a light-colored sweater that offset their dark complexion. They were bald but had a thick white beard. Since they weren't in a uniform, Adan guessed they probably weren't part of the Defense Force. "I guess I am, Citizen. It's my first visit to the Library."

The older citizen chuckled. "By the look on your face, I'd guess it's your first visit to any Library." They held out the books. "Here, take these and follow me. I'll show you around."

Adan nodded and grabbed the books while the citizen wandered around him into the aisle between the rows of shelves. They stopped about halfway in and pointed to their right. "They go in there. On the spines, there, you'll see stickers with a set of numbers printed on them. Put them on the shelves in the proper order."

Adan looked at the books. He didn't know what the spine was, but he saw the stickers on the narrow part of the cover. When he walked between the shelves, he saw the same stickers facing out on all the books. After a few minutes of searching, Adan found where both books belonged. One was a heavy volume about some kind of mathematics. The other was a mathematics book specifically about magnetic fields. When he emerged from the shelves, the older citizen was no longer there. Adan shrugged, then walked back toward the front of the Library. The citizen was seated behind a desk off to the side of the room.

They looked up when Adan reappeared. "Excellent work, Trooper. Top-notch problem-solving skills, reshelving books correctly during your first Library visit."

Adan wasn't sure if that was an insult or not. "Thank you."

The older citizen smiled. "I'm the Librarian, which means I manage things here, among other duties. My name is Kapo Pelota, and I use he and him pronouns."

"I'm Provisional Trooper Adan Testa, also he and him."

"So, Testa, what brings you here?"

Adan wasn't sure how to answer that without insulting the Librarian. "It's my first liberty period, and I'm not allowed to do anything physically strenuous for the next two weeks."

The Librarian nodded. "How refreshingly honest of you, Testa. Since it sounds like you could be a frequent visitor, I'll give a brief rundown of how things work."

"Thank you, Librarian Pelota."

Pelota nodded again, then stood. He walked around the desk and led Adan to a cabinet full of small drawers. In each of those drawers was a set of cards organized by book titles. Each card also held the number for each book's location on the shelves. The shelves were organized by subject. If Adan knew a book's title, he could look it up in the cards. If he only knew what subject he was interested in, he could just browse the shelves.

"That seems easy enough," Adan commented.

"It's an old system that predates even our landing on Neska. But it still works just fine for our needs."

Adan hadn't expected to hear that. "Really?"

Pelota laughed. "You're surprised by that? Then you'll be shocked to learn that almost all of our technology and many of our social practices would be considered archaic by our First Explorer ancestors." Pelota turned back to the card cabinet, opened a drawer, and searched through the cards. Then he pulled one out and handed it to Adan. "Here, Testa. This is the first book you should read."

Adan took the card. The title on it read *Landfall: The Story of Settling Neska*. He looked up at Pelota. "First book?"

Pelota laughed again. "I like you, Testa. You have a sense of humor." Then he started walking back to his desk. "It's either that," he said over his shoulder, "or you start helping me shelve the books."

Adan chuckled, then headed into the shelves to find the book on the card. It wasn't very thick. And it had a nice painting of the Osbak Mountains on the cover. He opened the cover and flipped through the pages until he found one with a short paragraph written on it.

This volume comprises the collected testimonies of the first explorers to land on Neska. These stories were played back and recorded by hand for reproduction in this book in anticipation of the few remaining mem-stores breaking down.

Adan had already learned about the First Explorers. The subject was regularly talked about in the weeks approaching Landfall Day. But it could be interesting to learn more about them, he supposed. Adan snapped the book shut and returned to the Librarian's desk.

"Is there somewhere here I can sit and read this?"

The Librarian, busily making notations in a ledger book on his desk, looked up in irritation. "Why not take it back to your room and read it there?"

"Take it?"

Pelota nodded. "Yes, yes. Just take the card from inside the back cover, fill out your name and the date on the next available line, then hand it to me. You're allowed to check out any book for up to two weeks, but you can keep that one until you're finished if it takes longer."

Adan opened the back cover and saw a lined card sitting in a paper pocket that had been glued inside. He slipped the card out and looked at it. The book had only been checked out a half-dozen times, and no one had taken it in several years. Then he noticed the second name on the card. Cristina Sala. The Commander had checked out the book eighteen years ago. She'd clearly not been a Commander yet. She was only a Provie then, like him. Interesting. Adan took a pen from the cup on the desk and wrote his name and the date. Then he put the pen back and handed the card to the Librarian.

"Here you are."

"Thank you," the Librarian commented when he took the

card. "If anyone else is interested in books, feel free to bring them with you when you next come back."

"I will. Thank you."

Adan left the Library and headed back to his barracks room. As soon as he was back, he took off his boots, lay down on his bed, and started reading. It had been more than a year since he'd read a book, and he'd never done it for any reason other than to complete his lessons. It was slow going. He wasn't a strong reader. But he found himself engrossed in the stories of the first, and only, explorers to touch down on Neska.

The first chapter was a series of transcriptions made from the logs of Chander Sanyal. He was the Captain of the CSF Samuel Jennix. That was the exploration ship that crashed near a place they eventually named after him. Most people vaguely understood the location to be somewhere west of the Osbaks. Still, only the Union knew precisely where it was. Or, so they claimed. Adan figured that the government in Port Abarra probably knew its location, too. But reading actual words spoken by Captain Sanyal more than five hundred years ago seemed surreal. Adan was a Neskan by birth. But, to Sanyal, Neska was a strange and alien place.

Reading also served to quiet Adan's anxious mind, and he found it harder and harder for his eyes to stay open. By the time the rest of the squad returned from their liberty time, Adan was fast asleep.

Official Log of Captain Chander Sanyal

Neskan Colony, Day 118, Year 1 (Neskan Calendar)

We really need to start using an official calendar instead of just a day count. But so far, no one has been able to break into Bowen's secure files. Why would he have our damn calendar locked up?

We detected another instance of magnetic field fluctuation. One of the Orbital Net sensors picked it up about 100 kilometers off the eastern Ateri coast. It wasn't nearly as wild as the one that downed the Jennix, but it was still cause for concern. Even our rad-hardened systems would still be vulnerable. Zhao thinks he can repurpose some of our active EM shield generators to protect against it. Why didn't Colony detect any of these fluctuation events in the initial surveys? Or did they, and just didn't tell us? Neska is ideal in every other way. Even the majority of the local plants and wildlife are edible. That's a good thing because the animals were all on the Fleet vessels. At least we're still able to print some viable seeds for farming.

Chapter 8

"Who can tell me what the Three Principles of Union Citizenship are?" Everyone in the squad knew the answer. Or, at least they should have. But no one raised their hand. The instructor's too-thin lips widened to a creepy smile. "Come now. Surely, you're not all too shy to answer in front of the class?"

Even the instructor's voice gave Adan chills. They'd introduced themself as Citizen Ren, with no mention of their proper pronouns. The only other information they shared about themself is that they were from the Union Bureau of Citizen Affairs. But it was clear they were a Pincher. Having had a few recent dealings with the secretive organization, Adan had grown a sense for them. They appeared very ordinary. Too ordinary, in Adan's view. Ren was dressed in dark gray trousers, a light gray shirt, and simple, shiny black shoes. Their rosy brown face was clean-shaven, and their short black hair was slicked back with some kind of oil.

Only their dark, piercing eyes stood out, darting around the room like spin flies.

Jenra raised her hand, undoubtedly responding to Ren's thinly veiled insult toward her squad. The instructor pointed at her, and she stood. "Balda Tomari's Three Principles," she started, name dropping the first Union Committee Chairperson, "are purity of the mind, steadfastness of the spirit, and loyalty of the heart."

Citizen Ren smiled again, and Adan suppressed an involuntary shiver. "That's correct, Trooper Tabata. I'm glad you mentioned the name of Honored Chairperson Tomari as well. It was through careful application of Tomari's Three Principles that the Union has grown into the strong, productive State that it is today." Ren continued with a speech that Adan had heard in one form or another at least once a quarter in the Instruction Center.

When Adan learned that their lesson topic for the day was Citizenship, he inwardly groaned. Bo always called the subject Indoctrination. And he was right. The annual reminder of Union philosophy and policy through repetitive slogans was hard to see any other way. Adan supposed that some citizens may appreciate the regular reminders on how to best serve the State. But he didn't know any of them.

Adan's biggest reservation was his fear that the Pincher would recognize him. There was nothing Ren could actually do to him. Or, at least, nothing that Adan could think of. But, despite any assurances to the contrary from Bo, Adan knew full well that they both had giant Pincher targets on their backs. Yes, the Bureau of Justice had sentenced them, and they were serving that sentence. According to Balda Tomari himself, no citizen was perfect. And no citizen, once they'd properly atoned for their mistakes, should ever be shamed or treated as any less than anyone else. But that philosophy had never been equally applied. All citizens were supposedly equal in the eyes of the State. Some were just more equal than others.

"Trooper Testa?"

Adan hadn't been paying attention, and the instructor had just called on him. "Yes, Citizen Ren?"

"You're a recent addition to the squad, yes? I don't recall your face from our previous lessons."

"That's correct, Citizen Ren."

The instructor's spin fly eyes had stopped darting this way and that to focus solely on him. Adan suppressed another shiver. But there was nothing he could do about the bead of sweat running down his back. "Your surname sounds familiar to me. Is it possible that you have a relative in the Bureau of Citizen Affairs?"

Was Ren messing with him? "Not that I'm aware of, Citizen Ren."

The instructor nodded. "Ah, my mistake. Well, since you're new, you have not yet recited the Oath of Citizenship for us. Please stand and do so now."

Every citizen knew the Oath. Or, they were supposed to. And every citizen knew to be ready to repeat that Oath when any officer of the State requested it. Citizen Ren had made no such claim, and they were practically daring Adan to call them out on that. Ren obviously knew who Adan was and was testing him. Would he comply?

Adan stood and cleared his throat. "I pledge my loyalty to the citizens of the Union and the Committee that provides for them. I pledge to honestly and faithfully serve for the good of the people and the glory of the Founders." He remained standing after he'd finished, looking directly at the instructor. Adan had recited the Oath as requested. But he'd used the original Oath that the first Committee had created, not the more modern version that had been introduced a few decades ago. That was when lines like "to the citizens of" were removed to clarify who you were expected to be loyal to. But it was still valid in spirit, if not in practice.

Citizen Ren's thin-lipped smile returned. "You honor the Founders with the original Oath? I wasn't aware it was even taught at our Instruction Centers any longer."

"Yes, Citizen Ren." Would Ren return to the Bureau and dig through their records to find out which instructor at which Center had taught it to him? Would that instructor end up in a cold cell carved into the mountain bedrock?

"Thank you, Trooper Testa. You may be seated."

Adan took his seat, careful not to let his rebellious pride show on his face. It was one thing to bend the rules. But it was better not to boast about it. Citizen Ren spent the next few minutes discussing the importance of following proper citizenship protocols in the Defense Force. Then they passed out blank sheets of paper and pens.

"Please write down three paragraphs about the importance of being a good citizen," they instructed the squad.

Adan wanted to groan. He could tell by the expressions around him that he wasn't the only one. But he was only a half-year out of his last Instruction Center, where he'd also been asked to do that at least once a quarter, too. One instructor shared the essay's secret around the second or third time he'd gotten the assignment. Adan didn't know whether she'd intended to or not. The trick was that the instructors never really read them year over year. So Adan wrote down essentially the same thing he had the time before. Then he did it again. And every time after that, he used the same three boring paragraphs. No one ever called him on it. By that time, he half expected to be praised for his consistency.

Adan picked up his pen and began writing. Those essays always asked for three paragraphs because they mirrored the Three Principles. So he wrote short paragraphs about the mind, spirit, and heart. Adan wasn't a good writer. But he'd had a lot of practice with this test. Once he was done, Adan set his pen down and waited for the rest of the squad to finish.

Uso was the last one to complete the assignment. By that time, the lesson was practically over.

"Pass your papers and pens to the front," Ren instructed them. "Once I've collected them all, you're free to go."

Adan was surprised the squad didn't bolt out of the classroom. And there was so much pent-up tension in the hall it almost set off his fight or flight instincts. Then he spotted Jenra near the front of the group and hurried to catch up to her.

She smiled when she saw him. "That was quite the stunt you pulled in there, Adan."

"You mean the Oath?"

Jenra chuckled. "What else would I mean? I'm glad the instructor let it go, or I would've been the one who had to discipline you."

"Discipline me? That's a perfectly valid Oath."

"I know. And I would've pushed back if it came to that. But you know how the Citizenship Bureau can be."

Adan groaned. "Okay, yeah. But something tells me that Ren's office is closer to the Pinch than it is to Bolvar House."

Jenra's eyes went wide, and she shook her head no. "I don't think the Bureau's down that way." Then she tapped her ear. Someone could be listening to them, she reminded him.

He nodded. Of course, that was true. Adan couldn't believe he'd let his guard slip like that. Maybe it was surviving a run-in with the Pinchers that made him feel like he could get away with a bit of rebellion. "Yeah, I was thinking of the wrong place."

She reached up and rubbed the top of his head. "It's alright. You'll learn where everything is soon enough."

Once the squad checked into the Mess Hall, everyone started eating their lunch. Garun kept silent throughout the meal like he had all day. None of the others seemed to mind. Nobody tried talking to him either. After lunch, the squad moved on to physical training, but Jenra excused Adan to report to Third Chief Osaben.

Adan didn't actually know where the Chief was. He went to Osaben's office, but no one was there. Then he went back to the Physical Training Center and found First Trooper Mannix, who told him that Osaben was at the Gun Range. That was in another building, so Adan had to pass through two ID checkpoints to even get there. But Osaben wasn't in the Gun Range itself. He was in the Armory instead.

Once Adan found him, he stood at attention and saluted. "Reporting as ordered, Chief."

Osaben saluted back. "Your form is improving already, Testa. Stand at ease."

Adan relaxed his stance. "Thank you, Chief."

"You haven't been cleared for firearms yet, and I don't want you firing a gun with a healing concussion anyway. But we can still work on your clearance. How are you with small parts?"

"Chief?

Osaben smirked. "Come with me."

The Chief led him over to a table set up between long sets of gun racks. Adan had never seen so many weapons in one place. He could count the number of times he'd seen a real gun on one hand. Osaben instructed Adan to sit on one of the stools set up at the table, then sat down opposite him. A pair of long wood and metal guns were sitting on the table, along with a small toolkit, a stack of white cloths, and several small bottles of different liquids.

Osaben picked up one of the long guns. "This is the Bolvar Defense Force Standard Battle Rifle, a DF16 Mark 3. It's a selective-fire rifle with a gas-operated, rotating bolt action that fires standard 5.7 mm rounds from a twenty-two-round magazine. It weighs 4.9 kilograms when fully loaded." He held it out toward Adan. "Here, Testa. Feel how much it weighs."

Adan carefully took it and lifted it a few times. It didn't seem very heavy, but he knew that could be deceiving. He might feel differently about it if he had to carry it around all day. He handed it back to the Chief, who took it and flipped it around, inspecting it from the underside.

"I know that most of that meant nothing to you, right, Testa?"

Adan nodded. "Sorry, Chief."

Osaben waved off his apology. "I'd be more surprised if you knew what I was talking about." He set the rifle back down. "As I said, we're not firing these today. Instead, we're going to clean them." The Chief lifted the rifle, pressed his thumb on a catch, and slid a rod out from the top near the trigger. Then he set that down and started taking the rest of it apart. When Osaben was done, he had a set of pieces sitting in front of him. Then he repeated the same process with the second rifle, explaining to Adan each step as he went along. Once Osaben was finished with that, Adan had the same collection of parts sitting in front of him.

"Don't worry about remembering all that," Osaben shared. "You'll have a formal lesson at some point. But this should make it easier. Now, grab a cloth. Use the clear oil to clean the metal parts and the amber oil for the wood furniture."

"Yes, Chief." Adan grabbed a rag, put some amber oil on it, and started to wipe down the long, wooden piece in front of him.

"So, how are things now that Tabata is in charge of the squad?"

Adan's mouth suddenly went dry. How was he supposed to answer that? "She's a capable Squad Leader, Chief."

"Speak freely, Testa. If there are any problems, it's better that I find out now before she hauls off and punches you, too."

Adan almost smiled at the Chief's joke. "I stand by my answer, Chief. She already had the squad's respect, even before you put her in charge. That hasn't changed."

Osaben nodded. "Outstanding. Is Mostok still pouting everywhere he goes?"

Adan smiled at that and nodded. "Yes, Chief. He hasn't said a word since yesterday. But he hasn't caused any trouble, either." Thinking back on his day, Adan remembered a few times he forgot Garun was there. He knew that wouldn't last,

147

but it was nice while it did.

Osaben nodded again. "He'll come around. Or, he won't. But it always seems to happen with the citizens from up around Gallur. You're from the Lowers?"

"Yes, Chief."

"I grew up in the Flats. I think there's something about growing up on the west side of the Daralsha that gives you a certain practical sensibility."

Adan wasn't sure what to say. He'd been given permission to speak freely, but he didn't actually know how free that meant. "May I ask a question, Chief?"

"Go ahead."

"How long have you been in the Defense Force?"

"Longer than you've been alive, Testa."

That wasn't exactly clear. But it also wasn't what he really wondered about. "Why did you stay on after your five?"

"It's been a good way for me to serve the Union. I was already a Third Scout by the end of my mandatory service. And it's taken me places most citizens will never go."

"You mean over the wall?"

Osaben stopped what he was doing and looked at Adan with narrowed eyes. Then he nodded. "Yes, Testa. It's important to remember the wall's there for a reason. It's a dangerous world out there. There are people who don't have the Union to protect and provide for them. So they try to take from us. Every one of them would be welcomed into Bolvar with open arms if they simply came to the Gate and asked. But they attack our resource expeditions instead. And it's our job to keep our people safe. Do you understand?"

Adan knew that things couldn't be that simple. Nothing in the Union ever was. But Osaben was a believer. You had to be if you wanted a career with the Gray Coats since there was no other advantage to it. The Gray Coats had a dangerous job, and their only reward was the same promise of food and housing every other citizen got. Adan nodded anyway. "Yes, Chief."

Osaben smiled. "Outstanding. There might just be hope for you, after all, Testa."

Once they'd each cleaned their collection of parts, the Chief walked Adan through reassembling everything. Osaben explained each part and had Adan repeat their names as they went along. He had no illusions that he'd remember all that or be able to do it again without supervision. But Osaben seemed pleased with what Adan had done.

Then the Chief excused him to rejoin his squad for their daily duty assignment. The squad was still cleaning the classrooms, and Adan was put on mop duty. He understood then why the Training Center had seemed so clean. It was scrubbed and polished on an almost daily basis. Jenra partnered him with Simi, who moved the desks and chairs to one side of each room while Adan mopped, then repeated the process with the other side. Simi was light-hearted and fun and had an endless supply of jokes and quips. At one point, he had Adan laughing so hard he almost slipped on the wet floor and fell. That made them both laugh even harder, and Mannix came in to check that they were okay. They received a stern warning from the First Trooper about taking their work seriously and quietly chuckled to themselves for the remainder of their work.

After their evening meal, Bo invited Adan to join him for their liberty time in the Physical Training Center. Because of Bo's sling, he'd been forced to avoid any strenuous physical activity, too. So Bo suggested using the running track that looped around the Center to walk together. The two of them kept to the outside of the track, leaving the rest for the Provies who wanted to run.

The PTC was also an excellent place to talk to each other privately. It was a generally noisy space, which would make it harder to eavesdrop. Plus, they were moving around enough that it would be obvious if anyone else was trying to listen in.

And Adan was happy to spend some more time with his best friend. "This is way better than what I did yesterday. Although that wasn't bad, either."

"What did you do?"

"I went to the Library."

Bo looked surprised. "They have a library here?"

Adan nodded. "Not a library," he corrected, then emphasized the capitalized letter. "A Library. It's actually pretty big. And the Librarian is alright. He recommended a book with transcriptions of the recordings the First Explorers made after Landfall."

"As in, their actual words?"

Adan nodded again. "Yeah. Or, well, what the person who wrote it claims they are."

Bo sighed. "I suppose, yeah." Then he grinned. "Still, I'll have to check it out."

Adan groaned at his friend's attempt at humor. "Maybe they have a book of bad puns, too. But it will be a good place to do some research. Even if everything in there is Union approved, there could still be information there we could use."

Bo kept quiet as another Provie jogged past them. "Yeah,"

he agreed after they were alone again. "That, too. So, what did you end up doing during physical training?"

"I took a rifle apart."

Bo's eyebrows rose up in surprise. "Seriously?"

Adan nodded. "Osaben taught me how to take one apart, clean it, and put it back together."

Bo sighed again. "That actually sounds like fun. Maybe I'll get a crack at it, too. I haven't gotten to take anything apart like that since I got that timepiece."

Adan was about to ask what happened to it when he realized he probably knew the answer already. "They took it?"

Bo nodded. "The Pinchers did, yeah. They probably didn't want me knowing how long I was in my cell or something. But they never gave it back."

"I'm sorry."

Bo shrugged. "It's fine. It was just a dumb old timepiece anyway."

Adan knew that wasn't true but didn't want to push things. "Osaben has a nice one."

Bo nodded. "I've seen it, yeah. Do you think he got it from the Gray Coats?"

"Anything's possible. Osaben told me he's been serving since before I was born." Then Adan shared the conversation he'd had with the Chief, including the Chief's story about why he stayed in the Defense Force.

"So he's a believer," Bo confirmed, echoing Adan's own conclusion.

Adan nodded. "That's what I thought, too. He's nice enough when you're one on one, though, so it wasn't too bad spending the time with him. I didn't expect that."

"Nothing here is what I thought it would be like. I mean, I expected the parading around as a squad and the ID checkpoints and stuff. But the lessons? I didn't know Gray Coats had to know mathematics."

"That's what you studied today?"

Bo nodded. "What about you?"

"We had geography yesterday, which was interesting. Did you know that there are permanent Defense Force camps on the other side of the Osbaks?"

Bo looked at Adan in surprise. "For real?" Adan nodded. "They never taught us that before. But it makes sense, I suppose. I wonder how you get assigned to a posting like that."

Adan shrugged. But he knew what his friend was thinking. Another possibility for escape. "I don't know. Osaben must've been assigned to one of them at some point. Maybe, if he keeps giving me gun cleaning lessons, I'll ask him."

"Just don't be too obvious."

Adan felt a sudden flash of annoyance. As if he would be too obvious? It wasn't like one of his contacts had turned them in to the Pinchers. Then he realized that he was angry about that. Angry at Bo. Now that his friend was safe and accounted for, his worry had been replaced by anger. But he kept it to himself for the moment. It was probably too soon to share it with Bo, considering he was still recovering from his injuries, too. It was probably time to change the subject. "What about your physical training?"

"Mine was physical therapy." He lifted his left arm a bit, still in the sling. "The Medic had me doing some exercises to help me get mobility back in my shoulder. They said I would probably only have to wear the sling for a few more days."

Adan smiled. "That's good."

Bo nodded, then glanced over at Adan and examined his face. "That black eye is looking nasty." It was. Overnight the dark purple had spread out into some awful shades of green and yellow. "But that's how they go, right? They look worse before they go away?"

"I suppose, yeah. But my head is feeling better. So far today, it's only ached a little. The worst headache was from today's lesson, actually."

"What was it?"

"Citizenship."

Bo groaned loudly. "You're kidding?"

Adan shook his head. Then he described the instructor from the Bureau of Citizen Affairs to Bo.

"Pincher," Bo commented.

"Had to be, yeah. I spent the whole class wondering if they knew who I was. And they asked me to stand and do the Oath." Then Adan told Bo which one he'd done.

Bo laughed. "You didn't?"

Adan nodded, smiling. "I sure did. I couldn't tell if they were angry or impressed that I knew it. And they told me my name sounded familiar and asked if any Testas worked at the Bureau."

"Damn. That wasn't subtle. What an ass."

It wasn't at all. The more Adan had thought about it, the more he was sure that the Pincher was reminding Adan that he had a reputation at Utrogg House now. "A complete ass. Don't worry. I'm sure you'll get your turn, too."

"I can hardly wait." Bo reached up and massaged his strained shoulder for a few moments. "So, did your Squad Leader say anything about me today?"

153

Adan stopped himself from laughing. Jenra had already asked him the same thing about Bo. Leave it to his best friend to get sentenced to extra mandatory service time and use it to start looking for a girlfriend. "As a matter of fact, she asked me the same thing about you."

"Really?" Bo didn't look over when he said that. He was trying very hard to seem casual. But Adan knew him well enough to see through the act.

"Anything I should report back to her? Do you want me to slip her a note later?"

Bo rolled his eyes. "Come on, Adan. I was just asking."

Adan shrugged. "Ask all you want. It doesn't mean I won't judge you for setting your sights on the first pretty girl you meet serving your five."

"Serving my six-point-five, you mean," Bo corrected. "And we all have our ways of coping. I look for pretty girls. You get into fights with your Squad Leader."

Adan winced. "Okay, ouch."

Bo looked at Adan with a frown, then put a hand on Adan's shoulder. "Sorry. That was kind of a low blow." Bo kept his hand in place for a moment, then self-consciously let his free arm fall back to his side. "But what about you? There are plenty of pretty boys here, too."

Adan looked down at his feet as they shuffled along. "We've only been here for a day. And I don't know that I even want to get attached like that if we're not planning on staying."

Bo smiled. "There's no law that says you have to get attached."

Adan jokingly huffed, then lightly bumped into his friend. "Come on. You know my love is precious and pure."

Bo snickered. "Oh, sure. You're as pure as an Osbak

154

snowcap."

A loud whistle chirp suddenly interrupted their back and forth. "Listen up, Provies!" The First Trooper's voice carried well across the PTC. "We'll be holding a Flux Storm Drill in five minutes. Since some of you are still new here, now would be a good time to figure out where your storm shelters are."

"We should probably go find our squads," Adan suggested.

"Yeah," Bo agreed. "Same time tomorrow?"

Adan smiled. "I wouldn't miss it." Then he spotted Jenra standing near the weightlifting equipment and headed her way. She nodded in acknowledgment when she saw Adan approaching.

"I suppose you're wondering where you need to go," she commented when he was within earshot. Adan nodded. "We shelter by squad, of course, although that depends on where you are when the alarm goes off, too. The number one rule is to get to any shelter you can. But for drills, it's always by squad. We shelter with Squad Nine."

"Alright. Should we wait here for the alarm?"

Jenra shook her head. "No, we may as well avoid the rush. Come on." She turned and started walking toward the PTC entrance. "I saw you talking to Bo." It wasn't a question. That was probably implied.

"Yes, fearless Squad Leader, he asked me about you. He asked me if you asked about him, in fact."

Jenra's golden-brown cheeks reddened slightly. Then she laughed. "You're saying I should just talk to him?"

Adan laughed. "I'm saying that maybe I don't feel like the youngest person here anymore."

Jenra looked at him with a single eyebrow raised. Adan

could never make his do that, no matter how many times he tried it. "Well, you are." She pointed down the right side of a corridor Adan hadn't explored yet. "Our shelter is up here. There's one near each building entrance and each major gathering location. You know, in case you find yourself away from the squad during a real alert."

"Good to know."

A few people had already gathered near a door up ahead. Adan recognized some of them. The rest must've been from Squad Nine. Heading to the shelter before the drill even started kind of violated the spirit of the drill. But it was a good time to learn where the shelters were, which was the most critical part of flux storm procedures.

Garun was one of the people waiting by the door. Adan still hadn't spoken to him. He wasn't even sure what he'd say to his former squad leader. Should he demand an apology? Or just make it clear that Garun deserved every bit of the punishment he'd gotten? Garun must've noticed Adan's attention and turned his way. Garun looked at him, expressionless, for a moment, then turned away.

Well, that was something, Adan thought. They still hadn't spoken, but Garun had finally acknowledged his existence.

Then the alarm klaxon sounded. Adan jumped, even though he'd been expecting it. It was louder than he thought it would be. Jenra reached for the door handle as the other squads came running up. The door opened onto a stairwell that led down into darkness. Then a light came on at the base of the stairs, and Adan could see the opening of the shelter door. It opened inward like every other shelter he'd been in. They were always over-pressured inside to help keep the door closed.

Adan followed Jenra down the stairs. The shelter was a smaller version of the one at the laundry plant. It didn't have to hold nearly as many people, but it could still hold many more than just two eight-member squads.

Adan grabbed a seat on one of the benches lining the long side walls. Others took their seats as they gathered inside. There was no rush since everyone was already outside when the alarm sounded. And, even if they somehow didn't make it into a shelter, the worst that would happen would be disciplinary action from their squad leader.

"Testa."

Adan turned to see Garun seated next to him. Apparently, he'd chosen that moment to finally break the silence between them. It wasn't a bad choice since they were both trapped in that space for the whole drill. But it also meant that whatever they said wouldn't be private. "Garun."

"Adan," Garun corrected himself. "I know I haven't said anything to you since yesterday and that I owe you an apology. I needed some time to get my thoughts together and do it right."

"Okay," Adan cautiously replied. It was a promising start.

Garun took a deep breath and nodded. "I'm sorry for hurting you during our sparring yesterday. And I'm sorry for being an ass to you in general before that. You didn't deserve any of that."

Adan nodded. All in all, it was one of the better apologies Adan had received. It was thoughtful and well said. Adan was impressed. "Alright. I accept your apology. But can you at least tell me why you did all that?"

The quick acceptance of his apology must've surprised Garun. If he was anything like Adan, Garun hadn't planned

157

on it and didn't know what to say next. "I don't know." Then he sighed and shook his head. "No, that's not true. It's like this. I've been groomed for the Defense Force since I was young. My sister works for our great uncle, who sits on the Committee. My brother is studying experimental physics with the Bureau of Mechanics and Sciences. And I'm the child that joins the Defense Force and becomes a Commander." He stopped to see if Adan was following along.

Adan nodded. "Okay."

"Everything seemed to be going how it was supposed to," Garun continued. His voice was tight and controlled. "Then you showed up. And suddenly, everyone was paying attention to you, and I was jealous. Then I was angry. Not at you, but because of what you forced me to see. You made me realize how much I hate being here and how much I hate that I have to stay here after my five."

That was an unexpected moment of honesty from Garun. And it was strange for Adan to hear someone like Garun admit all that. Here was a person who had every comfort a citizen could have. Things Adan had never had access to. And yet, in the end, he was just as unhappy as Adan was. Hopefully, Garun was smart enough to know that, while Adan could relate somewhat, Garun would never get any pity from him. "I have to be honest and say I have no idea what any of that feels like. Except for the part about not having any choice about being here, of course." He smiled to let Garun know he was making a bad joke.

Garun smiled and shook his head. "I know we'll probably never be friends or anything, Adan. Not after how I behaved. But I at least want to be able to work alongside you without all that tension."

For the second time, Adan saw the Garun he'd first seen the morning he was dropped into the squad. Before they'd spoken and Garun had snapped at him. His former squad leader was undeniably handsome, especially when quiet and earnest. Adan had accepted his apology, and he knew that he'd forgive him for his actions at some point. He wasn't ready to do that just yet, but he was willing to move forward with Garun. His former Squad Leader had been punished and seemed to accept his part in what he'd done. And what had Balda Tomari said about a citizen who'd properly atoned for their mistakes?

"I don't know about friends, either, Garun. But I appreciate your honesty right now. And if we deal with each other like this going forward, we won't have any problems."

Garun smiled again. "I can accept that." Then he held out a hand. "Shake on it?"

Adan took his hand and shook. It felt good to finally have that episode behind them.

Private Log of Captain Chander Sanyal

Neskan Colony, 32 March, Year 2 (Neskan Calendar)

I'd rather be a farmer. It was always part of my plan to take up farming once Colony leadership took the reins from me after landfall. But I'm the Colony leader now, which means I've had to put my farming dreams on hold. The same has been true for most of the bridge crew, so I've kept my disappointment to myself. Even Marketta, our only physician, has had to take on the duties meant for a team of doctors, nurses, and techs. Everyone except Sander, I suppose. He was always going to be our first Security chief. And he's been indispensable, breaking up the inevitable fights and quarrels that come from perpetual struggle. One would think that the difficulties we're facing would unite us. But when have people ever really acted that way?

Chapter 9

When it came time for Squad Ten to have their monthly evaluation, Adan was only required to participate in the classroom portion. He'd finally been examined and cleared by the Medic to participate in physical training the day beforehand. But he hadn't done any physical training except walking around the running track with Bo during their liberty time. So First Trooper Mannix gave him a medical exemption but told him that his performance during the next Monthly had better be exceptional.

It wasn't like Adan slacked off during physical training. Far from it. He'd taken apart, cleaned, and reassembled several different firearms. He'd peeled so many potatoes that he never wanted to see another one again. And he'd spent many hours in the Library assisting Citizen Pelota by cleaning the shelves. That was the most challenging of all his extra work since he had to remove all the books from a shelf, clean them and the shelf, then put them all back in the proper order. But

Adan didn't have to do it alone. After he'd mentioned to the Chief that Bo was also excused from physical training, the pair ended up doing most of their tasks together. Osaben admitted that it was easier to watch them both when they were together. Even if that directly contradicted what the Commander had told him on his first day at the DFTC.

Adan hadn't seen the Commander since that day. There were ten other squads besides his to manage, so he imagined she was busy. Plus, the new Provies were starting their five at the beginning of the month. But if she was watching his progress, she wasn't making it obvious at all.

On the day of their Monthly, Mannix told Adan and Bo to report to the Librarian once their squads completed the classroom exams. Everyone in Squad Ten finished in the allotted time, which was a good sign. Despite the Commander's absence, Adan held on to her promise that she would share the fate of his parents. And the threat that, if he performed poorly, she wouldn't.

Once his squad was finished, Adan joined them all in the corridor outside the classroom. Bo's squad, Squad Eleven, had also just finished. Adan spotted Bo talking with Jenra. The two had gotten friendly shortly after Adan jokingly complained about being their go-between. Nothing serious had developed between them yet. But anyone could see that it was only a matter of time. Adan knew Bo well enough to tell that he was flirting with Adan's Squad Leader. There were Defense Force rules about relationships between different ranks, but they didn't apply to Provisional Troopers. Jenra outranked them both, but that rank was only Provisional.

Watching them flirt made Adan a little uncomfortable. He and Bo had discussed a few different ideas about how they might make their escape from the Gray Coats. But they needed more time before they could come up with anything serious. Their whereabouts were constantly monitored. And neither of them had any illusions about walking out the front door. But Adan couldn't think of flirting as anything but a distraction. Bo had been the one to push them to try their original plan, the one that had gotten them caught.

"It's not really my place to say anything, but if you don't stop staring at Jenra and Bo, they're going to notice."

Adan turned to see Garun standing next to him. The two of them had come a long way since Garun had given Adan a black eye. They weren't proper friends yet. If that ever happened, it was still a ways off. But they'd been friendly with each other since Garun had apologized in the storm shelter. "I didn't realize I was being that obvious."

Garun smiled. "You were too focused to realize it. Jealousy can be like that."

Adan scoffed. "I'm not jealous. They're both my friends. And they can talk to each other as much as they want."

Garun's smile disappeared, and he nodded. "If you say so. But you should try to let it not bother you so obviously next time."

Adan huffed. He knew Garun was right, and Garun knew that he knew it. "I guess you know a little about that."

"I sure do," Garun agreed with a crooked smile. "But I should go get ready for the Physical exams. Wish me luck."

"You'll do fine, Garun." Especially if you're required to give someone a black eye, Adan thought but didn't say.

"He will do fine," Jenra agreed. She and Bo had walked over without Adan realizing it. "He's one of the best in the squad."

Jenra was right. Removing Garun as Squad Leader had

turned out to be a good thing for his performance. No longer burdened by watching over the squad, Garun was free to focus on his own training. Only Uso outdid Garun in raw physical strength, and Sabina was the only Provie who ran faster. And no one had been able to beat him in grappling except Adan.

Garun smiled. "Thanks, Tabata. Are we ready to head to the PTC?"

Jenra nodded. "Looks like it." She looked at Bo and Adan. "You two enjoy whatever it is they've cooked up for you this afternoon."

"I'm sure it'll be delightful," Bo said with a grin.

"Yeah," Adan agreed, "so don't let us keep you. Go show everyone our squad is the best in the Defense Force."

Jenra laughed. "Alright. I'll catch you both after. Come on, Garun."

While they joined the squad to head for the PTC, Adan and Bo walked to the Library.

"Is there anything you want to tell me?" Bo asked on the way.

"What do you mean?"

Bo frowned. "I saw you looking at Jenra and me."

If only Garun had warned him earlier. "Sorry. I didn't mean to stare."

Bo laughed. "I don't care about that. I just want to make sure you're okay."

"I'm fine," Adan assured him. He wasn't sure that was true, but Bo didn't need to know that.

"If you say so." Bo didn't look any more convinced about it than Adan felt. "Just remember that we're friends. Best friends. And that comes before anything else, as far as I'm concerned."

Adan nodded. "I know. Same here."

"Good." Bo flexed his arm, then stretched it out from the shoulder. He stopped wearing the sling more than a week prior and seemed to be doing alright.

"Your arm feeling better?"

Bo nodded. "I think so. I've been doing the stretches the Medic taught me and haven't felt any pain or tightness for a while."

"That's good," Adan commented as they walked into the Library.

Citizen Pelota was standing there waiting for them. He looked unusually excited. "Good day, Troopers. How did the exams go?"

"I feel good about mine," Adan answered.

"Same here," Bo agreed.

"Outstanding. Well, since this is a special day, I've got something special planned for you both."

Adan raised his eyebrows in curiosity. "No cleaning shelves today?"

"No shelves," the Librarian confirmed.

He hadn't said no cleaning, Adan noticed. Of course, they'd still be cleaning. It would just be something new. Pelota asked them to follow him, then walked through the Library to a locked door in the back that Adan had never used. After Pelota unlocked it, Adan saw that it led to a stairwell with a long service corridor at the bottom.

"We're heading underground," Bo commented.

"That's correct, Trooper Shen," Pelota confirmed despite Bo stating the obvious. "We're passing under the main DFTC building right now."

Pelota led them down the corridor to another stairwell at the far end. At the top of the stairs, a locked door opened to a chamber that Adan immediately recognized.

"This is the Old Tech Museum," Adan said with a gasp.

Pelota looked very pleased with himself. "Yes, it is, Trooper Testa. And it needs to be cleaned before next month's Instruction Center tours."

That was why Adan recognized it. He'd been on one of those tours as a child. He looked around the darkened space in wonder. Glass-enclosed exhibits lined the walls of the long chamber. Each glass case held a relic that the Union had recovered from all over Neska. It was all equipment that had once been used by the First Explorers.

"Founder's grace," Bo quietly swore. His eyes were wide with fascination. "What do you need us to do?"

Pelota led them to a nearby supply closet, where he retrieved a pair of spray bottles full of blue liquid and a stack of white cloths. They were to clean all the glass in the exhibit hall, he instructed them. Or as much of it as they could manage in the time they had. While they did that, Pelota would organize all the educational handouts they gave students on their tours.

Adan and Bo decided to split up the work, with each taking one side of the hall. Adan doubted they'd be able to do all of it, not if they wanted it done well. But the two of them could probably clean most of it. Adan picked up one of the bottles and half the rags and got to work.

The first case was smaller than the next few beyond it. Adan sprayed one side of the glass and started wiping. As he wiped, he examined the device within. It was about the size of a book but thinner and made of glass with a narrow white band around the edges. The sign mounted on the stand beneath the case said it was a portable, handheld computer terminal commonly referred to as a tablet or pad. Adan didn't know what a computer terminal was. He knew that compute meant the same thing as calculate, as in mathematics. But he couldn't figure out how a piece of glass could help with that. The sign explained that computers were sophisticated decision-making devices that used billions of tiny circuits that could be programmed to solve problems with something called software. Adan knew what circuits were, but he hadn't ever seen any small enough that they'd be invisible. It still amazed Adan that, in the five centuries they'd lived on Neska, the people had lost so much of what they brought with them.

The next exhibit held a larger device called a Bio-printer. Adan remembered seeing that one before. Like the tablet, it was controlled by a computer. But it knit together tiny bits of matter to create any biological substance that its computer brain knew how to make. Adan marveled at the idea that you could press a button on a box, and it would make you a bowl of marsh pig stew. But he doubted that it would be anywhere near as good as Mother Agra's stew.

The exhibit after that one held something called a Diagnostic Field Scanner. According to the sign, the Scanner emitted special, invisible waves that would bounce back to a detector. Then the computer brain would be able to tell what kind of injury you'd suffered and how to treat it. That made it sort of a Doctor. And he remembered from his childhood visit that a Diagnostic Field Scanner could identify every bit of matter that made up a lifeform, down to its atoms.

Adan hadn't been able to get a close look at it when he was there before since there was a whole class of children on tour. Up close, the Scanner was just a white, sort of mallet-shaped object that could be easily carried in one hand. It had a black square of glass on one side of the top end and a square of silvery mesh on the other. The extended portion on the bottom was clearly a handle. Even though that one had been thoroughly cleaned, it was well used. Adan leaned in even closer. He could see parts of the white handle with a grayish tinge and a scratch on the black glass.

A tiny green light appeared on the black glass. For a moment, Adan thought it was a spot on the glass case and moved his cloth to wipe at it. But the green light flashed several times before disappearing. Then it was replaced by tiny squares and symbols made of colored light. Adan let out a loud yelp and jumped back.

"Adan, what happened?" Bo called out. "Are you alright?"

"I don't know," Adan replied, his voice cracking with anxiety. Something felt very wrong. "This thing just lit up."

Bo looked confused and walked over to Adan. "What do you mean?"

Adan pointed. "Just come here and look."

Bo shook his head and stepped up to the display case. "Founder's mercy! The damn thing is lit up. How did that happen?"

"I don't know. I didn't do anything!" Adan kept backing away, fearful that his very presence was causing the problem. "It just happened!"

Then all the commotion finally caught the attention of the Librarian. "What's going on down there? You're being too loud!"

Adan stopped where he was standing, looking back and forth between the Librarian and the Diagnostic Field Scanner exhibit. What would Pelota think about it? Was Adan about to get into even more trouble?

Bo rushed over to Adan and grabbed him by the arms. "Calm down. This will be fine. You didn't do anything. You couldn't have. The damn thing is covered in glass."

Adan gulped and nodded. Then he took a deep breath. "Yeah. You're right."

Pelota stopped near the two of them, his hands on his hips. "This behavior is very unbecoming, Troopers. What's going on?"

Bo looked at the Librarian, then back over his shoulder at the lit-up Scanner. "We were just cleaning the glass, Citizen Pelota. Then that thing just started to light up."

Pelota furrowed his brow in confusion. "What are you talking about, Trooper?" Then he looked over at the exhibit in question, and his jaw dropped. "Founder's grace." He rushed over the Diagnostic Field Scanner and practically shoved his face against the glass. "This shouldn't be possible." He looked back over his shoulder. "You're saying neither of you touched this in any way?"

Adan shook his head. "Not at all. How could we with the glass? I was just cleaning, and it lit up all by itself."

Pelota slowly nodded. "You were the one. You were standing here, and it lit up?"

"Yes," Adan confirmed. "I didn't touch it, I swear."

Pelota stared at Adan for an uncomfortably long moment. Then he turned to face the Scanner again and let out a deep sigh. After muttering to himself too quietly for Adan to hear what he said, he walked back over to the two friends. "Let go of him, Trooper Shen."

Bo looked at his hands in surprise, as if he'd forgotten he

had a hold on Adan. He let go of Adan's arms and stepped back. "What's happening, Citizen Pelota?"

"That's what I'll attempt to discover." Pelota looked at Adan with a calm, focused expression. "Trooper Testa, please remain calm. You're not in any trouble. Do you understand?"

Adan tried to calm his breathing and nodded. "Yes.

"Good." Pelota reached out and lightly took hold of Adan's arm. "Come with me, Trooper." Then he gently led Adan over to the exhibit behind him.

Inside the glass case was a rifle. It was all made from the same dull, white material as the Scanner and looked more like a toy than any rifle Adan had recently seen. But he'd worked with enough firearms to understand that he was standing next to a weapon.

Pelota guided him closer until he stood right next to the display case. "Place your hand on the glass, Trooper Testa." Adan looked at him with an unsure expression. Was he being serious? "Go ahead, Trooper," the Librarian added. "It's fine."

Adan gulped and nodded. Then he lifted a hand and carefully put it on the glass. He winced when his hand made contact as if it would shatter under his touch. But nothing happened. He started to pull his arm away when Pelota reached out and grabbed it.

"No," the Librarian firmly said. "It's been dormant for a long while. Give it a moment."

Dormant? Did he mean the rifle was asleep? Then a tiny green light suddenly lit up. It flashed a few times, then a series of green and yellow lights came on all over the device.

Pelota let out a loud gasp. "Impossible!" He looked at Adan, his eyes narrowed in suspicion. "How could this be? Who are you?"

170

Adan was suddenly very frightened. He tried to pull his arm away from the glass, but Pelota tightened his grip and held it in place. "Let me go!" Adan called out.

Bo rushed over and grabbed onto the Librarian. "You heard him. Let go!" Then he managed to get Pelota's hand off of Adan. Pelota scowled, then turned and shoved Bo hard. Bo stumbled and fell backward onto the hard stone floor. Whoever Citizen Pelota was, he was more than a mere Librarian. That much was clear.

Adan quickly stepped back from the rifle exhibit, and the lights slowly went off. He desperately wanted to be somewhere else, anywhere else, besides the museum. But there was nowhere he could go.

Pelota stood looming over Bo. "Stand at attention, Trooper Shen," he commanded. His tone left no room for argument. Pelota turned to face Adan as Bo scrambled to his feet. "Stand at attention, Trooper Testa." Adan instinctively straightened his stance and held his arms firmly at his side. "You both will remain here until dismissed," he ordered them. His voice was a throaty growl. Then he flashed an almost evil grin. "After all, where would you even go?" Then he huffed and rushed back toward the front of the museum.

Once the Librarian was out of view, Adan relaxed his stance. Bo moved over to him with a look of concern on his face.

"What's going on, Adan?"

Adan frantically shrugged. "How in the Founder's name should I know? Where did Pelota go?"

"To call in more Troopers, of course. And probably the Commander."

Commander Sala. She said she knew Adan. She went out of her way to visit him in the Pincher prison cell. She saved

171

him from the firing squad. Did she know something about what was happening? "Oh. Damn," Adan muttered.

Then Pelota started walking back toward them. When he saw that they'd moved, he shook his head. "I see you follow orders like the Provies you are."

Bo whirled around to face him. "You're only a citizen. You don't have the right to give us orders."

Pelota laughed. "I let you believe that I'm only a citizen, Trooper Shen. But do you honestly think that a mere citizen would be responsible for the most important First Explorer artifacts in all of Bolvar?" He stopped short a few meters from the pair, then pointed to the side of the chamber. "Both of you take a seat over there until you're told otherwise. Regardless of who you think I am, I assure you that you'll regret it very much if you disobey me again."

Adan saw Bo stiffen, then reached out to grab his arm. "Come on, Bo. We may as well sit down."

Bo huffed, then nodded. "Fine. I guess you're right. Like he said, it's not like there's anywhere else to go."

The two of them walked over to the side of the gallery. Then they sat down with their backs up against the wall. Adan noticed that the stone floor was pleasantly warm. The museum staff kept the environment tightly controlled with the many 500-year-old artifacts in the room. So the pair sat there in silence for a few minutes, each deep in their thoughts.

"You know," Bo finally announced, "I've never been in here before today."

"Really? You never went on a student tour for one of your lessons?"

Bo shook his head. "No. I got shuffled around a lot as a kid. I must've missed out on the class tour because of that.

We toured the hydroelectric plant, though."

Adan chuckled. "I think I would've enjoyed that more as a kid. I was here when I was, I don't know, six or seven? It was right after I'd moved into the group home. I kept getting stuck in the back of the group as we walked through here, and I wasn't tall enough to really see anything."

Bo suddenly inhaled sharply. "Balda's ass! Imagine if this had happened back then!"

Adan opened his eyes wide with shock. He'd never considered that. "Damn. Yeah, thank the Founders it didn't." Adan had no idea what was about to happen. But the kind of fear he would've felt about it back then would've probably broken him.

They heard the sound of the door to the underground tunnel opening, then the distinctive click-clack sound that Adan heard on his first day in the DFTC. The Commander was coming. Adan leaned out to see who might've been with her. Commander Sala was flanked by Third Chief Osaben and the Librarian. A younger citizen wearing a long, white lab coat walked behind the Librarian. Two Troopers in their gray battle uniforms marched behind them all. Both Troopers carried the same type of rifle that Adan had taken apart two weeks prior.

"He's just up here, Commander," Pelota announced as the Commander stopped in front of Adan and Bo.

"Provisional Troopers Testa and Shen," the Commander announced, her voice dripping with sarcasm. "Imagine my surprise to see you both here."

The Chief looked down on them and frowned. "Stand at attention for the Commander, Provies."

Adan and Bo jumped to their feet, saluted, and stood at

173

attention.

Commander Sala regarded them for a few moments, then turned to the Librarian. "Show me, Sub-Commander."

Of course, the Librarian was no ordinary citizen. He was a Defense Force Sub-Commander. Was his name even Pelota?

"Yes, Commander Sala. It's this one here." He held out his arm toward the weapon display.

Sala nodded and walked over to see the white rifle. She looked at it carefully, then turned back to Pelota. "Open the case."

Pelota gasped. "But, Commander, that's highly–"

"I said open it," Sala interrupted. "Now."

Sub-Commander Pelota sighed, then pulled a neck chain out from under his shirt. A small key hung from the chain. He slipped the chain over his head, then inserted the key into a hidden keyhole at the top of the base and turned it. Adan heard a clicking sound. Pelota looked back at Osaben. "Help me with this," he instructed the Chief.

Osaben nodded and walked over to the display case. He grabbed it with his hands on two opposite sides. Pelota grabbed the same sides, and the pair of them lifted the glass case off the top of the display column. Then they moved to the side and set the glass down on the floor. Commander Sala stepped forward and leaned over the rifle, looking at it closely. Then she reached out and took it in her hands. Adan heard the rifle make a quick buzzing sound, then all the lights on it turned red.

"Tricky," the Commander said to no one. Then she turned to Adan. "Step forward, Trooper."

Adan took a single step forward. Sala glared at him until he walked all the way over to her.

The Commander nodded. "Chief, draw your weapon and keep Trooper Testa in your sights at all times. If he deviates in any way from my next set of commands, you are to put him down. Am I understood?"

The Chief drew his pistol from a holster at his waist. Then he released the safety and pointed it at Adan. "Yes, Commander."

Sala smiled. "Good. Testa, I'm going to hand you this rifle. Once I do so, I want you to point it at that pillar." She stopped and pointed a finger at a meter-wide pillar halfway up the chamber gallery. "Then I want you to fire the weapon. Do you understand?"

Adan furrowed his brow in confusion. "I don't know how to do that, Commander."

Sala scoffed. "Come now, Trooper. It may not be one of the rifles you've seen before, but it's clearly still a rifle. This is the end you point at your target, and this is the trigger. Understand?"

Adan nodded. "Yes, Commander."

"Good. Remember, if the Chief thinks you're about to do anything other than what I've ordered you to do, such as point that weapon at me, he will kill you."

"Yes, Commander."

Sala nodded, then held the rifle out for Adan. He took it from her, careful to keep his movements slow and deliberate. The Chief had claimed to like him at one point, but Adan had no doubt Osaben would kill him as ordered. The Chief was a believer, after all.

The white rifle felt strange. It was half as light as the DF16, and the material didn't feel like either metal or wood. Perhaps it was some kind of plastic strong enough to make a gun out of. And it was surprisingly warm to the touch. Adan looked up at the pillar, then at the Commander, who was in the way. She smiled, then stepped well back.

Adan placed the butt end of the weapon against his shoulder as he'd seen others do, then lifted it and pointed the barrel at the pillar. The moment he placed his finger on the trigger, the rifle emitted a quiet beep, then the red lights on it all turned back to green and yellow. That was interesting. Before, he only needed to stand near it for it to activate. Once the Commander held it, he needed to touch the trigger for it to become active again.

He took a deep breath, braced himself, and pressed the trigger. The barrel emitted a bright flash, and a chunk of stone the size of Adan's head blasted away from the pillar. He'd been expecting a boom. But the sound was more of a high-pitched pop.

Osaben was still pointing his sidearm at him. Adan carefully took his finger from the trigger and lowered the weapon. He glanced over at the Commander to see a look of sheer amazement on her face. Pelota and the other Troopers each had a similar expression. Bo was standing behind him, but he didn't have to turn around to know that his friend was shocked, too.

"Commander Sala?" Adan carefully asked.

Sala looked at Adan with surprise, and something close to awe. Or maybe even fear. Then her smile returned. "Osaben," Sala said without turning away from Adan, "take that weapon from Testa and keep him under guard."

"Yes, Commander." He lowered his pistol and stepped forward. Adan carefully held out the weapon for him to take.

Sala turned to Pelota. "Sub-Commander, summon a squad of my Troopers and get all of these display cases open."

Pelota looked at her as if he didn't understand the order. Then he nodded. "Right away, Commander." He walked off toward the front of the chamber.

Then she turned to the Troopers who were already there. "One of you, place Provisional Trooper Shen into custody and keep him under guard."

The Trooper on the left saluted her. "Yes, Commander." Then they marched over to Bo and placed a set of shackles on his wrists.

"What are you doing?" Adan asked before he could stop himself.

The Commander smiled at him. "I can't very well have Trooper Shen talking to anyone about what happened here, can I? As for you?" Her smile grew even wider. "You're going to try using everything in here."

Neskan Colony Official Census Record

1 May, Year 2 (Neskan Calendar)
   Deaths (to date): *32 Colonists*
   Deaths (prior month): *2 Colonists*
   Li Yimu, Accidental Poisoning (poisonous plant-type added to Colony Ag Records)
   Petri Betelu, Construction Accident/Structural Malfunction
   Births (to date): *2 Colonists*
   Kari Soro (P1: Hilda Soro, P2: Sharad Nayar–Deceased)
   Salli Aho (P1: Lumi Aho, P2: Gregory Aho)
   Births (prior month): *1 Colonist*
   Salli Aho (P1: Lumi Aho, P2: Gregory Aho)
   Total Population Count: *157 Colonists*

Chapter 10

"Again!"

Adan huffed and wiped the sweat from his brow. He no longer noticed the Trooper fireteam that had their weapons trained on him. They would shoot him, or they wouldn't. He didn't care. With a grunt, Adan hoisted the long, heavy tube over his shoulder and pointed it at the target. The Commander and her team had since moved on from having him fire at stone pillars, especially when Pelota noticed a new crack in the ceiling. Sala had some people bring in a set of massive, metal plates that they'd fixed together into an impenetrable wall. Adan had enjoyed that part. It gave him a chance to eat and use the bathroom. He was glad the Commander realized she needed him, at least for their current exercise. Once the need was gone, he knew he was headed for a cell like Bo's. Or worse.

The tube was called a Heavy Ordnance Launcher. Adan was surprised to find out just how many of the artifacts the

Union had recovered were weapons. It hadn't even been on display but was stored in a vault attached to the Museum's gallery.

The Launcher had so far refused to actually launch anything. According to a carefully preserved paper manual, the weapon used the same technology as the Bio-printer but printed ammunition instead. Only it didn't seem to be working. And the Commander was growing frustrated.

Adan pointed the Launcher at the metal wall before him and pressed the top-mounted switch that acted as its trigger. The Launcher made the same buzzing noise it made every other time he'd tried it, and Adan sighed. He set the Launcher down onto a makeshift stand next to him as two of the technicians who worked with Sub-Commander Pelota rushed over.

One of them leaned over to check the square of black glass on the weapon. The display screen, they'd called it. "I don't understand," the technician exclaimed. They sounded exasperated. Adan could relate. "All of the indicators are green. The Launcher has produced the requested ordinance and loaded it into the firing chamber. This should work."

"We're obviously missing something," the other technician stated.

"Founder's grace, of course, we're missing something," the first technician exclaimed. "Otherwise, we'd know what it is. Don't you have anything helpful to add?"

The second technician scowled, threw up their hands, and walked off muttering to themself. Pelota suddenly appeared from the shadows next to them. Adan could see he was trying to calm them down. He looked back as the first technician scribbled notes into a small book.

They'd all been at it for hours. When Commander Sala told him he would be testing everything, she wasn't kidding. Adan didn't think she ever kidded about anything. He was tired, and his back was starting to hurt. "Can we take a break," he asked the technician. "I need to sit down. I need some water."

"No, no," the technician answered without looking up from their scribbling. "Leave your hand on the device."

"I'll bring you some water, Testa." It was the Chief. He'd been there the whole time. At first, he seemed just as excited as the Commander. But, eventually, he'd grown tired and bored, too.

The problem was that no one else could use anything. As soon as Adan put an item into someone else's hands, it stopped working. They only worked for him. The ones that still worked at all, that is.

Chief Osaben walked back toward him with a metal cup full of water. But when he crossed in front of the Launcher, it beeped.

The technician raised their head. "What was that? What did you do?"

"I didn't do anything," Adan answered. "You can see me standing right here."

"Something happened." They spat back. "What happened?"

What had happened? The only thing Adan could think of was the Chief walking over with the water. The Chief. He was armed. "Chief!" Osaben stopped and looked at him. "Can you walk back about a meter? This thing beeped before when you walked by."

The technician snapped their fingers. "Of course! Yes! Third Chief Osaben, please do as Testa has asked."

181

Osaben scowled but nodded. Then he backed up along his original path. As soon as he was in front of the Launcher, it beeped again.

"It needs a target," the technician murmured. "Thank you, Third Chief," they called out. "That will do." The technician snapped their book of notes closed and hurried off.

The Chief nodded, then brought the cup over to Adan. "What was all that?"

Adan took the cup and drank from it. "The technician said that the launcher needs a target," he said after he swallowed.

"And that was me?"

Adan nodded. "That's what it looks like, Chief."

Osaben nodded again, then walked off. Adan stood there with one hand on the Launcher and drank the cold, metal-tasting water with his other. Adan glanced over each shoulder to see what was happening behind him. The Chief, Pelota, the technician, and Commander Sala spoke out of hearing range. There were still two Troopers with rifles aimed his way. The Troopers were periodically swapped out with replacements so that they'd stay fresh. Adan wished he could be swapped out with a replacement.

"Testa," the Commander called out. He looked back her way to see that the conference had ended. "Get ready to try again."

"Yes, Commander." He set the water cup down on the floor, then stood and lifted the Launcher over his shoulder again. Then he heard some commotion to his right.

"No! Are you crazy? I'm not doing it." The technician who'd angrily stormed off before was arguing with Pelota. Then the Chief walked up, pulled out his sidearm, and pointed it at the technician's head.

"Either you do as you're asked," the Chief said with an eerily calm voice, "or I'll shoot you in the head."

The technician suddenly seemed very afraid. Everyone stood by silently and waited for them to answer. "Fine," they finally said. "I'll do it."

They turned and walked toward the metal wall with the Chief behind them, gun in hand. Then they stood next to the wall in the path of Adan's Launcher. There was no beep.

"Fire now, Testa," the Commander ordered.

Adan realized what they were doing. They were testing the Launcher's computer brain. He squeezed the trigger switch, but the weapon only buzzed. Nothing launched.

"Alright. The technician can go." She turned to one of the Troopers guarding Adan. "Trooper–"

"No, Commander," Osaben called out. She looked at him, more curious than upset. "I'll do it."

Sala considered the offer, then nodded. "Fine. Take your position and be ready to move."

The Chief nodded, then walked up to where the technician had been. The weapon started beeping as he approached, with the beeps getting more rapid the closer he got until he stood where the technician had been. Then the beeping was so rapid it was almost a steady sound. Curious, Adan pointed the Launcher slightly to the right. The beeping slowed. He pointed it back toward the Chief, and it increased again. Somehow it sensed the Chief's presence and that the Chief was armed.

"Are you ready, Chief?" Adan shouted.

"Give me a three count," the Chief replied.

Adan nodded. "Counting down now, Chief. Three, two, one–" he squeezed the trigger switch, and the Launcher spat fire. Osaben was already diving to the side when the ammunition hit the wall. It shredded through the metal like it was paper before hitting the great stone blocks that had been set up behind it.

Adan immediately set the weapon down on the stand. "Chief! Are you good? Chief?"

Then he saw Osaben stand and dust himself off. "I'm fine, I'm fine."

The first technician hurried over to the Launcher with the Commander right behind them. "Incredible," the technician called out. "A smart targeting system." They must've been referring to the weapon's computer brain. "Alright, now let's try it with–"

"No," the Commander interrupted. "We've already attempted it enough times to know what will happen."

"But, Commander–"

"I said, no."

The technician obviously wanted to try the next phase of their experiments. But Adan had no idea what else there was. They'd already tried to get the Old Tech artifacts to work for someone else. They'd attempted it in a variety of ways, but it never worked. If anyone else made contact with a device, it wouldn't work even if Adan held it. One of the technicians had called it a security protocol. Apparently, it had something to do with Adan's genes. Or, at least, that's what they were saying.

Adan knew that genes were some of the smallest parts of him, smaller than cells but bigger than atoms. But that was the extent of his knowledge on the subject. They'd already taken blood from his arm. That was part of the reason Adan was tired. But Adan learned from their murmured conversations that genes were a problem. Specifically studying genes. They had the knowledge. The First Explorers had called it genetics, and much of the information had been passed on over the centuries. But they didn't have the equipment. Genes were too small to see with the instruments they had. And they didn't know how to make the Diagnostic Field Scanner do anything.

"Well, Testa." The Commander had already stopped addressing him as Trooper. "I'd say that today has been unexpectedly productive. We've begun to determine what does and doesn't work with these artifacts, as well as some of their functions. But we need to know more. And we still lack the answer to the most important question. Why?"

"What's going to happen next?" Adan had stopped asking for permission to speak. If they were going to throw out the rule book, he wouldn't follow the rules, either.

"We have a great deal more studying to do, of course. But I think we're done here for the day."

Adan let his shoulders slump. "Does that mean I can eat something?" He had no idea what time it was, and he hadn't eaten since his morning meal.

But the Commander ignored his question and turned to the Chief. "Third Chief Osaben, see that Testa is placed in a secure location. I'd prefer that you do so without any fanfare, if possible."

"Understood, Commander."

The Commander nodded and turned to Pelota. "Sub-Commander Pelota, I need you to–"

Adan tuned her out. He'd been running on empty for hours and didn't have the will or patience to protest any further. The Chief approached Adan with a softer than usual expression on his face. "Do I need to shackle you for this, Testa?"

Adan sighed. "I've been standing for hours, and I haven't eaten since this morning. I can't see how I'd put up any effective resistance. But you do what you have to, Chief."

Osaben grinned. "Not too tired to talk back to your superiors, eh?"

"Sorry, Chief."

Osaben waved off the apology. "Don't worry about it, kid. It's been an odd day for all of us." He held his hand out to the right. "This way, please."

Adan nodded and stepped off the small platform he'd been standing on all day. His legs and back were stiff, so his steps were slightly off balance. "Where are we going?"

"There's another service corridor over here. It leads to some of the facilities located under the DFTC."

After a lifetime of thinking the Pinchers held all the secrets, Adan was mildly surprised to discover that the Defense Force was just as secretive. "Why is all this here, Chief? I mean, I always thought it was odd for the Old Tech Museum to be at the Training Center."

"I wouldn't share the answer to that even if I knew it. And it's not my job to know things like that." Adan stopped at an unmarked door. "Let me get that," the Chief added.

Adan stepped aside as the Chief pulled a set of keys from his pocket. Osaben used one of the keys to unlock the door then pulled it open. It was at least twice as thick as Adan had expected. It opened to a stairwell that led down, just like the one he and Bo had taken in the Library that morning. The Chief stepped back and gestured toward the stairwell. Adan nodded and walked through the door.

The corridor wasn't as long as the earlier one had been. There were no stairs at the end, either, just another door with an armed Trooper standing guard. What a tedious job that must've been, guarding a lonely corridor that almost no one in the building above them knew about. The guard saluted the Chief as he and Adan approached them. Adan felt a slight breeze when they opened the door as chilled air rushed out into the corridor. The other side was kept over-pressured like the storm shelters.

Adan walked through the door into a short, bright, white-walled corridor. The floor was tiled with light gray squares of a material Adan had never seen before. It was almost soft, and Adan's boots made no sound as he walked. Two more armed Troopers were standing guard at the t-intersection end of the corridor. They saluted as the Chief approached, too.

"Head to the left, Testa," the Chief instructed him.

Adan turned left and saw a half-dozen doors evenly spaced along the right side of the short corridor. The doors were numbered. The first door was number one.

When they reached door number three, the Chief stopped. "This is the one," he shared. Then he pulled out his keys again, chose one, and used it to unlock the door. After he opened it, Adan stepped through into a small room, maybe two and a half meters square. He saw a small bed, a tall locker, and a simple chair. Adan walked over to the bed and sat down for the first time in hours.

"I hate to keep asking about food, Chief–"

Osaben waved his question off. "Someone will be by shortly with food and a change of clothes. I'll arrange for access to a shower and bathroom, too. If you need anything else, just use the intercom by the door."

"Intercom?"

The Chief turned and pointed to a small, rectangular metal grill fixed to the wall next to the door. "That's an intercom. It's like a two-way wireless. You press and hold the black button while you're speaking, then let go so you can hear the answer. Someone will be monitoring it at all times."

"Okay, Chief."

Osaben nodded. "Outstanding. In the meantime, get some rest. Someone will come to collect you in the morning."

"What time is it now?"

The Chief looked at the timepiece on their wrist. "It's five o'clock in the evening."

He and Bo had shown up at the Library just after eleven in the morning. That meant he'd been at it for seven hours. "Alright. Thanks, Chief."

Osaben smiled, then walked out into the corridor and closed the door. After a moment, Adan heard him lock it. He lay back on the bed. The mattress was too stiff, and the sheets smelled a little musty. But he was alone, at least. Except for whoever was monitoring him, that was.

"Adan?"

His eyes shot open at the sound of his name. Adan hadn't realized he'd closed them. He sat up, but no one was in the room with him. "Hello?"

"Adan, it's Bo."

Bo's voice sounded like it was coming from under his bed. Adan got off the bed and crouched down to look underneath it. He saw a dim light shining through a small metal vent set into the wall in the darkness under his bed. "Bo? Are you in the room next to mine?"

"I guess so. I could hear you come in with the Chief. But I waited until he left before I said anything."

His knees hurt while he crouched, so Adan sat down on the floor. "Are you okay?'

Bo laughed. "Am I okay? Of course, I am. I'm just really bored. What about you? Is it really five o'clock?"

"That's what the Chief said. I'm alright. Tired and starving, but okay otherwise."

"That's good."

Adan sighed. "I'm sorry you've been stuck in there all day because of me."

"It's not the most exciting place to be, but it's better than the last place I was locked up." He paused for a moment, and Adan thought he heard a quiet sigh. "I wonder what they told our squads."

Adan hadn't thought about that. He'd been too focused on the Old Tech all day. "That's a good question. Probably nothing. You know how it is. Did they even tell you anything?"

"No. What did they have you doing all day?"

"I don't know that I should tell you. We're being monitored. The more you know, the less likely that you'll get out of here."

Bo chuckled, but it sounded sad. "What makes you think I'm ever getting out of here? I already know too much." Then Adan heard him sigh again. "But you're probably right. The less I know, the better. As long as you're doing okay, that's all that matters."

Suddenly there was a knock on the door. Adan scrambled back up onto the bed. Then he heard the door unlock, and a Trooper walked in carrying a metal tray with food on it. "On the chair?"

Adan nodded. "Sure." There wasn't any table, so that was the best option besides the bed.

The Trooper set the tray down. "Someone will come collect that and bring you to the showers later."

"Thank you, Trooper," Adan said out of habit. While he was happy to have food, he didn't feel particularly grateful.

The Trooper nodded, then walked out of the room and locked Adan's door. There was no keyhole on his side. He was stuck in there until someone out there with a key let him out.

Bo's voice floated up from under the bed again. "Did they bring you food? The stew isn't bad."

Adan laughed. "Has captivity turned you into a food critic?"

"I'm bored. I ate. I napped. I stretched my shoulder and did some push-ups. The only other stuff I can think of to do are not things I want to do while I'm being monitored."

Adan laughed again, then grabbed the tray off the chair and set it on the bed. On it was a bowl of stew, maybe Ridge Fowl, a lump of bread, and a cup of hot tea. The stew smelled good. He grabbed the spoon, dipped it in the bowl, and took a bite. "You're right. It is good."

"See."

Adan took another bite, then ripped off a chunk of bread and dipped it in the bowl. He washed the bread down with a sip of tea. "I wonder what they're gonna do with me tomorrow."

"They didn't tell you?"

"No." Adan took another bite, then another swallow of tea. "My guess is probably more of the same as today." He remembered what the Commander had said. They hadn't discovered the why. And Adan was sure that was something they'd want to know.

Adan and Bo kept chatting throughout Adan's meal. They struggled with what to say. Neither one of them wanted to talk about the details of Adan's experiments. A couple of minutes after Adan finished eating, the same Trooper came to collect his tray and bring him to the showers. They led Adan back up the short corridor then continued down the other side. Just before it turned a corner to the left, the Trooper led Adan through a door into a small locker room. A pair of long benches sat in the middle, and a dozen wall-mounted lockers were mounted on each side. Adan spotted a pile of folded clothing and a towel on one of the benches. He walked over to inspect the clothing and discovered that it was his. Someone had gotten it from his locker in the barracks. Adan started to take off his uniform jacket, then looked back at the Trooper.

"Sorry," the Trooper said, guessing Adan's unspoken question. "I have to stay with you while you shower. But I'll stay here in the locker room."

Adan nodded. "It's fine." Then he stripped down to his undershorts, grabbed the towel, and walked through the open doorway in the back of the room. There he saw a set of showers on one side and a set of toilet stalls on the other. Adan visited the toilets first then took a steaming hot shower. The hot water helped to loosen up his tight shoulders. By the time he was done, he felt almost human again. After drying off, he wrapped the towel around his waist and walked back to the locker room. The Trooper made an effort to look away while Adan dressed. It didn't matter. Adan was already used to communal living facilities, but he appreciated the Trooper's efforts anyway.

After getting dressed, Adan collected both the clean and dirty clothes and followed the Trooper back to his room. Or was it his cell? Probably the latter, but Adan wasn't ready to call it that yet. The longer he could pretend things were normal, the longer he could hold it together.

Once the Trooper locked the door again, Adan put his clothes into the new locker, then sat down on the bed.

"Hey Bo, have they taken you to the showers yet? They're not bad, and the water is hot." Bo didn't answer. "Bo?" Adan waited a moment, listening carefully. Then he got down on the floor and crawled under the bed to the vent. There was no light coming through it. He waited there for several minutes, listening for any noise, but there was nothing. Bo wasn't there. Adan knew he hadn't been taken to the bathroom or showers unless there was another set somewhere in the secret facilities. That meant they'd moved him while Adan was out of the room. But where?

Adan crawled out from under the bed and climbed back on it. Then he laid back, resting his head against the musty-smelling pillow. His best friend was gone again. They could've moved him to a different cell to keep them from talking to each other. They could've taken him to a different location altogether. Bo could've even been sent back up to the DFTC with a promise to keep quiet about everything. Or they could've made him disappear. All were real possibilities.

His breathing was starting to get heavier as Adan got more upset. He took several deep breaths, trying to calm himself. But he couldn't shake the feeling of suddenly being very alone. For the first time in a long time, Adan started crying. Eventually, he cried himself to sleep.

Private Log of First Officer Marta Kanerva

Neskan Colony, 14 October, Year 2 (Neskan Calendar)

I'm worried about the Captain. When we first proposed enacting the Colony Emergency protocols from the Charter, Chander privately shared his fear that he didn't know enough about running a settlement. He probably doesn't remember that. And I can see now how much that role has stressed him. I spoke to Marketta, but she claims that his health is fine for someone his age. But we can all see the toll this has taken on him. I'll speak to Clarinda about it tomorrow. We need to have a plan for succession in place, just in case.

I've heard some troubling rumors from Sander. He says that some households are talking about breaking away and establishing a new settlement. Not officially, of course, since they would have to rely on us for support. But I'm afraid that the Chander's naysayers are starting to get bold about their opposition to his leadership.

Chapter 11

"I think we're done with that one, Testa." The strain in the Commander's voice was evident. After three solid days of "pick this up and use it while we stand really close by and observe," Adan could relate.

After the first day of testing in the Museum gallery, the Commander moved the Old Tech testing to a large room in the secret underground facility. It was smaller than the gallery but was set up specifically for the sorts of things they were doing. And mainly what they were doing was testing weapons. The technicians still had him working with other devices, too. Mostly scanners and similar devices. But it was the weapons the Commander was most interested in. She wanted to know as much as possible. What did they do? What firing modes did they have? How long would they go before running out of ammunition? What materials protect against them?

Since Adan was the only one who could make any of the

weapons work, he was the one that had to pull the trigger. Every single time. The novelty had worn off long ago, both for him and the technicians. At one point on the second day, an annoyed technician suggested that they try rendering Adan unconscious and rig up a system forcing his finger to press the trigger using small electric shocks. Then the Chief suggested they test that system on the technician first since Adan was essentially irreplaceable. That technician had been unfailingly polite to Adan after that.

But the fact that they were already proposing ways to use Adan without his input was chilling. He could already see that people were no longer thinking of him as a person. Adan was just another device. And, unlike the Old Tech devices, he needed inconvenient things like food, water, and bathroom breaks.

The sides being drawn up were also becoming clear. The Commander wanted weapons. The technicians wanted data. The Chief was the only one who seemed to be concerned for Adan's general welfare. But Adan knew that concern was entirely dependent on Adan's usefulness. If the best thing for the State's interests was for Adan to not be alive, the Chief wouldn't hesitate to pull the trigger.

Adan set the weapon down on the table next to him and reached for his water cup. He'd been careful to balance his thirst with the trouble involved in taking a bathroom break. But the cup was empty. Adan tipped it back to get the remaining few drops to fall into his mouth.

"Here you go, kid."

Adan looked over to see the Chief standing near him with a full water cup in his hand. He smiled and took it. "Thanks, Chief."

Osaben smiled as Adan took a long drink. "May as well finish it. I can get you more while we're waiting to hear what's next."

Thinking that meant he could get a bathroom visit soon, he emptied the cup in a few gulps. The water made him burp. "Sorry, Chief."

"It's no problem, Testa." Osaben took the water cup and set it down on the table. "I want to say that I appreciate how helpful you've been the past few days. You've been an excellent example of a Defense Force Trooper."

The Chief had always been nice to him, but that was unusual for him to say. "Sure thing, Chief. Not that I've had much choice."

Osaben suddenly looked uncomfortable. "No, of course not. The Union asks, and the Union provides."

"All hail the Union," Adan responded out of habit.

"And sometimes the Union asks more of us than of others. And, like it or not, the Union is asking a lot from you."

Adan sensed that the Chief wasn't talking about his efforts as a standing trigger machine. "What do you m–" Adan stopped, overcome with a sudden wave of dizziness. He tried to grab the table, but it seemed out of reach. Then he felt the Chief grab his arms.

"Go ahead and fall, Testa," he heard the Chief say as everything faded to black. "I've got you."

The next thing Adan knew, he was lying on a stiff bed in a bright room. As his vision slowly adjusted, Adan realized he was in a medical examination room. How did he get there? He tried to lift his head, but it was too heavy for his neck. So Adan turned his head to the side. He found a flexible tube sticking out of a needle in his arm. It led up to a clear, liquid-filled bag hanging from a slim metal stand. His forearm had a bandage wrapped around it. And his wrist was wrapped in a thick cuff and buckle. So was his other wrist. Adan was strapped down to the bed. Then he realized he wasn't even wearing a shirt. His chest looked dull and ashy, like he'd been sick and was dehydrated. Adan spotted another thick, white bandage taped to his right hip sticking out the top of his trousers. What had they done to him?

Adan remembered the Chief giving him the water then acting strangely. They'd drugged him. The Chief had drugged him. Osaben must've felt guilty about it, giving Adan that stupid, apologetic speech. Not guilty enough to keep from giving him the drugged water, though.

As his strength returned, Adan lifted his head and looked around the room. It was smaller than the exam room in the DFTC but otherwise looked the same. Walls covered in pale, blue-green tile, bright overhead lights, assorted gray cabinets, and a metal sink.

Adan wanted to sit up. His mouth and tongue were dry enough to want another cup of water, despite his recent experience. He experimentally tugged on the wrist cuffs, but they were too strong for him to break out of. Someone would have to release him.

Then the door opened, and the Commander walked in. The Sub-Commander came in behind her. "I see you're awake," Sala announced. Adan huffed and let his head fall back onto the bed. "And in good spirits," she added.

Adan growled. "What in the Founder's name did you do to me?"

Sub-Commander Pelota angrily surged forward. "See here–"

But the Commander stopped him with a raised hand. "It's alright. Testa has every right to be angry with us." She stepped right up next to the bed and leaned down over him. She was close enough that Adan could smell the mildly floral scent of whatever soap she used. Then Sala reached out and cupped a hand under his chin. Adan tried to pull his head away, but she tightened her grip enough that it hurt. She turned his head to face her. "But your cooperation is no longer necessary. Not that I don't appreciate how willing you've been to assist us in our research. It made things so much easier for both of us." Commander Sala let go of his chin and stepped back. Then she turned to Pelota. "Fetch the Doctor, Sub-Commander. And Testa's guards, if you please."

Pelota bowed his head. "Right away, Commander." Then he walked back out of the room.

"You're not going to tell me what you did?"

The Commander frowned, then looked down at his chest and the bandage on his arm. "We've hardly done anything yet. We took some blood and bone marrow samples. And we implanted you with a tracking device. You're a precious asset to the Union, Adan Testa. Your ability to activate and operate Old Tech makes you unique. Until we discover how you can do it, that is."

Meaning, Adan assumed, that they planned on experimenting on him. He groaned when he realized that he should've seen that coming. He'd spent the past three days handling highly advanced artifacts and weapons that could've easily taken out everyone in the room. Sure, he probably would've been shot by one of the Troopers guarding him. But that would've saved Adan from whatever Sala and Pelota had planned for him. "You're a real marsh pig's ass, Commander."

The Commander laughed. "I'm glad to hear there's still some fight left in you. You're going to need it."

The door opened again, and Pelota walked in with two Troopers and someone wearing a long, white lab coat. The room suddenly felt crowded. The older citizen in the lab coat must've been the Doctor. They turned to the Troopers. "You two," they commanded in a rough voice, "go wait in the corridor until you're needed."

The Troopers both looked to Sala for confirmation. She nodded her head toward the door, so they went back through it into the corridor. "Remember your place, Doctor Naris."

The Doctor whirled on her and scowled. Their deep brown face was flushed, presumably with annoyance. "Don't you start with me, Cristina. Either take me out and have me shot or stand back and let me do my job. I highly doubt you have a long list of geneticists waiting to take my place."

Adan almost laughed. It was the first time he'd seen someone talk back to the Commander like that. But she took the dressing down in stride.

"Of course, Doctor Naris," she said with her usual smile. "I was merely reminding you that my Troopers only answer to me."

"Bah," the Doctor croaked. "Founders, save us from your bumbling Troopers." They stepped up to Adan's side, then reached up and stroked the thin, silver beard sprouting from their chin. "How are you feeling, Testa?"

"Thirsty."

Naris nodded. "Of course, you are. We drew a liter of your blood." They looked back at Pelota. "You, Sub-Commander, fetch a cup of water for this one."

The Sub-Commander frowned and looked at Commander

Sala. "You heard the Doctor, Pelota."

He huffed, then stepped over to the cabinets and started looking through them.

Doctor Naris nodded and turned back to Adan. "Alright, let me look at you." As if Adan had any choice. They reached out and placed the back of their hand on Adan's forehead. "Temperature seems normal." They felt the glands at the base of Adan's jaw. Then they gently probed the skin above Adan's hip bandage. "Any soreness here?"

Adan shook his head. "No."

"That's the pain medication. It'll be a little sore for a few days. You'll want to avoid any highly physical activities."

"Something tells me that won't be an issue, Doctor."

Naris looked briefly surprised at Adan's response, then nodded. "Yes, of course." They looked at the Commander. "He'll need food and rest. If you're interested in keeping him alive, we'll have to wait at least thirteen hours before we attempt any additional procedures."

The Commander lifted her eyebrows in surprise. "A half-day, doctor?"

The Doctor turned back to Adan, then reached across him and inspected the fluid bag hanging on the hook. "If you don't plan on killing him, yes. Normally I would tell a patient to wait three weeks after a blood draw of that volume before taking any more. But I don't believe we'll need any more blood tomorrow."

Commander Sala nodded. "Alright, fine. I'll have him brought back to his room and feed him there."

Pelota turned on the sink and filled up a cup he'd found. Once it was full, he turned off the water and brought it to the Doctor. Naris reached under Adan's head with their free hand and lifted his head. Then they held the cup to Adan's lips. "Here you go, drink this. Slowly, please."

Adan sipped the water in the cup. It was cold but tasted faintly of metal. At least he knew it wasn't drugged. What would be the point anymore? He could barely move. They could do whatever they wanted. Once he'd taken a few swallows, the Doctor pulled the cup away. "That's enough for now. Let's get that needle out of your arm." They walked over to one of the cabinets and grabbed a puffy white ball and bandage from it. Then they stepped around to the other side of Adan's bed and carefully removed the needle from his arm. Once it was out, they tied a knot in the clear tube, then they pressed the white puff against the tiny wound on his arm and taped it down the bandage. After inspecting the bandage, they turned back to the Commander. "Alright, you can call your soldiers back in here. He'll need assistance to get to his room. And, if you don't mind, I'll get back to my lab."

The Commander smiled. "Of course, Doctor. Have someone fetch me if you learn anything important. Otherwise, we'll be seeing you again tomorrow."

Naris nodded and waved her off dismissively before walking out of the room.

Sub-Commander Pelota snorted. "You should have him shot for speaking to you like that."

Commander Sala shook her head. "I'd sooner have you shot, Pelota. Doctor Naris is the Union's foremost geneticist. And, as he correctly pointed out, there's no one to replace him."

Pelota's mouth grew tiny as he angrily pursed his lips. Then he forced his face to relax. "Yes, Commander. I'll get the

Troopers."

Once the Troopers were back in the room, and after some shuffling around, they had his cuffs removed and helped Adan to his feet. Then each of the Troopers took one of Adan's arms and walked him out into the corridor. Adan recognized where he was right away. He'd been marched around the square loop of the underground facility enough times to know where pretty much everything was. But he let the Troopers help him around to his room anyway. Adan wasn't sure he would've made it on his own. Then they helped him inside and onto his bed.

After Adan was situated, the Troopers began to leave. But one of them turned back at the door. "Someone will be back shortly with food and water, Adan." Then they walked out, shut the door, and locked it.

Adan sighed and sat there for a moment. The fury he'd felt back in the exam room had drained out with the effort to walk back to his cozy prison cell. He shivered from a sudden chill, then looked down and realized he was still shirtless. With a sigh, he forced himself off the bed and stood, then shuffled toward–

That Trooper had called him Adan. Not once since everything started had anyone called him anything except Trooper, Citizen, or Testa. How would that Trooper even know his first name? Adan tried to remember their face, but his memory was just a blur. It had to mean something, but Adan didn't know what.

He shuffled the rest of the way to his locker, opened it, and pulled out a gray undershirt. Once he managed to get that on, he went back to his bed and sat down. At least he had a clean shirt to wear. Sometime the day before, somebody had taken his dirty uniforms and had them laundered. Adan suspected that wouldn't happen again.

Someone knocked on his door, then Adan heard them unlock it. A Trooper stepped inside carrying a tray of food. He thought it was the same Trooper who'd called him Adan, but he wasn't sure. He hadn't been paying attention before, but he made an effort to start. "I have your food," they said. Instead of putting it on the chair, like the Troopers usually did, they set it next to him on the bed.

Adan's guard immediately went up. He could do nothing if the Trooper attacked him except put up a weak struggle. But his dulled instincts still told him something was happening.

After putting the tray down, the Trooper walked back to the door and pushed it closed. Then they quickly turned back around. "Adan Testa, my name is Rune Tabata. I'm going to get you out of here."

Tabata. "Jenra?"

Rune nodded and took off their helmet. "I'm her brother."

Adan saw the resemblance right away. Rune had the same narrow face and small, striking hazel eyes as his sister. His shoulders were broader than hers, and his build was sturdier. But Adan would still call him willowy. "You are, aren't you?"

Rune set his helmet down as he nodded again. "We don't have much time. First, we need to get rid of that tracker in your arm."

Adan was afraid it would start with something like that. But he hated that it was there, so he nodded and held out his bandaged arm. Rune reached down and slid the tray back on the bed. Adan hadn't noticed it before, but it had been sitting on a slim, shiny, black, rectangular object. Rune reached out and grasped two of the object's corners and pressed on them.

The top swung up and open. The object was some kind of case. Inside were two palm-sized, black metal discs attached to folded, black straps, along with a small knife, forceps, and white medical tape.

Rune grabbed Adan's arm, then peeled the bandage away. "It'll be quick because it's fresh," he explained. "But it's still going to hurt. Are you ready?"

Adan nodded. Rune picked up the knife and used it to slice through the pair of cross stitches that held the wound closed. Then he dropped the knife back into the case and picked up the forceps. Adan took a deep breath, then clenched his jaw in pain as Rune used the forceps to pry open the wound, dig inside for the tracker, and pull it out. He dropped the bloody tracker in the case. It was smaller than Adan expected—maybe three centimeters wide and less than ten centimeters long. Rune quickly grabbed the tape, tore off a strip, and used it to close the wound back together. Then he added two more strips before finally replacing the bandage.

"That's it for that," Rune explained. Then he grabbed the two discs and lifted them from the case. "Now for the interesting part. Can you stand?"

Adan nodded and pushed himself up. "What are those? And who are you, really? Jenra never told me her brother was a Gray Coat."

"Lift your arms, Adan." Adan did so, and Rune reached up and slid the straps from one disc around his arms, then lowered them until the disc was centered on Adan's chest. "She never told you because I'm not really a Gray Coat. I used forged credentials to take a post in this facility." Rune pulled the straps tight until they fit Adan like a harness. Then Rune reached around Adan's torso and grabbed the other strap, pulling it around his waist. Adan got a strong whiff of Rune's scent and became instantly distracted. He was suddenly very aware of how attractive Rune was. Adan closed his eyes, willing himself to relax and focus on what was happening. It wasn't the time for boyish crushes.

Once Rune attached the strap to the other disc at his waist, he pulled it tight until it sat there like a belt. "It's my understanding that you can make Old Tech work, right?" Adan nodded. He had no reason to keep that secret anymore. "Good," Rune confirmed. "This is a unique piece of tech that the Union doesn't know about. If you can make it work, then I think I can get you out of here. But we have to hurry. It's only a matter of time before someone notices I'm not at my post."

Adan looked down at the disc on his chest. "What do I do?"

Rune frowned. "I don't know. I thought you would."

Great. Here he was in the middle of a surprise rescue that required him to operate Old Tech he'd never seen. Adan grunted and shook his head. Then he reached up and grabbed the disc. Nothing happened. He ran his fingers around its glossy, smooth face and felt a slight depression right in the center. He pressed a finger into it like it was a button. It didn't move, but the disc suddenly lit up blue around the edges. He reached down and did the same with the disc at his waist, and it lit up, too. But that was it. Frustrated, he grunted again. "I'm sorry, Rune. I don't know how this works. I don't know how to activate–"

The second he said activate, something happened. Both discs started to whir and vibrate. Adan pulled his hands away, and Rune took a step back. Then Adan heard a snick, and thin bands of hard, dark material flowed out from the disc. Snick,

snick, snick, the bands kept coming until they appeared to blur as they spread out across his chest and down his legs. "What's happening?"

"Founder's mercy," Rune quietly whispered before recovering himself. "It's armor of some kind, Adan. That's all I know. Just let it happen. You'll be okay."

"How do you know that? You said you didn't know what it was."

Rune shook his head. "No, I never said that."

But Adan stopped paying attention to him. His legs were completely covered with the black bands. They had formed around his trousers, fitting tight against him like an extra layer of muscle. Adan felt it as they flowed down his arms. It was the strangest sensation, like putting on a heavy jacket. They continued until they reached and then covered his fingers. Then he felt the bands coming up his neck and started to panic. He tried to reach up and grab them, but the material suddenly stiffened, forcing his arms to remain in place. Adan quickly took a deep breath and squeezed his eyes shut. But he couldn't feel the material on his face. Instead, the bands seemed to flow around the edges until they covered the rest of his head. He took an experimental breath and tasted fresh, clean air. Then he opened his eyes and almost fell back onto the bed.

Something was covering his face. The room looked as if he was viewing it through a darkened window. But Adan could still see Rune standing in front of him. Then words made of blue light appeared in the air in front of him. The letters were familiar, but the words they spelled were gibberish. "I can't read that," he said aloud.

"Read what?" Rune asked. "Can you hear me, Adan?"

Adan nodded and the text moved with his head. "I can. Can't you see those words?"

Rune shook his head. "I only see you. You're completely armored now."

"There are words made of light floating in the air in front of me, but I don't understand the language."

Rune nodded. "Of course! This is Old Tech, so they may not be written in Neskan." He lightly patted the top of his head while he thought. "What did they used to call Neskan? Oh, yeah. Ask it to give you English."

Adan didn't know what that meant, but he tried anyway. "Give me English, please."

The text suddenly scrambled, then reappeared in Neskan so Adan could read it. Or, a version of slightly misspelled Neskan. *Please identify user.*

"My name is Adan Testa."

The text changed again. *User Adan Testa not recognized. Creating a new profile. Specify visual or audio interface.*

Adan didn't know what interface meant or what a profile was supposed to be. But he knew visual or audio. "Audio interface."

Suddenly a genderless voice flooded his ears. "Audio interface initiated, Adan Testa. Please specify your circumstances. Are you in immediate danger?"

"I'm in danger, yes. But the person in the room with me is a friend." He hoped.

"Designating the specified individual as friendly." Suddenly a green square appeared in the air around Rune's face.

"The armor's speaking to me, Rune. Do you hear it?"

Rune shook his head. "I can only hear you. That's amazing enough since I can't see any openings in your armor."

Suddenly the door flew open, and a Trooper rushed in with their rifle in hand. "What's going on here, Kossam? You were supposed to return to your post."

Rune lunged at them before they could say anything else. He knocked the rifle down with one hand, then struck the Trooper in the face with an open palm. The Trooper fell backward and hit the wall.

"Hostile identified," the armor announced as a red square appeared around the Trooper's face. "Defense protocol initiated." Suddenly Adan felt the armor move, with him inside it. He rushed toward the Trooper and stomped hard on their booted foot. Then his arm bent and swung out until he hit the Trooper's throat with the edge of his hand.

The Trooper gasped, dropped their rifle, and reached up to their throat as they struggled to draw in a breath. Adan felt the armor move his arm again as he reached up and grabbed the Trooper's head with a fistful of hair, then slammed the Trooper's head down hard into his knee. Once the armor released Adan's grip, the Trooper slumped to the floor.

Adan immediately jumped back and looked at a shocked Rune. "I didn't do that," he explained. "It was the armor. It was controlling me."

Rune shook his head, then smiled. "Then I think we may have a chance to make it out of here after all." He reached down and grabbed the fallen Trooper's rifle, then held it out for Adan.

Adan looked down at it and watched as a red outline appeared around it. Then the red outline flashed. "The weapon is unnecessary," the armor stated. "Onboard armaments will be sufficient."

"The armor says I don't need it," Adan said to Rune.

Rune took a deep breath and nodded. "Fine. It seems to know what it's doing."

"What is this armor, Rune?"

Rune looked down at the rifle, checked the chamber for a load, then flipped off the safety catch. "All I know is that it's called Smart Combat Armor. It must have a computer brain, which is what's speaking to you. When we found out who you are and what you can do, we smuggled it here in case you could use it."

"What do you mean we? Who are you?"

Rune grinned. "You haven't worked that out yet? I'm with the Motari."

Official Log of Captain Chander Sanyal

Neskan Colony, 29 February, Year 3 (Neskan Calendar)

We lost an entire crop this week. We planted early due to the favorable weather, hoping to get a second crop out of the field later in the year. But the seedlings all died practically overnight. Jun says that it was an error in the printing process, resulting in a faulty genome. His team has already fixed it and is printing new seeds. Until then, he said, we'll have to let the field remain fallow. I had to look that word up, by the way. Maybe it's better that I'm not a farmer.

More troubling is the news that the Bio-printer is starting to show signs of early breakdown. Jun said it was never designed to support an entire colony on its own. He's been able to print replacement parts from the remaining Service-printers, but those, too, won't last forever. We need to make a fallback plan for when we have to service and repair items without having any new replacement parts.

Chapter 12

Adan couldn't believe what he'd just heard. Had the underground really sent someone to rescue him? And Jenra's brother, of all people. "You? You're really Motari?"

Rune nodded. "Yes. And as much as I'd love to give you our recruiting pitch, now isn't the time. We seriously need to go if we're going to make it out of here."

"Damn it," Adan murmured. "Alright, I'm with you."

Rune nodded again, then pulled open Adan's cell door and hurried out into the corridor. Adan stepped over the downed Trooper and followed Rune. Everything outside of his cell seemed unusually calm. There were no flashing lights, alarms, or any signs of trouble. It was eerie.

Then the armor spoke to him again. "I detect multiple armed individuals in your vicinity. Please designate them as friendly or hostile."

Two more armed Troopers rushed around the corner. They didn't look friendly.

"They're all hostile," Adan spat as he took an instinctive step backward.

"Designating all contacts as hostile," the armor announced while Rune lifted the rifle and fired twice. Adan could barely hear the shots. The armor must've muffled their sound.

One of the Troopers took a hit from Rune's rifle, flew back, and hit the floor hard. The remaining Trooper pointed their rifle at Adan and fired. Adan didn't even have time to duck or dodge before the shot hit him with a dull thud. He cringed, expecting a sudden, searing pain. But it felt like nothing more than taking a punch.

Then the armor took over again. Adan found himself rushing toward the remaining Trooper. They fired at him again, but the armor twisted Adan out of the shot's path. Then Adan was on them. The armor made him grab the rifle barrel and shove it up. The Trooper cried out in shock and pain as the weapon smashed into their nose. Then Adan tore the rifle from the Trooper's hands, flipped it around, and slammed the butt end into the Trooper's bloody face. They flew back onto the tile floor and didn't get back up.

Adan struggled with a sudden burst of conflicting feelings. He was excited at his unexpected victory and frightened with his sudden violent outburst. But it wasn't his outburst, Adan reminded himself. It was the armor. The armor had been controlling him, and he was just along for the ride.

"You move like a machine."

Adan turned back to see Rune standing there. His expression was either awe or fear, but Adan couldn't tell which. Adan looked down at the rifle, then switched the safety back on and dropped it to the floor. "That's because it's a machine that's moving me around. I'm just the passenger here."

"Then take control," Rune suggested. "Tell it what to do."

That was easy for him to say. Rune was a trained fighter. Adan was a trained janitor. But he wasn't helpless.

"Armor, or whatever I should call you–"

"I am called a Battlefield Enhanced System Intelligence."

That name was way too long. Adan needed something shorter. "How about Besi?"

"I will answer to Besi."

"There are Old Tech weapons nearby. The weapons are the same technology as you, I mean. Can you detect them?"

"Yes."

"Show me where they are," Adan commanded.

"Follow the Augmented Display prompts."

An arrow appeared in the air before him.

"Come on, Rune," Adan directed the Motari spy. "We're going to make a detour."

Rune furrowed his brow. "Are you sure? It's only a matter of time before someone activates the alarm, and this place is crawling with Gray Coats. Remember, only one of us is wearing impenetrable armor."

"I know. But this is important."

Adan didn't wait for Rune to argue further. He rushed forward, following the arrow down the corridor until it swung to the left. Adan wasn't sure if they kept all the weapons in the testing room or not. He suspected they were locked up elsewhere when they weren't being studied. As he was about to turn the corner, the armor spoke again.

"Alert. Enemy combatants ahead."

"You said this thing is armed, yeah?"

"Affirmative."

"So let's use that."

Adan felt a sudden pressure on his forearms, then twin bulges, one on each arm, rose from the bands of armor. "Extend your arm to aim," the armor instructed him. "Squeeze your fist to fire."

He peeked around the corner and saw two more Troopers rushing down the corridor toward him. Red squares appeared around their faces as he stuck his arm out toward them. Then Adan pointed his fist at the closest Trooper and squeezed. He heard a quick pop and saw a blue-white flash. The Trooper briefly gyrated in place before collapsing to the floor. The other Trooper stopped and tried to raise their rifle, so Adan shifted his aim and squeezed again. Then that Trooper went down, too.

Adan pulled his arm back and looked at the black knob. "What just happened? Are they dead"

"It is a Variable Ion Pulse Emitter. You fired it at its most lethal setting. Your targets are dead."

Adan didn't understand what the name meant. And he was getting tired of not really knowing what the devices he used were. "Fine. Now, the Old Tech weapons?"

The arrow reappeared, and Adan followed it around the corner. He approached the door that led to the testing room, but the arrow directed him further forward. After another few meters, it flipped and pointed to a door on his right. Adan reached out and tried the handle, but the door was locked. "Will the pulse weapon work on door locks?"

"No," Besi replied.

"Let me," Rune offered. He put a hand on Adan's chest and gently pushed him back. Then Rune stood back, pointed his rifle at the door lock, and fired. The shot burst through the door, leaving a hole where the lock was. "Is this where they're storing all their Old Tech?"

"Yeah," Adan replied as he pushed the door open. Then he heard more voices in the distance. "Watch my back," he added. "I won't be long."

Rune took cover just inside the doorway as Adan stepped into the darkened room. "Where are the lights?" Adan muttered while he looked for the switch. Then the room suddenly lit up. No, that wasn't right. Everything became visible, but it was fuzzy and drained of color. Adan's ability to see in the dark must've been another of the armor's wonders. Adan immediately spotted the racks of the Old Tech artifacts he'd been testing. He quickly searched through them and found the Old Tech handgun. When Adan picked it up, it recognized him and activated even though he was armored.

He heard Rune fire his rifle. "Besi, can I attach this to the armor somehow?"

"Yes. Place it near your hip, and it will connect there."

Adan held it against his hip, and it stuck there as if he was sticking a magnet to a piece of metal. He let go of the weapon, then reached out and grabbed one of the rifles. It sat next to the Heavy Ordnance Launcher, but Adan's shoulder ached just from thinking about lifting that. The rifle activated at his touch as it had before.

"Can you tell me how to set the firing mode on this, Besi?"

"I can mesh with the weapon's control unit and manage it directly."

That was handy. Then he heard Rune fire several times. "Set it for semi-automatic fire, please. Now, can you tell me if anything in here is explosive?"

"Everything in here is explosive under the proper circumstances."

That was what he'd been hoping to hear. Adan shared what he had in mind, and Besi told him what to do. After another minute, everything was ready. He picked up the rifle again and joined Rune at the door. "We need to go."

Rune huffed. "That's what I've been trying to tell you."

"No, I mean we have three minutes to get out of this facility before it all goes boom." Adan shouldered his rifle and leaned out into the corridor. A rifle round zipped by his head, then a red square appeared over the Trooper who'd fired it. Adan pointed the Old Tech rifle at the Trooper and pressed the trigger. The rifle's blast struck the Trooper and threw them back hard into the wall behind them. Then a second square appeared, floating in front of the wall near the corner. Was someone hiding there? "Come on out. I'll cover you." Adan fired a pair of warning shots at the corner as Rune moved out behind him.

"Three minutes?" Rune asked. "What did you do?"

Adan ignored him for the moment. "Besi, how do we get out of here?"

"Take the corridor behind you for three meters, then turn and follow the next corridor for ten meters to a door on your right. There is a stairwell there that leads up from this level."

Adan kept the rifle pointed at the hidden Trooper and started backing up. "I'm taking away all their toys, Rune." he finally answered. "They were about to start experimenting on me, and I'm not letting them get away with it." The red square started to move. Adan waited until he saw the Trooper peek around the corner, then fired again. He missed but earned them a little more time.

"My sister's up there, Adan."

"I know. We're going to get her along with my friend Bo."

216

Adan glanced at the timer counting down in the corner of his view. Two minutes. They had to hurry. He flipped around to face the upcoming corner and moved forward.

"Enemy combatants detected ahead," Besi informed him as three small squares appeared to his left.

"What do you mean we're going to get her?"

Adan grunted and put his back to the wall. "There are three more Troopers around the corner," he announced as Rune backed up next to him, "so stay behind me. And I mean, we're getting her and Bo out of here, too." Then he firmed up his grip on the rifle and stepped around the corner.

He'd caught the Troopers by surprise. So Adan pointed his weapon at the closest one and fired. The first Trooper fell while another aimed their rifle at Adan and fired back. But Adan's armor just absorbed the hit as he continued down the corridor. Adan aimed, fired again, and the second Trooper went down. He pointed his rifle at the remaining Trooper, then hesitated. It was Third Chief Osaben. The Chief fired three times, each shot hitting him in the center of his chest hard enough to knock him off balance.

"Besi?"

"Your armor integrity is holding. You are only feeling the kinetic force from the impact."

Adan didn't know what kinetic meant, but he understood force. He stepped forward again, pointing his weapon at Osaben. "Don't make me shoot you, Chief."

The Chief didn't fire again but kept his rifle pointed at Adan. "Is that you in there, Testa? You know I can't let you out of here."

Adan kept advancing as the timer counted down. "And I think you know that you can't stop me, Chief. Just put the

217

rifle down and walk away so you can tell this story to the next class of Provies."

"I'm afraid can't do that, Testa." Then the Chief fired again, hitting Adan in the helmet hard enough to knock his head back and stop his advance.

Adan shook his head to regain his balance, then started forward again. "Last warning, Chief."

But the Chief stood his ground. "I'm not moving from this spot. Do what you have to do, Testa."

Balda's ass, but the man was stubborn. After all, he was a damn believer. And, like him or not, the Chief was willing to drug Adan so that his superiors could perform whatever experiments on Adan they needed to do. "Damn it, Chief."

Adan fired, hitting Osaben right in the forehead, killing him before his body even hit the floor. There was nothing else Adan could've done. The place would blow soon, and the Chief would've been just as dead anyway.

Adan glanced at Rune, then rushed over to the door that led to the stairwell. Adan tried the handle just in case, but it was locked. So he stepped back, pointed the rifle at the door handle, and fired. Then Adan shoved the door open with his shoulder and rushed into the stairwell. Rune was right behind him. The timer was almost at zero as they reached the landing halfway up the stairwell.

"Brace yourself," Besi warned.

Adan grabbed Rune and pushed him up against the wall, putting his armor between Rune's body and the facility. Then the time bomb Besi had helped him set went off with a deafening roar. At least, Adan assumed it was deafening. The armor muffled the sound to a dull boom. But the force of the blast blew the door at the bottom of the stairwell apart, and Adan felt the stairs beneath him tremble.

"That'll get their attention," Adan predicted as he backed off of Rune. He hadn't realized how close they'd been to one another. If it weren't for the armor–

No. It still wasn't the time for that line of thought.

Rune raised an eyebrow at Adan as if he somehow knew what Adan was thinking. Then he shook his head and wiped some of the dust and debris off his trousers. "You should've told me about the bomb. If we're going to make it out of here, you can't be doing things like that. You need to trust me."

Who exactly did Rune think he was talking to Adan about trust? "Trust you? I don't even know you." Emboldened by his sudden frustration, Adan leaned in closer to Rune. "Everyone who's had any power over me has abused it. And I'm done with that. If you want my trust, you need to earn it."

Rune raised his hands in surrender. Or as an apology. "Alright, alright, I'm sorry. But I gave you that armor, didn't I? That has to count for something."

Adan huffed. "It's a start."

Rune nodded. "Good enough. But we need to get out of this stairwell if we want any chance of getting to Jenra and Bo before the Commander does." Then he tapped a finger on Adan's armored chest. "And you should take that armor off."

"Take it off? It's how I survived this long."

"Yeah, down here." Then Rune pointed up the rest of the stairs. "But, up there, you'll be outnumbered and outgunned. Not to mention how much you'll stand out. You look like a walking machine."

Besi chimed in before Adan could protest any further. "Your companion is correct. While you would likely survive most attacks in this armor, it is not invulnerable. And any attention you draw would potentially be lethal to anyone who was near you."

"Okay, yeah. You're right." Adan looked down at his rifle. "But what do I do with this?"

"I don't know," Rune replied. "Maybe we can wrap it in my uniform jacket?"

"It is collapsible," Besi shared, "as is your other weapon. I will initiate the process now." Adan's rifle suddenly shifted in his hands and then collapsed in on itself. When it was done, it had turned into a solid white and gray box no longer than his forearm. "It can be fixed to the back of your harness. The hand weapon can be attached to your belt strap. I will retract the armor now, but I will remain active. When you need it again, simply say the words 'Activate armor.'"

"And you'll be able to hear me?"

"Yes." Then the piece in front of his face retracted as the armor rapidly returned to its hidden home in the harness and belt he wore. "You will hear me as well. I can use a directed sound field to communicate with you privately."

By the time Besi was done speaking, Adan was completely unarmored. He suddenly felt very naked, and the bravado he had when he rushed up the stairs was gone. He looked down to see the handgun, collapsed into a white rectangle the size of a soap bar, attached to his belt. Adan lifted the collapsed rifle over his shoulder and set it against the back of his harness, where it stuck fast.

Rune looked Adan over, smirking as he shook his head. "Okay, for a while there, I forgot you were just a kid."

Adan scowled. "Hey, I–"

Rune held up a hand to stop him. "I didn't mean anything

negative. I just met you and forgot what you looked like. That's all. Now, let's get upstairs." He turned and started rushing up to the door ahead. "If things look like they're about to go wrong, I'll pretend to take you prisoner. That will confuse things enough to give us some time."

Adan could already hear the alarm sounding through the door and imagined how chaotic it must be in the DFTC. "Alright." He doubted a ploy that like one would work for more than a few seconds, but that might be just enough to give them a chance to take some kind of action. Or get away.

The door was unlocked when Rune tried it, so he opened it and walked through. Adan followed him into chaos. Troopers and Provies scrambled every which way, and no one seemed to notice the two of them in their confusion.

Rune turned back to Adan. "Be on the lookout for the Commander and any other Troopers who might recognize you." Adan nodded. "Where would my sister and your friend be?"

Adan shrugged. "I've been locked in the basement for three days. And who even knows with everyone running around like this? But we should probably try the barracks first."

Rune slung his rifle's strap over his shoulder, then gestured for Adan to take the lead. Adan nodded before realizing he wasn't sure where in the DFTC they were. He looked around as he went until he recognized the corridor that led to the Library. Adan shook his head in wonder. The Commander's secret facility really was right beneath the DFTC. But Adan finally knew where he was, so he took off toward the barracks.

"Besi, can you still hear me?" he whispered.

"Yes," Besi replied. It sounded like someone speaking over

221

his shoulder. He turned his head in surprise, half expecting to see someone there.

"I don't suppose you can alert me if Commander Sala or First Trooper Mannix are nearby?"

"I do not have biometric data for those persons. But I can listen for mentions of those names."

That would have to do. It could give them at least a few seconds of warning. "Do it. Also, listen for Jenra Tabata and Bo Shen."

"Affirmative."

"It's still talking to you," Rune mentioned, "but I can't hear it."

Adan nodded, then stopped at a corridor intersection. He wanted to peek around the corner to see who was ahead, but he knew he looked suspicious enough as it was. At least Adan was in uniform trousers and boots, even if he wasn't wearing his jacket. "It uses something called a sound field. I don't know what that is."

Adan stepped around the corner and started walking toward the barracks. He held his breath as several Troopers rushed by, but no one paid him any attention. Feeling more confident, Adan picked up his pace as they neared the door for his squad's room, then stopped in front of it. Adan pointed at the door. "This is the one."

Rune slipped the strap off his shoulder and took hold of his rifle. "Okay, ready."

Adan opened the door and rushed in. The rest of Squad Ten was mostly gathered nervously on the left side of the barracks. They were all watching First Trooper Mannix, who was shouting something at Jenra in the back of the room. At least Mannix was facing away from the door. Jenra's jaw dropped when she recognized Adan and, to her apparent shock, her brother.

"Adan? Rune?" Jenra called out.

Mannix whipped around at the sound of Adan's name. But Rune was ready and had his rifle pointed at them.

"Everyone stay where they are," Rune commanded. "Let's see those hands, Mannix."

The rest of the squad remained frozen in place, unsure of what was happening.

Mannix scowled and lifted up their hands. "Tabata. Of course, it's you."

Garun seemed to understand before the others. "You're Jenra's brother?"

"We can do the introductions later," Adan said. "Jenra, we're getting out of here, and we came to get you."

Jenra's sudden confusion was obvious. For a moment, Adan was afraid she wouldn't respond. Or that, if she did, she'd say no.

Mannix used that awkward moment to make their move, lunging to their side and tackling Jenra. Rune followed the action with his rifle but couldn't shoot for fear of hitting his sister. Adan reached down to his belt for the collapsed handgun without thinking. It started to reassemble itself and was ready once it was in his hand. Besi must've been paying attention.

But neither of them had to do anything. The rest of Squad Ten finally jumped to action. Maybe seeing Mannix attack their Squad Leader was enough for them to overcome their fear of Rune's rifle. Rune swung the rifle to the side, looking for a new target, but Adan put a hand on his shoulder.

"Wait," Adan advised.

Garun and Uso rushed over to the scuffle, took hold of Mannix, and pulled them off Jenra. Mannix managed to shake Garun off but was no match for Uso, who was heavier and stronger. He wrenched the First Trooper's arm behind their back, then used the extra leverage to push them down to their knees. Jenra jumped up and stepped over to the kneeling Trooper, reached down, and grabbed their sidearm from the holster at their belt. Adan hadn't even realized they were armed. Jenra's face was surprisingly calm as she flipped the safety switch off and pointed the gun at the First Trooper's head.

"You're crazy if you think you'll get away with this, Tabata," Mannix growled. It wasn't clear which of the Tabatas they were referring to. Maybe it didn't even matter.

Jenra smiled. "You're crazy if you think I won't shoot you, Mannix." Then she turned to face the rest of the room. "Squad Ten, we're leaving. I need someone to tie the First Trooper up. Anyone else who wants to stay behind will have to be tied up as well."

Adan's squadmates seemed to accept Jenra's order without question. Rune lowered his rifle as several of them rushed back to their lockers. "We can't take everybody, Jenra. This was supposed to be a simple operation."

Jenra shook her head. "This is what's happening, Rune. It's all of us or none of us."

Rune looked to Adan for support, but Adan shook his head, too. "She's my Squad Leader. I can't say no."

Rune groaned, then nodded. "Fine. Adan, help them secure Mannix. Jenra and I will go find your friend Bo. I assume she knows who he is?"

Adan shook his head. "No, I should be the one to–"

But Rune was already slinging his rifle over his shoulder. "No, you need to stay out of sight," he reminded Adan, cutting him off. "You're the only reason I'm here." He turned to his sister. "Come on, Jenra. We need to find someone called Bo. And only Bo. No one else."

Jenra nodded while Garun and Uso gagged Mannix with a shirt. Then they used a few of their belts to secure the First Trooper's hands and ankles. Jenra hurried over to Rune and Adan, then took Adan's hands. "They wouldn't tell us what happened to you. Bo only said that he wasn't allowed to talk about it."

Adan was relieved to hear Bo had been brought back upstairs after he disappeared. "Does that mean he's alright?"

Jenra nodded as Rune grabbed her shoulder. "Let's go."

"We'll be right back," Jenra promised. Then her brother opened the door to the corridor, and they both left.

Mannix struggled with their bonds as Uso and Garun laid them on Jenra's bed. Wellan and Simi sat on their beds, lacing up their boots. Sabina and Fan were arguing with each other. Adan realized he was still holding onto the Old Tech handgun, probably giving off the wrong impression. Or the right impression, but not the one he wanted to give. So he slapped it back onto his belt and watched it collapse back into a small rectangle.

"And I'm telling you this can't work!" Sabina shouted.

Fan threw up their hands in exasperation. "And what do you think will happen if we stay behind?"

"I'll tell you what will happen," Adan called out. Both of them looked at him in surprise. "Or, at least, I'll tell you what happened to me. You see, there's a secret, secure research facility right underneath the DFTC. Or, there was until a

225

few minutes ago. But that's where the Commander kept me locked up for the last few days." He lifted up his shirt and showed them the bandage on his hip. "That's where they extracted some of my bone marrow. They also took a pint of my blood. And those are just the first experiments they had planned for me." Then Adan held out his arm and showed them the bandage there. He noticed that some blood had soaked through, but he ignored it. "And that's where they implanted a wireless tracker. That's how important I am to the Commander. So you can count on the fact that she'll want to learn everything you know about me. And that she probably won't ask nicely."

Everyone fell silent. Their shock and confusion were evident on their faces. Everyone except Mannix, who kept struggling against their bonds.

"Well, that seals it," Garun announced. "We're all going. Right, Sabina?"

"Yeah, fine, you're right," Sabina reluctantly agreed. Then she lunged toward the door. Adan moved to stop her, but she was too fast. Sabina threw open the door to see Jenra standing with Bo and Rune. Jenra scowled and shoved Sabina back into the room.

"Stupid," Fan spat as they pulled a belt from their locker. Uso, shaking his head, grabbed Sabina and held her down on her own bed while Fan bound and gagged her, too.

But Adan didn't see any of that. Instead, he rushed over to Bo, who pulled Adan into a tight embrace.

"You're here?" Bo gushed. "And you're okay? Founder's grace, I didn't think I was going to see you again."

"Same here," Adan agreed. "I was so worried. No one would tell me what happened to you."

Bo let Adan go, then took a moment to inspect Adan's injuries. He shook his head. "What are these bandages? Were they running tests on you?" Adan nodded, and Bo shook his head again. He looked close to tears. "I wanted to tell everyone! But the Commander told me that if I said anything about you, she'd put both our squads in front of the firing squad."

"That's still a real possibility," Rune announced, "if we don't get this next part right."

"What's the next part?" Jenra asked.

"About that," Rune replied. "My original plan is already ruined thanks to Adan and his Old Tech. But I've been thinking about what to do next. And, now that I know what I'm working with, I think my new plan might actually work."

Official Log of Captain Chander Sanyal

Neskan Colony, 6 June, Year 3 (Neskan Calendar)

The eastern settlement officially broke ground today. They're calling it Bowen Valley after Nestor Bowen, one of the colony lander casualties. Marketta was livid about the name. Bowen was to be the original Colony Administrator, of course. She thinks it's a deliberate snub against me. She may be right about that. But Nestor was also my friend, and I'm glad some of the colonists have chosen to honor him that way.

The Officer Council initially voted to deny the request. But I overrode the dissenting votes to allow it. I understand Marketta's reason for voting no. We have to carefully monitor and distribute our remaining resources if we're going to survive. But she misses the bigger picture. I know that the colonists are motivated by their need to break away from my leadership, even symbolically. And they're right to do so. This isn't the Chander Sanyal colony. This is a colony for all Neskans. And their plan was sound. They surveyed a lovely site nestled in a small valley about 100 km from here. There's plenty of arable land for farming, and the valley shelters them from the worst of the winds that kick up on these plains. We'll still be printing the supplies they need, of course. We need their plan to work as much as they do if we're ever going to have a future as a colony.

Chapter 13

Adan waited at the corner for a ten-second count, then cautiously peered around into the open corridor. The Troopers he'd hidden from had moved out of sight, so Adan quietly rushed across to where the rest of the squad was waiting. Jenra and Bo were right on his tail. Once they were all through the door, Rune swung it shut and flipped the locking bar down.

Earlier, after Rune had quietly explained his plan to them, the squad ensured Mannix and Sabina were sufficiently secured. Then they all emerged from the barracks room into a DFTC very different from the one Adan expected. The klaxons had gone quiet by that time, and the Provies had all been ushered into their rooms. It was eerily quiet. You'd never know there'd been an Old Tech explosion right below their feet. The thought of Commander Sala discovering the loss of all those precious artifacts brought a malicious smile to Adan's face as he ducked behind a stack of metal boxes just beyond the door.

"Two Troopers detected," Besi announced. The armor's computer brain listened to everything and had adapted its terminology. "Twenty meters to your right."

Adan tapped on Rune's shoulder. When the Motari operative turned his way, Adan held up two fingers then pointed them to his right. Rune nodded, then turned to pass the info to Jenra. Adan was suddenly struck by how much the brother and sister really looked alike. Even more so than Riela and Tavi back at the group home. Then Adan almost laughed. He hadn't thought about the group home in weeks. He wondered if any of his old housemates had been told about what happened to him and Bo. Probably not. They were just two more thatch rats from the Lowers who got swallowed up by the city one night.

Rune tapped on his shoulder. When Adan turned toward him, he leaned in close and whispered in Adan's ear. "It's time. Are you ready?"

Adan nodded. It was hard to ignore the effect Rune's closeness had on him. But he needed to stay alert. They weren't out of danger yet.

Rune turned back to his sister and gave her a nod. Jenra moved off and led the rest of the squad back into the darkness. Adan and Rune crept the other way, hiding behind boxes and crates where they could.

"Five meters," Besi said.

Adan stopped and listened. He heard the muffled sounds of a quiet conversation up ahead. Then he turned back to Rune and cupped his hand behind his ear.

Rune nodded. "Let's go," Rune whispered.

Adan stood and clasped his hands behind his back as if

he were shackled. Rune stood behind him and pulled his borrowed uniform jacket down. He'd taken it from Mannix, who was both shorter and thicker than he was, so it didn't quite fit. But it had the First Trooper stars on the shoulder. Adan wore a uniform jacket he'd borrowed from Garun. It helped him blend in and, more importantly, covered the Old Tech armor and weapons. Rune grabbed his arm and started to lead him forward. As soon as the two Troopers standing guard came into view, Rune switched on his act.

"Why in the Founder's name are you just standing there?" Rune yelled. "You were told to sweep the facility for strays." He roughly pulled Adan forward. "Like this one."

The Troopers looked at Rune, then each other, confused. Rune's commanding tone and the apparently shackled Provie had their desired effect. "We were given no such orders, First Trooper," said the one closest to them.

"No such–" Rune spat, then calmed himself and began to step forward. "These orders came from the Commander herself," he added with a growl. "A whole squad of Provies is still unaccounted for, along with Third Chief Osaben."

"Chief Osaben?" The other Trooper asked. "We weren't told–"

But Rune cut them off, shoving Adan toward the closest Trooper while he lunged toward the farther one. Adan's Trooper stumbled back in surprise, then tried lifting his rifle off his shoulder. But he was already too late. Adan swung his armor-protected arm out and cracked his elbow across the Trooper's cheek. Then he swung his elbow back, connecting with the bridge of the Trooper's nose with an audible crunch. The Trooper howled and fell to their knees. Adan grabbed their head and bashed them in the temple with his knee.

When Adan let go, they slumped to the cold floor.

Adan glanced at Rune to see that he'd already dealt with the other Trooper. Then he reached down and took the Trooper's rifle.

"All clear of combatants," Besi informed him.

"All clear," Adan repeated aloud.

"Perfect. Find the controls for this door and get ready to open it. Jenra!"

Adan followed Besi's whispered directions to the door controls while Jenra appeared from the shadows. "We're loaded up and ready to go," she confirmed.

"Perfect. Adan, how are we with that door?"

Adan stopped where Besi instructed and found a wall-mounted box. He opened the front panel and saw the large, push-button switches. "Got it. Just tell me when."

"Now, please."

Adan pushed the button marked Open, and the massive roll door lifted with a creaky rumble. He turned and hurried back to where Rune and Jenra stood, then followed them to where the heavy truck was parked.

Rune grabbed the rifle from Adan's hands, pulled his rifle from his shoulder, and handed both to Jenra. "You're in the back with the others," he instructed her. "Make sure you all stay down and out of sight, but be ready to protect our backside if we're followed."

Jenra frowned but nodded. "Alright." Then she took the rifles and walked to the back of the truck. The Defense Force had modified the heavy flatbed hauler with side rails and a thick canvas top to transport Troopers. The cab had room for three, but only Rune and Adan would be in it. Jenra didn't look excited to be stuck in the back, but she agreed that someone back there had to be in charge. Bo had suggested that he could drive, but Rune refused. Only he knew where they needed to go. Adan would be his gunner. Since he had the Old Tech weapons, he had a better chance of stopping any forward attacks than anyone else.

Adan opened the passenger side door and climbed inside. He wished he'd taken the Heavy Ordnance Launcher. But Rune assured him that the Old Tech rifle would be more than enough.

Rune climbed in behind the wheel, then reached forward and pressed the starter button. The truck's big engine rumbled to life. He turned to Adan. "Armor up, Adan. I'll need your extra senses."

"Besi, activate armor." The process still took him by surprise that time, even though he knew what to expect. By the time he settled his jangled nerves, Adan was staring out from the inside of his black helmet again. "Can you show me what's out there?"

"Affirmative." The night suddenly lit up, bathing the yard beyond the garage in faint silver light. Then a series of glowing red squares, circles, and triangles appeared before him with small words next to them printed in light. Besi could detect everything from building entrances to Troopers to alarm sensors. It was overwhelming.

"That's too much," Adan complained. "Just show me the main threats between here and the main gate." Most of the shapes disappeared, leaving only a few for the Gray Coats stationed nearby. "Rune, there are four Troopers on patrol about a hundred meters to the left and four Troopers stationed at the gate."

"How far is the gate?"

"Just over two hundred meters away."

"Perfect." Rune reached back and slid open the small partition between the cab and the truck's rear. He relayed the Trooper positions to Jenra and told her to hold on. Then he switched on the forward lights and put the truck into gear. Adan reached behind his uniform jacket and pulled the rifle off his back. It had reassembled itself by the time he had it in front of him.

Rune nodded at Adan and pushed on the accelerator. The truck lurched forward, and Rune backed off the pedal slightly. Even he'd never driven a truck that big. But he quickly got the hang of it and steered them out of the garage toward the main drive. Rune turned right when he reached it, then started accelerating.

Adan rolled down his side window and leaned out with the rifle. Besi displayed flashing circles to show him the places that would disable the gate so they could force the truck through it. Adan aimed toward the first circle, using a red cross that indicated where his gun pointed. When he had the cross centered on the circle, Adan pressed the trigger. Once the gun flashed, he moved to the next circle, then fired again. By that time, the Troopers at the gate were rushing out of the gatehouse. The unfamiliar bright flash of the Old Tech rifle's shots no doubt took them by surprise. Adan hit the third target then aimed for the fourth when a rifle round smashed through the truck's windshield. He hesitated for a moment.

"Ignore that!" Rune shouted. "Just get us out of here."

Adan grunted and fired at the fourth target. With the truck's lights and his helmet's enhanced night vision, he watched the gate tip forward and fall to the ground. "We're good. Let's do it."

Rune pressed hard on the accelerator, and the truck surged forward. A series of rifle shots peppered the truck cab. Adan leaned out with the Old Tech rifle again, found one of the Troopers, and fired. He had no idea if he hit them or not before the truck bumped up over the edge of the heavy gate. Then they were past it and back down on the road.

Adan heard the sounds of gunfire behind him. He leaned up to peek through the partition. A few of his squadmates were firing at the guards back at the gate. But he didn't see any trucks or autos following them yet. Adan turned back toward the front. "That felt too easy."

Rune chuckled darkly. "That's because it was the easy part. We still have to get out of the Pinch. And then we have to get away."

A small canyon inside the Valley, the Pinch was infamous for its one narrow access point. That's why Utrogg House, the home of the Pinchers, and the Defense Force's secret facilities were located there. No one got in or out without them knowing. Adan had heard it said the Pinch was like its own walled city, able to even defend against siege or an attacking army if necessary. "But how come it was that easy?"

"Because the Defense Force never expects for attacks to come from within. If anyone dares to speak out or act against them or the Union, they get taken in by the Pinchers. Then they disappear." Adan nodded. He'd seen that for himself. "Now, stay on the lookout. I expect them to at least put something in our path before we get out of here."

"I detect several possible threats," Besi chimed in. "Two large vehicles left that compound behind us in pursuit. There is additional activity near the canyon entrance as well."

Rune took them wide around the perimeter of the Pinch

to avoid Utrogg House. Even the Motari were scared of that, Adan guessed. But they would soon have to turn back onto the main road in and out of the Pinch, a narrow gauntlet with three and four-story buildings on either side. Then more gunfire pelted the truck from behind. It sounded louder than the rest.

"Damn," Rune muttered.

"Detecting large caliber weapons fire," Besi confirmed.

"Uso and Simi are hit!" Jenra called out.

Damn! "What can I do, Besi?"

"Use the passthrough to fire back at them," Besi responded. "I can set your weapon for maximum power. Tell your companions to keep low."

Adan jumped up and pointed his rifle through the partition. "Everyone get down!" he shouted. A pair of flashing circles appeared in his vision just as more shots pounded their truck. Adan took a breath and aimed at the larger circle. It was one of the smaller gray trucks with some kind of extra-large super rifle mounted on the top. He lined up the cross with the circle and pressed the trigger. The resulting blast lit up the back of their truck for a moment. Then the front of the pursuing truck lit up in a great fireball as it skidded and crashed off to the side of the road.

"Founder's mercy!" someone shouted from the back. But Adan ignored it, aimed at the second flashing circle, and fired. The circle jumped to the side at the last second as the driver veered out of the way. His shot struck a post instead. Adan re-aimed and fired again. This time his shot went low, but it still hit the second truck in a fiery blast and flipped it into the air.

"Anything else, Besi?"

"There is possible danger ahead."

Adan grunted and turned around just as Rune steered them onto the main road. He caught a pair of flashes from the rooftops on either side of the gauntlet just before two more shots pierced the windshield. One struck just to Rune's right and dug into the bench seat. The other struck Adan in the chest. Even with the armor, it felt like he'd been hit with a hammer. Adan groaned from the pain. But there was no time for misery. He ignored the discomfort and leaned out the window, pointing his rifle at the flashing circle on the right. Then Adan pulled the trigger. Suddenly the top floor of the building exploded in flames.

"Besi!"

"This is no time for subtlety, Adan Testa. You still have another target."

Adan groaned while leaning out far enough to target the second circle as it rapidly grew smaller. Were they running away? But he fired again and destroyed a second rooftop.

"We're almost there," Rune called out, "but they're blocking the road."

Adan looked ahead to see the narrow canyon entrance blocked by a pair of black vans. He didn't even need the flashing circles for those. He aimed at one and fired twice. The explosion was enough to flip the van into the air and knock the other one away.

Rune gasped. "Balda's ass!" Adan looked over to see him grinning. "Remind me to never get on your bad side, Adan."

"More vehicles are in pursuit," Besi warned him. "I have designated a new target. Aim for it, but wait for my signal to fire."

Adan looked out and saw the edge of a flashing object at

the top of his view. He looked up to see a flashing circle in the sky. No, not in the sky, he realized. It was marking the top of the canyon's edge. Adan took a breath then pointed the cross at the circle, keeping it there as the truck moved. Then, just as they were about to pass underneath it, Besi gave him the command.

"Fire now."

Adan pressed the trigger and watched as his shot hit the rocky canyon edge. Then he heard a loud crack and a rumble. While Rune spun the wheel to make a sharp left turn, a piece of rock the size of a building came crashing down and completely closed off the entrance to the Pinch. Adan slumped back into his seat in wonder. Now they'd finally get a chance to test out that siege theory, Adan thought.

"Besi, can we turn the power back down now?"

"Yes," his armor's computer brain replied. "We have nearly depleted that weapon's charge. It will need an hour of direct sunlight to recharge to maximum capacity."

Putting it in the sun gave it power? The First Explorers were truly masters of science. "Okay, then let's deactivate it for now. Please deactivate the armor, too."

Adan felt the truck slow as his rifle collapsed into its box shape and his armor retreated back into his harness and belt discs. He reached back and stuck the collapsed rifle to his harness. Then he turned to Rune and saw the bullet hole in the seat behind him. "Are you alright?"

"One of those shots almost hit me. But I'm fine."

"What now?"

"Now," Rune said as he turned another corner, pointing them toward the Lowers, "we have to ditch this truck. I'm sure a hundred frantic calls for help have gone out on the

239

wireless by now. Every Pincher not trapped behind your rock will be on the lookout for us."

"How far is it?"

"Not far. Could you check on your Troopers?"

"Oh, yeah." Adan turned back to the opening in the partition. "How is everyone back there?"

Bo crawled up to speak with him. "Everyone except for Uso and Simi is okay. Uso is badly hurt. And Simi is dead."

Adan's heart sank. He'd foolishly hoped everyone would make it out alright. Maybe a hardened Gray Coat like Osaben would call a single death a success, but not Adan. "We're almost wherever Rune is taking us. Then we can get help."

"But you're alright?"

Adan nodded. "I am. So is Rune." Technically, Adan had been hit, but it hadn't injured him, so it didn't matter.

"That gun is really something, Adan. Did you make that rock fall down from the canyon?"

Adan couldn't help but grin. "Yeah. That was me."

"No wonder the Commander was so stuck on sucking you dry."

Bo didn't know how close that statement was to the truth. "She's probably so upset right now."

Bo chuckled. "Yeah. But I'm sorry you never found out about your parents."

Adan hadn't even considered that. After everything that happened with the Old Tech weapons, the thought hadn't crossed his mind. Somehow it didn't seem important anymore. "Yeah, there is that. But maybe I'll still find out someday. I'm just glad I'm not there for the Commander to experiment on anymore."

"The Union provides," Bo joked.

Adan snorted. "All hail the Union."

The truck slowed again, so Adan turned to see where they were, but then the lights went out. He slid back into his seat, wishing he still had his helmet on so he could see in the dark. "The lights are off," he observed.

"It's about the only way to hide a truck like this driving through the Lowers. Thankfully, it'll be gone by the time any of the Pincher's informants will get word back to their handlers." Rune leaned forward and squinted. "Ah, there they are."

Adan spotted the silhouette of someone holding a portable torch. They shined it at the truck, then down and to Adan's right. Rune slowed to a crawl as he drove closer to the torch holder, then cranked the wheel hard for a sharp right turn. That took them off the narrow street and into a downward sloping driveway. Rune stopped the truck just after starting the turn and rolled down his window.

"Think it'll fit?" Rune asked whoever was standing outside.

The unseen person laughed. "What? You couldn't find a bigger truck?"

Rune jokingly scoffed. "I can leave it out on the street if you prefer."

"Don't you dare. It'll fit. Just go slowly."

"That's the only way I go," Rune replied. "Get your Medic ready. We've got wounded." He pulled forward toward the entrance to an underground garage tucked underneath a building that could've been a small warehouse. Adan didn't think the truck would fit into the opening, but Rune carefully pulled it forward until the nose poked through. Then he spun the wheel to the left and somehow squeezed them into a space that didn't look any bigger than the truck was.

"I'm impressed," Adan admitted.

Rune looked at him and winked. "I'm a person of many talents, Adan Testa. You haven't even seen half of them yet."

In the dim, orange lighting in the garage, Rune looked dark and mysterious. Adan forced himself to smile. It was no use fighting it anymore. He had a crush on Rune, and there was no stopping it.

A knock on Rune's door made him look away from Adan. "Damn, Soto, I'm coming."

"Take your time Tabata," called out a voice from outside the truck. "It's not like you've got the entire Defense Force on your tail."

Rune chuckled as he opened his door. "Don't forget the Pinchers," he said as he climbed out of the truck.

"Ah, of course. The military and the secret police? Should we just assume the Clubbers want in on your little game, too?"

Adan opened his door and climbed out. They were parked in an oversized garage. Or maybe a small warehouse space. And it felt like the floor was moving, although that could've just been Adan's nerves. He walked to the back of the truck to see two citizens in ordinary worker's dress helping Jenra, Garun, and Wellan lift Uso down onto the floor. Then one of the helpers knelt down next to Uso, reached into a nearby black bag for a pair of scissors, and started cutting his shirt open. Fan climbed out next. They had a fraught expression on their flushed face as they tried kneeling down next to Uso. But Jenra and Garun held them back. The worker inspecting Uso's wounds needed space. Bo finally climbed out and looked around until he spotted Adan.

"Do you know where we are?" Bo quietly asked him.

Adan shook his head. "No, only that we're in the Lowers. We must be near the river, too."

Bo nodded. "Yeah, I could smell it when we stopped back there."

Then Adan thought he felt the floor move again. He flashed a questioning look at Bo. "Did you feel that?"

Bo nodded again. "I did. Are we on some kind of boat?"

"You're on a barge, to be specific," said the voice that had spoken to Rune. Adan turned to see an older citizen dressed in plain dark trousers and an old gray sweater. The tight curls of their black hair were buzzed close to their dark brown scalp, and they had a neatly trimmed black beard. The citizen slapped the side of the truck. "This beast is a little more than she usually carries, but she'll hold it for as long as she needs to. Welcome aboard, at any rate." They offered a hand in greeting. "I'm–"

"Soto Pavola," Bo interrupted.

The older citizen looked surprised. "That's right. Do I know you?"

"You're the Thatcher we were supposed to bring the bashki to."

Pavola laughed. "That was you? I'd heard you were nabbed by the Pinchers. And now here you are."

"Here we are," Bo repeated. "I'm Bo. This is Adan."

Adan took Pavola's still extended hand and shook it. "Nice to meet you. I'm sorry that we're late."

Pavola laughed again. "And you brought me a truck full of wounded Troopers instead of bashki."

"Are you with the Motari, too?"

Pavola's eyes suddenly went wide, and he signaled for Adan to keep his voice down. "I work with them from time to time," he quietly replied. "But we don't like to use that word around here."

"Don't let the old Thatcher fool you," Rune suggested as he rounded the front of the truck. "He's got his fingers in more winefruit pies than just us." He stopped and clapped Pavola on the back. "Did you prep everything like I asked?"

Pavola huffed. "I'm a man of my word, Tabata. You should know that. Although it looks like you're going to need more than what you asked for."

Rune smiled bashfully and rubbed his hand through his thick, black hair. "Well, things didn't exactly go according to plan. But if you can accommodate us, you know my people are good for it."

Pavola nodded. "That's true. And it's a good thing because getting rid of this beast," he said as he slapped the truck again, "is going to cost you."

Jenra finally left Uso and the others to join Adan and Bo. Rune smiled, then went to her and gave her a hug. She accepted it with a smile, then stepped back and looked the four of them over. "Well, that could've gone better."

Rune nodded. "Maybe. But it could've gone much worse, thank the Founders. How's your Troopers?"

Jenra frowned. "Poor Simi took a round right in the chest." She paused for a moment, shaking her head. Then she took a breath before continuing. "But Uso might be okay. He got hit in the side and leg, but that citizen has already started dressing his wounds."

"Mitri has field medical training," Pavola shared. "If he says your friend will be okay, then he will be. Mitri knows what he's about."

Jenra looked relieved. "Thank the Founders." She glanced

back at Uso one more time, then returned her attention to the group. "So, now that we've completely trashed the Pinch and are probably the most wanted people in the Valley, what next?"

Rune nodded. "I need to get Adan out of Bolvar. As for the rest of you, we'll have to discuss that."

"Wherever he goes, I go," Bo declared.

"That's right," Adan confirmed.

Rune looked the pair of them over. "Well, two of you, I can manage. But I can't take all of you."

"Take all of us where?" Garun asked as he joined the discussion.

"Yeah," Adan added. "Where?"

A look of frustration briefly crossed Rune's face, then he sighed. He must've realized that it was too late to protest at that point. "We have a settlement to the west on the other side of the Osbaks. And we have an Old Tech expert there that could help Adan understand what he can do."

Adan frowned. "Not like the experts you just rescued me from, I hope?"

Rune shook his head. "No, nothing like that. It's all voluntary. And they know more than your Union friends. A lot more."

"That's great," Jenra commented. "But what about the rest of us?"

Rune shrugged. "Like I said–"

"No," Jenra interrupted. "None of us can go back there now. We'll be tortured for information about you and Adan, or we'll see the wrong side of a firing squad."

"Or both," Garun added,

Rune sighed. "I know."

Pavola, who had been listening intently, suddenly looked over Adan's head. "I'm afraid this discussion will have to continue elsewhere. They're ready to shove off, and I'd rather not have you aboard while they deal with your truck problem." He gestured behind himself past the front of the truck. "If you'll just come with me–"

"What about Uso?" Jenra asked.

"Your injured comrade? They'll be brought in with us. Now, please."

Pavola turned and led the group away from the truck. They approached a small ramp that led up to a doorway. There must've been one leading off the driveway, too, Adan realized. It was an easy way to load and unload goods from the barge since it was essentially the lowest floor in the building. The doorway led to a small office with a ramp sloping up on the far side. Pavola took them up the ramp to a large warehouse space then up a stairway into a long corridor.

"Use the last door on the left," Pavola instructed them. "Rune, you'll find the supplies you requested there. I'll come join you once the barge has been launched."

Rune nodded as Pavola turned and walked back down the stairs.

The door Pavola mentioned opened to a comfortably sized room set up with a table, four chairs, and several cots. A wooden crate sat in one corner. Rune went to it right away, lifted the lid, and looked inside.

Adan went to sit on one of the cots. Bo joined him while Jenra and Garun took seats at the table. The door opened after a few moments, and two of Pavola's crew helped Fan and Wellan carry Uso inside on a metal-framed canvas stretcher. They set the stretcher down on one of the other cots before

246

Pavola's crew departed. Wellan sat next to Uso on the cot. Fan pulled one of the empty chairs next to them and sat down.

"How is he?" Jenra asked.

"The damage wasn't as bad as it looked," Fan answered, the fatigue evident in their voice, "especially with all the blood. But he won't be tossing around any First Troopers any time soon."

"What about Simi?" Garun asked.

Wellan sighed. "They're going to leave Simi's body in the truck when they sink it."

"Founder's help us," Garun said, shaking his head. "But I suppose that's the best thing to do. Does anyone know his family?"

Wellan glanced down at Uso. "I'm pretty sure he does."

"Maybe we can figure out a way to get word to them somehow," Jenra suggested.

"If you give me their names, I can have someone do that," Rune offered as he came to join the group. He pulled the last chair out to the middle of the room and sat. "But right now, we need to decide what you're all going to do. I've got equipment and supplies for myself, Adan, and Bo. Pavola says he can get more if we need to, but I still can't take all of you with me."

"Take us where?" Fan asked.

"Outside the wall," Rune replied. "Somewhere I can keep Adan safe while we help him figure out why he can do what he does. But I can't take everyone with me. Maybe a couple more of you, but that's it."

Wellan hooked his thumb toward Uso. "He won't be able to walk for a while, let alone cross the Osbaks. And I don't think I really want to."

Rune nodded. "We've got safe houses around the Valley. I can get you access to one of them while my contacts arrange for new ID cards for you."

"Your contacts in the Motari?" Fan asked.

Rune nodded again. "Yes."

"What about work? Do we have to start working with you, too?"

"With the Motari?" Rune shook his head. "No, at least not right away. You're too much of a target. But, once things settle down a bit, then maybe."

Fan considered that for a few moments. "Alright. I'd rather stay with Wellan and Uso, anyway."

"I'm going," Garun announced.

Adan looked at him in surprise. "You are?"

Garun nodded. "The way I see it, this is mostly my fault. If I hadn't done what I did, you would never have been in the Museum that day."

"How did you–"

"Once we were in the truck," Bo shared, "I told everyone what happened."

"Okay," Adan said, sounding unsure, "but you don't owe me any–"

"But I do," Garun interrupted. "So I'm going."

"Me, too," Jenra said.

Rune looked at her and frowned. "Jenra–"

"Don't," Jenra warned him. "Whatever plans we may have had about embedding me in the Defense Force are over. And I've got no place else to go now. So, I'm coming. "

Rune's frown grew even deeper, then he nodded. "You're right, of course. Okay, five of us I can manage. I'll get Pavola to arrange the rest of the supplies. In the meantime, I suggest you all get comfortable. This room is your new home, at least for the next few days."

Official Log of Medical Officer Dr. Marketta Palo

Neskan Colony, 33 December, Year 3 (Neskan Calendar)

We aren't making enough babies. I say it to every patient who comes to see me. I post it to the InfoNet's social feed every chance I get. I just held my third community learning session this year to explain that to everyone.

I don't know how to say it any more plainly. I could go on about heterozygosity and healthy growth rate models. But the short version is that everyone who's able to get pregnant should be getting pregnant. The loss of an entire Colony Fleet puts us in a significant bind, mainly because we now have a tenth of the genetic material we planned on. And add to that the loss of our Obstetricians, Pediatric Specialists, and Geneticists? I can't stress it enough. If we aren't making more babies, all the work we're doing to produce the resources for a viable colony will be a wasted effort.

On a side note, I've run the required gene assays on our newborn Neskans. The germline edits bolstering our immune systems are successfully being passed on to our offspring so far. But Colony's gene-lock sequence that identifies us as colonists to our equipment is not. It's most likely a sequencing error. Once things start to settle down a bit, I'll try to investigate it more thoroughly and develop a solution. It's not like our toddlers need to access the Bio-printer.

Chapter 14

The squad waited in that room for four days. They were mainly allowed out to use the shower and toilets. They were also let out in pairs to walk around on the empty barge once it returned. Uso woke up the following morning, and Wellan explained what had happened. Uso cried when he found out about Simi. He agreed that staying behind in a Motari safe house was the best thing for him to do.

Pavola sent up meals, usually sandwiches or stew and bread, with tea in the mornings and beer in the evenings. He also checked on them periodically and updated them on the situation outside the warehouse.

The news, what little there was of it, was grim. The rockslide that blocked the entrance to the Pinch was officially called a freak accident. Engineering crews set up the next day to start clearing out the blockage, which would take days at the very least. And new checkpoints had been set up all over the city. According to Rune, the Pinchers were desperate to find Adan. His contacts were reporting all sorts of Pincher activity, and the Motari operatives in the city were all lying low. Many of Rune's contacts had also gone dark.

The Defense Force, for their part, had begun conducting daily practice drills around Bolvar House and other sensitive areas of the Valley. The drills were a sham, of course. The Defense Force was just afraid of what Adan and his Old Tech weaponry might do if he attacked them. The idea sounded crazy to Adan. Why would he attack anywhere? The only people he'd hurt so far were the ones who tried to stop him from leaving the DFTC. Adan wasn't about to become a one-man army and take on the whole Bolvaran Union single-handedly.

Adan mostly divided his time between hanging out with the remaining members of Squad Ten and quietly talking with Besi to learn more about the Old Tech. That was when Adan learned how to interact with Besi without giving himself away.

"You can communicate with me without speaking aloud," Besi informed him. "It's similar to the way you unconsciously sound out words while you are reading them. This is called subvocalizing. Try it now by saying 'I understand' as if you are reading it to yourself."

Adan thought about how he would do that, but thinking about it got in the way of doing it. Instead, he just relaxed and did what Besi suggested, saying the words silently to himself like he was reading them off a page. "I understand," he subvocalized.

"That was excellent," Besi shared, making Adan feel surprisingly proud.

Bo and Jenra spent more time together now that they

weren't stuck with DFTC schedules and rules. That left Adan mainly hanging out with Garun. At least his former Squad Leader was serious about repairing their friendship. And without the pressure of being Provies, Garun was actually nice to be around.

"But you still knew your parents, right?"

Garun and Adan sat on the barge's edge, dangling their feet over the side. Since they'd offloaded the truck, it sat high enough in the river that they wouldn't get wet.

"I did," Adan answered. "I was almost six when they disappeared."

Garun frowned. "That's rough. I'm sorry."

"It's fine. That was ten years ago. They were good people, as far as I remember. But the fact that Commander Sala knew them makes me wonder."

Garun shook his head. "Don't. Sala is a total rock eel. She probably made that up just to scare you."

Adan wanted to hope that was true, but he wasn't so sure. "Maybe."

The two of them sat in friendly silence for a while, enjoying the cool river breeze.

"I wonder what my parents think of me after what we did," Garun suddenly announced. Then he sighed. "I doubt they really care much."

Adan looked at Garun with furrowed brows. "I thought they wanted you to be a Gray Coat?"

"No, they expected me to be a Gray Coat. But that's only because I wasn't good enough to do anything else. And having an eventual Commander in the family would be advantageous, in their minds."

Adan chuckled. "Oh, so that was a foregone conclusion?"

Garun laughed. "Doubt me if you want, but family connections are no joke in the Valley. As long as I managed to stay alive for long enough, then, yeah, it would happen."

"Do you regret leaving?"

Garun shook his head. "No. I regret how I treated you at the beginning, but I never actually wanted to join up. Who really does? I was serving my five, just like everyone else."

Garun looked away upriver, staring out at the bubbling white caps. He had an undeniably handsome profile. Garun's strong nose and chin were both weaknesses for Adan. And, except for that incident on the first day, he'd been nothing but gracious and kind. But Garun hadn't given Adan any indication on where his interests lie. And Adan wasn't about to kindle a romance with his former bully, handsome or not.

Garun smiled. "I can feel you looking at me, Adan."

Adan laughed. "Just because you think the world revolves around you–"

"It's alright," Garun said, cutting him off. "I don't mind." Okay, that might have been an indication. "But maybe we should get back in and let some of the others have their turn? If you can tear yourself away from the view."

Adan scoffed. "Tear myself away?"

Garun smiled and got up. "I'm gonna walk away now. You know, in case you want to watch."

Then he did walk away, but Adan didn't turn around. He wasn't going to be won over by a little sarcastic flirting. Even if he wanted to be.

On the third day, Rune shared what he'd learned about Adan and Bo's arrest. The Motari had discovered the name of the person who'd snitched on them to the Pinchers. "It was someone called Calin Dambolen."

Bo was understandably upset. "Aunt Calin? No, that's not possible. She's like family to me. My only family."

"She was recently seen in the company of a Pincher Commander. And she was very much not under arrest at the time."

Bo frantically shook his head. "But I don't get it? She's gone out of her way to protect me my whole life. Why would she do something like that now?"

Rune shrugged. "Who knows? Could she have been in some kind of trouble, maybe?"

Bo shook his head and looked away. Adan could see that his friend was close to tears, so he put an arm around him.

"But it could be a misunderstanding," Adan suggested. Then he made deliberate eye contact with Rune. "Right? Calin supplied us with forged papers. Maybe the Pinchers were just watching her?"

Rune didn't respond right away, so Adan kept staring at him.

"That's possible," Rune finally admitted. "But the Union is very good at inspiring loyalty. Or, if that doesn't work, coercing it. I mean, I grew up with Mannix."

"They didn't seem very happy to see you," Adan commented.

Rune nodded. "The feeling was mutual. But, even if it wasn't Dambolen that set you up, the Pinchers were definitely on to you. What I don't get is why they didn't follow you all the way here."

"Is it possible that Pavola was in on it?"

Rune shook his head. "No, I've known Soto too long and worked with him too many times to think that. No, not even with you here, Adan. I bet the Pinchers would be extremely grateful if someone were to turn you in."

"And he probably would've done that already if he was going to," Adan agreed.

"The Pinchers were sloppy," Bo suddenly snapped, "and gave themselves away too early. So, we ran and made them chase us."

"Oh, you mean the incident with the bashki barrel? Balda's ass! You two were the talk of the underground for days. I've even heard people joking about tossing a barrel at you. I bet the Pinchers hate it."

Bo reluctantly smiled and patted Adan on the arm. "You've got this one to thank for that move."

Adan shrugged. "If I have to be famous, I'd rather it was for that."

"I doubt you'll be famous for anything else," Rune admitted. "I haven't heard a single word about you and Old Tech out on the street. Only that you managed to escape from the DFTC during your service training."

Adan wasn't surprised. With all the effort Sala put into keeping her research facility a secret, Adan doubted that she'd spread the word about what Adan could do. He was glad about that, in a way. Even having his former squadmates know about it made him uncomfortable. It was silly to feel that way. Adan knew he was being childish. But the fewer people that knew about it, the easier it was for him to pretend he was still the same person as before.

That night, a pair of unknown citizens showed up with a delivery van and parked it down on the barge. They were some of Rune's contacts and presumably part of the Motari. They also ran a safe house that would take in Fan, Uso, and Wellan. The three of them shared a tearful goodbye with the rest of Squad Ten before climbing inside the van. While no one came right out and said it, everyone knew it was probably the last time they'd ever see each other.

But it was one more trying day for Adan after a long series of them. Once he was lying on his cot, Adan felt a sudden flood of emotions threatening to drown him. He'd been stuffing down his feelings and putting off dealing with everything for too long, and Adan could no longer hold it back. After the tears started, Adan tried to keep quiet since everyone else was sleeping. But he whimpered before he could stop himself. When Adan heard the sound of someone shifting on their squeaky cot, he held his breath. Then he heard them get up and quietly walk over to him. It was Bo, who'd taken to sharing a cot with Jenra. His best friend climbed over him and lay down behind him. And when Bo wrapped an arm around Adan and pulled him close, the floodgates finally opened. Adan quietly sobbed while Bo held him in his arms.

Bo was still there when Adan woke up the following day, although he'd rolled over onto his back sometime during the night. It had been a long time since the pair of them had shared a bed. They used to do it all the time when they were younger, especially on those days when it felt like it was just them against the world. It had felt like that for Adan a lot during recent days. It must have for Bo, too. With everything that had happened, Adan was grateful that his friendship with Bo hadn't really changed.

Adan carefully pulled the blanket off himself, making sure the Bo was still covered, then got up. Still in his trousers from the day before, Adan stumbled to the toilet, tired and half awake. When he was finished, Adan washed his face and hands before returning to the room to get a shirt. The silvery light peeking through the curtains over the window was barely enough to see by. It must've been early. Adan slipped on a shirt and sweater, gifts from Rune courtesy of his arrangement with Pavola, then walked down the hallway to the small kitchen at the other end. Someone had already boiled water and made tea. Adan grabbed a mug and poured some for himself. Then he made his way down to the bottom level barge and found Rune sitting on a box near the open edge, drinking tea and looking at the river. Rune turned around when Adan approached him. Then he smiled.

"You're up early today." Rune slid over to the side to make room for Adan to sit.

Adan nodded then took a seat next to the Motari rebel. "I think all this sitting around and waiting is finally getting to me."

Rune nodded. "I'm kind of surprised it's taken this long. I've been anxious to get going myself." He took a sip of his tea, let it cool in his mouth for a moment, then swallowed it. "That was you I heard last night, yeah?"

Adan looked down into his tea. "Sorry. I didn't realize I was being so loud."

"Don't be sorry. You've been through a lot. I get it. It wasn't that long ago when I was your age. And I wasn't much older than you are when I joined the Motari."

"Really?"

Rune nodded again. "I imagine that a lot of what motivated you and Bo to try your escape plan was similar to what pushed me to join them. My five was coming up, too, and I couldn't see myself blindly marching to the beat of the Union's drum."

259

Adan half-heartedly smiled. "If only we'd known someone in the underground."

Rune shook his head. "But, don't you see? This is the best thing that could've happened for you. And it might never have happened if you joined the Motari. We get a lot of young, frustrated citizens looking to change the Union somehow. And we lose a lot of them, too. But, you're in a position to actually change things."

That idea had been circling the edge of Adan's thoughts for a few days. But it was so far outside of what he'd ever seen himself doing, he didn't know how to accept it yet. "What if I don't want to change things? The Union works fine for plenty of citizens. Just not for me."

"Then don't. I'm not telling you what to do, Adan. I'm just showing you the possibilities. It's up to you to figure out what to do with them."

Adan chuckled darkly. "That's a first."

Rune laughed. "I think you'd be surprised at how many people feel the same way."

Adan thought about the people he knew who'd somehow managed to make things work in the Union. Mother Agra found her place making the best Marsh Pig Stew in the Lowers. Bo's friend Min enjoyed their job driving corpses around. Jurda was probably getting ready for his next shift at the Laundry. But, had any of them been given a choice? And, if they had one, what would they choose?

"Too much to think about?" Rune asked after his last sip of tea.

Adan looked down again, embarrassed. "Sorry. Still early for me, I guess."

Rune reached over and gave Adan's shoulder a squeeze.

"It's fine. And it's good that you're up early. You can help me start getting ready. Today's finally the day."

Adan immediately perked up. "Are you serious?"

Rune nodded. "I am. I just got word from my contacts." Then he slapped the box they were sitting on. "And Soto came through with the extra supplies and gear we need."

"Thank the Founders. What do you need me to do?"

"Finish your tea. Then head upstairs and wake everyone up while I get this box open."

Adan nodded and stood up. "You got it." The dreariness of the early morning was suddenly gone. He gulped down the rest of his tea then rushed back up to his room. Bo and Jenra were awake and sitting on their cot, quietly whispering. Garun was still asleep, so Adan walked over to his cot, leaned over, and gently shook his shoulder.

Garun groaned and rolled over to see who was disturbing him. "Adan? What's happening?"

"It's time to get up, Garun. I just talked to Rune. Today's the day."

"For real?" Bo asked.

Adan nodded. "He got word from the Motari. And Pavola came through with the extra supplies."

Bo and Jenra both smiled. But Garun groaned again. "If we're about to sneak past the wall and spend a week in the mountains, then I'm sleeping for another hour. Who knows when we'll even get to sleep inside again?"

Adan laughed. Then he reached down and shook his shoulder again. "Sorry, Garun. Unless you plan on staying behind, it's now or never."

He sighed. "Fine." Then he kicked the covers down so he could sit up, giving Adan an excellent view of his chest and stomach.

Adan quickly turned away. As much as he wanted it, he didn't need that kind of distraction. Instead, Adan walked over to his small pile of things on the floor. He pulled his sweater off and set it on the cot. Then he grabbed the Old Tech armor pieces and strapped them on. If Rune was going to share their plan of action, he wanted Besi to know about it, too. Once he had everything fastened, he put his sweater back on over it.

"What does it feel like to have that on?"

Adan glanced back to see Bo standing behind him. "It feels like a harness and belt."

Bo rolled his eyes. "You know what I mean, you ass."

Adan laughed. The whole time they'd been at Pavola's, Bo had asked Adan about the Old Tech stuff less than a handful of times. "It's like wearing a thick, heavy uniform, I guess. Except it's not actually heavy at all. It even helps me move, so I can go a lot faster when I'm wearing it. And it talks to me."

"For real?"

Adan nodded again. "It has a machine brain." He looked down at his chest where the disc sat under his sweater. "Although I don't have the slightest idea how it works."

"Can I hear it?"

Adan didn't actually know the answer to that. "Maybe? Let's see. Besi, are you there?"

"I am, Adan Testa."

"Can you make it so Bo can hear me?"

"Are you authorizing me to communicate with this individual?"

"I am."

"Hello, Citizen Bo Shen. I am a Battlefield Enhanced System Intelligence. You may refer to me as Besi."

Bo's jaw dropped, then he instinctively looked over his shoulder. "It's like someone is standing right next to me speaking. That's really eerie."

Adan smiled and nodded. "It takes some getting used to."

"How does it do that?"

"I use a directed sound field," Besi replied, "that compresses and directs the sound waves so they're only audible to you."

Bo looked at Adan like Besi was speaking a different language. Which, in a way, it was. Adan smiled again. "You get used to that, too."

"You might," Bo retorted, "but I doubt that I would. It's probably a good thing you're the one it responds to."

Jenra, who'd stepped out of the room, walked back in with two steaming mugs of tea. She handed one to Bo. "I just talked to Rune. He wants us to gather everything and bring it down to the warehouse. Then we can divide it up and get it all packed."

Bo took a sip of his tea then handed it back to Jenra. "Sounds good. But I've got to use the toilet first."

Jenra and Adan laughed as Bo rushed out of the room. Jenra offered the tea to Adan, but he shook his head. "I've had plenty already, thank you."

"Suit yourself." She walked over to her cot and sat down, placing the extra mug on the floor. "I noticed that you stole my bedmate last night."

Adan didn't know how to respond to that. Was she jealous? "It's not really–"

But Jenra laughed. "It's fine. I'm not trying to make anything out of it. I know you two are best friends."

Adan exhaled. "I was having a rough night, and he must've heard me. It's something Bo and I used to do back in the group home when one of us was feeling bad."

Jenra nodded then took a sip of her tea. "I think it's sweet. You two obviously care about each other a lot. I might be a little jealous."

Adan smiled. "We've already been over that. I'm not his type, remember?"

Jenra nodded. "I know. That's not what I meant. But you both have that connection. It's not a physical thing, but it's still love, right? I don't think I've ever had that with anyone."

Adan walked over and sat next to Jenra. "Bo's been sharing your bed. I've never seen him do that with anyone but me before. I think it's safe to say that he likes you."

"Sure, except it could just be proximity and convenience."

Adan grinned and shook his head. "I thought you were supposed to be older than me."

Jenra barked out a laugh. "Oh, so you're saying I'm just a lovesick schoolgirl?"

Adan laughed along with her. "No, I'm saying that I know Bo better than anyone. Trust me when I say you can trust him."

Jenra looked at Adan for a moment, then nodded. "Fine. I'll trust you. It's silly anyway. As if we're not about to get smuggled over the wall. We could all be in a Pincher prison cell by this time tomorrow."

Adan grimaced. "Well, trust me when I say you definitely don't want that."

Jenra laughed again. "From your lips to the Founder's ears. Speaking of trust, what's going on with you and Garun?"

"What do you mean?"

Jenra shook her head. "Don't get all coy on me now, Citizen Trustworthy. We've been sharing a tiny room for the last four days."

Adan sighed. "Fine. I don't really know what's going on. I can't decide if Garun is flirting with me or messing around. What do you think?"

Jenra shrugged. "I don't really know. I've only known him a couple weeks longer than you. And we never talked about the sorts of people he's interested in. But it looks to me like he's interested in you. And, if that's true, it kind of explains his initial reaction to you."

Adan furrowed his brows. "So you're saying he beat me up because he likes me?"

"First of all, he hardly beat you up. And no, he did that because he's an ass."

Adan nodded. "Okay, because I was about to question your judgment."

"But he would hardly be the first person to react badly when they realized they were attracted to a rival."

Adan frowned. "That's why I still can't figure out what he's up to."

"Good. I wanted to tell you not to rush into anything. But it sounds like you've got no plans to."

Adan shook his head. "No, not at all."

Jenra smiled. "But he is very handsome, isn't he?"

Adan groaned. "Don't remind me. That's the last thing I need to be thinking about right now. But, between Garun and your brother–"

"My brother?"

Adan grinned. "What? I thought you said he was gay?"

Jenra rolled her eyes. "He is. But he's also more than seven years older than you."

"Says the person who's sharing a bed with a younger man."

Jenra frowned. "A year younger. That's not the same."

Adan laughed. "I know, I know. And I'm not trying to start anything with Rune. I'm just saying he smells terrific."

Jenra sighed. "Why does everyone say that? Founders save me."

Adan chuckled. "Speaking of your brother, I'm anxious to hear what he has in store for us."

"You and me both, Adan. You and me, both."

Official Log of Captain Chander Sanyal

Neskan Colony, 14 April, Year 4 (Neskan Calendar)

We had a ten-minute warning before today's magnetic field fluctuation event. When Jun impressed on me the need for a team to study Neska's magnetic field, I almost turned him down. We're so short on experts in everything that it seemed like a waste of time and effort for something that hasn't hit us since landfall. Yesterday I was so glad I'd allowed it I nearly cried.

The localized fluctuations in the normal levels of electromagnetic radiation are unprecedented in all of Colony's history. We've started calling them Flux Storms. Jun's active EM shielding modifications thankfully helped prevent significant damage to the Colony's most sensitive equipment. But we finally lost the Bio-printer. The team had it out of the lander for some reason. I don't remember why. And we can't manufacture another one.

There's also been no word from Bowen Valley. We assume the Flux Storm must've affected their communications equipment, so I've sent Sander and his team to check on them.

Chapter 15

Adan was surprised to find another cargo truck parked on the barge. But this time, it wasn't a stolen Defense Force truck. Or, at least it wasn't a Defense Force truck. Adan couldn't say if it was stolen or not. But it was hopefully the truck that would carry them past the wall. Adan hoped that wouldn't mean getting shot at in the process.

"I don't understand," Jenra asked when she saw the truck. "We're going past the wall in this?"

Rune and Pavola both laughed. They'd been doing a lot of that as they explained the plan to the others. It got more irritating every time. By the look on Jenra's face, she was near her breaking point with it.

"By the Founders, no," Pavola replied. "Trucks such as this are never allowed outside the wall. Only Bureau and Defense Force trucks ever leave the city." He slapped the side of the truck bed. "No, my young Trooper, this is to get you across the city. New checkpoints have been established all around

Bolvar since you all made your dramatic exit from the Pinch. It's almost certain that our truck will be inspected at some point on our journey."

"Every Pincher and Clubber in the city is looking for you," Rune added, then looked at Adan. "Especially you. They've printed and distributed your picture everywhere. My contacts say that the Clubbers are even taking in citizens who resemble you in case it might be you in disguise. So we're going to hide you."

Adan's anger immediately flared. Now people were suffering just because they looked like him? The Union was obviously desperate. Sala was desperate. But a small voice in his head reminded Adan that he could end all of that by turning himself in. If it didn't mean handing the Defense Force his ability to use Old Tech, Adan might have considered it.

All the Union's attention to finding the four of them meant they couldn't travel out in the open. Thus, the truck. It looked like an ordinary vehicle meant for hauling goods around the Valley. But Pavola's crew had modified it by adding hidden storage sections underneath the bed, each large enough to hold a single person and their gear. Well, large enough for most people. Uso would never have fit. It was a good thing he'd chosen to remain behind.

"On our journey to where?" Adan asked.

Pavola shook his head. "I'm sorry, but that I can't tell you. It's best if you don't learn anything more about my operation than you already know. In the unlikely event that you're recaptured, of course."

"Best for who?" Garun asked.

Pavola spread his arms and smiled.

"But it's okay for us to know about this place?" Bo challenged him.

"You already knew about this place," Pavola reminded Bo. "It would be inconvenient to abandon this facility, but I would if necessary."

Jenra huffed. She was definitely getting tired of Pavola and her brother's attitude. "And it's at our destination that you'll take us over the wall?"

Pavola nodded. "It's where I'll take you outside the city, yes."

It was a subtle difference in wording, but Adan noticed it. They weren't going over the wall. Adan guessed that meant they were going under it. Pavola was a Thatcher, after all. And the profession was named for the Thatch Rat, which had abandoned the old city's thatched roofs for its underground sewers long ago.

"So, when do we leave?" Garun asked the remaining important question. His expression said he was tired of the question-and-answer session.

"An hour after sundown," Rune responded.

That made sense. Darkness would be helpful. While it allowed the black-clad Clubbers and Pinchers to sneak around the city, it would do the same for the squadmates and Pavola's crew.

Pavola looked down at the timepiece on his wrist. The move immediately reminded Adan of Chief Osaben, and he thought back to their standoff in the secret facility. It made Adan upset all over again—angry at the Chief for stubbornly refusing to give way and sad that Adan had only been left with the choice to shoot him. Adan grunted and tried to shake the memory off, earning him concerned looks from

270

Bo, Jenra, and Garun.

"That gives us a few more hours to prepare," Pavola said when he looked up. "So eat, use the toilet, or do whatever you need to. Once you're locked into your hiding spaces, you won't be getting back out again until we let you out." Then he pulled Rune aside, and the pair quietly chatted while they walked back toward the building's truck entrance.

Adan turned around and looked out at the broad expanse of water. The Daralsha was at least a kilometer wide at that point, the eastern bank rising sharply from the water's edge for dozens of meters before the buildings started. It was a surprisingly private location, given that it was next to everything and out in the open.

Bo walked up and stood next to him. "Are you feeling alright? I saw a look there towards the end."

Adan nodded. "Yeah. Just something that made me think about the Chief."

Bo frowned and nodded. "That ass. I mean, I know he was only doing his job, but–"

"It's fine," Adan interrupted. "I've already relived that moment enough for the day."

Bo looked away. "Sorry."

"Don't be." Adan reached out and put his hand on Bo's arm. "And thanks for what you did last night, by the way. I didn't realize how much I'd been holding everything back. I really needed that."

Bo smiled and nodded. "Me, too. Things have changed so much for us. And so quickly. I didn't know how much I missed the way things used to be. Or how much I missed my best friend."

"There's always Jenra."

FOUNDER'S MERCY

Bo looked back at her at Adan's mention of her name. She was talking with Garun about something. "I really like her, Adan. And I think she likes me. But this situation isn't exactly ideal for a newly budding romance, right? So she thinks we should take things slow." Bo turned back to face Adan. "But you're my best friend. You may as well be my brother, you know? No matter what, it'll be you and me to the end."

Adan smiled. "You and me to the end. And may that be a long way off."

Bo laughed. "A long, long way off."

"What's a long way off?" Jenra asked as she approached the pair.

"Just how far we're imagining the walk will be after we're outside the wall," Bo replied.

Jenra groaned. "Oh, don't start that now. I just got used to not going anywhere."

Bo chuckled. "That doesn't sound much like the Squad Leader I remember."

"I was never your Squad Leader, Bo Shen. But I was hoping I could steal you away for a bit if that's alright?"

Adan thought about their conversation from that morning. He wanted Jenra to know that he wasn't jealous of her and that the two of them weren't competing for Bo's attention. Adan nodded. "He's yours for the taking, Squad Leader Tabata."

She rolled her eyes. "Don't you start with that, Testa."

Bo put his hand on Adan's shoulder and lightly squeezed. "Alright, we'll be back, I guess." Then he walked off with Jenra, leaving Adan alone.

"And, once again, it's just us." Okay, not totally alone. Garun walked up and took Bo's place on the edge of the barge. "There's something I want to show you." He pointed out over the water. "See that tower there? The tall one with the big wireless transmitter on the roof?"

Adan looked in the direction Garun was pointing. The tower he mentioned belonged to one of the Union's Bureaus, although Adan couldn't remember which one. "Yeah, I see it."

Garun moved his hand to the right. "Follow the line from the top of that building all the way up to Gallur, and you'll see a big domed building."

Adan knew that building well enough. Everyone did. It was where the Union Committee Chairperson lived. "Sure, I know that one."

Garun nodded. "Okay, then continue past the dome, and you'll see a boxy building with big windows in a line across the top."

Adan squinted as he looked for the building Garun described. Then he spotted it. It was smaller than the domed building, although it was too far away for Adan to know how big it really was. But it was higher up than the Chairperson's Residence, so it must've had a lovely view of the Valley. "What am I looking at?"

"Home. My family's home."

Adan lifted his eyebrows in surprise. "Are you serious? How many people are in your family?"

Garun chuckled. "You don't get up to the Heights much, eh? It's just my parents, mother's parents, siblings, and me. Well, not me, anymore, I guess."

Even at that distance, Adan could tell that Garun's house was at least half again as big as Adan's group home. But it was meant for less than half as many people. Adan thought about all those times he'd looked up Daigur toward Gallur Heights, imagining how nice it was. But he never imagined it was like that. "Wow. You mean it was just your family living in a place that big?"

Garun shrugged. "And some of the people that worked there, too. Cooks, cleaners, maintenance workers."

Adan looked at Garun in confusion. All of those people just to make Garun's life easier, and he walked away from it? "You come from all that, and you're here with us? Why give that all up?"

Garun sighed and looked down at his boots. "I've never known what life was like for someone like you. The only people I was ever around were just like me. Spoiled. Privileged. And I hated it the whole time."

Adan frowned. "Come on, Garun. You hated it?"

"I know. Why would I hate never wanting anything I couldn't have?" Then Garun frowned as if saying the words left a bad taste in his mouth. "But I did. Except hating it all didn't actually change anything. And I never tried to change it. I never refused any of it. I was silently resentful of my privilege, but I still took everything they handed to me." He looked at Adan, then shrugged and looked back down. "And I know what that made me."

Adan knew, too. "That made you worse than the others."

Garun nodded. "Exactly. I was a hypocrite. After I was an ass to you and hurt you, something inside me finally broke. That piece of myself that was holding me back, I guess. And I knew it was time for me to stop being an ass and start changing the things I hate."

"And that's why you came with us?"

Garun laughed. "Balda's ass, Adan! I came with you because

I didn't want to get tied up like Mannix and Sabina. But that's why I decided to stay. And it's why I'm still here."

"Because you can change something?"

Garun nodded. "Yes." Then he shook his head. "No. I don't know." He finally settled on a shrug. "I mean, I guess I want to help you because I don't think I'll ever be able to change anything. But, maybe you could."

Was Garun being honest? If not, he was a convincing liar. "Do you really think so?"

Garun nodded. "I do. Don't ask me why, because I don't know. But I definitely do."

Adan cracked a modest smile. "Alright. In that case, I'm glad you're here."

Garun flashed a smile that lit up his whole, handsome face. "Really? If you really mean that, then thank you."

While Garun's self-doubt was surprising, Adan could at least relate to that. All he'd wanted was a way to avoid serving his five with the Gray Coats. Instead, he found himself in the middle of a centuries-old mystery and a player in a deadly game with rules he was only beginning to understand. Adan didn't know how to play chess, but he knew enough about it to know that he was a pawn in the Union's game. Even the source of his greatest strength was a piece of Old Tech that moved him around like a puppet.

Adan reached out and gave Garun's shoulder a gentle squeeze. "I do mean it."

Then Rune appeared, walking down from the driveway onto the barge. "I hope I'm not interrupting anything, but I'd like a few minutes alone with Adan. If that's alright."

Garun smiled again, then ducked out from under Adan's grip. "It's fine. I should probably spend some quality time with that toilet before you lock me in a box." He turned, and Adan watched him walk away. Like him or not, it was a nice view.

Rune waited until Garun was out of earshot before speaking. "Everything good between you two? Jenra mentioned there was an incident back at the DFTC."

Adan nodded. "It's fine. Honestly, that seems like it was so long ago now."

Rune smiled. "That's what living a life of adventure will do to you. Your time gets marked by these grand, exciting events so much that you start to lose the small ones. But the small moments end up being the ones you want to hang onto the most."

Adan thought he understood Rune's point, even if it sounded a little cliché. "So you're a revolutionary and a philosopher?"

Rune laughed. "All the best revolutionaries are, my friend."

"Is that what you wanted to talk about? Philosophy?"

Rune shook his head, then his expression turned dark. "No." He walked over to stand at the very edge of the barge. Adan got a distinct impression that Rune was about to make a grand statement, just like Garun had. And Bo, come to think of it. Was everyone worried that they might not survive the night and wanted to leave behind a piece of their wisdom, just in case? "I wanted to discuss what will happen if things go wrong tonight."

That didn't sound good. Or much like a grand statement. "What do you mean? You don't expect anything to go wrong, do you?"

Rune shook his head and turned to face Adan. The lighthearted adventurer that Adan had developed a crush on

276

was gone. In his place was a tired and battle-weary Motari operative that kind of scared Adan a little. "Of course not. We've gone out of our way to ensure that things don't. But, based on my experience with you, I need to be sure that you don't throw any last-minute spanners into the works. Understand?"

He was talking about the bomb back at the secret research facility and Adan's insistence that they rescue Bo and Jenra. Both of which led to everything else that happened that night. "I understand."

"Okay. Because if things do go wrong, there won't be any detours to rescue your friends. You're the only thing that matters, which means you matter more than they do."

Adan immediately wanted to protest, but Rune's expression told him it wouldn't make any difference. He tried anyway. "Even more than your sister?"

Rune nodded. "Yes. More than Jenra. More than me, even. I need you to understand that because I'm not sure you do yet. What you're capable of doing, Adan? It's going to change everything. It's already started to change things here. And I want to be sure that it doesn't change them for the worse. If the wrong group gets their hands on you, there's no telling what they'll do with you and your gift. But it won't be good for all the citizens out there just trying to live their lives. That much I know." He stopped to let his words sink in for a few moments.

What Rune said about Adan not understanding wasn't true. Adan had spent a lot of the quieter moments in that warehouse thinking about the implications of him and Old Tech. Even the few times he'd used it had ended in a lot of fire and destruction. Adan didn't think that any innocent people had gotten hurt. Except that the soldiers he'd shot were kind of innocent. They were just doing their jobs, and it wasn't like they chose those jobs. The Union did. After all, the Union provides, and you do what the Union commands in return.

In the end, all that thinking led Adan to the same conclusion Rune had. If the Union captured him again, they wouldn't have those same concerns about innocent lives. The good of the Union was the only thing that mattered to them. Even if a few citizens got lost in the process.

"I know, Rune," Adan quietly agreed. "Believe me. I've had plenty of time to think these last few days. What do you suppose I've been thinking about?"

Rune examined Adan's face for a moment. Then he nodded, and the dark expression went away. Suddenly Rune was the lighthearted adventurer again. "Good. I just needed to be sure. It's nearing the time to get ready, so do what you have to before we go."

Adan nodded before Rune walked away, leaving him finally alone on the barge. He couldn't think of anything else he needed to do to get ready. He'd already packed up his gear in the backpack Pavola had given him. He'd taken a shower earlier in the afternoon. And he was already dressed in the undershirt, thick sweater, heavy trousers, and sturdy boots that made up half his new wardrobe. Adan wasn't really hungry, either. He thought about making some tea but decided against it since he didn't know how long it would be before he could visit a toilet once he was in the truck. There wasn't much else to do but wander around and wait.

Eventually, everyone was gathered back on the barge. Once Rune had confirmed that they had everything they needed, it was time to get locked into the secret hiding places in the truck.

Garun volunteered to go first. "Thanks, I could really use a nap," he said with a wink as they replaced the wooden plank over his hiding place. Bo went next, followed by Jenra. Then it was finally Adan's turn.

"You're wearing your harness and everything?" Rune quietly asked him as he helped Adan into the tight space. It wasn't even tall enough to lay his head on his pack. That got stuffed down between his feet.

Rune meant the Old Tech armor and weapons, of course. Adan had been wearing them under his sweater all day. "I am," he answered.

"Good. Remember, this is all about you." Then he handed Adan a small, folded piece of paper. "Keep this with you. If everything goes sideways, get yourself out of the city any way you can. Then have your armor direct you to the coordinates on the paper. They're old, First Explorer style, so it should understand them well enough. Wait there until someone from the Motari meets you, and they'll lead you to our settlement."

Adan couldn't even begin thinking about doing all that himself. But he nodded anyway. "Alright."

One of Pavola's workers lowered the plank on top of him and began to nail it down. Then Adan heard the shuffling sounds of boxes and crates being set onto the truck bed. Pavola had arranged an actual shipment as cover for the truck's drive through the Valley. The driver would have proper papers authorizing the shipment that matched the crates' goods. Clubbers at a checkpoint may want to inspect the boxes, but none of them were the size and shape a person would easily fit inside of. Even if they offloaded the whole shipment, the Clubbers would have to inspect the bed for any signs of the people underneath it. Since the planks on the bed were all nailed down, it was unlikely that they'd notice anything.

Rune was the only one who would ride in the front with the driver. He was dressed as a worker and had a false ID card identifying him as someone assigned to Pavola's operation. It was a risk, but he insisted on being able to react if needed and Pavola was wary enough of the Motari to allow it.

"Besi," Adan subvocalized, "can you sense what's happening outside?"

"I can. If you were wearing the armor, I could show you."

Adan thought back to the night of the escape when it seemed like nighttime turned to mid-day. But the space was tight enough without the armor. "Have you been listening enough to understand our plan?"

"Yes, including the coordinates in your pocket."

"I hope it won't come to that."

"There's an old saying the Captain often repeated. Expect the best, but plan for the worst."

"The Captain?"

"Captain Chander Sanyal of the CSF Samuel Jennix."

Adan recognized the name from the book he'd gotten from the Library. Sanyal was the Captain of the First Explorers ship that originally landed on Neska. Although he didn't remember reading that particular phrase in the printed Captain's logs, it certainly sounded like something the Captain would've said. The fact that Besi referred to him made Adan suddenly wonder how old the Old Tech armor really was.

Then Adan heard the truck start up and felt it begin to move. The rumble of the engine and transmission was muffled by the wooden box surrounding him. But he still felt every bump the truck passed over. It was going to be a long ride.

"You really knew Captain Sanyal?"

"I have knowledge of the Captain."

That was a strange answer. But Adan was talking to a machine brain. "What was he like?"

"First Officer Marta Kanerva described the Captain as sharp-witted enough to outsmart a nav computer and stubborn enough to make the very ground move out of his way."

Adan knew that Kanerva was another of the First Explorers. "But what did you think about him?"

"I do not think. Not in the way you mean."

"I thought you were an enhanced system intelligence?"

"I am a smart program that uses natural-sounding language to communicate with people. I am designed to solve problems and assist with battlefield strategy. But I do not think in the sense of developing original concepts or ideas. And I do not form opinions."

Once again, a lot of that fell outside Adan's understanding. Besi had already tried explaining what a program was to him. It needed a computer to work, which he'd seen examples of in the Old Tech Museum. But the idea of how that worked eluded him. The whole time he'd been talking with Besi, he essentially pretended he was talking to someone on the wireless as if there was an actual person on the other end. But there wasn't.

Adan felt the truck slow down and then stop. They could've just been at an intersection, he figured. But then Adan thought he heard muffled voices outside the truck.

"What's happening out there, Besi?"

"Several armed individuals commanded this vehicle to stop. One of those individuals is querying the vehicle driver's authorization while another is inspecting the cargo."

Clubbers. Adan heard the sound of boots walking around above him, then a box getting shoved around. He held his breath, even though he could probably scream and not be heard. Probably. Hopefully, the Clubbers weren't desperate enough to start ripping the truck apart. If Adan somehow managed to escape the city, he wondered how long it would take before it came to that. Or before the Union gave up the search. Even if they did so, they'd never truly give it up. The Union had a long memory. And, if what Commander Sala said about knowing the truth about his parents was true, so did she.

Then the boots got closer until they were almost right above him. "Open this one," one of the Clubbers said before kicking the box that was on top of Adan's hiding place.

Adan heard another pair of boots thud as they hit the truck bed and walked over to stand near his hiding place. Then he heard the unmistakable squeal of a pry bar being shoved in the narrow gap between pieces of wood, followed by a crunch as the box's lid was torn free. Adan had no idea what was actually in the boxes, only that it was a legitimate cargo transfer.

"You need to exhale," Besi said, and Adan almost jumped. "You've been holding your breath for too long." He quietly exhaled, then forced himself to slowly breathe in rather than instinctively gulping down air.

"Is it correct?" asked the Clubber Adan had already heard.

"The transfer order said something about parts," replied a

second Clubber, "and these look like parts to me."

"Parts for what?"

"Don't ask me. I'm no damn engineer."

The first Clubber laughed. "That's true enough, but did you check the whole container for hiding spaces?"

The second Clubber loudly grunted, and Adan heard the hard clink of metal hitting metal. "Are you serious? Just one of these things must weigh five kilos. If someone is hiding under all of this, then they'd be crushed."

"Let me feel that." There was a quiet pause when the Clubber holding the part handed it over to the other. "Alright, yeah. That's heavy. Put it back and seal it up."

After a few minutes of shuffling and pounding, the noise above Adan stopped.

"The armed individual querying the driver has approved their authorization," Besi announced.

"You can hear them?"

"Yes. The sound of their voice travels through the vehicle frame as vibrations. I have an algorithm that filters out all the other noise."

Algorithm. Was that like algebra, meaning it was math? That seemed more likely than rhythm, making it music. But wouldn't it be interesting if that was how Besi actually worked?

"Besi, can you make music?"

"I cannot make it. But I have many music files in my memory. Would you like to hear one?"

"Yes, please."

Suddenly Adan was surrounded by noise. It was music, but it sounded like he was standing in the middle of the band. He didn't recognize the style, but he recognized most of the instruments. Especially the guitar. He'd never heard one sound like that before. "What is that?"

"The song is called Mi Amor es una flor, or My Love is a Flower, by Hector Escrivá, recorded in 2371. Escrivá specializes in a style known as Spanish Guitar. It was added to the Jennix memory storage by Nav Officer Clarinda Osoria."

"It's beautiful. How did you know I'd like it?"

"I did not. I chose it at random."

But Adan really did like it. When it was done, he asked Besi to play another one like that. And then another. He'd never understood the appeal of music before. But he'd never heard anything like that before, either. Bolvaran music was serious and heavy, intended to be marched around to and inspire loyalty. But Spanish Guitar music was soft and delicate. No, soft wasn't the right word. It was–he didn't know. Adan just didn't have the words to describe it. But he passed the time discovering sounds he never knew even existed until the truck finally came to a stop again.

"What's happening?" Adan asked.

"The driver and passenger are exiting the vehicle," Besi replied. "There are two other individuals here, both armed but not hostile."

"Alright, then keep the music coming."

By the time someone got around to prying up the plank that covered his hiding place, Adan was more calm and relaxed than he could remember feeling in a long time.

"Why are you smiling?" Rune asked as he reached out to help Adan get up.

"Just happy to finally be here. Speaking of which–" Adan looked around to see that they were inside another warehouse. "Where are we?"

"Settler's Rise." That meant they'd traveled all the way past the other side of the Flats. And that they were near the Western Gate. "Grab your gear and follow me. This will be a brief stop."

Adan leaned down to grab his pack, then followed Rune to the edge of the truck bed. The rest of the group, including the driver and the two other citizens Besi mentioned, were gathered off to the side. Adan jumped down to the floor then walked over to join everyone.

"Alright," Rune said, "that was the easy part."

"Easy?" Garun questioned him, chuckling. "Those Clubbers were all over that truck."

"They opened the box right on top of me," Adan mentioned.

"But they didn't suspect anything," Rune countered. "And all you had to do was lie there and be quiet. Which you did very well. But this next part will be a little more physically challenging." Rune turned to the two citizens waiting for them. Both were dressed in civilian versions of Gray Coats gear and tall rubber boots. "These two are our guides, so you must listen to them and follow their instructions." Their guides. Adan smiled as he realized that he was finally standing in front of the people who would lead him out of the city. Although he'd taken a roundabout way to get there, Adan was still exactly where he'd hoped to be all those weeks ago when he and Bo had attempted to pull off their bashki heist. "You can call them Rico and Delan," Rune added, "he and her."

The one Rune called Rico smiled. "Those are not our real names, and we don't want to know yours. The less we know about each other, the better, in case someone gets caught."

"And you should keep any chatter to an absolute minimum," Delan added. "Sound travels weird down there, so you don't know who might hear us."

"Down where?" Jenra asked.

"The sewers," Adan guessed.

"That's almost right," Rico said. "We're actually using old Flood Control tunnels, so they may be wet, but they won't be full of waste."

Delan nodded. "But that doesn't mean they won't smell. I hardly notice it anymore, but you probably will."

"So," Garun said, "not a sewer and not full of waste, but still wet and stinky?"

Delan nodded again. "Pretty much." Then she stood aside to reveal a small table with a stack of portable torches sitting on top. "They're also very dark, so you'll need these. There may come times when we tell you to go dark, which means it's lights out until you hear otherwise."

Adan furrowed his brows in confusion. "There may come times?"

"We don't use the same route every time," Rico replied. "And, given the state of things out in the Valley right now, it's possible the Clubbers may have decided to monitor the tunnels."

Rune shook his head. "My information says otherwise."

"So does ours," Delan agreed, "but that doesn't mean we won't be ready for it. It's our job."

"Of course," Rune agreed.

"Good enough, then," Rico said. "Everyone strap on your packs, button up your coats, and grab a torch. Then follow me."

Things quickly got busy as everyone checked their jackets

and put their backpacks on. Then Rune pulled Adan aside and leaned in close. "Remember that these two have no idea why we're doing this," he quietly shared. "So keep your gear under wraps, so to speak, unless you absolutely need it."

Adan nodded. "Got it. Have you ever done this before?"

"I have, but not along this route. Otherwise, we wouldn't need the guides."

Rune left Adan to check on the others. Then Adan noticed Bo standing nearby with a big grin on his face.

Adan couldn't help smiling back at him. "What's that look about?"

Bo rolled his eyes. "Don't you get it? This is what we wanted. If things had worked out with the bashki, we would've been doing this anyway."

Adan smacked his forehead in mock surprise. "Oh, you're right! I never thought of that."

Bo frowned. "Don't be an ass, Adan."

Adan laughed and threw his arm around Bo's shoulders. "Of course, I was thinking the same thing. We're finally going over the wall."

"Under the wall," Bo corrected with a smile.

Adan shrugged. "Over? Under? As long as it's out, I don't care."

"If you two are done," Rune called out from the table full of torches, "we should really get going."

The pair looked at each other and laughed again. Rune rolled his eyes and turned back to the others.

"Alright, you heard him," Bo said as he tried to stop laughing. "It's time to go."

Adan grinned. He could hardly wait to get down into the tunnels.

Official Log of First Officer Marta Kanerva

Neskan Colony, 14 April, Year 4 (Neskan Calendar)

Bowen Valley is gone. Sander told us that a lander had crashed in the town center, destroying most of the valley. It must've been in the air during the Flux Storm. Someone at Bowen Valley must've found it somehow but didn't report it to us. We still don't know exactly why. But, Chander is devastated. We haven't recovered all the bodies yet, but it looks like we lost everyone there. If so, that's four-dozen Neskans lost, including a pair of newborns. Plus, all the equipment and materials, just gone. I don't know how we're going to recover from this. The only good news is that the fields were unaffected. I'll have to talk to Clarinda about getting a team out there to bring those crops in if we can spare anyone.

Chapter 16

Given the Union's obsession with security and defense, the entrance to the flood tunnels was almost laughably insecure. It was simply a larger than average sewer cover sitting in the paved-over area behind the warehouse. The cover was fixed to the top of the tunnel access pipe with secure, locking bolts to prevent unauthorized entry. But Pavola's crew had procured one of the Union's special socket spanners to open them.

Once they unlocked and removed the cover, the crew descended one by one down the long ladder of metal rungs bolted to the sides of the access pipe. The access ladder was about thirty meters long, including the descent down to the tunnel floor. The tunnel itself was at least three meters in diameter. Adan had plenty of room to stand and couldn't even touch the top at its highest point. A shallow layer of standing water pooled on the tunnel floor, and the sounds of everyone walking through it echoed off the smooth, concrete walls. Adan suspected voices would easily carry in there, too.

After everyone climbed to the bottom, one of Pavola's crew members replaced and secured the cover. Then inky darkness descended on them. Even with the combined lights from everyone's portable torches, Adan could no longer see the tunnel ceiling.

Rico quietly put everyone into a marching order, with himself as the lead and Delan bringing up the rear. Adan was third in line, walking behind Rune. He suspected that Rune may have mentioned Adan's importance to their guides, earning him his place near the front. Or Rune may have simply insisted on it. Jenra walked behind Adan, followed by Bo, Garun, and Delan.

"I can map your path as you go," Besi suddenly announced. "Tap your thigh twice to confirm." Adan tapped his thigh. "Affirmative. I will commence mapping."

Adan had no idea how Besi would do that since the machine brain was buried under his sweater and jacket. Then again, he still had no idea how Besi could even speak to him without anyone else hearing it, either.

The group walked along in a line behind Rico until they reached a spot where the tunnel split in two. It was hard to tell how long it took to get there since there were no landmarks or any other way to judge how far they'd gone. Rico shined his torch down each fork for a few moments before choosing the left one and continuing onward until the group reached another fork. After investigating both forks with his torch, Rico chose the right one, and the group followed him. When Adan asked Besi how long they'd been at it, he found out it was only fifteen minutes. He'd thought they'd been at it for longer than that. But that still put them more than a kilometer away from the tunnel entrance at an average walking pace.

Adan wondered where they were relative to the warehouse. The city wall sat away from the edge of the actual city, separated by open ground at least five hundred meters wide. A similar space cleared of all rocks, trees, and other obstructions surrounded the wall on the outside. Evenly spaced guard posts on the wall were staffed by Gray Coats serving their five monitoring both sides for any trespassers. That's what made going over the wall next to impossible. You'd be totally exposed approaching the wall from either side since there was nowhere to hide. The tunnels presumably traveled under the wall at some point, emerging somewhere safe enough for Pavola and his crew to ferry citizens in and out of the city without going through the Gate. Adan was glad Besi was mapping his progress. If he had to go it alone, he'd at least be able to make it back to the starting point.

"I am getting unusual readings up ahead," Besi declared. "Something about the composition of the concrete lining the tunnel walls is interfering with my scans. But the ambient temperature differential is enough to suggest that people are waiting ahead of us."

Besi's announcement made Adan immediately tense up. He wished he was armored. Not only would he be protected from attack, but he'd also be able to see. At least he had his–

"Motion detected," Besi suddenly warned him. "You are in danger."

Adan's mind suddenly fell into panic as he swung his torch back and forth, trying to spot whatever it was that Besi warned him about.

"Behind you," Besi announced.

Adan swung around in time to see the butt of a rifle slam into the middle of his forehead. The world flashed around him as his head exploded in pain. He fell backward onto the wet tunnel floor, dizzy and unable to make his body follow his mind's commands.

The sounds of scuffles and quiet violence suddenly surrounded him. The group was being attacked. Was it the Clubbers, laying in wait in secret tunnel hiding places? Adan hadn't seen enough to be sure.

"Get up!" someone called out nearby, their voice echoing down the tunnel.

"No, not that one," someone else said. "The one behind him."

"Activating Battlefield Impairment Protocol," Besi said. "Verbal override only."

Adan lifted his hand to his head and moaned. "What?"

Then Adan's armor shot out from its hiding places in his harness and belt. After a few moments, the helmet closed around his head, surrounding him in silent darkness. His enhanced view returned, revealing a large, heavily muscled citizen looming over him. Their expression immediately changed from anger to shock.

"Balda's great brassy ass! What's all this?"

The attacker reached down to grab for Adan, but Besi was in control and ready. His armor moved, flexing like a hardened layer of muscle surrounding his body. Adan felt himself roll toward the reaching citizen, crashing into their legs and knocking them forward. Once Adan was on his stomach, the armor made him reach out and push himself up to a crouch. Green and red squares flared to life in his view, marking the members of his crew and the people attacking him. Adan tried to count the number of attackers, but Besi had him moving before he got past two.

Adan suddenly found himself on his feet, turning to the next closest attacker. A red square framed the face of a shorter, older version of the muscled citizen that tried to grab him. As Adan felt himself lunge toward them, he noticed they were standing next to Rico. Then Adan understood what had happened. Rico had led them into a trap.

"Both of them are enemies, Besi."

The green square surrounding Rico's face immediately changed to red as Adan felt his arm reach out. His hand stretched out flat and slammed into the short attacker's throat with a dull crunch. As his first target dropped, Adan felt himself twist into a spin and reach out with his other arm. His hand squeezed into a fist as he swung his arm around. Then Adan smashed the side of that fist into the bridge of Rico's nose. Rico's head flew back as he fell to the tunnel floor with a surprised grunt.

A red light flashed on the right edge of Adan's vision. Adan turned to see his original attacker getting back to their feet. Adan felt himself turn to the rising attacker, then launch toward them. The citizen fumbled at the rifle hanging from their shoulder, trying to point it at Adan, but Adan was too fast. He felt himself duck down and ram into the attacker's belly with his shoulder. The citizen fell back with a wheezy oof and slammed onto the tunnel floor. Adan put out a knee as he fell forward, planting it on the attacker's chest. The armor made him yank the rifle from their hands, hoist it up, then bash the butt into their forehead. Adan grinned. It felt good to get a little payback.

Then another rifle boomed. The shot slammed into Adan's

shoulder and knocked him backward. But he still kept hold of the attacker's rifle as he fell.

"Adan!" someone shouted behind him.

He looked over to see Rune. Adan held the rifle up, momentarily controlling his own body again. "Take this," he commanded, "and get everyone out of here. I'll handle the rest."

Rune grunted and grabbed the rifle from Adan's hand. Apparently, he already knew better than to ask what "handle the rest" met.

Adan felt himself jump up as soon as the rifle was free from his grip. Then he heard another shot and felt himself shift to the left just before being struck by another bullet. "Did you just move me in front of that shot?" Adan complained.

"Your armor can withstand it," Besi reminded him. "Your companion's body cannot."

Adan grudgingly accepted Besi's logic. As irritating as it was, the actual damage would be little more than a bruise. More red and green squares splashed across his field of view as Adan felt himself dodge back to the right then surge forward. One of the squares turned orange. It was Delan. Was she involved along with Rico? That was an unknown factor, but he or Besi would work it out when it came time.

The armor made Adan reach for his Old Tech handgun. Besi must've judged the action to be safe enough. Hopefully, all of his friends were on the ground, leaving them out of the way. The gun reassembled in his hand as Adan felt himself point it toward the attacker who held the rifle.

Blam! Adan's view flashed white as he pressed on the trigger. Then the rifle-toting attacker went down. Adan aimed toward the next red square and fired again. Then he shifted his aim and fired again. Finally, he was left with Delan and her orange square.

"Don't shoot her," Adan commanded, "unless she makes a move."

"Complying. Suspending Battlefield Impairment Protocol."

"Delan," Adan called out, "it's over. Get down on your knees and put your hands behind your head." She frantically waved her torch around until the beam landed on him. Then her eyes grew wide with shock and fear. Adan could only imagine what he must've looked like to her. "I'll give you one more chance, Delan. Down on your knees, hands behind your head."

Delan took a deep breath and nodded. Then she knelt on the wet tunnel floor, set the torch down, and put her hands behind her head. Adan glanced to his side to see Jenra on the ground next to him, looking up at him in wonder mixed with fear.

"Jenra," he said calmly, "please get that rifle and make sure Delan doesn't move."

She nodded, then carefully got back to her feet. "This is what they were after?"

Adan nodded. "I'll explain once we've got everything else sorted first."

Jenra still hesitated, then gave him a quick nod and pointed her torch toward the downed attacker, looking for the rifle. Once she'd picked it up and pointed it at Delan, Adan lowered his gun and exhaled some of his pent-up tension. His head hurt. Hopefully, he didn't have another concussion. And Adan had no idea what they were going to do next.

"Bo, Garun," Rune called out. "Help me get these three tied

up."

Adan was surprised at first to hear Rune speak so loudly. Then again, there didn't seem to be any reason to keep quiet anymore. If all that gunfire didn't draw the Clubbers or Gray Coats down on them, a little shouting certainly wouldn't.

Since Rune seemed to have his part under control, Adan walked over to where Delan knelt. He kept the weapon in his hand but let it hang down by his side. As he got closer, Delan looked up at him in fear.

"What are you?" she whispered.

"You mean they didn't tell you?" Adan responded. "Why am I not surprised?"

Delan shook her head. "I only learned about the plan just this morning. And Rico didn't give me any details."

Adan could see her struggling with where to look and wondered if people could even see his face behind the helmet. He realized he had no idea what he looked like in the armor. But that would have to wait. "Who arranged all this? Was it Pavola?"

Delan shook her head again. "No, Pavola would kill me if he knew about this." Then she sighed. "Will kill me, I mean."

"You haven't answered my first question."

"I don't know." Delan sighed and almost dropped her arms before catching herself. "Rico, I guess. He didn't tell me why, but I heard some of the others talking about a reward for your capture."

"What reward?"

"The Pinchers have been telling their informants that they'll wipe anyone's record who helps them capture you."

That figured. What else could they offer? But had the attack really just been an attempt to earn some goodwill from the Pinchers? Everyone knew you couldn't count on them to keep their word when they promised you anything.

Adan heard Rune approaching him from behind. "Bo and Garun are securing the others," Rune said. Then he stopped next to Adan and shined his torch down on Delan. "Did she talk?"

"Yes," Adan replied. "She claims that Rico set this up on his own. I guess the Pinchers are offering a reward for my capture."

Rune nodded. "That figures. If Pavola wanted to turn you in, he would've just done it without going to all this trouble." Rune inhaled sharply, then looked at Delan while he let his breath out with a low, throaty growl. "How much farther is the exit from here?"

Delan squinted as she looked into the light from Rune's torch. "About fifteen minutes farther ahead. There's a cistern at the end of the tunnel with a hatch to the surface."

"And are there any more ambushes ahead of us?"

"No, I don't think so."

Rune kept his light pointed at Delan for a few moments more. "Alright," he finally said. "Here's what's going to happen. You'll lead us to that exit. If we get there and get out of this tunnel without any more trouble from you, we'll let you go. Do you understand?"

Delan nodded. "I understand." She looked out toward where Bo and Garun were securing the others. "What about them?"

"They'll stay here. You can come back for them once we let you go." Rune glanced toward the bodies lying nearby. "You can deal with those, too, I suppose." Then he turned his attention to Jenra. "Are you alright?"

She nodded. "A little shaken and probably bruised, but fine otherwise."

Rune sighed with relief. "That's good. I'll take Delan up front with me. You and Adan take the rear. Adan, you may as well stay in your gear. That's the only way we'll know if anyone tries to sneak up behind us."

That wasn't actually true, but Adan didn't think he wanted to correct Rune at that point. Too many people Adan was supposed to trust had turned on him recently. The less people knew about what he could do, the better.

"Come on." Rune grabbed Delan and helped her up. "Which way is it?"

She pointed toward the way they'd come from. "Back this way."

"Alright," Rune confirmed. "You two make sure the others are ready," he said to Adan and Jenra, "and head to the rear of the group."

Adan and Jenra nodded, then Jenra slung her rifle strap over her shoulder. As they walked away, Garun flashed his torch over the pair of them.

"Damn, Adan," Bo exclaimed. "That's quite a look."

Garun grinned and nodded. "Yeah. Remind me not to get on your bad side again."

The two of them had tied and gagged the group's attackers. Both were still unconscious, but Rico had come around and struggled against his bonds. Adan walked over to him, knelt, and pushed a hand down onto his chest.

"You may as well get comfortable," Adan explained. "Once we're gone, your friend Delan will be back to release you." Rico tried to complain but couldn't manage more than a gurgled moan through his gag. "And don't even think about trying to come after us. I'll be watching for you. Next time, I won't just break your nose."

Rico suddenly went quiet. Adan nodded and stood up.

Jenra looked at him curiously. "I feel like I'm seeing a different side of you, Testa."

Adan shrugged. "I'm tired of getting ambushed by people who claimed to be my allies. That's one thing I'll say about the Commander. At least she doesn't pretend she's not a villain."

Jenra frowned. "Yeah, I suppose that's true."

Then Rune announced they were heading out, so everyone formed up into their new marching order and followed Delan back up the tunnel.

Jenra glanced over at him as they walked. "Is now a good time to ask what in the Founder's name you're wearing?"

"I suppose." Adan gave her a brief explanation of the armor and what it could do. But he kept his story light on specifics since he was still smarting about his ambush. It wasn't like he suddenly distrusted Jenra or anyone else in their group. But Adan wanted to protect them, if possible, by limiting what they knew. "There's still a lot about this stuff that I need to learn. Hopefully, your brother's Motari friends can help with that."

Jenra didn't look so sure. "Nothing against the Motari, and certainly nothing against Rune, but I wouldn't recommend getting your hopes up too much." She looked at him and showed the same confusion Delan had about where to focus her gaze. "And don't forget that the Motari have an agenda, too," she finally added.

"I hear you," Adan agreed. "But we all have some kind of agenda, don't we? And I'll finally be out of the Valley, at least.

So whatever I end up dealing with, it won't be inside Bolvar's walls. That's what I've always wanted."

"So, you and Bo were serious about that, then? With your bashki theft and all that?"

Adan nodded. "Yeah, we were. We both hoped we could avoid everything we've been doing for the last month. But, at least we'll have a chance to stop doing it anymore."

Jenra nodded, then went silent for a few moments. Adan watched the bouncing light from her torch as she walked. "I gotta ask you," she finally said. "You know you have the chance to really make a difference here, right?" Adan assumed by here she meant Bolvar. "If the Motari asked you for help, would you give it to them?"

That was a tricky question. But it was one Adan had already thought about. There were many things about the Union that he didn't mind. Everyone was fed, housed, and clothed. There was no real crime to speak of unless you counted crimes against the State. And he knew a lot of good people there. But the price you paid for all that, living under the oppressive thumb of the Union Committee and their enforcers, was often too high.

"I don't know," Adan finally answered. "It would depend on what they asked me to do. I agree that the Union could be a lot better than it is. But I'm not ready to start a war to get that. Too many people have gotten hurt already." Gotten hurt, he heard himself say. As if he wasn't the one who'd hurt them.

Jenra nodded. "I guess that's fair. Honestly, I never intended to be more than a convenient access point into the Defense Force for my brother. And now, thanks to you, here I am marching off to join the cause."

"I'm sorry."

"No, don't be," she assured him. "It's for the best. Just because the system hasn't abused me the way it's abused you doesn't mean it's not abusive."

"You are approaching the cistern," Besi quietly announced.

"We're getting close," Adan said. "Shine your torch up ahead."

Jenra pointed her torch past the people ahead of her, and Adan saw where the tunnel ended in an opening to a darkened cavern beyond. "Well, that doesn't look scary at all," Jenra jokingly commented. Her view probably looked a lot different than his.

"It'll be fine," Adan assured her.

The group gathered near the opening, shining their torches around to get an idea of the cistern's size. It was massive. Adan didn't understand how it could lead to an exit. It turned out that it technically didn't.

"There's a narrow ledge," Delan explained. "You follow it around to the right. Just past the second corner, a ladder leads up to a small access shaft then to a ground-level opening on the far side. It's about a kilometer away from the wall and half that from the exclusion zone."

Rune frowned. "It's safe to exit there?"

"It's safe enough," Delan replied. "As long as you don't go out of the way to call attention to yourself. But be sure that you're ready to move on once you're out. When you close the hatch, it stays closed. You can't open it from the outside."

Rune nodded. "So, to get back into the city, you need someone from inside the wall to open it for you."

Delan nodded. She'd given up any pretense about guarding the tunnels' secrets. "That's right."

"I see." Rune held out his hand toward the dark opening. "After you?"

Delan's mouth fell open. "You want me to go first?"

Rune laughed. "Did you think we'd leave you here? No, it's best if you show us the way. As I said, once we're outside, then you can go."

"I've never done it before," she muttered. "I'm always the one who stays behind as a lookout."

"Then today's your lucky day," Rune replied with a smile. He turned to the group. "Same marching order as before. Adan, are you still okay taking the rear?

Adan nodded. "You can count on me."

"Good enough. Let's go."

Delan took a deep breath, stepped through the opening, and disappeared. Then Rune followed behind her. Once Adan was the last one remaining, he stood at the edge and watched the bobbing torches spaced along the impossibly long wall to his right. Then Adan looked down. Slipping from the ledge would surely reward him with a fall of at least 100 meters. Besi could probably tell him for sure, but Adan didn't want to know. It was a fatal drop, that much was sure. The good news was that the ledge was wider than Adan expected, extending nearly a meter from the wall. That made the idea of the coming walk easier to deal with.

Adan glanced back over his shoulder to double-check that the way behind him was still clear. Then he stepped out onto the ledge and hurried as quickly as he dared to catch up to Jenra. As long as he kept looking ahead instead of down, he didn't even mind that he was skirting the edge of a lethal fall.

It only took Adan a minute to reach the first corner. By that time, Delan and Rune were almost to the next one.

Then Adan looked back and realized that the depth of the cistern was nothing compared to its length. A half-dozen more openings were spread out along the wall behind him, each from its own flood tunnel. When the river flooded, Adan guessed that the water would pour into the cistern and fill it up instead of the city streets. But the ones he saw couldn't be the only flood tunnels. The Daralsha ran the length of the entire city. This must've been in just one of many underground cisterns in the area.

"I detect motion behind you," Besi announced, interrupting Adan's thoughts. "They are close."

"Already? Damn." Adan pulled his Old Tech rifle from his back then aimed it at the opening. "We've got company," he called out. "Everyone hurry and get out. I'll cover you."

A pair of red squares materialized near the tunnel opening. Whatever it was interfering with Besi's sensors in the tunnels had allowed their pursuers to get close. Adan steadied his aim and pointed the red cross into the center of the largest red square. Then his target appeared in the tunnel opening. It was Rico. Despite having his rifle taken from him earlier, Rico somehow managed to get his hands on another one. Adan snarled, remembering his promise to Rico back in the tunnels, and fired his weapon. It flashed, and Adan saw Rico get hit and thrown back into the tunnel. Another attacker emerged in Rico's place, rifle ready. Adan fired again, knocking them from his view.

Then a shot rang out from the tunnel opening, striking the torchlight on the wall between Rune and Garun. "They're aiming for the torches," Rune shouted as his light went out. Everyone behind him quickly followed suit and turned their torches off.

That made it harder for the shooter to see, but Adan still couldn't see where the shooter was. He was at the wrong angle. Adan hurried along the ledge until he caught up to Jenra at the final corner. When Adan looked back, he saw a small red square and aimed for it.

"They are still too far away from the tunnel opening for you to hit them," Besi confirmed.

Someone ahead of Adan cried out. He looked over to see Delan and Rune struggling in each other's grip. Was Delan after Rune's weapon? Adan pushed forward around Jenra as he tried to get to Rune. When Rune's torch came back on, Adan realized it was really what they'd been fighting over. Then another shot rang out from the tunnel entrance and struck Delan, who bounced off the wall and fell back over the side of the ledge, dropping to the far bottom of the cistern.

Adan whirled toward the tunnel opening, aimed for the red square, and fired off a series of blasts. The red square disappeared. Adan stood there for a moment, waiting for someone else to appear.

"Is there anyone else back there?" he asked.

"I detect one possible additional combatant," Besi replied, "but they are too far for me to get a fix on their position. And they seem to be moving away."

"We're clear for the moment," Adan called out. Then he backed up to the wall to give Jenra room to pass around him.

"Thanks," she said as she went by.

Adan watched the tunnel opening for signs of activity until Jenra finally got her chance to start up the ladder. Then he reattached his weapon to his back, grabbed a ladder rung, and pulled himself up after her. It was a ten-meter climb to the top of the cistern, then another 100 or so up the access tube. Everyone had to pause while Rune figured out how to get the access panel at the top open, then he climbed out.

"It's clear," Rune called down to the others, who all then started to follow him up and out.

Finally, it was Adan's turn. He reached from the top rung to the edge of the opening and pulled himself up through it. Once he got a foothold on the edge, Adan crawled out into the night air. After Adan stepped away, Rune pushed the access panel until it swung closed with a dull thud. The panel was smooth and flat, with no obvious way to lift it from the outside. That was fine. Adan would be okay if he never saw the inside of those tunnels again.

Adan surveyed his immediate surroundings. It was still nighttime, although his armor allowed him to see as well as he could at early dusk. They were in a wooded area, surrounded by a loose stand of trees and bushes. As he turned around, the city came into view, spread out ahead of him along the Valley floor under a blanket of twinkling lights.

"Open up, please, Besi."

Frigid air flooded his nostrils as his helmet disengaged and folded back into his collar. His surroundings returned to darkness, making the city's lights stand out even more.

Garun came up and stood next to him, admiring the same view. "It's even more beautiful here than it is at home."

Adan chuckled. "I always wondered what that view was like."

"It's good," Garun assured him. "But, this one is much better since we're on the other side of the wall." Then he turned and left Adan to join the rest of the group.

But Adan remained standing there. If that was the last time he would ever see Bolvar, he wanted to appreciate it for a few moments longer.

Official Log of Captain Chander Sanyal

Neskan Colony, 4 March, Year 5 (Neskan Calendar)

The Officer Council (well, mainly Marta and Clarinda) asked me to consider extending the Colony State of Emergency for another year. But I've refused. It's time for me to step down and give the colonists a chance to choose their next leaders. Everyone knows they'll choose Marta (or maybe Clarinda if she stands) anyway.

It's been nearly a year since the Broken Valley disaster—that's what everyone calls it now—and we're still here. Between the new births and the people that are currently pregnant, our numbers will soon be back up to the landfall level. Dr. Palo is cautiously optimistic. And we've harvested our first whole crop from non-printed seeds. There's still a lot that can go wrong, of course. But it's time for someone else to take over the leadership. I've done all I can. And I'm tired.

Chapter 17

"So what happened back there with Delan?"

Adan walked behind Rune on the nearly invisible trail. Once they were all out in the open, Rune quickly determined where they were and which way they needed to go. After hiking a safe distance from the city, Rune informed the group, they'd make for the rendezvous point where other Motari operatives would pick them up.

The air was cold enough that Adan opted to leave his armor on for the added warmth. But he kept his helmet off and could see his breath every time he exhaled. Adan was amazed at how much colder it was outside the city.

"She was worried that leading us to the exit would make Rico assume she turned against him," Rune answered. "My guess is she thought that she may be able to delay us long enough for Rico or his allies to do something to stop us."

"But then someone shot her."

Rune nodded. "Someone did. They may have been aiming

for me and missed. Or it may have been deliberate. We'll probably never find out which." Then he sighed. "That, and what Pavola hears about what happened."

Adan had already told Rune that he had shot Rico and another of their attackers. But someone else had likely gotten away. Adan wasn't sure if Rune was more bothered that Rico and Delan were dead or that one of their attackers had escaped. But he assured Adan everything was fine and not to worry about it.

"But, what can they even say?" Adan asked. "That we attacked them for no reason even though they were giving us what we asked for?"

Rune shrugged. "I don't know. But I'm not too worried about it. Pavola's not so easily fooled. He's smart. You have to be to run an operation like his under the Pinchers' noses for as long as he has. Well, smart, or with their blessing."

"I thought you said we could trust him."

"Yeah, I said we could trust him. But I don't know if that holds true for everyone."

Adan shook his head. "Founder's grace, Rune. I don't know how you manage this."

"Manage what?"

"All these games of who can trust who. It feels to me like every time I think I've got a situation handled, it goes wrong. I can barely keep up."

Rune nodded. "I hear you, and I'll let you in on my secret. I don't trust anyone."

"Anyone?"

"Okay, that sounded more extreme than I meant it to. I trust everyone to do what's in their best interest. And if that happens to be the same as my interests, then I'm good."

Adan laughed. "I'm not sure if that version sounds any less extreme."

Rune grinned. "No, I suppose it doesn't. But that's what gets me through days like the ones we've been having lately, you know?"

"I guess so."

It was a really negative way to look at things, thinking that everyone was only out for themselves. But maybe Adan was being naive, thinking that not everyone was like that. It was hard to say. Adan knew some people who weren't like that at all. Maybe Rune claimed he was. But Bo wasn't. Adan didn't think Jenra was, either.

They were so different, the brother and sister. One was a Motari operative, and one was a Defense Force Trooper. Well, a Defense Force deserter, now. In the end, maybe they weren't so different. But Adan couldn't see Jenra having her brother's negative attitude about everyone. Not yet, at least.

"How much farther is it?" Garun asked from behind them. Garun was still a question mark for Adan. He'd been kind, helpful, and even a little flirty with Adan since they'd made their escape from the DFTC. But Adan was still reluctant to trust him.

"I'm going to make you walk an extra kilometer for every time you ask that," Rune responded.

"Sorry. I'm just feeling a little left out. You two are talking strategy, and Bo and Jenra are, well, I don't know what they're talking about." Bo and Jenra were bringing up the rear of the group. They'd been nearly inseparable ever since the group had started hiking up the mountain. Maybe their recent brush with danger made them want to connect. Maybe it was what made Garun want to connect, too.

"Alright, fine," Rune conceded. "I don't know exactly how far it is. We'll get there when we get there."

Adan slowed down a bit to let Garun catch up to him. Despite the cover from the treetops, both moons shone brightly in the darkness overhead. Arga, the larger of the two, floated directly overhead. The smaller one, Yuli, sat just over the mountaintops up ahead of them. Adan could hardly remember the last time he'd been that far from the city lights. And the combined light from Neska's moons gave Garun's skin an enchanting, almost silvery glow.

"Have you ever been outside the wall before?" Adan asked him.

Garun shook his head. "No. I used to play in the woods by my house as a kid, but that doesn't really compare." He looked up. "Even with the trees, I can see so many more stars."

Adan looked up. Arga was so bright that the sky looked like it did in the Lowers. An exceptionally bright, slightly reddish star sparkled close to it. "I can see Araba up there." The first planet in the Pamuan system wasn't suitable for life like Neska was. But the First Explorers had mapped it anyway for possible colonization in the future.

"What about you?" Garun asked. "Have you ever been outside the wall before?"

Adan nodded. "My parents took me to Lanbro Falls when I was young."

"Are you serious? Mine never even did that. How did yours manage to get a pass? What do they do?"

Garun had asked where they worked, but he really wondered who they knew. But Adan couldn't answer either question. "I don't remember. I don't know that I ever really

311

knew."

Garun frowned and looked down. "Oh. Sorry, Adan."

"It's alright." That was the problem with meeting so many new people lately. He had to keep explaining his greatest source of trauma to them. Or, his second greatest, given recent events. "I wish I could've found out something about them ."

"And Sala never told you what she knew."

Adan shook his head. "No. And once she found out I can activate Old Tech, I doubt she ever planned to."

"Maybe so. Do you know what Sala did before taking over the DFTC?"

"No, I don't know much about her at all."

Garun grunted. "She led some kind of secret Union task force. My father talked about it sometimes. He claimed that she led a special Gray Coats unit that hunted down raiders and rebels. He also claimed that she was very successful at it. But then, one day, Sala got transferred to the DFTC. My father thought it was really odd and that maybe she'd pissed off the wrong Committee member." He fell silent for a few moments as they walked along. "But I doubt he knows anything about that secret research facility. What if she wasn't hunting raiders at all?"

Adan nodded. "What if she was hunting Old Tech?"

"It makes sense," Garun confirmed.

"That does make sense," Rune agreed. "Although she did hunt raiders. But, with what we recently learned about the DFTC, my guess is that she only hunted certain kinds of raiders."

"Raiders who'd gotten their hands on Old Tech," Adan offered.

Garun let out a low whistle. "I can still hardly believe all of that was going on right under our feet."

Adan shivered involuntarily at the thought of it. He'd come way too close to being a scientific experiment for his liking.

"Ah!" Rune suddenly exclaimed. "There it is." He stepped off to his left and grabbed something hanging from a tree branch. It was a white ribbon. "There should be a clearing just up ahead. It's the rendezvous point for our pick up, so we should make camp there."

"Finally," Garun said with a smile. "I can't wait to get a fire going. I'm freezing."

Rune frowned. "Sorry, no fires. It would give away our position to any spotters on the wall."

"Balda's ass!" Garun complained. "So we're just supposed to freeze out here?"

Rune laughed. "Spoken like a true Gallur boy. No, there are chemical heating packs in your backpack. Slip one inside your sleeping bag, and you'll be plenty warm." Then he walked off into the brush.

Garun frowned. Adan doubted that he enjoyed the Gallur insult. "I guess that'll have to do."

"What's going on?" Bo asked as he and Jenra walked up behind them.

"Rune said we're at the rendezvous point," Adan answered. "He's looking for the clearing for us to set up camp."

Bo patted his arms and shivered. "Thank the Founders. Now we can finally light a fire."

Garun laughed. "Get ready for some bad news. Rune said something about chemical heating packs."

"Oh, I've used those before," Jenra commented. "They're alright." She turned to Bo. "You and I should consider

313

doubling up our sleeping bags. That would be even better."

Bo grinned. "Now, there's an idea."

Garun turned to Adan with an eyebrow raised.

Adan shook his head. "No way."

Garun grinned and shrugged. "Can't blame me for trying? It's damn cold out here."

Before Adan could protest any further, Rune emerged from the woods, brushing some leaves and twigs from his jacket. "Come on, the clearing is right through here." Then he turned around and went back the way he came.

Adan walked off the trail and found the gap between the tall bushes Rune had used. After a few moments of ducking under branches or pushing them out of the way, Adan stepped into a small, flat clearing with several boulders arranged in a circle near the middle. Rune sat on one of the boulders pulling several items from his pack.

Garun, Jenra, and Bo emerged from the brush right behind Adan. Suddenly the campsite was crowded.

Bo nodded in approval. "I like it. How long will we be staying?"

"The white ribbon means someone will be coming by to check on the area by tomorrow," Rune explained. "So, this is where we'll stay for the night. You've got rations in your packs if you're hungry. If you just need to piss, make sure you're downhill from the camp. And if you need to relieve yourself, I've got a small shovel for you to dig a hole. Adan, you and Bo have got small tents in your packs. I'm afraid Soto couldn't get enough for everyone. But they're big enough for two, so you can double up."

Garun looked at Adan expectantly, who quietly groaned. "Alright, fine. You can share my tent."

Garun smiled. "Thank you. Really."

Adan shrugged. "It would be dumb to take you this far just to let you freeze to death."

Garun chuckled. "I suppose that's true."

Adan pulled his pack off and sat down on one of the boulders. He undid the straps, lifted up the top flap, then reached inside to pull out his sleeping bag. It was Defense Force issued, like the pack he kept it in. That meant it could handle the wide variety of conditions found in and around the Osbaks. The pack also held a clean shirt, a change of socks and undershorts, a small medkit, a few packs of Defense Force rations, and a thick bundle at the bottom. That must've been the tent. Adan grabbed it and pulled it out. When he set it on the ground next to his sleeping bag, he heard some rustling in the nearby bushes.

"It's just a family of ridge fowl," Rune commented. "I saw their nest not far from here."

Ridge fowl were harmless and were a common source of protein in the Valley. They were smallish, rarely growing taller than a person's knee, and scampered around on their four hind legs in the brush. Their forelimbs were long and flat, resembling the long, soft, grayish-brown scales that covered their bodies. Ridge fowl were abundant throughout the Valley and surrounding foothills. The prowlers in the Valley, their primary natural predator besides people, had been hunted almost to extinction. It made Adan a little sad to think about how much people had bent Neska to their needs. But he was also grateful that he didn't have to worry about a pack of prowlers sneaking up on him in the middle of the night.

Adan looked down at the tent, then over at Bo and Jenra,

who were setting up theirs. "Garun? Can you help me with this?"

Garun nodded and stood up from his boulder seat. "Sure." He walked over and knelt near the tent pack. "Have you set one of these up before?"

Adan shook his head. "No, but Rune has, so we just have to copy him. I'll grab it, and you pull the carry bag off it."

"Alright."

The two of them got it out of the carry bag and unrolled it. Then, following along with Rune as he set up his tent, they set out the pieces, slotted the frame poles into the loops sewn onto the outside, and finally got it upright. It was a low, long, wide half-tube that looked barely big enough for two.

"That's gonna be cozy," Adan commented.

Garun frowned. "If you'd rather I didn't–"

"No, it's fine. At this point, I'm too tired to care."

Garun nodded. "Yeah, same here. I'm gonna go pee. I'll be right back."

"I gotta go, too," Adan shared. "I'll go with you."

The pair of them headed for the downhill side of the clearing and stepped around the bushes. Then Adan found a private spot away from Garun. He didn't mind having someone else there, having spent most of the last month sharing showers and a restroom with seven other people. But it was nice to get a quick moment alone anyhow.

Once he was done, he zipped his trousers back up and walked back to the campsite. Jenra and Bo were already climbing into their tent. Then he saw Rune emerge from the brush on the other side.

"I thought you said to pee downhill," Adan commented.

Rune held up the white ribbon from the tree branch near

the trail. "I was just swapping this out for a blue one to let the others know we're here when they arrive." Then he knelt down and unzipped the entrance to his tent. "Sleep well tonight. We've got a lot of hiking to do tomorrow."

Adan groaned and nodded. "You're always full of good news."

Rune smiled, then slipped into his tent. Adan knelt and unzipped the flap for his own tent as Garun walked up behind him.

"Should we zip our sleeping bags together?" Garun asked. "Looks like it would be a more efficient use of space."

Adan thought about it for a moment, but he knew Garun was right. The tent would fit the two of them, but trying to cram two separate sleeping bags in would probably make it uncomfortably tight. "Yeah, we probably should."

So they each unrolled their sleeping bags and managed to zip them together into one, larger bag without getting them too dirty. Then they shoved it into the tent. Adan crawled in after it, then sat at the entrance and took off his boots. He set them outside the tent and crawled farther inside so Garun could do the same. Then Garun crawled in and zipped the flap closed. Once Adan stripped off his jacket and sweater, he removed the Old Tech weapons from his back and hip, setting it all inside the jacket. After some slightly complicated maneuvering, Adan and Garun managed to get inside the sleeping bag together.

"This isn't so bad," Adan commented.

"No, it's not," Garun agreed. "Thanks again for sharing."

"I already told you, it's fine."

"I know how inconvenient it would be for me to freeze to death out there."

Adan snorted. "Not really. We could just roll your body down the mountain and let the Gray Coats collect it at the bottom."

Garun chuckled. "That's considerate of you." He fell silent for a few moments before speaking again. "You know," he quietly added, "I appreciate that you've been so nice to me, considering everything I did."

Adan was about to dismiss the idea but stopped himself. Why not be truthful? Garun had openly acknowledged his mistakes and worked to correct them. Adan could at least be honest with him in return. "It's because I've forgiven you for that. I won't forget about it, but I'm not going to hold it over your head, either. You've been acting like a friend to me practically the whole time since then. I guess maybe we are friends now."

Garun stayed quiet for a few moments. All Adan could hear was the sound of his breathing. "Well, 'maybe friends' is pretty good," Garun finally said.

Adan heard the "but," even if Garun didn't say it. "But?"

Garun sighed. "But, what about more than that?"

Finally, there it was. Garun had been flirting with him for a reason. "Why don't you start by telling me what you want, Garun?"

"Right now? I want to kiss you. After that? I don't know. Things are pretty complicated at the moment."

Adan laughed, then stopped himself. "Sorry, I'm not laughing at you. Just how fitting the word complicated is for everything."

Then Garun laughed, too. But, complicated or not, Adan still had a decision to make. Should he let Garun kiss him? The idea was tempting, especially lying there next to him in a shared sleeping bag inside a tiny tent.

After a moment, Adan rolled onto his side to face Garun. Then he reached out, grabbed Garun's shoulder, and gently pulled him onto his side so that the two were face to face. Adan could hardly see him in the filtered moonlight inside the tent. But he could smell the musky scent of Garun's body, and he could feel the warmth of Garun's breath on his face. Then he put his hand behind Garun's head, running his fingers through his thick, short hair, before pulling him closer until their lips touched.

Their connection was immediate and electric. Adan hadn't kissed many other people in his life, but he had kissed a few. And the kiss with Garun was by far the best. Garun's lips were soft and warm. His tongue tasted a little sour, but not in an unpleasant way. And Adan doubted that his tasted any better. After what felt like minutes but was probably just a few moments, Adan pulled away.

"Founder's grace," Garun said. "That was amazing."

Adan smiled. "I don't think anyone's ever invoked the Founders after one of my kisses before."

"I don't believe you," Garun said, chuckling. "And it might be because I haven't kissed many people before."

"Well, I don't believe that. You're handsome and privileged. I'd think people are throwing themselves at you."

"That doesn't mean I want to kiss them back."

"Are you sure you want to kiss me back?"

"I'm sure I want to do it again."

Garun leaned forward and put his mouth on Adan's. The electric spark from the first kiss had turned into a warm fire, spreading down from his lips through his body. Feeling playful, Adan pulled Garun's lower lip into his mouth and lightly bit down. That made Garun squirm and push himself into Adan even harder. Adan ran his hand up Garun's arm, then over his shoulder and down his back. Even with the bulky sweater Garun was wearing, Adan could still feel the muscles he'd spied on that first night in the barracks.

Then Adan felt Garun's hand reach behind his head and run his fingers through his hair. It was Adan's turn to squirm. Adan pulled Garun closer until their bodies were touching. He could feel the heat building between them and knew it was probably time to stop.

Adan pulled back from Garun's mouth, grinning uncontrollably. Then he reached up and ruffled Garun's hair on top of his head. Garun smiled, then bit his lower lip. His breath was heavy, and Adan could see his shoulders rise and fall.

"I don't know about you," Adan said, "but I almost didn't want to stop."

Garun's smile stretched into a wicked grin. "Then why did you?"

"Because I'm too tired for anything else, and we have a long day of hiking ahead of us."

Garun exhaled through his nose, and Adan felt the warmth on his face. Then Garun nodded. "You're right. I'm tired, too. Plus, I'm dirty, and I probably smell like a marsh pig."

"You smell fine. And we still need to keep warm, right?"

Adan rolled over to face the other way, then backed up and nestled himself under Garun's shoulder. Garun reached across Adan's chest and held him tightly. It was warm and comforting but felt entirely different than when he shared a bed with Bo. There was the kissing, for one. And there was the excitement of the shared attraction. For how tired he was,

Adan wondered if he'd even fall asleep. But his exhaustion soon caught up with him, and within minutes Adan was sleeping wrapped in Garun's arms.

Official Log of Colony Administrator Marta Kanerva

Neskan Colony, 26 October, Year 6 (Neskan Calendar)

We lost Captain Sanyal today. His health had been failing for months, despite Dr. Palo's best efforts. But every one of us owes our lives to him. I have no doubt that we've only made it this far because of his strength, insightfulness, and courage, especially in the first few years. Some of the colonists have been talking about naming the community after him. So I've asked Sarita to propose the idea at our next Council meeting. Maybe it will help me feel better when I go by his empty house.

Chapter 18

Adan woke to the sound of someone unzipping the flap on his tent. He looked over to see that he was alone. Then Garun poked his head through the opening and climbed inside.

"Sorry to wake you," Garun said, "but nature called. And Rune says we need to get up anyway. He's bribing us with hot tea."

Adan perked up at the mention of tea. "Wait. I thought there was a no-fire rule?"

"It turns out Rune's been holding out on us. He has a portable stove, and he's boiling water as we speak."

"That ass. What else has he been hiding from us?"

"It's four to one. We could probably hold him down and search his pack."

Adan laughed, which turned into a groan and stretch. He could feel some stiffness in his back and shoulders from sleeping on the ground. At least he had a long walk ahead of him to work out the kinks in his muscles. "I don't know. It might make things awkward when his Motari friends show up if we've got him tied up."

Garun chuckled. "Yeah, you're probably right. We should probably just ask him. Anyway, I'm gonna get some tea in my belly before I attempt one of those awful ration bars." Then he leaned in and kissed Adan on the cheek. Adan could feel the cold coming off him and caught the woodsy scent of blackfern trees mingling with Garun's body odor. "Good morning, by the way," he added with a smile, then crawled back out of the tent.

Adan laid there for a minute or so, working up the nerve to brave the cold, mountain air. Even with Garun gone, the sleeping bag was nice and warm. Despite the stiffness from lying on the ground, Adan slept well enough. The combination of a warm, friendly body next to him and his sheer exhaustion from the day's adventures had worked their magic.

Adan felt surprisingly okay about kissing Garun. A small part of him expected to feel guilt or shame about it. But he had nothing to be guilty about or ashamed of. He was almost seventeen and already a member of the Defense Force. Former member, that is. But he was old enough to decide who he wanted to kiss, which was the point.

Then a knot in his guts suddenly twisted itself loose, and Adan knew he'd have to wrap up his relaxation soon. So he sat up, wormed his way out of the sleeping bag, and crawled toward the front flap. Then Adan reached out to grab his boots and slip them on before climbing outside. The cold air hit him like a punch to the face. Then his stomach loudly gurgled.

"The shovel's over there," Rune announced and pointed

toward an empty boulder. Adan looked at him strangely, but Rune just shrugged. "What? You don't think that was the first thing I did when I got up?"

Adan huffed and nodded, then went to collect the shovel. There was a packet of wipes sitting next to it, which he also grabbed. Then he marched out into the brush to find a spot to take care of things. After several awkward minutes, Adan returned to the campsite and set the shovel and wipes back on the rock. Then he noticed a small sanitizer bottle sitting there, so he rubbed that liberally around on his hands.

Bo wandered over with a metal cup full of steaming liquid and handed it to Adan. "Here you go, hot and fresh. Well, powdered, not fresh. But recently brewed, at least."

Adan took the cup and had a careful sip. It tasted enough like tea that he was satisfied, so he took another. "It'll do. Thanks."

Bo nodded. "So," he said innocently, "how'd things go with Garun last night?"

"Why? What did he tell you?"

Bo grinned. "Nothing, you ass. You don't think I can tell when my best friend wakes up happy?" He reached behind himself and rubbed his hand on his lower back. "And I know it can't be from sleeping on the ground."

Adan rolled his eyes and took another sip of tea. He wished Bo had at least waited until he'd had a whole cup before interrogating him. "We kissed, alright?"

Bo nodded. "And?"

"And, it was really nice, okay?"

Bo chuckled. "Nice? Balda's ass, Adan. It's me, remember?"

Adan frowned. "Alright, sorry. Still waking up, I guess." He sipped his tea again. "It was great. Garun's a good kisser.

And he cuddled me while we fell asleep."

Bo smiled. "Good. That makes me happy, even if that used to be my job."

Adan laughed. "Yeah? Well, now the job requires kissing first, so I think you've been replaced. Speaking of kissing, what about you and the Squad Leader?"

Bo's smile turned guilty, and his golden-brown cheeks reddened. "Yeah, we got up to a bit of that ourselves. That was it, though. I don't know about you, but I feel like I haven't bathed in a week."

Adan sniffed the air. "That's what it smells like to me."

Bo laughed and playfully smacked Adan in the arm. "You're one to talk. Are you sure you haven't caught your own scent?"

Adan shrugged. "Probably, but I don't care. This is my first day waking up outside the wall. And, unless you're a Union spy, I know for sure that no one is listening in."

"Who's a Union spy?" Rune asked as he walked up to join them.

"You are," Adan replied, "unless you tell us what else you've got hidden in that pack."

Rune chuckled. "You mean the dozen spiced sweet buns I've got stuffed in the bottom?"

Bo groaned. "Ugh, you had to say spiced sweet buns? Now I'm gonna think about them all day."

Rune laughed and put an arm around Bo's shoulders. "It's part of my torture training in spy class. Now let's get you two over with the rest of us so I can share what's going to happen today."

"Fine," Bo grouched. "As long as I can eat something while you do it."

Rune nodded. "The breakfast ration bar isn't that bad,

especially if you dip it in your tea."

"Ration bar?" Bo grumbled, then winked at Adan.

Adan chuckled as they all walked back toward the portable stove. Garun and Jenra were sitting nearby, eating their ration bars out of the wrapper. They were both joking and laughing, which made Adan smile. Everyone seemed to be so much happier since they'd escaped from the city. Adan knew he was. There were still many things that could go wrong for them, but, for the moment, everything was good.

After they were all seated near the warm stove, Rune outlined what they could expect for the day. Since he'd found a white ribbon tied to that tree, it meant that a Motari team would visit the rendezvous point every two days. No one was waiting there for them, which meant they were on their way.

"So, what?" Garun asked. "They just walk back and forth between here and their hideout until someone shows up?"

Rune flashed a quick glare at Garun for interrupting and shook his head. "No, genius. They rotate through a set of teams for it, and only during a planned pick-up window. We're expected, so they're coming. Now, stop interrupting."

Garun mumbled an apology while Adan, Bo, and Jenra hid their grins. They don't stay and wait around, Rune added, because it wasn't wise to stick to one place for very long around there. Although they were outside the city, they were still well inside Gray Coats territory. It wasn't unknown for patrols to show up when you weren't paying attention.

"So, pay attention," Rune commanded.

Once the other Motari operatives arrived, they'd lead the group over the mountain to a hidden staging point. There, everyone would board a truck and drive to the Motari outpost.

"Over the mountain?" Jenra asked.

"It's not an easy hike, but it's safer than trying to get a vehicle this close to the city," Rune answered.

"How long will it take?" Adan asked.

"That depends on you all, but it shouldn't take more than a few hours. Now, everyone, eat up and take care of whatever else you need to so we can break down this camp."

Adan got up, went to his tent, and reached inside to grab his pack. Then he dug through it until he found the ration bars. Those were also Defense Force issued and were helpfully labeled with their contents. The bar labeled Breakfast was cereal grains and dried winefruit. It actually wasn't that bad, especially once Adan dipped it into his tea. He had a second cup of that mixed from Rune's packet of dried tea powder.

Once he was finished, and after a second visit to the bushes, Adan and Garun took down the tent. It broke down more easily than it went up, but it took the pair of them much longer to get it rolled up and back into the carry bag. The way they laughed and playfully touched each other while doing it didn't help things go any faster, either.

Things had obviously changed between Adan and Garun since the previous day. Adan found them slipping into an easy way with each other, making the tension between them feel like old news. He didn't know how that would play out over the long term. Or even the short term, for that matter. But it was a nice feeling to have in the moment.

Eventually, the group broke down and packed up the whole camp, leaving the portable stove for last while it cooled on one of the boulders. Adan almost wished he could have one more cup of tea, but he'd already peed twice since waking up, and he didn't want to end up stopping every hour while they were hiking. Hopefully, they wouldn't have to wait long for their guides to show up. And, hopefully, those guides wouldn't turn on them and attack like the last ones had done.

Adan reflexively reached for the Old Tech handgun at his hip, then stopped himself. But he couldn't stop himself from recalling what he'd done with it the day before. Adan understood the need to shoot those people. They were trying to hurt him, and they wouldn't stop because of any persuasive arguments or insults he might offer. But Adan hated the feeling afterward. He hated the knowledge that he'd hurt someone else. Or killed them. It was why he'd wanted to avoid serving his five in the first place. Somehow fate or the Founders had conspired against him by giving him the rare and coveted gift of activating Old Tech. That made the Union see him as a much different tool than a simple Trooper or laundry worker. But how would it make the Motari see him?

He didn't have to wait very long to find out.

"Two armed individuals are approaching on foot from the northwest," Besi suddenly announced.

Adan reached for his weapon but stopped himself again. That was becoming a disturbing habit. "We've got company coming," he said instead. "They're approaching from the northwest."

"That'll be our Motari friends," Rune declared. "If it was the Gray Coats, they'd be coming up from the city." Then he stood up. "But be ready, just in case."

Adan stood as well, wondering precisely what being ready meant. Getting his gun out? Activating his armor? Making more tea? He flashed a look at Bo, who shrugged. So much for their Defense Force training.

After a few minutes of anxious waiting, a pair of individuals emerged from the brush surrounding the campsite. One was taller, with deep brown skin and a short dark beard. The shorter one had a sandy brown complexion and long black hair tied back behind their head. They were both dressed in plain-looking cold-weather clothing and boots. And they both had rifles slung over their shoulders.

Rune burst into a grin the moment he saw them. "Asta! Elo!" He walked over and wrapped his arms around the shorter one, then hugged the taller one as well. "Did you make it okay?"

The taller one laughed. "Did we make it okay?" they repeated in a deep voice. "We just walked here. What about you?"

Rune shook his head. "Pavola's hired guides tried to double-cross us, but we handled it."

"That doesn't sound like Soto," the shorter one commented.

"I don't think he had anything to do with it. But, I don't know for sure."

"You can let Asona know when you check in," the taller one told Rune. "She can have someone do a little digging and find out more." Then they turned to the group. "This is a sizable crew you brought. More than we expected, at least."

Rune nodded. "The original plan went a little sideways."

"Like they always do," the shorter one said with a grin.

Rune chuckled. "No comment." He turned to the rest of the group. "Alright, introductions. He's Elo Rigari," Rune said, pointing to the taller one, then pointed to the shorter one. "And she's Asta Koro. He's Garun Mostok," Rune added, pointing at Garun before continuing to the others. "He's Bo Shen, and he's Adan Testa. And, of course, this is my sister,

Jenra Tabata."

Elo and Asta both smiled. "Nice to meet you all," Asta said. "Especially you, Jenra. We've heard so much about you."

Jenra smiled. "All good things, I hope."

Asta nodded. "Yes. Your brother practically idolizes you."

Rune shook his head. "I wouldn't say that."

Asta laughed. "No, of course, you wouldn't. Now, which of you is the one we originally came here for?"

Adan raised his hand. "If you mean, which of us has all the neat tricks, that's me."

Asta nodded, then turned to Rune. "So, it's true?"

"It is. You should catch him in action, too. It's like nothing I've ever seen before."

"I can only imagine," Elo proclaimed. "But we'll have to save the demonstrations for when we reach the outpost. We caught a glimpse of some Gray Coats action down near the exclusion zone. They must've found out about your attempt to cross the wall. So, if you're ready to go, we should start heading back."

Rune nodded. "We're all ready."

"Good," Elo confirmed. "It took us about four hours to get here at a steady pace. Since most of you are inexperienced mountaineers, I'd say we should plan on at least five to six hours for the return trip." Then Elo arranged them into an informal walking order, with himself, Asta, and Adan near the front. Rune and Jenra took the rear since they were both armed.

Adan was a little wary at first of being left along with the two new Motari operatives. But, soon, the boredom of endless hiking set in and took over. The first hour of the march was a steady incline on a relatively easy trail through the forest. Adan managed to work the kinks out of his back in time for his legs to start complaining. His lungs were also unhappy. Bolvar already sat at around 1,200 meters above sea level. Adan guessed they'd come close to doubling that elevation since exiting the tunnels. But Elo and Asta didn't seem to mind it at all. They were obviously not inexperienced mountaineers.

Once they were well underway, Asta spent some of the time politely interrogating Adan and seemed highly interested in what he had to say. He'd grown used to the many questions even if he no longer enjoyed them. But he appreciated Asta's efforts to keep things light. At least until they got to the part of his story involving Commander Sala and the Defense Force. Then Asta's face turned hard.

"Do you know her?" Adan asked.

"I know of her. Her relentless pursuit for Old Tech artifacts is well known among the Motari. As is her cruelty."

"That sounds like her," Adan agreed.

"And she just showed up in your Pincher cell like that?"

Adan nodded. "Yeah, like she was visiting a friend in the Medical Center. I didn't realize how easy it was for someone like her to get inside Utrogg House."

"It's not," Asta corrected him. "It's quite tough, in fact. For all that nonsense about how every piece of the Union machine works together in harmony, that's all it is. Nonsense. I'd guess that she had to pull a lot of strings to make that happen. And then to get the Magistrate to basically turn you over to her, too."

Adan shrugged. "It seemed like a good thing at first."

"Until all the experimenting started, right?" Asta flashed him a grin. Then she turned serious again. "But she couldn't have known about your ability, or else she would've had you testing out Old Tech on the first day."

"Yeah," Adan agreed. "I wondered about that, too. She claimed to know what happened to my parents. They disappeared one day when I was young, and I never found out how or why."

"Did she tell you what she knew?"

Adan shook his head. "No, of course not. I kind of doubt that she knew anything."

"She must've known something, or else why go to all that effort on your behalf?"

Adan shrugged. "Maybe she was just that impressed with my barrel maneuver during our bashki heist?"

Asta looked confused. "Barrel maneuver?"

Adan explained what he'd done when he and Bo were in the van being chased by Pinchers. Asta had a good laugh about it. "That was you? Rune told me about that. I'm impressed."

"See?" Adan commented.

Asta shook her head. "Sure, I'm impressed. But that story wouldn't get me to risk my life to bust you out of the DFTC. No, she had to have known something about you already."

Asta had to be correct. It didn't make much sense otherwise. "Alright, but what? My parents weren't Motari, were they?"

"Your family name is Testa?" Adan nodded. "No, not that I know of."

But was his name really Adan Testa? He thought about Bo and how his aunt had changed his name from Neren to Shen. Had his parents used different names, too? But Adan kept those thoughts to himself. He wasn't about to risk spilling Bo's secret to the Motari without his permission. "Well, I've lived with the mystery this long," he finally said. "She can keep her secrets if she wants."

"Honestly, what she knew or suspected about you may not even have anything to do with you, as strange as that sounds. Sala plays the long game. With you, she may have just been setting up another move she'll make in the future. Then she lucked into discovering you were also special."

Adan grunted. "That sounds like chess. I prefer Tik-Tix."

Asta nodded. "Sure. There's a time and place for both styles of play. But it's important to know the difference. You don't want to get caught playing one game when you should've been playing the other."

"But, how do you know which one to play?"

Asta laughed. "You guess. Welcome to adulthood, Testa."

Adan smiled and shook his head. He reminded himself that there was no one to tell him what to do anymore. Which was what he wanted. Or, thought he wanted.

"I detect a group of armed soldiers approaching from the rear," Besi announced. "They are hunting you."

Adan suddenly stopped. "How do you know that?" Adan subvocalized.

Asta turned to him in surprise. "Why have you–?"

Adan held up his hand to stop her and shook his head.

"They are using unencrypted wireless communications, which I have intercepted. I estimate you have three minutes before they are within visual range. You should leave the trail and take cover."

Three minutes? How had they gotten that close already? And they were close enough to hear the group if they made too much noise. Adan waved to get everyone's attention, then held a finger to his mouth to request silence. "There's a group of Gray Coats approaching from behind us," Adan said to Asta and Elo. "They're less than three minutes away."

He could see that Asta wanted to ask how he knew that, but she didn't. Instead, she nodded, then rushed back to tell Rune.

"Let's get you off the trail," Elo quietly suggested. "Follow me."

Adan hesitated for a moment. He'd just met this person, and yet they asked to lead him away from the group. Adan was growing increasingly reluctant to trust strangers after recent events. But he also had to think of everyone else, too. "Okay."

"The others will hide, too," Elo assured him as he led Adan into the trees and brush. "But hiding as a single group only makes us easier to find."

That made sense. Adan followed Elo until they were about thirty meters away from the trail. Elo spotted a pair of old bowleaf trees with thick trunks and directed Adan to hide behind them. So, Adan ducked behind the closest one, then carefully leaned out to catch a view of the trail. He couldn't see much around the brush and tree branches that blocked his view. But he couldn't see the others in his group, either. Hopefully, that meant everyone was hidden. Then he heard the unmistakable sounds of people approaching and caught his first glimpse of the Gray Coats on his tail. It was an entire squad of eight soldiers. One led them, slowly walking ahead of the group while looking down at the trail.

"Damn," Elo whispered next to him. "They have a tracker. They'll spot our footprints for sure. You'd better get ready to fight."

Adan exhaled his stifled groan. He'd love to go a whole day without fighting anyone. And these were trained Gray Coats, which also put his friends in danger.

"There is another option," Besi informed him. "I can project a sound field to the lead soldier tracking you, making it seem as if your group is behind them. That may cause them to briefly turn back."

Elo reached for his gun, but Adan stopped him with a gesture. "Wait. Be ready for that, but let me try something first," Adan whispered. Then he switched to subvocalizing. "Do it, Besi."

"Confirmed. Activating directed sound field."

Adan held his breath as he watched and waited. Suddenly the tracker looked up and then back. They raised their hand to stop the group, then motioned for silence. The tracker craned their neck to point their ear back down the trail. After a few moments, they raised their hand and circled it around through the air before walking toward the Troopers behind them. The rest of the squad soon followed them.

"What just happened?" Elo asked him.

"Just being a little tricky. But I don't know how long we have before they realize they've been tricked."

Elo didn't seem to like that answer, but he nodded anyway. "Alright. Can you gather everyone here without letting the Gray Coats know?"

Adan nodded. Elo must've guessed something about Besi's trick. He had to know about Adan's armor. Rune said he'd gotten it from the Motari.

"I understand your companion's request," Besi shared. "Would you like me to do as they ask?"

"Please," Adan subvocalized.

"Acknowledged. I will direct the others in your group to your location."

"They're on their way now," Adan informed Elo.

Elo nodded but kept quiet. After a few moments, Bo and Jenra emerged from the downhill brush and squatted next to Adan. Then Adan saw Rune, Asta, and Garun sneak across the trail and quickly climb up to join the rest of them.

Once everyone was close by, Elo waved to get their attention. "We have a few minutes, maybe more, to get far enough from the trail that we might be able to lose the Gray Coats. They have a tracker, so we'll need to get somewhere we won't leave any footprints or trail markers." Then he looked at Asta. "Any ideas?"

Asta pursed her lips for a moment, then nodded. "If we move fast, we can lead them to Rami's Pinch, then climb up and double-back to the proper trail while we're up on the ridge."

Elo nodded. "Yes, that could work. Alright, we're going back to the trail. I need you all to follow me and stay close." He looked at Rune and Jenra. "You're rearguard, so keep your ears open." Then he looked at Adan. "Same for you." Adan nodded. "Good enough. Let's go."

Everyone in the group stood and followed Elo back down to the trail, where they all broke into a jog. After a few minutes of light running, they came to a fork, where Elo led them to the left. The trail rose sharply from that point, slowing their progress, with rocks and boulders scattered about among the thinning trees. At one point, Adan misstepped and slipped on some loose gravel. But Garun grabbed onto him and kept him from falling.

"Thanks," Adan blurted, his breathing heavy.

Garun smiled. "It would be dumb to take you this far just to let you fall off the mountain," he joked as they started off

337

again, running to catch up to their pack leaders.

Soon enough, the group reached a rock face at least ten meters high with a small, narrow gap sliced through it.

"Rami's Pinch?" Adan asked.

Asta nodded. "It's slow and tight in some spots, so we need to hurry and get in there. But watch your footing."

Elo slipped into the gap first, then Asta went in after him. Adan followed after Asta, stepping into the gap in the rocks. It was just wide enough for him to walk normally, but there were frequent twists and turns. After a minute or two, the gap began to narrow, forcing Adan to turn his shoulders a bit to fit through some spots. If it got any slimmer, he'd have to take off his pack and slide through sideways.

Then Adan spotted Elo and Asta up ahead. He moved up right behind them and waited there as the rest of the group caught up to him. Once everyone was close enough, Elo spoke again.

"Asta is going to lead you all up the side. It's not a beginner's climb, but if you pay attention, you can follow her hand and footholds easily enough. Rune, you're with me. We'll continue leaving a trail through the Pinch, then climb up and come back across the ridge. Everyone understand?"

Adan nodded. He understood the basic plan, and his part seemed obvious.

"Follow me," Asta said. She reached up, grabbed a small ledge on the right side of the gap, and pulled herself up to a foothold below the ledge. Then she grabbed another handhold and climbed farther up.

Adan reached up and grabbed the same ledge. When he pulled himself up, it took a moment to find the first foothold. Then he looked up to see Asta waiting above him. She pointed down to the ledge she'd grabbed, and Adan reached for it. Once Adan pulled himself up, Garun started the process below him. Adan kept following Asta through the series of hand and footholds up the side of the gap. Some of them he didn't see until Asta grabbed for them or pointed them out. An experienced rock climber might have noticed them, but Adan was sure Asta had climbed that spot in Rami's Pinch before. Maybe she and Elo had practiced for the very situation they were in.

It felt like it took forever, but then Asta helped pull Adan up to the top of the climb. He stood there on the rock ridge, breathless, while he waited for the others. The view was extraordinary. Adan could see all the way down into Bolvar Valley. He could also see down the other side to either a narrow river or wide creek that wound down from the higher Osbak peaks.

Garun came up next, followed by Jenra. After a few more minutes, Jenra helped pull Bo up to the top of the ridge, and everyone was present. Asta motioned for them all to follow her, then she ducked down low as she quickly walked away from the gap. The ridge was easier than the climb had been, but Adan still had to watch his footing around small cracks in the rock. Twice he had to jump across gaps that were too large to step over. Adan didn't know how long they'd been moving when Asta brought them all to a stop on a smooth, flat shelf of rock under a slight overhang. But it must've been past midday since their shadows had grown longer. Adan was happy to stop. He'd already gotten sick of hiking.

Asta looked at Adan. "Are we clear?"

She was asking if they were being followed. Besi hadn't made a sound the whole time. "Yeah, we're good."

339

Asta nodded. "I know you're all probably tired, so we can take some time to rest and stretch. But we have to go as soon as Elo and Rune get here."

Bo groaned. "Balda's ass. All that climbing and awkward running is killing my calves."

Jenra chuckled. "I always said you should've been doing more squats in the PTC."

Bo shrugged and rolled his eyes. "Yeah? If only you'd been my squad leader at the time."

"Uh oh," Jenra joked. "Sounds like someone is getting cranky."

Then Adan felt a hand on his shoulder. He turned to see Garun standing behind him. "Come with me," Garun suggested. "You should see this." Adan turned and let Garun lead him to the edge of the rock shelf. Then Garun pointed toward the north end of the valley. "There, that's Lanbro Falls."

Adan squinted to bring it into focus. But, even at that distance, he still recognized it. "It looks so small from here."

"We've climbed up pretty high. At least a few kilometers. Not to mention that we've traveled at least that far from the city."

Adan swept his gaze across Bolvar Valley. The Eastern Osbaks framed his view, their snow-capped iron peaks pointing toward a deep blue sky. He knew the Eastern Ocean lay beyond the mountains, but he wasn't high enough to see it. Adan had never seen an ocean except in photos. He wondered what it looked like in person. "The view is beautiful from up here," Adan admitted.

"Not as beautiful as it is from here," Garun replied.

Adan turned to see Garun looking right at him. He wished

Garun hadn't used such an obvious line. But Adan was still flattered, and he could feel his cheeks suddenly get warm. "You don't have to do that, but thank you."

Garun looked confused. "Do what?"

"Compliment me."

Garun smiled and shook his head. "Do you think I said that because I had to?" He reached forward and softly caressed Adan's cheek. His hand felt cool to the touch. "I only said it because it's the truth."

Adan didn't know how to react. People didn't normally try to flatter him like that. And no one had ever told him he was beautiful before. If they weren't in the process of escaping from a Gray Coat squad–

"Your remaining two companions are approaching," Besi suddenly alerted him.

"Okay, thank you," Adan subvocalized. Then he reached up and caressed Garun's cheek in return. "Thank you. Now, we should get back. Elo and Rune are almost here."

Garun groaned. "If it weren't for those damn Gray Coats."

Adan laughed. "The Union provides."

"I wish the Union would provide me a little more time alone with you."

Adan leaned in and lightly kissed Garun on the cheek. "Later." Then took Garun's hand and led him back toward the rest of the group.

"It was very odd when your machine spoke to me earlier," Garun mentioned as they walked. "It felt like someone was speaking just over my shoulder. What do you call her?"

"Besi. Why do you think it's a she?"

Garun shrugged. "I don't know. I guess the voice is neutral enough to be any gender. I just thought she felt feminine.

341

You gave her a feminine name."

"It stands for Battlefield Enhanced Systems Intelligence. It's not a person. It doesn't think or feel like we do. It just runs off an alga–, no, algo–"

"Algorithm," Besi prompted.

"An algorithm. That's like a super complex math problem."

Garun chuckled. "I know what an algorithm is."

"Good, then maybe you can explain it to me. They didn't teach us about stuff like that in my Instructional Center."

Garun grinned. "I'll do it for another kiss."

Adan smiled as he felt his cheeks get warm. "Deal. But, later."

"Later," Garun groaned. "Always later."

Elo and Rune crested the ridge just as Adan and Garun returned to the group. Asta waived when she saw them.

"I'm glad to see you all made it here," Elo shared when he was close enough to be heard.

"Same with you both," Asta replied. "We haven't had any contact with the Gray Coats at all."

Rune smiled. "That's because your plan worked. We hid out long enough to see the tracker lose our trail on the other side of the passage."

Asta smiled. "That's a relief. Do you need to rest before we go?"

Elo shook his head. "No, I don't want to lose any more daylight. We should've been there already."

Asta turned to address the group. "You heard Elo," she announced. "It's time to move out."

Bo groaned as Jenra helped him to his feet, but no one else complained. Adan wasn't excited about more walking. But he was ready to get the rest of the hike over with. Being out in nature was nice enough, but he wanted to put the Bolvar Union as far behind him as he could. And maybe sleep in a bed.

Asta led the group around the rock shelf to another passage. It was also narrow but wider than Rami's Pinch. Even the few turns were roomy enough to walk through normally. The group emerged from the passage onto a broad field that sloped uphill. The trees were smaller and more sparse than before, clumped with brush and shrubs growing around their trunks. It made for easier hiking than the wooded trails but left them more exposed.

"Are we okay here?" Adan asked Besi.

"The only movement I can detect is animal life." Meaning ridge fowl and the other small creatures that populated the Osbaks, Adan guessed.

Everyone kept silent as they walked along. Adan was too tired to talk, and he imagined the others felt the same. When they reached the top of the slope, Adan looked down on another small valley. There was no sign of the stream he'd seen earlier. But there were plenty of trees, and it didn't take long before they were on another forest trail. Adan felt the temperature drop once they passed into the shadows from the tree canopies. It was going to be another cold night. Hopefully, they'd spend it indoors.

After walking downhill on the wooded trail, the group came upon a small clearing. Elo called for a break, giving people time to stretch and take a piss if need be. Adan sat on a downed tree trunk. Then he dug a ration bar labeled Midday Meal from his pack and tore the wrapper open. It tasted faintly of ridge fowl stew. As he chewed, he noticed Rune, Elo, and Asta standing to the side of the clearing, quietly talking with one another.

Then Bo came up and sat next to Adan. "What do you think they're talking about?"

"I don't know. Probably me."

"Can you listen in?"

Could he? "Besi," Adan subvocalized, "can you let me hear what those three are saying?"

"Yes," Besi replied. After a moment, he heard Rune's voice as if he was right next to him.

"–did I tell you about his abilities?"

"You were right to take the risk," Elo replied. "Even from the little I saw, it's clear that Testa has full command of the battle unit."

"What do you think it means?" Asta asked.

"I don't know," Elo admitted. "But Kitola probably will."

Who was Kitola? Were they the Old Tech expert Rune had mentioned? Hopefully, they wouldn't be as bad as that Defense Force doctor had been.

"They're definitely talking about me," Adan confirmed.

"Anything we need to worry about?"

"Not yet. But, if there is anything, I suspect we'll find out about it soon enough."

Official Log of Colony Administrator Marta Kanerva

Sanyal, 17 December, Year 6 (Neskan Calendar)

A few months ago, I asked Jun and his team to prepare a long-term plan for our failing equipment. Our supply of replacement processors and mem-stores from the Jennix is dwindling fast, especially since we can no longer print them. And the working equipment is being used far beyond its intended capacity. It's all breaking down faster than it should. Jun confessed to me privately that the reliable alternatives they're developing will be a significant step backward in technology. Think shielded copper wire. After all, there's copper in abundance in the Neskan crust, along with countless other metals and minerals. As for the mem-stores, our primary alternative would be magnetic drives. Obviously, that presents an unacceptable risk with Neska's temperamental magnetic field. So, Jun suggested that we start making paper.

Chapter 19

After another hour of walking, the group finally arrived at the Motari staging point. The Motari operatives had hidden it well. Elo led the group past a dark green canvas tent nestled among the trees to the truck parked next to it. They'd camouflaged that, too, with loose branches stacked around and on top of it.

Elo asked the squad to help Asta clear the branches from the truck then invited Adan into the tent. The light coming through the open flap did little to brighten the tent's interior. Then Elo turned on a lantern hanging from the tent's peak. The light revealed a pair of cots and several small crates. Elo went to one of the crates, lifted the top off, and reached inside. He pulled out a small white device and held it up for Adan to see.

"Do you know what this is?"

Adan immediately recognized it from the Old Tech Museum collection. The only difference was that Elo's looked brand new, with a bright red cross printed on one side.

"It's a Diagnostic Field Scanner," Adan replied.

Elo nodded. "You recognize it?"

"The Union has one, too."

Elo held it out to Adan. "Can you make it work?"

Adan took it and looked it over.

"It is inoperative," Besi volunteered. "It needs to be charged."

Adan shook his head. "No. There's no charge."

"Can you charge it?"

Assuming it was like his weapons and armor, Adan thought he could. "Yes. It needs to sit in the sun."

Elo raised a curious eyebrow. "Sunlight charges it?"

"Yes."

Elo nodded. "Alright. Hang on to it for now, and we can charge it up back at the outpost." Then he turned to replace the lid on the crate.

"Is there any other Old Tech in here?" Adan subvocalized.

"I do not detect any. But if it were inactive or shielded, I would not."

So, maybe there was some. But certainly, nothing that Adan could activate without charging it.

Asta poked her head through the tent flap. "We're ready out here."

Elo nodded. "Alright, let's get going."

The truck was similar to the one they'd taken from the DFTC, but there were no Union or Defense Force markings on it. Elo, Asta, and Rune all rode up in the cab while the rest of them climbed into the back. The covered back end had long benches for seating running along each side. So, Bo and Jenra took one side while Adan and Garun took the

347

other. They had about an hour's drive ahead of them, Asta had shared. She also warned them to hang on in the back since it would get bumpy sometimes.

As soon as they started driving, Garun stretched out on the bench and closed his eyes. Adan felt the temptation. But, as tired as he was, the desire for sleep wasn't there. So, he got up and carefully made his way to the open back, sitting on the truck bed so that he could look out behind them. There were still at least a couple hours of daylight left, and they were traveling west, which might buy them a little more. But the light was weak in the wooded valley, making it harder to see.

After a few minutes, Adan felt someone moving up behind him. It was Jenra, who sat next to him on the truck bed. "Mind if I join you, Citizen Moody."

Adan snorted and shook his head. "Don't start with that. Bo's asleep?"

"Yes. I don't know how those two can sleep in this thing."

"Bo can sleep anywhere. It's a gift of his."

Jenra quietly laughed. "That's good to know."

Adan smiled. "I know pretty much all of his secrets, so if there's anything you want to know, now's a good time to ask."

Jenra snorted. "As tempting as that sounds, I'll let him keep his secrets until he wants to share them."

Adan shrugged. "Suit yourself."

"You trust him and care about him. That's good enough for me."

Adan smiled, then looked back when Garun loudly snorted. "I don't know if it should be. Recent evidence suggests that I'm not a good judge of character."

Jenra smiled. "Do you like him?"

"It's complicated."

Jenra nodded. "That's fair, given everything that's happened. But, if I met him today, I'd never guess he was anything like the way he was back at the beginning."

Adan nodded, then turned back to look at her. "Me neither. That's what makes it complicated. I like him as he is now. But I remember how he was."

"There's no reason you need to forget it. And if it keeps you two from growing any closer, that's perfectly okay. But we've all got some darkness within us, Adan. Don't forget that, either."

Adan nodded. He knew what she meant. From the moment he'd put on the armor, he'd become someone he never knew he could be. A killer. He knew it was justified. He did it because he had to. Adan would still be strapped to a bed being experimented on in that secret underground facility without the armor and the Old Tech weapons. If he was even still alive. But all the valid reasons and excuses didn't change that one simple fact. He'd killed people.

"I know," Adan finally said. "I've been thinking about that a lot lately."

Jenra looked at him with concern. "I'm not singling you out, here. If I were in your position, I have no doubt that I would've done the same things you have. Honestly, I might not have shown as much restraint as you do." Adan looked at her in shock. "It's true," she confirmed. "You only resort to firing your weapon when there's no other option. I've seen you do that multiple times. So you're probably not the monster you think you are."

Adan was caught off guard by her last statement. "How can you say that? How many people have you killed?"

"Not as many as you," Jenra acknowledged. "But I watched you offer Delan and even Rico a chance to walk away. I wouldn't have done that. That's what I mean. You also rescued me, Bo, and Garun, too, when you didn't have to."

"But I did have to."

Jenra shook her head. "No, you didn't. You wanted to. You had to escape, but the rest was your choice."

That was a good point. Rune had no plans to help anyone escape except for Adan. It was Adan's idea to go for Bo and Jenra. He could even claim that all of the violence he'd committed, starting with the escape, had been things he was forced to do by others. Thinking that way would free him from any guilt or responsibility. But it would also mean he had no choice, and he didn't like how that felt. Adan had chosen to do those things, even if the only other choice was to tell Rune no and stay behind. But Jenra was right, too. If Adan hadn't left Rico alive, Rico wouldn't have come after them. And Delan might still be alive. Until Pavola found out about what she did. It was all so confusing.

In the end, it still came down to his choices. Adan knew he made the best ones he could at the time. And he had to live with the results. Going back and examining every time he'd fired his weapon didn't help. Adan just had to keep making the best choices he could and then live with the consequences.

Jenra chuckled. "That looks like it hurts."

Adan blinked back into focus and shook his head. He hadn't realized he wasn't paying attention. "Sorry. I guess I just had my own mini flux storm there."

Jenra laughed. "No worries. We're all out of our element these days."

Adan smiled. "Thanks."

"Speaking of flux storms, that reminds me. We're pretty far away from any storm shelters, so I asked Asta about that. As in, what do we do if a flux storm hits? It turns out that the Union has been inflating the danger of flux storms, at least when it comes to people. According to Asta, in the five centuries people have lived on Neska, there's only been one incident where a magnetic field flux was strong enough to harm someone."

Adan's jaw dropped in surprise. "Are you serious?"

Jenra nodded. "That's what she said, at least. Asta also told me that the Union has even faked flux alerts before so that they can do secret things out in the open."

Of course, they did. It totally made sense that the Union would do something like that. "While everyone is locked in the shelters?" Jenra nodded. "What sort of things?"

Jenra shrugged. "I didn't ask. But I think we've seen enough to know that it's probably true."

Adan sighed. Just when he thought he couldn't be any more disappointed with the Union, they surprised him.

As the two of them talked, the truck climbed steadily upward, winding its way around a narrow switchback. Adan watched the forested valley disappear below them as they went along and felt the temperature drop right along with it.

Adan soon started to shiver and see his own breath. "Founder's mercy, I'm freezing."

"Me, too," Jenra agreed. "Let's get the sleeping bags out."

Adan nodded, then got up and went for his pack. He pulled the sleeping bag out, unrolled it, then unzipped it to open it up wide. Adan looked down at Garun, who shivered while he was asleep. Adan sighed. Then he reached down and lifted Garun by his shoulders. Garun briefly stirred while Adan wrapped half of the sleeping bag around him. Then Adan sat down beside Garun, wrapped himself in the other half, and let Garun rest his head on his shoulder.

When Adan looked over at Jenra, he saw that she'd done the same thing with Bo but had closed her eyes as well. He smiled. Adan enjoyed seeing the two of them together. He hadn't always liked the people Bo had shown interest in. The ones he'd met, at least. So it was nice that he didn't have to fake it with Jenra. Adan was already friends with her on his own.

He looked down at Garun resting on his shoulder. Adan couldn't deny that it felt good to have him there. And Jenra had made some good points about the darkness in people. He'd seen that darkness in Garun, but he'd seen it even more so in himself, too. That made Adan feel better about letting go of what happened between him and Garun. And maybe about seeing where things might go between them, too. Depending on how everything went with the Motari, of course. And whatever happened after that, which was something that Adan hadn't spent any time thinking about. It was all happening so fast. After a life of the same routines–one after another, day after day–his life had become nothing but constant change.

It was better just to appreciate the moment, Adan decided. He reached up and ran his fingers through Garun's thick, black hair, and Garun stirred, nestling himself deeper into Adan's shoulder. Then Adan felt a yawn coming on, and–

A bump woke Adan up. He didn't even realize he'd fallen asleep. He looked out the back to see that they'd descended the other side of the mountain pass and were traveling through rolling hills covered in long grass. Adan could see the end of the switchback road behind them, though, so he couldn't have been asleep that long. Twenty minutes, maybe.

Adan glanced at the other side of the truck and saw that Bo and Jenra had switched places, with her asleep leaning on him.

Bo smiled at him. "That bump woke you, too?"

Adan nodded and yawned. "I can't believe I fell asleep at all." He pulled the sleeping bag off himself, carefully slipped out from under Garun, and stood up to stretch. Another bump nearly knocked him over before he grabbed onto the metal frame holding up the canvas cover.

Bo laughed. "As graceful as ever."

Adan huffed but ignored the jab. "Besi," he subvocalized, "how long have we been traveling? How close are we to the outpost?"

"You have been traveling for just over fifty-eight minutes. I am picking up localized EM activity and wireless transmissions that suggest you are about to arrive at your destination.

"We're almost there," Adan informed Bo. "Maybe we should wake the others?"

Bo nodded, then softly prodded Jenra to wake her. Adan knelt next to Garun and gently shook his shoulder. "Look alive, sleepy. We're nearly there."

Garun smiled but didn't open his eyes. "Are you sure? Because I really liked using your shoulder for a pillow."

Adan smiled and shook his head. "I'm sure. Based on the past couple of days, I figure you'll want to be awake and alert in case everything goes to hell."

Garun frowned and opened one of his eyes. "Yeah, you're probably right." Then he yawned and stretched before pushing himself up to a sitting position. "What does your machine friend think will happen?"

Adan furrowed his brows in frustration. Why hadn't he thought to ask Besi that? "I don't know. Besi, what can you tell us about the outpost? What should we expect?"

"Based on my sensor readings," Besi answered aloud for everyone to hear, "I estimate at least fifty persons present at the outpost. EM and wireless readings suggest a communications hub for additional personnel. At least one section of the outpost is using EM shielding that I cannot penetrate at this distance."

"Is that Old Tech?" Garun asked.

"That is unlikely. It is passive shielding, possibly physical in nature. I suspect a simple Faraday shield."

Adan recalled hearing that term in one of his DFTC lessons but couldn't think of how it worked. He looked at Garun, who shook his head. "I don't know what we're walking into, Besi. What's your recommendation?"

"Context suggests that this group bringing you to the outpost will protect you from Union Defense Force attacks. Context also suggests that your value to this group is based entirely on your ability to interact with Colony tech. My recommended strategy is to limit the amount of information you share until they have earned your trust."

Adan smiled. "So I should keep my counters close," he said, referencing the old Tik-Tix saying.

Garun nodded. "I agree."

"So do I," Bo added. "You're only here because that computer will talk to you. And we're only here because you asked us to be. We should play it slow and controlled."

"He's right," Jenra agreed. "I trust my brother, but he tends to put the needs of the underground over his own. The others have to be like that, too."

Adan nodded. No matter what happened, he was the only one of them protected by the armor. But that also meant the Motari's attention would mostly be on him. "Alright. I assume they'll separate us when we get there, so let's use that as best we can. Jenra, find out what you can from Rune about their organization. How many of them are there? Where are the other outposts?"

Jenra nodded. "Will do."

"Bo, Garun, see what you can learn about the outpost layout? If we need to get out quick, what are their weak points?"

Bo smiled and nodded. "Founder's mercy, Adan. You're turning ruthless."

Garun chuckled. "Yeah. Is it bad that I kind of like that?"

Adan grinned. "I've been locked up three different times in the last month. I'm not letting that happen again if I can help it."

Then the truck slowly came to a stop. Adan held tight to the metal frame until they were stationary. After a moment, the truck moved forward again, rolling at barely more than a crawl. Adan looked out the back end and saw them pass through a low, metal gate that two people were swinging closed. Once they pulled at least a truck length from the gate, they stopped again. Adan heard one of the truck doors open. Then, after a few moments, Rune walked into view at the back of the truck.

"We made it," Rune said with a smile. "I hope the ride wasn't too bad."

Adan smiled back, pushing down the intense feelings of suspicion he'd built up while discussing their plan. "No, but you could've warned us about the cold."

Rune rubbed his head sheepishly. "Sorry, I forgot about that. But I'm glad to see you made it work. Why don't you all jump out so we can bring you to the outpost commander? I'll have someone pack up your stuff and bring it to your tent."

"Tent?" Garun asked with a frown.

"It'll be fine," Rune assured him. "You'll see. Now, come on." Rune unlatched the gate at the rear of the truck bed, opened it, and stepped back.

Adan helped Garun stand up before he walked toward Rune. Then Adan jumped off the back of the truck onto the hard-packed ground and stepped away from the truck. His first look at the Motari outpost wasn't very awe-inspiring. Adan could see a pair of large, sandy-brown tents set up on either side of the entrance. They definitely weren't the tiny tents he and the others had slept in the night before. These were the size of small buildings.

Adan walked around to the side of the truck and saw Asta standing outside the cab, talking with someone he didn't know. The dirt road the truck was parked on extended out past a small, central square with more tent buildings set up along its sides. They were in a tent city. Power lines ran alongside the road and into each tent. Electric lights set on posts outside some tents were just starting to come on, although it wasn't quite dark enough to need them.

But the view beyond the outpost was wondrous. Adan saw a western sky ablaze with low clouds painted in rose, orange, and crimson hues. Even with the rolling hills surrounding them, the horizon seemed impossibly flat. Adan had never seen the sun so low before. He was used to the tall mountains that surrounded the Valley hiding the sunset's last hour from view.

Bo walked up beside him to see what he was looking at. "Founder's grace. That's amazing." Then he looked around at the tent city. "But this place is hardly Bolvar, is it?"

"As long as there aren't any Pinchers sneaking around," Garun added as he joined them, "it's an improvement."

Adan glanced over his shoulder and saw Jenra talking with her brother. When he turned back to Asta, Adan saw her walking toward him. The person she'd been talking to was gone.

"Welcome to Samu Outpost," she said with a smile. "I know it's a lot different than you're used to, but it's more comfortable than it looks."

Adan smiled back at her. "Are all the sunsets like that?"

Asta turned to look west as if she needed to remind herself what it looked like. "That's not bad," she claimed as she looked back at Adan. "You should see one after a thunderstorm. Those are impressive."

"But we didn't come here to enjoy the view," Adan noted.

"No," Asta agreed. "If you wouldn't mind coming with me, Adan, I'll take you to the person who runs things around here. Garun and Bo, you should go with Rune, and he'll take you to your tent. I promise I'll have Adan back to you in time for dinner."

"There's dinner?" Garun exclaimed.

Bo chuckled. "Come on, Garun, before they realize that you're a marsh pig in disguise."

"Okay, fine." Garun leaned forward and kissed Adan on the cheek. "Be careful," he whispered.

Adan smiled and nodded, then stepped forward to follow Asta as she walked down the dirt road.

"Garun seems nice," Asta commented.

"He seems that way, doesn't he?" Asta flashed a concerned look at Adan. "Sorry," he quickly added, "that was just a bad joke. It's been a rough few days."

Asta nodded. "I understand. I grew up in the Union, too. I probably wasn't much older than you when I left."

Adan didn't know how old she was, but he guessed she was probably in her mid-twenties. That meant she'd been living outside the wall for years. "Why did you do it? Leave, I mean."

"I never meant to. I was looking forward to serving my five and then continuing in the Defense Force after that. I wanted to protect the resource scouts and engineers from all those horrible raider attacks." She gave him a quick wink to show she was kidding, then her expression turned hard. "But my brother got caught up in a Clubber raid on a tea house. They said it was a known Motari sympathizer hangout, even though my brother was the farthest thing from that. But he tried to run, and they shot him." She paused for a few moments as they crossed over the open square, which was little more than an intersection. Adan could easily imagine her brother's situation. He'd seen Clubbers and Pinchers in action, so he knew what it was like.

"And then you decided to switch sides?"

Asta nodded. "I was furious. First, that they'd shot him. Then, that they'd convicted him of treason anyway. That meant my father lost his Bureau assignment and got sent to work the marsh pig pens." Adan raised a confused eyebrow, and she shook her head. "Don't get me wrong. All work is worthy," she added, quoting the Union saying, "but he was old, and the work was too much for someone in his condition."

Adan noticed that she said "was" and thought of Jurda back in the laundry plant. Jurda claimed to enjoy the work, but Adan wondered if he'd been sent there for a similar reason. "I'm sorry to hear that."

"The Union provides, right? But that was years ago, and I've happily served here this whole time instead." She stopped in front of a tent with a sign that said Commander on it. "This is it. Come on, Asona is great. You'll like her."

She reached out and grabbed the flap, pulling it open for Adan to step through. The inside of the tent felt even more like a small building. It had a wood plank floor with a threadbare rug on it. There was a desk with a lamp and stacks of papers on it and some cabinets and chairs nearby. A canvas sheet hung from the ceiling to block off the back half.

Someone sat at the desk with a piece of paper in one hand and a steaming mug in the other. They looked older than Asta in the lamplight, maybe in their late thirties or early forties, if the streaks of gray in their shoulder-length black hair were any indication. They had a warm, friendly, russet face and well-shaped brows sitting over deep-set, brown eyes.

"Commander Asona," Asta said as she stepped in behind him. "I've brought someone to meet you."

The person at the desk looked up with a curious expression, then set the paper down and smiled. "Of course. I was so focused on this report I didn't notice you. Please, come in and sit." They put their mug down, then stood and walked around the desk. "I'm Asona Belasco, the leader of this little outpost. But you can call me Asona. Or, if you prefer, Commander Belasco. She and her pronouns, either way."

Adan wasn't sure what that meant. "If I prefer?"

Asona smiled. "Sometimes people fresh over the wall need some time to adjust to our less formal way of doing things. Giving me a title makes them feel more comfortable."

Adan nodded. "Ah, okay. I'm Adan Testa. He and him, but no title."

Asona laughed politely. "No, but you have a reputation, don't you? Some of the folks here have started calling you the Old Tech Master."

"People here are talking about me?"

Asona laughed again, and Adan wasn't sure if it was with him or at him. "Once we received word from Rune about you, you're all people have been talking about."

Adan didn't know what to say about that. "Oh. Well, thank you?"

"You're certainly a charming one. I'll give you that." Asona moved to sit on the edge of her desk, reminding Adan of Commander Sala on his first day in the DFTC. "We'll hopefully have plenty of time to work with you on this, but I'd be grateful if you'd indulge me with a little demonstration. You're wearing the artifact we sent you, I assume."

So much for keeping his counters close. She was asking him to play his best ones first thing. But it was why they'd risked so much to get him out of Bolvar, he reasoned.

"Alright," Adan agreed. He took off his jacket and sweater and set them on a nearby chair. "Besi," he subvocalized, "activate the armor."

The bands of black material quickly unfolded from the harness and belt until they completely covered him. Asona couldn't hide her obvious shock at what she saw. As he looked at her through the visor of his helmet, Adan noticed the spot Besi highlighted on her waist where she wore a handgun hidden under a long jacket.

"That's astounding," Asona quietly murmured. "Absolutely astounding."

Adan watched her look him over and spot the handgun at his waist. He glanced over his shoulder at Asta, who was openly amazed.

"All the time we studied that artifact," Asona finally added, "and we could only guess what it really was. I'm glad we were right. You can take it off, or deactivate it, now. I don't think we're quite ready for everyone here to see you like that."

"If you wish," Adan said. "Besi," he subvocalized, "deactivate." First the helmet, then the armor bands collapsed into themselves until they disappeared back into his harness and belt.

"Astounding," Asona repeated. "I'm delighted to have you here, Adan. Very glad. If you're willing, I'd like you to meet with our lead Old Tech researcher tomorrow. I'm sure she'll have a million questions for you. But that's for tomorrow. Tonight, we'll let you get some food and rest." She stood and reached out, offering her hand. "Welcome to Samu Outpost, Adan Testa."

Private Log of Colony Administrator Clarinda Osoria

Sanyal, 33 December, Year 10 (Neskan Calendar)

This is a thankless job. Every time we get on top of a problem, another one surfaces to take its place. I can see why it drove Marta to early retirement. But we're so close to creating a stable system. I can feel it. Food production and population numbers are good. But the sudden shift from a highly advanced, space-faring society to a planet-bound, agrarian one has challenged even the best of us.

Sander wants to mount another search for the missing lander. He always thought that Captain Sanyal gave up on that too soon. He's probably right, in hindsight. But, at the time, it just didn't seem necessary. Sander's convinced that the clues he needs are in orbit. If he can get the uplink in the Broken Valley lander working, Sander claims he might have a shot at tracking down the one that's still lost. I doubt that's true. Captain Sanyal wouldn't have overlooked anything. But the idea of finding it is too tempting to ignore. And we may have missed some usable parts or resources in Broken Valley, anyway.

Chapter 20

Asta led Adan from the Commander's tent into the rapidly cooling nighttime air. She didn't comment on Adan's meeting with Asona or her obvious reaction to seeing Adan in the Old Tech armor. Instead, Asta described the outpost facilities and services as she led Adan to his assigned barracks tent. Adan would've noticed her omission more if he'd bothered paying attention to what she was saying. The meeting with Asona had completely set Adan on edge. He couldn't point to any specific reason for it. Or, at least, not any single reason. But it surprised him that Asona was armed. Even Commander Sala walked around the DFTC unarmed. What were things like here that someone sitting in their tent reading reports needed a sidearm? The Commander had been unfailingly polite, even friendly. And then he'd shown her the armor. The way she looked at Adan as if he was a shiny new toy made him very uneasy.

The result of their meeting was that Adan didn't trust

the outpost Commander. Of course, Adan could've been projecting his own insecurity onto her. Just because so many of the people he'd recently met ended up double-crossing him didn't mean that she would, too. But Adan resolved to keep his guard up for a while anyway. What was it that Captain Sanyal liked to say? Expect the best, but plan for the worst.

After their walk through the outpost, Asta left Adan at the entrance to his barracks tent and wished him a good night. The tent was building-sized like all the others. Adan stepped through the entrance flap as Asta walked away and saw the rest of the squad waiting inside. The space looked the same as Asona's, down to the wood plank floor and hanging canvas partition in the rear. But it was set up like a mini barracks room, with four beds, two on each side, facing the center. Each bed had a footlocker next to it. A small lamp hung from the tallest point in the center casting warm, yellow light on the space. A narrow table stood at the far end with a large ceramic bowl, a glass pitcher full of water, and several glasses on top.

Garun, Jenra, and Bo all jumped from their seats on the beds as soon as Adan came in. After assuring them that he was okay, Adan explained what happened in the Commander's tent. But he kept his reservations about the meeting and the Commander to himself. Everyone was already on edge as it was. There was no need to worry them any more than they already were.

When Adan finished his update, Jenra asked if he wanted to wash off and shared that their tent had a small shower rigged up on the other side of the flap. Adan noticed that everyone was clean except for him and considered a shower, but his hunger won out. He felt like he'd already burned through the pair of ration bars he'd eaten earlier. But Adan promised to shower off before he went to sleep.

So the squad went out to track down the mess tent. It was several times bigger than the Commander's tent and easy to find. Adan thought it was the largest one he'd seen so far in the outpost. The Motari had set up a dozen tables inside with benches for seating on each side of them. Someone had arranged a small buffet on another table set off to one side of the tent. Adan grabbed a bowl of savory-smelling ridge fowl and noodles, a pair of dark bread rolls, and a mug of dark amber liquid that smelled like beer. He took it to an empty table and was halfway through eating before the others even sat down.

"Slow down, there," Bo suggested as he sat down. "You look like a prowler loose in the marsh pig pens."

"Can't talk," Adan replied between mouthfuls. "Too busy eating."

Bo and the others chuckled as they started on their own meals. Adan took a break from his noodles to tear off a chunk of bread and stuff it in his mouth. He washed it down with the beer, which was light and refreshing despite being so dark. Then Adan noticed the others had stopped eating.

"What's going on?" Adan asked.

"Everyone's looking at us," Jenra explained.

"No, everyone's looking at Adan," Garun corrected her.

Adan glanced around the tent. Some of the tables were occupied with diners, maybe a dozen people in total. And they were all looking right at him. "Speaking of prowlers loose in the marsh pig pens."

Then Rune walked into the tent. "Founder's mercy, everybody. Are you trying to make the new kids feel like outcasts? Finish your meals and give them some space." Several diners mumbled that they were sorry as they all turned away. Rune nodded then joined the group at their table. "Sorry about them. We don't get a lot of newcomers. Especially not Old Tech Masters."

Adan huffed, then took another spoonful of stew. "I guess it's fine," he said after he swallowed. "It's not like I'll be sticking around here for very long."

Rune seemed surprised by that. "Really? And where do you plan on going?"

Adan looked over at Bo. "I don't know. West, I guess? Port Abarra."

Bo nodded. "That's right. That was our plan all along."

Rune didn't seem convinced. "I see. Well, I came to let you know that Dr. Davi Kitola would like to meet with you tomorrow if you're willing. She's our lead Old Tech researcher. Our former Old Tech Master, I guess."

Adan narrowed his eyes suspiciously. "If I'm willing?"

Rune chuckled. "I don't think anyone's planning on drugging you and strapping you to a table."

"That would be an improvement if it's true. Alright, I'll meet with your researcher on one condition. You seriously need to stop calling me the Old Tech Master."

Rune chuckled again. "Deal."

"Are you sure about that?" Garun asked. "I think it gives you a nice sense of mystery and authority."

Adan smiled. "Okay, Garun can still call me that. But no one else."

Rune shook his head and chuckled as he got up to leave. "Alright, then. I'll come find you in the morning, Adan.

Everyone have a good night."

After Rune left, the rest of the group reported what they'd learned about the camp to Adan. Adan pretended to pay attention to them, nodding during the pauses and occasionally grunting. But his mind was stuck on what he'd said to Rune. Specifically about what he planned on doing next. Adan and Bo had always planned on going to Port Abarra once they escaped from the Bolvar Union. Now that they'd actually gone over the wall, the main hole in their original plan was obvious. The pair had never figured out exactly how they would cross Ateri, including the vast Adak Desert that spread across the middle of the continent. But Adan figured that there had to be a way. Did anyone regularly cross between the grasslands of the Tepani Plains and Port Abarra? If so, maybe they could help.

Surprisingly, that wasn't the part that bothered Adan the most. It was the Old Tech armor. What would happen to the armor if he left? Would Adan have to give it back to the Motari? Did he even want to keep it? Adan's ability to use it had saved his life multiple times. And, even though Besi wasn't a real, thinking person, Adan liked having access to the machine brain. But his ability to use the Old Tech was also what put him in that danger in the first place. It was a problem that would take some thought. But Adan didn't have to decide anything right then. First, he needed a shower and some sleep in a bed.

Once the squad finished eating, they walked back to the barracks tent. Adan checked out the facilities then took a quick shower. Bo warned him that the hot water wouldn't last. But Adan managed to finish his final rinse off before the water got too cold. Then he changed into his clean shirt, undershorts, and socks. By the time Adan walked back into the main part of the tent, the rest of the group had pushed the beds together to make two from the original four.

"Rune told us the tents can get cold at night," Jenra explained as she climbed into one of the beds with Bo.

"And doubling up worked so well last night," Bo added.

Adan laughed, "Sounds like a good plan to me." He draped his damp towel on the rail at the foot of the other bed and noticed Garun watching him from under the covers. "What?"

"Just enjoying the view," Garun admitted with a grin.

Adan rolled his eyes and climbed into his side of the bed. "Damn," he swore as he slid between the freezing sheets. Then he slid closer to Garun to take advantage of the warmth. Garun rolled onto his side and pulled Adan close to him, cuddling him tightly.

"Are you alright?" Garun quietly asked, lifting his head from the pillow.

"What do you mean?"

"I mean, things are weird here, right? We've all noticed it. This outpost feels like it's been here for a long time. There's power and running water in every tent. So, what happens when the Defense Force spots them, and they have to fight back or pack up and move?"

Adan hadn't considered that. "I don't know."

Garun snorted. "I wasn't asking you that. It was a rhetorical question. But you seemed a little shaken and distracted after meeting with the outpost Commander. So I'm asking if you're alright."

Adan didn't think his anxiety about the situation was that obvious. But it sounded like Garun had really been paying attention to him, even if he guessed wrong about what was bothering Adan. That was another point for the "stay with Garun" column.

"I think I'm alright," Adan finally admitted. "It's been a long day, and I just need some sleep."

"Do you want me to give you some space?"

Another point for Garun. "No. I want you right where you are."

Garun laid his head back down on the pillow then gave Adan a gentle squeeze. Adan's racing thoughts suddenly slowed to a crawl as a day full of hiking, climbing, and running had finally caught up with him. He was asleep by his third breath.

"Adan Testa."

His eyes shot open, but there was nothing to see. Garun had rolled back over at some point and was facing the other way, quietly snoring. It was still too dark, and the camp was too quiet for it to be morning yet.

"Adan Testa." It was Besi speaking to him.

"Why did you wake me?" Adan whispered. He didn't know if subvocalizing would work when he wasn't wearing the harness.

"I detect movement from at least two armed individuals beyond the outpost boundaries. Their trajectories indicate they are approaching this location from the west."

Was the outpost about to be under attack? Or was Besi being overly cautious about Motari scouts on patrol. "What does this have to do with me?"

"Their profiles suggest that they are Union Defense Force soldiers."

Gray Coats at the outpost already? Had they followed him there? No. If that were the case, the Union would've sent a lot more than just two soldiers. More than two squads, even. Something about the situation was off. "What are my options?"

"You could alert someone from the camp. Or, you could suit up and go investigate it yourself."

Unfortunately, neither of those options was falling back asleep and pretending nothing happened. Not that Adan would be able to fall asleep knowing that his hunters were out there stalking him at that very moment. Adan sighed, then carefully rolled out from under the covers and off the bed. He didn't want to bother getting dressed, so he slipped the belt and harness over his shirt and undershorts. Once he gave Besi the command to activate, the armor bands rapidly extended until they covered his whole body. Adan finished by attaching his Old Tech weapons to his back and waist.

"Give me control," Besi instructed him. "I will assure you that you remain undetected."

"Alright, take control," Adan responded. He felt the armor flex, then it moved him out of the tent onto the road. Adan didn't spot anyone nearby, but Besi still moved him around to the back of the tent quickly and quietly. The motions felt weird. "Why are you moving me like that?"

"My programming allows me to reduce your sound profile. It will help you avoid being heard by anyone who may be nearby."

Adan thought that was an overly technical way to say tiptoeing because that's what his maneuvers felt like. That, or dancing.

Besi snuck him over to the back of the neighboring tent. Then something changed with his vision. The dim, grayish appearance of his enhanced night vision suddenly took on strange colors. They were in the shapes of people, he realized. "What am I seeing?"

"I have enabled filtered infrared detection. That allows you to see past your normal visual spectrum. The colors represent heat, from red to yellow. Yellow is the hottest."

So Adan could see people asleep in their tents. But not everyone that he saw was asleep. Some people moved around, and some weren't in their tents at all. As Besi took him closer to the edge of the camp, Adan spotted a pair of red-orange silhouettes standing near the main gate to his left. They must've been guarding the gate. Another pair walked away from him along the tall, corrugated metal fence to his right. They must've been patrolling.

The whole outpost had felt like a military encampment. Even though nobody wore uniforms and the Commander went by her first name instead of her rank, Adan still felt like he was back at the DFTC. It seemed the Motari were trying very hard to pretend they weren't something they really were.

"In a moment, I am going to move you very fast," Besi informed him. "Do not be alarmed."

Before Adan could even respond, he felt himself leap forward into a fast sprint. He was heading directly toward the metal wall and had to fight against his urge to throw his arms up and shield himself. Then Adan did throw his arms up, right before he leaped off the ground. He felt his hands grab the top of the wall with inhuman precision, pull himself into the air, and flip over the top. Adan continued through his flip until he landed feet-first, then ducked into a forward roll into the tall grass beyond the fence. Adan never would've imagined climbing over the wall that way, but it was faster and quieter than he could've done under his own power. It

371

also made him a little sick to his stomach.

"The intruders are ahead and to your right. They have stopped 100 meters from the fenceline."

Adan looked to his right and saw the reddish blobs of two Gray Coats crouching like he was. Or, at least, he assumed they were Gray Coats. He couldn't make out enough detail to be sure. "Can we get closer?"

"Yes." He felt himself begin to move, then suddenly stop. "Stand by. I have detected movement near the fence. Two individuals armed with rifles are patrolling outside the camp."

Damn it. "We have to warn them!"

"Doing so would alert the intruders to your presence. That would be counterproductive if they were here to secure you. It could also put the patrol into greater danger."

Adan huffed. Then he reminded himself to listen to Besi. He had no mind for battle tactics. "Alright."

"But we should move closer."

Adan felt himself creep to the right, crawling on his hands and feet like he imagined a real prowler would move. Even he could barely hear himself. He was pointed slightly up the incline where the Gray Coats were waiting. Then he stopped again.

"One of the outpost patrollers has broken off and is walking toward the intruders."

"What? We need to warn them now."

"No. They are walking directly toward the intruders. They must know the intruders are there."

Adan felt a knot forming in the pit of his stomach. The Gray Coats had someone on the inside–probably more than one someone. And then, suddenly, the camp's existence made sense. They'd been able to avoid a Union attack because the

Gray Coats had deliberately avoided attacking them. Instead, they must've been using the outpost to gather information on the Motari. But how did the Motari not realize that? So, not everything made sense yet. There was still a missing piece to the puzzle.

"Can we get closer?"

"I can amplify any dialogue they may have."

"I know. I want to be close enough to take action if I need to."

"Affirmative."

Adan felt himself move again, slinking along through the tall grass like a silent predator. As he got closer, he could make out more detail. But the colors were getting in the way. "Can you deactivate the colors? I can't see any details."

"The ambient light at this location is not enough for a clear enhanced view. It will be grainy."

Adan didn't know what that meant, but he didn't care. "That's fine."

The colors dropped away, and Adan was left with a fuzzy, grayish picture. Then he realized what grainy meant, like a poor quality photograph. Adan watched as both of the Gray Coats stood up. One of them had some kind of visor over their eyes. It looked like binoculars. "What are they wearing?"

"That appears to be a crude infrared device."

Adan suddenly panicked. Could they see him, blazing red-orange in a field of black? "Am I–"

"You are safe. The suit stores your waste heat while in stealth mode, making you appear to be the same temperature as your surroundings. That is why you feel warm even though you are not fully dressed."

Adan sighed with relief. There was still so much about Besi and the armor he didn't even know.

Besi brought Adan to a stop about ten meters from the Gray Coats. And he could see that was definitely who they were. Both of them were wearing the mountain standard battle dress he'd seen in one of his lessons at the DFTC.

Adan turned his head to look at the Motari casually approaching them. They had no apprehension at all. It had to be a scheduled meeting. As the Motari got closer, Adan could make out the details of their face. Then he recognized them. It was Elo. Founder's mercy!

"I need to hear them, Besi."

"I will amplify their audio and record it."

"You can do that?"

"Yes."

Adan watched as Elo walked right up to the two Gray Coats. The one wearing the infrared device removed it. Then they reached out and offered Elo their hand. Elo shook it.

"You're late," said the Gray Coat in a low voice.

"It was just a complication with the guard rotation. Security has been tightened now that the asset is in place."

"Then your assignment was a success?"

"Nearly not," Elo complained, sounding frustrated. "That other patrol practically stumbled on us. But we were able to avoid them."

"You knew that was always a possibility. The regular forces have been ordered to capture Testa on sight."

Regular forces? Were these not actual Gray Coats? Or was one part of the Defense Force acting against the rest?

"Well, as I said, we were able to avoid them."

"And your Commander?"

"She understands what she needs to do. As long as Sala keeps feeding us your patrol routes and keeps you off our backs, Belasco will get you what you need."

Adan's heart sank at the mention of Commander Sala. To hear that she was still a part of everything felt like a weight placed back on his shoulders. Had Sala allowed his escape? Had she even arranged for it? Did Rune know? Adan felt his breathing quicken and heard his heartbeat pounding in his ears.

"You need to calm down, Adan."

"Calm down? You heard what they said!"

"You still do not have all the facts. And you need to be calm so that you do not overload your armor's waste heat sink. If you are captured, you cannot keep yourself and your companions safe."

Keep them safe. Besi was right. They weren't safe. Or, at least, they wouldn't be if Adan flew into a rage and took out his anger on the three standing in front of him.

"–will do as she's promised," continued the Gray Coat. Then they reached into a pouch on their belt and pulled out a small, white square of paper. "Here are the upcoming patrol routes. But Commander Sala expects results. We'll return in three days for an update."

"Three days? That's hardly enough time."

"Those are my orders. And now they're yours."

Elo huffed. "Alright, I understand. Three days. I'll inform Belasco." He looked back over his shoulder at the other Motari waiting for him. "If there's nothing else, I should get back."

The Gray Coat nodded. "Until then. The Union provides."

"Yeah, yeah. All hail the damn Union."

Elo turned and walked back to where his patrol companion was waiting. The Gray Coats crouched down into the grass but remained where they were. Besi kept Adan in place, too.

"What do we do?"

"We wait."

Adan huffed. He wanted to do something–whether it was attacking the Gray Coats, attacking Elo for betraying him, or just running back into the camp screaming that Elo and Asona were traitors. Except he didn't know who else was in on it. If everyone was in on it, Adan was in for some real trouble.

"That one's extremely disrespectful," Adan heard the other Gray Coat say. "Why do you allow that behavior from them?"

"It's their way," the first one responded. "I imagine it makes him feel better about being a traitor to his cause. I don't really care. As long as he keeps following through, I'll keep letting him get away with his meaningless acts of rebellion."

"Will he get us what Sala wants?"

"I couldn't say, but I hope so. It's getting harder to keep this outpost out of the regular force's line of sight. But the Commander thinks that, as long as Testa feels safe, he'll cooperate. She might be right. But we need to stay ready. The way Testa tore through the DFTC facility was no joke. Commander Sala was impressed."

So Sala was in on the whole thing, somehow. No wonder she was nowhere to be found that night.

"And if things go sour here?"

"We'll burn the place to the ground and move on to plan B." Adan watched the Gray Coat poke their head above the grass and look around. "We're clear. We should head back to camp."

"Understood."

Then both of them stood and started walking back toward the nearby foothills. Adan wanted to follow after them and see their camp, but he knew it wouldn't help things. He needed to get back inside the outpost, wake the others, and share with them everything he'd just learned. And then they needed to figure out what to do next. Adan smiled. He already had some ideas about that.

Private Log of Colony Administrator Clarinda Osoria

Sanyal, 14 January, Year 11 (Neskan Calendar)

Sander claims his trip was a success. I'm not sure if I agree. Thankfully we both agreed on the need for secrecy beforehand. He instructed his team to tell everyone they were on a resource scouting mission. It ended up becoming one, after a fashion, since they found a working household Bio-printer, a pair of Diagnostic scanners, and a half-dozen Tablets. Most of that will go to Dr. Palo.

But Sander got the uplink working and claims to know the missing lander's location. Now he wants to mount an expedition to retrieve it. I'm not sure if that's a good idea. I need to consult with Marta before I make my decision. In the meantime, Sander will keep the location to himself since he's the only one that knows. The last thing we need is for the people of Sanyal to start making their own plans to retrieve it. No one wants us to become the next Broken Valley.

Chapter 21

The rest of the squad took the news about as well as Adan expected they would.

"No," Jenra announced. "I don't believe it."

"Believe what?" Garun countered. "We all heard the recording."

Jenra scowled. "I know, I know. I'm not talking about that. I mean, I don't believe Rune would be involved in something like this. It goes against everything he believes in."

"Against everything he claims to believe in," Adan suggested. "What if he's not being honest with us? Or with you?"

Jenra shook her head. "That just can't be true. He's been a rebel since long before he joined the Motari."

Adan struggled to keep his face and voice calm. The last thing he needed was to turn Jenra against them. "He wasn't planning to rescue you, Jenra, or anyone else. He only came for me."

"That's because we had a plan for me already," she explained, sounding frustrated.

"Yeah," Garun agreed. "A plan for you to serve under Commander Sala, who has a secret deal with the leader of a Motari outpost where–"

Adan shot Garun a pleading look, and he immediately shut up. But the damage was done. Jenra loudly huffed and turned away from the group.

"There's really only one thing we can do here," Bo suggested. "We need to ask Rune."

Jenra turned back around to face them. Her frustration was still written all over her face, but she reluctantly nodded. "Yes. We need to ask him."

"And what if he's part of all this?" Garun asked. Adan tried stopping him with a look again, but Garun waved him off. "No. I'm sorry that this is an uncomfortable subject for everyone. But, my life is on the line here, just like all of yours. Just like they've been practically every day since we left the DFTC. And I'm not sure I'm willing to bet my life on this. Are you all? I say we just leave."

No one answered him, and the tent fell into an awkward silence. Garun was partly right. Even Jenra had to see that. Adan had been lied to and double-crossed enough times in the recent past that he was no longer willing to blindly trust a person based solely on someone else's word.

But Adan wasn't sure that leaving was the right answer. He wanted to put some faith in Jenra's trust, at least enough to talk to Rune first. And Adan didn't want to just slink off into the night, knowing that the fake Motari operation was still going on behind him. Not if Sala was involved. He'd never feel safe that way.

"I agree with Bo," Adan announced. "I say we give Rune a

chance to explain. We owe Jenra that much."

Jenra nodded. "Thank you."

"If Rune turns out to be working for Sala–"

"He's not," Jenra interrupted.

"But we don't know that yet," Adan persisted. "If he is, then we can tie him up to prevent him from warning the others about our escape."

Jenra's eyes went wide with surprise. "Adan–"

"And if he's not," Adan continued, cutting her off, "then we can offer to take him with us."

Jenra threw up her arms in irritation. "Oh, sure. You say that now, but if he says he's not, how do I know you'll even believe him. Are you telling me you'll know if he's lying or not?"

Garun nodded. "She's right. Which of us can tell if he's lying or telling the truth?"

Jenra shook her head. "That's not–"

"I can tell," Besi suddenly announced to the group. "With a reasonable degree of accuracy."

Everyone fell silent and turned to Adan, who looked down at the armor disc on his chest. "What are you saying, Besi?"

"I can detect and interpret many of the involuntary physiological signs commonly associated with deception."

Garun chuckled. "Did anyone understand that?"

Jenra nodded. "It's saying the body reacts in certain ways when you lie, ways that you can't necessarily control. And Besi can detect them."

Adan was impressed, even if he'd already known Jenra was the smartest of the four of them. "Alright. So we ask him, and Besi can tell us if he's probably telling the truth or not. And, then, Jenra will decide what we do."

Everyone looked at Adan in surprise.

"What do you mean, I decide?" Jenra asked.

"I mean exactly what I said. He's your brother, so you'll tell us how you want us to handle things."

Jenra narrowed her eyes suspiciously. "Just like that?"

"Yes. We're all biased here, except maybe for Besi. But, since Rune's your family, you're the most impacted. I think you should be the one to decide."

Jenra still didn't look convinced. "And if I decide to let him go or bring him along."

Adan shrugged. "Then, that's what we'll do."

Garun frowned. "And if she's wrong, and we get hurt or killed because of it?"

"Then, that's what happens." Adan made sure his tone left no more room for arguing. "There's no guarantee that we'll survive any of this either way. And I think we all realize that."

Garun thought it over for a moment, then nodded. "Alright. Yes, I agree that Jenra should decide."

Adan looked at Bo, who also nodded. "I vote yes, too."

Then everyone looked at Jenra. She looked back at each of them in turn, landing on Adan last. She shook her head. "I hate this. All this lying and deception. I liked things better when I didn't know about any of it."

"But?" Adan prompted her.

"But, I agree with your decision. I'll make the call."

Once everyone was in agreement, things began to move swiftly. Adan suggested that their first task should be to resupply themselves. Garun volunteered to go to the mess tent and find something that would work as travel rations. Bo said he would find out where they could get some clean clothing. And Jenra and Adan would remain in the tent until Rune arrived. Adan reminded Bo and Garun to act like everything was fine. Not everyone in the outpost was necessarily involved in the lie, and those who were wouldn't be aware that they knew about it.

Once the others were gone, Adan got dressed and repacked his things. Jenra remained quiet while she did the same thing, then she sat on her bed and looked at him.

"Thank you," she told him.

Adan nodded. "It was the only way I could see to do the right thing."

"I know. That's why I trust you. You made a difficult choice benefiting someone else that inconvenienced you. It's how things are supposed to be in the Union. The people with power and privilege should be the ones making the sacrifices instead of the other way around."

"Hopefully, that's what we'll find at the end of the road."

Jenra nodded. "I hope so. But, for now, we'll have to rely on each other. And we'll have to rely on you."

Adan was surprised to hear that. "On me?"

Jenra nodded again. "Like it or not, we're all here because of you. And it's your fate that's driving things here. So, I'm going to let you decide how to ask Rune."

Adan didn't understand what she meant by that. No, that wasn't true. He just didn't want to admit that he understood what Jenra said. "Are you sure?"

She sighed, then nodded her head. "I may seem calm right now, but, Founder's mercy, I'm so upset. And I don't know what I'd end up doing."

Adan nodded. She was afraid that she might do something rash that could hurt Rune. She needed Adan to assure that didn't happen. "Alright."

"He is approaching," Besi informed him.

"Rune's on his way," Adan repeated. "Get ready."

Jenra nodded, then stood and slid her pack under her bed. Adan moved over to stand next to the entrance flap, then pulled his handgun from his waist and activated it. Jenra carefully ignored him while he did that, working hard to keep herself composed. She finally managed a weak smile. It wasn't great, and Rune would know right away that something was wrong. But it was what Adan had to work with, so he would just have to make the best of things.

"Knock knock," Rune called out from outside the tent before pulling the flap open and stepping through. "Everybody decent?" He looked at Jenra, confused. "Where is everyone? Are you okay?"

Adan stepped out of the corner with his handgun pointed at Rune and pushed the barrel into the middle of Rune's back. "Don't turn around, Rune. You know what this is, right?"

Rune stiffened but didn't turn around. "What's going on, Adan?"

"You're going to slowly walk forward and then sit on the edge of the bed to your right, facing the back of the tent. Understand?"

Rune took a deep breath, and Adan prepared himself for action. But Rune simply nodded. "Alright. I'm moving now." He slowly stepped forward, careful to keep his movements deliberate. Adan was glad that Rune had seen enough of Adan in action to not put up a fight. Adan didn't want to think about what would happen if he actually had to shoot Jenra's brother. Adan followed Rune until he reached the side of the bed, stepping back once Rune sat down. Then Adan lowered his weapon and moved to stand in front of

Rune.

"Thank you for making this easy," Adan offered.

Rune frowned. "Are you going to tell me what in the Founder's name is going on right now?"

Adan nodded. "I need you to listen to something. And then I'm going to ask you a question."

Rune nodded, then Adan asked Besi to replay the recording from outside the camp. Rune listened as requested. At first, his face was neutral, but his expression got harder as the recording played out. By the time it was finished, he was obviously furious. When it stopped, he said a single word. "No."

"What do you mean?"

"I know what you're going to ask me. You want to know if I'm part of all that or if I knew about it. I'm telling you no, I'm not."

Adan's instinct was to believe him. But he needed to hear what Besi had to say. "Besi? Is he telling the truth?"

"There is a ninety-two percent probability that he is being truthful."

Rune suddenly looked shocked. "That thing can tell if someone is lying? Balda's ass, what can't it do?"

Jenra slowly walked over and stood between Adan and Rune. Adan expected her to look happy. Or, at least, relieved. But she looked like she was feeling neither of those things. Then, to Adan's shock, she hauled off and slapped her brother across the face. "How could you be so blind?" she angrily exclaimed. "You put all our lives on the line for a lie!"

She reached back to hit him again, but Adan grabbed her arm and stopped her. "That's enough."

Jenra turned on Adan in anger, then pulled her arm free

and stormed to the back of the tent behind the canvas wall.

Rune reached up and put a hand to his reddening cheek. "She's right. I should've seen it. I thought I was saving you all. Instead, I rescued you from one trap just to deliver you into another."

Adan sighed. "That might be so. But that's all done with, now. We have to focus on what to do next."

"That's easy," Rune commented. "We have to leave."

Adan shook his head. "Is that really how you want to play this?"

Rune tilted his head in confusion. "What do you mean?"

"I mean, this outpost is a Union front. Do we just leave things as they are? We know Elo and Asona are both in on it. But, who else is? And you brought me here to help me learn more about what I can do and why I can activate and control Old Tech. Sala still wants to know the answer to that, but so do I."

Rune huffed. "Alright, I see your point. Points. I don't know the answer to all of those problems, except maybe the last one."

"That's a start," Adan said.

Rune nodded. "We need to start with Davi. She's the one I'm supposed to take you to see."

"Davi?"

Rune nodded. "Dr. Davi Kitola, the Old Tech expert I told you about yesterday. I don't think she's part of the lie, but even if she is, she could still answer some of your questions."

"Why don't you think she's part of the lie?"

Rune smiled. "She's Abarran."

Adan couldn't hide his shock. "There's an Abarran here?"

Rune nodded. "She's a more recent addition to our Old

Tech team sent by the Abarran First Explorers Institute."

Adan was shocked. Port Abarra had only existed in his mind so far. It was the idea that a community on the other side of Ateri actually lived the ideals that Bolvar claimed to represent. But the Union would never have its citizens believe that. According to the Committee, Abarrans were decadent and selfish people who only cared about their own enjoyment. And Rune had just told Adan that he could meet an actual Abarran right in that very outpost.

Jenra emerged from behind the canvas wall before Adan could say anything else. "I'm sorry, Rune," she announced.

Rune nodded. "I know. Believe me. This situation is awful, and it kills me to think that I helped things along thinking I was doing good work."

"You are doing good work," Jenra assured him. "You rescued me, Adan, and the rest of us. And now you're going to help us escape again."

Rune smiled. "You're right. I am."

Rune stood from the bed to offer his sister a hug. Garun and Bo both returned from their errands then, followed by a brief, tense moment after they stepped inside the tent, wondering what had happened. Adan looked down and realized he was still holding his weapon. He quickly deactivated it and stuck it back on his hip. "Everything's fine," he said.

Garun and Bo both immediately relaxed.

"Founder's grace," Garun said. "I'm glad that part's over with."

Bo nodded. "Same here. Meanwhile, we were both successful." He held out an armful of clothing he'd managed to get. Garun held up two cloth bags presumably filled with rations.

Rune stood up. "Good. You three secure all that in your packs. While you're doing that, I'll take Adan to see Dr. Kitola. But we're going to have a much different conversation than we'd first planned."

Adan walked over to his pack and set it on the bed. Then he reached into it and pulled out the device Elo had given him. He held it up in front of him. "Besi," he subvocalized. "Is this safe? Are there any trackers or anything on it?"

"Nothing has been added to it beyond its original construction."

Besi was being cryptic as usual. Adan turned and held it out to Jenra. "This needs to be set in the sunlight to charge. Can you find a place for it that won't be seen by anyone else?"

Jenra shrugged, then took it from Adan. "I can try."

Adan nodded. "Good enough." He grabbed his jacket and slipped it on, then turned to Rune. "Should we go?"

"Yeah," Rune replied. "You three be ready," he added for the rest of the squad. "If one or both of us isn't back here in an hour, then we're probably not coming back."

"What do we do if that happens?" Garun asked.

Rune flashed a cryptic smile. "You run. Come on, Adan."

Adan stepped out to follow Rune but Garun grabbed his arm to stop him. "Hold on," Garun demanded as he turned Adan to face him. Then he leaned in and planted his lips on Adan's. Adan suddenly felt his knees go weak, but Garun held him tightly as they passionately kissed one another. For a beautiful moment, Adan forgot about the lies, the deceptions, and their upcoming escape plans. Then the kiss was over. "Sorry. But, if this is the last time I see you, I needed to do that."

Adan smiled sheepishly. "Well, now I'm going to make sure it's not the last time." Then he followed Rune out of the tent.

The pair were silent as they started walking. Adan was very uncomfortable. He felt like he had a sign on his back telling everyone that he knew their big secret. It didn't help that everyone Adan saw had to stare at him. He was the Old Tech Master, after all. The idea that anyone or everyone he saw could also have been part of a grand Union conspiracy led by Commander Sala didn't help things, either.

"So," Rune said, breaking the silence. "You and Garun, eh? Is that new?"

Adan chuckled, happy for the distraction from his paranoid train of thought. "I think it's been brewing for a while. But yes, it's new."

"I see. I guess I somehow thought that you and Bo were–"

"Bo?" Adan laughed. "No, Bo's breeze doesn't blow that way. He's much more interested in your sister."

Rune nodded. "Oh, believe me, I'm well aware of that. I just thought it was some kind of open arrangement."

"No, there's nothing like that. I mean, I love Bo, and he loves me, but only as friends. We've never even kissed."

"Huh. Well, I'm glad to see that you're still finding love amidst all this chaos."

Adan snorted. "I don't know about you, but growing up in Bolvar taught me that you take the good when you get it because you never know when it will come around again."

Rune sighed. "Balda's great brassy ass is that ever true. Now, who's the philosopher?" He grinned at his own joke, then he pointed out a tent slightly larger than the Commander's. "That's Davi's research lab. Are you ready for this?"

Adan nodded. "Yes. I mean, it's not like I have any new ideas about what to do. But, yes."

"I think I've got something. Just follow my lead."

Rune pulled the tent flap open, held it for Adan, and followed him through. The tent's interior looked eerily similar to the lab back in Bolvar, except everything was tan and gray instead of white. The only white in the room was a lab coat worn by the room's sole occupant. They were tall and thin, with broad shoulders and modest curves. Their coarse, black hair was tied back behind their head into a poofy ball, revealing a deep, dark brown complexion. Aside from the lab coat and hair tie, the only other accessory they wore was a pair of black-rimmed glasses.

"Hi, Davi. I brought someone to meet you."

The person in the lab coat looked up and smiled. "Rune! Nice to see you. And you must be Adan."

Adan nodded. "Adan Testa, yes. And thank you for not calling me the Old Tech Master."

Davi laughed. It was a charming tone, and Adan found himself immediately warming to her. "Yeah, well, some of the folks in this camp don't get out much." She set down the equipment she was holding and walked over to stand near Adan. Then she offered him her hand. "I'm Dr. Davi Kitola, but you can call me Davi. And I heard you're a he?" Adan nodded. "And I'm she. Alright." She turned, walked further into the tent, and gestured toward a nearby stool. "Please, have a seat."

"Actually, Davi," Rune interrupted, "there's something we need to talk about first."

Davi looked at him strangely, then nodded. "Alright. Based on your tone, maybe I'll have a seat instead. But, first, this."

She turned around and flipped a switch on a gray metal box sitting on the table. Then she sat on the stool.

Adan looked at Rune, who nodded.

"Besi, I'll need you to monitor Davi's responses for truthfulness," Adan subvocalized. Davi looked at him strangely, and Adan suspected she knew what he was doing.

"Davi," Rune said, getting her attention. "What would you say if I told you that this outpost is secretly a front for a covert Union operation with an unknown agenda?"

Dr. Kitola regarded Rune for a few moments. "I'd ask you how long you've known that and why you've only just now come to discuss it with me."

"I've known about it for less than an hour," Rune replied, then tilted his head toward Adan. "And I'd think the reason I'm discussing it with you is pretty obvious."

The doctor nodded. "Of course. And now you want to know if I'm involved." Then she looked at Adan. "And you have some Old Tech way of divining whether or not I'm telling the truth?"

Adan smiled. "Something like that."

"Alright. My name is Davi Kitola. I'm twenty-eight years old and was born in Port Abarra. I studied at AFEI, or the Abarran First Explorers Institute. Those are all control answers since they're all true, as far as you know. And to answer your implied question, I'm not involved in your Union conspiracy plot. But I figured it out shortly after arriving here. Now, what does your device say?"

"There is a ninety-two percent probability that Dr. Kitola is being truthful about all of her statements except her age. That was a lie."

Adan glanced back at Rune. "She's telling the truth." Then

391

he looked back at Davi. "Except she's not really twenty-eight."

Davi smiled. "Score one for the Old Tech Master," she said with a wink. "Now, that's a static field generator," she added, pointing to the device she'd switched on. "I use it to defeat the listening devices they think I don't know about in the tent. I suspect we've got between ten and thirty minutes before someone from Asona's staff mysteriously comes by to check on us." She nodded toward Adan. "Given your presence, it'll probably be closer to ten. And it might be Asona herself." She stood up and walked around the table to retrieve a large canvas pack.

Adan suddenly felt cold. "There's listening devices in the tents?"

Davi shrugged. "There are definitely some in here. There may be some in your tent, but I don't know. I suspect that if there were any, your Old Tech would've sniffed them out.

Adan sighed with relief. Besi would've noticed for sure.

Davi returned to her table and started putting various items into the pack. "So, what's your plan?" she asked.

Rune shrugged. "My plan ended with talking to you. We're kind of making it up as we go along."

Davi grunted. "What about you, Adan? What do you want?"

Adan was about to suggest that they make their escape from the outpost, then realized what she'd actually asked him. Not what his plan was. She asked what he wanted. He lifted up his sweater to show her the harness and disc. "I want to know why I can use this when no one else can."

Davi nodded. "Good answer. I can help you with that. But not here. So, here's what we'll do. I'm going to switch this device off in a moment. Assume that everything said after that will be overheard. Rune, you'll need to retrieve the others Adan came with. Then meet us at the test range near the west gate. And maybe bring a vehicle."

Rune nodded. "Understood."

Davi switched the device off. "And I can't wait to see how much more you can do. Thanks, Rune. I can take things from here."

"Alright, Davi. See you later, Adan." Rune winked, then turned and casually walked out of the tent.

"And, Adan, I think we need to take these experiments somewhere more appropriate. Somewhere you can really let loose, if you know what I mean? Can you help me out and grab that crate on the floor behind you? It's heavy, so you may need to use your armor to lift it."

She already knew what the armor was. The Commander may have told her about Adan's demonstration the night before. But Adan suspected that she'd known it all along. It was clear that Dr. Kitola knew a lot more than she let on.

Adan activated the armor while Davi watched. It wasn't as impressive as it could've been since he was still wearing a sweater and jacket. But Davi nodded in approval anyhow. Adan turned around, bent down, and lifted the case. He could feel the armor assisting him. The large crate felt like it weighed almost nothing.

Then a voice floated in from outside the tent. "Hello?" Someone parted the tent flap and stepped inside. It was Asona, just as Davi had predicted. "I hope I'm not interrupting anything, Dr. Kitola. I passed by Rune just now, who mentioned Adan was here with you."

Davi smiled at the Commander. "Not at all, Asona. I was just about to take Adan to the test range. I want to put some of this equipment through its paces somewhere that's a little more robust than this tent. Perhaps you'd like to join us?"

Adan was glad he was wearing his helmet, and Asona couldn't see his face. Davi was playing a suddenly dangerous game, and Adan didn't know the rules.

But Asona seemed pleased with the invitation. "If it's no trouble? I know how you don't like anyone looking over your shoulder while you work."

Davi nodded. "That's true. But, in this case, I'll make an exception."

Adan was sure things were being said between he didn't understand. But he didn't want to keep standing there just holding that crate. "So, should we head there now?"

Asona laughed. "Of course, you're excited to see what you can do. Yes, let's. I'll head there now."

"We'll be right behind you," Davi assured Asona as the Commander left the tent. Then Davi slung her pack over her shoulder. "Come along, Adan. It's this way."

"You want me to go out there in my armor?"

Davi nodded. "Yes." she quietly confirmed. "Right now, everyone is curious about you and half-scared. If this is going to work, we need them to be fully scared. Seeing you walk around like one of the First Explorers themselves while carrying a crate that two of them couldn't lift should do nicely."

"Alright. You're the expert."

"That's right," she agreed with a wink.

Private Log of Colony Administrator Clarinda Osoria

Sanyal, 29 January, Year 11 (Neskan Calendar)

After consulting with Marta, I've approved Sander's request to retrieve the missing lander. He was right when he said that his position is the easiest to replace out of all the senior officers. Sander already had a new Security Chief in mind, too. So we made it an official assignment and informed the colonists. The rumors were already flying anyway. Dozens of colonists volunteered to go with him, but Sander had already handpicked his team.

The day they departed almost felt like a party. But it was a bittersweet affair. Sander admitted that his chances for success were slim. He was facing a long journey west with limited equipment and supplies. But I have to admit it's been years since I've seen him look so happy and alive. And he might succeed. Even slim odds are better than none.

Chapter 22

Davi led Adan out of the tent to the packed-dirt track that passed for a road. The pair turned left at the open square and walked west away from the main gate. With his helmet on, Adan could see the second gate that he'd missed when he first arrived. It must've been the west gate that Davi had mentioned earlier. With Besi's aid, Adan could see many things about the outpost that he'd missed before. The armory, for one. It was in a tent the same size as the mess tent and was well stocked for whatever battles the Motari might face. Besi also showed Adan the outpost's underground wiring. The whole outpost was wired for power and communications. And you definitely didn't bother to bury your power lines if you weren't planning on sticking around. Asona and the outpost leadership could still maintain the fiction that the camp was temporary by using tents. But was that fiction meant for outsiders? Or was it there for the Motari who still didn't know they were dancing on the end of a string held by Commander Sala?

Adan glanced over toward Davi and saw nothing but relaxed confidence radiating off her. The way she'd calmly accepted Adan and Rune's clumsy interrogation was impressive. Even invulnerable in his armor, Adan didn't feel that confident. But Davi was older than Adan and from the other side of the continent. She must've earned the confidence she so easily displayed somehow.

"How old are you, anyway?" Adan asked.

Davi chuckled. "I'm really twenty-seven. I thought twenty-eight was close enough to the truth that I might get away with it." She hooked a thumb toward his chest. "But your computer assistant is too sharp for that."

"You mean Besi?"

Davi smiled. "You call it Besi?"

"It stands for Battlefield Enhanced System Intelligence."

"Of course it does. I didn't know that's what your system is called. Not to brag, but I'm probably the foremost Old Tech expert on Neska. And even I know very little. So much of what the First Explorers brought with them was locked away in their digital memories. All I've been able to find is stories and what they managed to commit to paper."

"Why is that?"

Davi snorted. "Don't get me started. That's a subject for another time. If we somehow manage to survive what we're about to pull, then I promise to tell you everything I know. Deal?"

"Deal. So what are we about to pull?"

"Rune's initial report mentioned that the Union had you testing all the Old Tech they possessed. Especially the weapons."

Adan groaned. "Don't tell me–"

"I'm afraid so. But I happen to have a particular weapon that will help us escape while harming the fewest people possible."

"Really? I like the sound of that. I've had to hurt way too many people lately."

Davi glanced over and looked at him. Unlike everyone else who'd tried, she somehow managed to look Adan in the eyes even when she couldn't see them. "Yes. But I suspect that those people wouldn't have gotten hurt if they hadn't tried to hurt you first."

Adan grunted. "I suppose that's true, but–"

"No," she interrupted. "We don't have time for complicated moral examinations, either. It's just what I hope will happen, and I'll explain more when we get to it. But I also have a few things that will do a lot of damage, if it comes to that."

Adan shook his head and sighed. "Founder's mercy. One of these days, I won't have to shoot anyone, Davi."

"You don't have to shoot anyone today, Adan. But then you also wouldn't be able to leave."

"I know."

They approached a large open area on the left side of the road that spanned at least 100 meters. It must've been the testing ground. Adan saw the metal wall and the other gate on the far side. The Commander was standing with Asta near the center of the space. Adan grimaced at the sight of Asta. Was she in on the deception? It made sense that she would be, considering that Elo was, too. That could've even been her out on patrol with him. But Adan hoped it wasn't true. He'd started to like Asta.

The Commander waved at them as they approached. Once

Adan and Davi got close to her, Davi signaled for Adan to set the crate down. Asona shook her head as she marveled at the example of his armor's strength.

"Asta," Asona said, "see if you can lift that crate."

"Commander?"

"Just humor me, please."

Asta nodded. Then she squatted near the crate, grabbed it, and tried to lift it. She managed to pull it back toward her but couldn't get it off the ground. "Sorry, Commander."

But Asona wasn't listening to her. "Astounding. Just astounding. Dr. Kitola, how does something like that work?"

"I can't say for sure until I've had a chance to examine it more closely. But I've read information about electro-muscular bands. They're an artificial material that reacts much like our muscles when an electrical charge is applied. Of course, they're much stronger than our muscles are."

"But where does the charge come from? And how is it applied?"

Davi smiled. "Remember the rule about watching over my shoulder?"

Asona nodded. "Of course, my apologies. I'll let you work."

"Thank you." Davi turned to Adan. "Please remove the lid from the crate. It's only nailed down, so it shouldn't be a problem for you."

Adan nodded. "Of course." He leaned down and grasped the sides of the lid. "Besi, see if you recognize any of the devices in this crate once I have it open." Adan pulled, but the lid didn't move. Only nailed down, eh? He tried pulling harder, which triggered the armor's assistance. The lid ripped from the top. After Adan held it up, he could see the nail points sticking out from the bottom.

399

When he looked down into the crate, Adan recognized some of the items for himself. Two rifles similar to the one he wore lay on top of everything. He also saw a Heavy Ordnance Launcher. But a lot of the devices weren't weapons. Adan spotted a Bio-printer, a Service-printer, and something that looked a lot like the tablet from the museum. Then text labels appeared before him, each one corresponding to a particular item. The weapons were labeled in red, and the general items were blue. Interestingly, one of the devices that looked like something ordinary was labeled in red as an Ion Pulse Generator.

Adan turned and set the lid on the ground. "Besi, I know you've been listening. We're going to make an escape attempt. My friends and Dr. Kitola must be unharmed, if possible."

"I understand. The weapon Dr. Kitola referred to earlier is probably the IPG. But I have devised several strategies for escape using the items in your possession and in the crate. I will advise you as needed."

"Now, Adan," Davi said, "do you recognize any of these?"

Adan nodded. "Yes. Those two are rifles like mine."

"Let's start with those." Davi turned to Asona and Asta. "You both will need to stand well away for your protection. I don't know the condition of these artifacts, and I would hate for either of you to be injured or killed."

Asona looked confused. "Surely that's not a concern?"

"Each of these artifacts is at least five centuries old. I'd be surprised if any of them worked at all. So it's better to be safe than sorry, yes?"

Asona nodded. "Of course."

"You should also inform your patrols that we'll be test-firing weapons so that there isn't any confusion."

400

Asona looked to Asta, who nodded. "On it, Commander." Asta took off running while Asona walked toward the eastern edge of the open area.

"Alright, Adan," Davi said, then leaned in close. "Let's try one of the rifles. And be ready."

"For what?"

"For Rune to make his move."

Adan nodded, then grabbed one of the rifles from the crate. As soon as he got near it, the lights came on. When he picked it up, it assembled itself into the usual rifle shape.

"This is an earlier model than the one you possess," Besi told him. "But it is operational."

Adan fit the butt against his shoulder and pointed the rifle at the metal wall. Then he pressed on the trigger. A white-hot blast shot from the barrel and struck the wall, leaving a scorched, blackened area behind.

"Excellent," Davi commented. "Set that one to the side and grab the other one."

Adan set the weapon down on the lid then reached for the other rifle. Nothing lit up when he got near it, and nothing happened when he picked it up.

"This weapon is damaged," Besi informed him. "I suspect the processor has been wiped."

"It's broken," Adan said aloud.

Davi nodded. "Set it aside, please. Is there another weapon in there besides the big one?"

Adan leaned in and moved a few things around until he spotted a handgun. "Yes, here." He grabbed it and pulled it out while it reassembled itself in his hand.

"Good. I don't know what's taking Rune so long, but I need to keep up the light show until he's ready."

401

"How will you know?"

Davi shrugged. "I've known Rune for as long as I've been here. He's quick and resourceful. I have no doubt he'll come through. Now, the weapon, please."

Adan nodded, then pointed it at the wall. He aimed for the spot he'd hit with the rifle, then pressed the trigger. Another flash and the blast hit the wall.

"I detect unusual activity on the other side of the outpost," Besi said.

Adan turned to Davi. "I think we're about to get our sign."

Davi smiled. "Alright. Very quickly, instruct your Besi to access and activate the Ion Pulse Generator. Set it for maximum dispersal with a sixty-second timer. But don't start the timer until I give the command."

"Do as she asks, Besi."

"Affirmative."

"Alright, Doctor. What next?"

Davi huffed. "It's time for the hole."

"The hole?"

Davi smiled. "Sorry. H-O-L."

Adan nodded. "Ah. If you insist."

He leaned over the crate and reached for the Heavy Ordnance Launcher. Then Besi interrupted him. "First, retrieve the tablet and give it to Doctor Kitola. Tell her that she will need it."

Adan grabbed the tablet and handed it over to her. "Besi says you'll need this."

Davi looked at Adan with confusion but nodded and took it. Then Adan heard shouting. He glanced back at the Commander and saw her looking away, too.

"Hurry, Adan," Davi suggested.

Adan pulled the HOL from the crate and watched it reassemble in his hands. Then he heard the sound of gunfire and looked back again.

"The gate, Adan," Davi implored him.

Adan lifted the HOL to his shoulder, aimed for the gate, and pressed the trigger. The end of the barrel flashed yellow-white, and the gate exploded from its hinges. Then he heard a shout.

"Doctor!"

Adan turned to see Asona, her face red with fury, and watched her pull her sidearm from her waist. It couldn't hurt him, but Davi wasn't so lucky. He dropped the HOL and reached for his pistol when Besi spoke.

"Give me control."

"Take it!"

Suddenly he felt his hand reach out, make a fist, and point toward the Commander. Then the weapon in his arm activated and shot a blue-white pulse directly at Asona. She screamed, then flew back and hit the ground. She didn't move after that.

"What was that?" Davi yelled.

"The weapon only delivered a stun charge," Besi explained. "Your target is not seriously injured."

"I stunned her," Adan explained as the sounds of more gunfire echoed throughout the camp. An engine roared, then the truck Adan rode in the day before tore down the dirt road toward them. Rune was at the wheel.

"Perfect." Davi reached into a pocket and pulled out a small, black device with a red switch on it. She manually extended a slim, silver antenna from the top, then pressed the switch. Adan heard a terrible boom and looked back in shock to see a fireball erupt from within the outpost. Was that Davi's tent?

Davi dropped the device then pointed at the HOL. "Bring that. And start the countdown now."

"Do it, Besi."

"Commencing countdown. You now have sixty seconds to reach the minimum safe distance."

Rune steered the truck into the testing area, aiming straight for Adan and Davi. Then Rune spun the wheel at the last moment, sending the truck into a sliding turn that Adan was afraid might tip it over. But it slid to a stop a couple meters from where he was standing, covering Adan in a cloud of dirt and dust.

Adan heard more gunfire and the ping of a shot hitting the side of the truck. Suddenly he was moving. Besi was still in control. Adan felt Besi move him in front of Davi just as a trio of shots rang out. Each of the shots struck his armor instead of her. Bo leaned out from the back of the truck with a rifle in hand and fired off a few shots. Then Garun jumped out, ran over to Davi, and grabbed her.

"We're taking her?" Garun asked breathlessly.

"Yes," Adan responded.

Garun nodded and quickly led her to the truck. A few more shots rang out, so Adan dropped the HOL and pulled out his sidearm. Then he aimed it at the closest shooter and fired, knocking them down. Another target appeared, so he fired at that, too.

"Adan," Davi shouted as Garun helped her climb into the truck. "Time!"

The countdown. Adan put his handgun away and grabbed the HOL from the ground, then rushed over to the back of the truck. He heard another gunshot, then watched in horror as it struck Garun in the back. Garun stumbled from the impact, so Adan tossed the HOL into the truck and grabbed him.

"Besi, help!"

Adan felt himself crouch, then leap straight over the tailgate onto the truck bed with Garun in his arms.

"Go!" Bo shouted, and the truck peeled into motion.

Jenra took Garun from Adan's arms and laid him down on the truck bed. In a fit of rage, Adan grabbed the HOL and pointed it back at the outpost. A half-dozen armed individuals, including Elo, ran up to the destroyed gate and pointed their rifles at the truck. Adan snarled, squeezed the trigger, and watched the ball of flame explode around them.

"Five seconds," Besi announced.

"Are we safe?"

"You will be."

Suddenly everything went silent, then there was a booming sound like the clang of a giant metal bell. A glowing, blue-white half-dome of lightning appeared inside the outpost and grew until it covered the whole camp. It kept growing, swallowing the ground and sky around it until the glow stopped just meters short of the truck. Then the lightning flashed out and was gone.

Adan stared out from the back of the truck as it sped away from the outpost. But he couldn't see a single thing moving. Did the bomb, or whatever it was, actually work?

Then Garun cried out. Adan dropped the HOL and turned back to find Jenra leaning over him. She pressed a shirt against Garun's shoulder, trying to stop the bleeding. Adan rushed over and knelt down next to him. Garun was cringing with pain, and his skin had a grayish, ashy tone.

"Besi, my helmet."

Adan felt a rush of cool, dusty air as his helmet collapsed back into his armor. Then he reached out and grabbed Garun's hand. "I'm here, Garun. You're going to be okay."

Garun cried out again and squeezed Adan's hand.

Adan turned to Davi. "Can you do anything?"

She shook her head. "Not that kind of doctor, I'm afraid. I don't even have a medkit."

Suddenly Adan remembered that he had one. "Jenra, do you have that device I gave you?"

She nodded. "Yes, it's in my pack. I set it in the sun for a little while, but then this all happened."

Adan turned to Bo. "Can you find it for me?"

Bo nodded, then grabbed a pack from under one of the benches and tore through it. After a moment, he pulled the device out and handed it over. "Here it is."

Adan grabbed it and saw tiny red lights come on. "Besi, tell me this will help."

"It will," Besi replied. "Activating it now."

The device split into several shapes, then reformed with a thick, rectangular head on top of a short handle. One side of the head was covered in silver mesh. The opposite side was a black, glass-like display screen. "Point the device at the injured area. It is not necessary to remove the temporary bandage."

Adan reached over and pointed the mesh head at Garun's shoulder.

"Accessing," Besi said.

The screen activated, and multi-colored words and symbols began to flow across it. Adan was too frantic to read any of them, so he just held the device over Garun.

"Scanning complete," Besi announced. "I am now building a treatment protocol. It will take several seconds."

Hurry, Adan mentally implored the machine brain.

"Treatment protocol prepared. Adan, remove any clothing covering the injured area. You may set the scanner aside for the moment."

Adan turned and handed the device to Davi. After Jenra lifted the shirt bandage from Garun's shoulder, Adan grabbed Garun's sweater. He gently tore the shoulder portion and right sleeve away. Then he did the same for Garun's shirt.

"Take the scanner and point it at the injured area approximately ten centimeters from the skin," Besi instructed him.

Davi handed the device back to Adan, and he did as Besi asked, holding it just over the wound in Garun's shoulder. Suddenly the screen flashed, and a grayish-white mist sprayed down, covering the affected area in thick, gray foam.

"Now, you must do the same thing for the entrance wound," Besi said.

"Someone help me flip him over," Adan called out.

Bo hurried up to Adan's side. Then he and Jenra rolled Garun onto his stomach. Garun thrashed and cried out in pain as they did so, but Adan did his best to ignore that. "Now, hold him still."

Bo and Jenra put their hands on Garun and tried to keep him steady. Then Adan reached out and held the device over the smaller wound where the shot struck him. After a moment, the screen flashed, and the same mist sprayed out, completely covering the wound with grayish foam. Then Garun suddenly stopped thrashing about. Adan panicked, thinking that he'd just killed him until Garun spoke.

"Founder's grace, the pain is gone," he whispered. Adan

almost didn't hear him over the sound of the truck.

"You must now wrap the affected area in a bandage," Besi advised. "Strips of clean cloth will suffice."

Davi smiled. "Now, that I can do." She reached back, picked up one of the shirts Bo had taken from Jenra's bag and tore a long strip from it. Then Davi moved around to Garun's other side. After working the strip under his arm, she wrapped it around once, then twice, before tying the ends together.

"Do I still have to keep lying on my face?" Garun suddenly asked. "These floorboards are filthy."

"You may move him now," Besi confirmed.

Adan reached out and carefully helped Garun flip over, then sit up. Garun flashed a weak smile. The color was already returning to his face.

"I'm sorry, Adan," Garun said. "They told me not to jump out of the truck. But I couldn't just sit here while you needed help."

Adan ran a gloved hand over Garun's cheek. With the gunfight, the strange bomb, and Garun's injury, Adan's feelings were a confusing mess. He didn't know whether he wanted to laugh or cry. "Don't apologize. It's okay. You're going to be alright." Then Adan smiled. "Just don't do it again."

Garun chuckled, then winced. "Oh, okay, the pain isn't entirely gone." He looked at the clean bandage on his shoulder, then at the bloody rag sitting on the truck bed. "What did you do to me?"

"I think I know," Davi claimed. "Those were medical nanites."

"You are correct, Doctor Kitola," Besi confirmed.

Davi nodded. "It's more Old Tech. Nanites are machines

so tiny that they can swim in our blood. Besi, you control them?"

"They control themselves. The scanner builds a genetic profile of the injured party. Then it provides that to the nanites, which repair any damage in the affected area. When the repairs are complete, they deactivate and pass harmlessly from the system."

"That's fascinating," Davi said. "I have so much to learn."

Garun didn't look quite as thrilled. "So I have blood machines inside of me?"

Adan chuckled. "Welcome to my world."

The truck started to slow and eventually came to a stop. Then the passthrough divider slid open, and Rune stuck his head through it. "Hey, so, I just wanted to say that I have no idea where to go at this point."

"That's okay," Davi responded. "I think I do."

Private Log of Colony Administrator Sarita Koskinen

Sanyal, 9 March, Year 35 (Neskan Calendar)

Tomorrow is my final day as Sanyal Community Administrator. After that, the first Neskan born Administrator will take my place. With the crop failure over in Malda and all the construction in Little Creek, they'll have their job cut out for them. Whoever they are.

I met with Dr. Palo today. She confirmed what most of us have suspected since the first generation of Neskans were born. None of our offspring have Colony's gene-lock sequence. Marketta can't explain it since she no longer has the proper equipment. But I'm not sure it really matters, either. Hardly any of the tech we brought with us on the Jennix even works anymore.

Chapter 23

The squad made their camp in a clearing atop a small rise in the ground. It wasn't tall enough to be called a proper hill. But they'd managed to put at least 300 kilometers between them and the outpost before they got there. Rune and Davi estimated that it would be a day, or maybe more, before the Union-backed Motari, or even the Union themselves, would be able to start after them. The Ion Pulse Generator had disabled any electronic systems in the base, and Rune had driven off in their only working vehicle.

Adan felt exposed camping out in the open. But it wasn't like they could hide. The Tepani Plains were so flat that the truck alone marked their position to anyone looking. Since they were near a stand of short, squat Redtail trees, the group gathered some loose branches and started a fire. It was almost warm enough to be unnecessary, but Rune assured them that they'd soon regret it if they didn't. The rations were still cold, but they could boil water for tea, which was nice. So everyone sat around the fire, drinking tea and enjoying the glowing flames.

Everyone except Davi, that is. It turned out that the tablet they'd taken from the outpost wasn't gene-locked like the other Old Tech. It only needed an authorization code, which Besi was able to provide. Davi was so thrilled it almost made her dizzy. After Besi told her how to start a tutorial program, Dave parked herself inside the truck with the glowing tablet in her lap, trying to figure out how to work it. When Rune asked her about where she thought they should go, Davi only answered that she needed to "look a few things up first." In some ways, she was just as cryptic as Besi. Then she shooed him off with a promise to tell everyone in the morning. "Let the kids have a night off," she suggested. "They could use one. We all could."

Adan, for his part, was unwilling to leave Garun's side. To come that close to losing someone he'd just developed feelings for was the scariest thing he'd ever experienced. It was also a good reminder that no one else in the group was invulnerable like he was. But the Old Tech scanner had done its job well. Garun could move his arm a bit after just a few hours. Ordinarily, a wound like that would've killed him out in the middle of nowhere. Even with proper Union medical treatment, his arm would've been in a sling for weeks, if not longer.

Garun didn't seem to mind the attention. That was fortunate because Adan had become a little clingy. He was still careful not to touch Garun too much. Garun had already complained about one of Adan's hugs being too painful. But he still managed to put his good arm around Adan and hold him close while they sat together.

The squad tried to keep the conversation as light and breezy as they could manage. But there was only so much the group could talk about that didn't lead them right back to more pressing matters. Nobody wanted to talk about what had just happened and what led up to it. But they couldn't avoid it forever. So, after one too many awkward topic shifts, Jenra had finally reached her limit.

"Alright," Jenra announced. "I'm calling it. We need to talk about what happened." She turned to Rune. "I know this is uncomfortable for you, but we need to figure out what the deal is with Asona and the Union. You know she's going to come after us."

"Not to mention Sala," Bo added.

Rune sighed and nodded, then took a sip of his tea. "You're right. It just makes me so upset to think about it. What role did I play in their plans without even knowing about it?"

"Well," Adan started, "we know it can't be all about me, right? It seems like this has been going on for longer than they've known about me."

"And they weren't ready for you, either," Garun suggested. "If they had been, then none of this would've happened."

Adan lifted his head from Garun's shoulder to look at him. "What do you mean?"

"There's clearly a connection to Old Tech," Garun answered. "First, there's Sala's secret facility right next to the Old Tech Museum. And there's Davi, at the outpost."

"But she had nothing to do with this," Rune pointed out.

"Not with the conspiracy, no," Garun agreed. "But she was there studying Old Tech. With her own collection and a lab to study it in. There's a connection there. But Adan wasn't part of the plan." Garun looked at Adan. "So, when you showed up, you forced them into action they weren't ready to take."

Adan thought about that for a moment. "Okay, but why all that trouble with orchestrating my escape just to get me to a Motari outpost Sala secretly controlled anyway?"

"Of course!" Jenra suddenly exclaimed. "It's because it's a secret."

Garun grinned and nodded. "Yes! That makes complete sense."

Bo huffed. "Can someone please explain it to those of us who went to school in the Lowers?"

Jenra playfully smacked him. "I went to school in the Lowers, too, you ass. But what I meant was that Sala's secret DFTC lab was secret from us. But the Motari base? That's a secret from everybody."

Suddenly everything came together in Adan's mind. "Are you saying even the Union doesn't know about it?"

Jenra nodded. "Exactly that. The official Committee policy on the Motari is to capture or eliminate them. Along with any so-called raiders. There's no way they'd allow a Defense Force Commander to use a Motari Commander to secretly study Old Tech."

Rune shook his head. "That seems awfully tricky, even for someone like Sala."

"But that's why they had you break Adan out," Jenra argued. "Otherwise, she could've just dumped Adan in a transport and driven him through the gate herself."

"Founder's mercy." Rune shook his head in disbelief. "But she took such a huge risk doing that. Look how close we came to getting turned in by Pavola's rebel crew."

"But did we really?" Adan asked. "They were hardly a match for Besi and the Old Tech weapons."

Bo nodded. "You're right. For all we know, Sala wanted a chance to see what Adan could do in the wild. I mean, she was already willing to lose her secret lab, not to mention one of her top Chiefs?"

"And she knew that we'd probably face Gray Coats on our way to the outpost, too," Adan added.

"Still," Rune objected, "it was a big risk."

"That's what I meant about forcing her to move," Garun replied. "It's like Tik-Tix when you misjudge your opponent's counters, thinking they're going for the spread, but they play a spinner."

Bo smiled. "So you drop whatever you have on the board and hope for the best."

Rune nodded. "Okay, you may be right about that. You have a scary mind for this sort of thing, don't you?"

"I'm only a couple steps removed from a Committee Member," Garun explained. "Don't let their appearances fool you. They're always jostling for power in Bolvar House."

"And why would a Commander who wants power be any different?" Jenra asked.

"Exactly," Garun agreed.

"So, who do you think was involved at the outpost, Rune?" Jenra asked.

"Obviously, Asona, Elo, and Asta," Rune answered. "Balda's ass, but Elo recruited me himself. Obviously not for my loyalty to the Union."

"But it's still a Motari outpost, isn't it?" Adan asked. "So they still need to have actual Motari there."

"You would think so," Rune answered. "But the Motari outposts and cells are very separate from each other. The leaders, like Asona, all meet with each other. But each outpost and operation is run independently. That way, if one cell gets broken by the Pinchers or Gray Coats, it doesn't compromise any of the others."

Garun grunted. "I hate to say this, but I'm starting to think the Motari aren't real."

Rune looked at him in shock. "Listen, kid, I can assure you that—"

Garun shook his head and interrupted. "No, no, that's not what I meant. Of course, you're really doing Motari stuff. It's just, if this outpost is compromised, what's to say they all aren't?"

Rune started to reply but stopped. Then he shook his head. "Alright, that's a possibility. But we've got no facts to back it up. Besides, the real issue isn't whether or not the Motari are real. It's that there are factions inside the Gray Coats."

Garun frowned. "Yeah. That's not something even I would suspect."

Adan nodded. "The Gray Coats I overheard said something about the regular force."

"Which implies the existence of an irregular force," Jenra added.

Adan scowled. "So one part of the Gray Coats, the part led by Commander Sala, is selling out the part of the Gray Coats hunting the Motari just so she can protect her Motari puppets."

Bo huffed. "Damn. Just thinking about that does my head in."

Adan felt the same way. He tilted his head up again and looked at the night sky. Even with the light from the campfire, the dark sky was alive with sparkling stars. There were no treetops overhead to block the view, either. At some point, five centuries ago, someone from the First Explorers' ship had looked up at that sky for the first time and noticed how strange it looked. And, as scary as it must've been, they still told themself that it didn't matter because they were there to stay.

Then Adan felt Garun yawn and realized how tired he was, too. Adan looked back at the group to see Jenra and Bo quietly talking.

"It may be time to call it a night," Adan said.

Garun nodded. "Definitely. All that strategic thinking used up whatever energy I had left."

Rune stood up and stretched. "I think I'm ready to turn in for the night. Do you all want to set up your tents out here, or do you want to sleep in the truck?"

After some discussion, the four of them decided to sleep in their tents while Rune would sleep in the back of the truck. Rune went to check in on Davi while the others retrieved their packs, then set up the pair of tents they had. After designating and using a toilet area on the other side of the small stand of trees, everyone was zipped up in their sleeping bags. But Adan decided to change things up since Garun was still injured. So he lay down and pulled Garun into his arms.

"I could get used to doing it this way," Garun shared. "This is nice."

Adan chuckled. "Oh, no, you don't. We trade off. It's only fair."

Garun snuggled himself closer to Adan's chest. "Alright. But not tonight."

Adan ran his hand through Garun's hair, then caressed Garun's cheek. "No. Not tonight."

They lay that way quietly for a while. Adan's mind was still racing from everything that happened that day. But Garun started snoring after just a minute or two. Adan understood. Even with the miraculous Old Tech scanner, Garun was still seriously injured. That took a lot out of a body. So Adan just held him while he waited for his mind to finally give up and quiet down.

Coming that close to losing Garun had done a number on Adan. Some things suddenly seemed a lot clearer to him. If none of the Old Tech stuff had happened and they were still back at the DFTC, Adan was pretty sure things still would've developed between them. But they would've gone much slower. And each of them would've been more cautious. How long would it have taken for Garun to lay sleeping wrapped in Adan's arms? More than a handful of days, certainly.

Was he making a mistake by acting on his feelings? Adan didn't doubt that he felt things for Garun. But he knew he didn't have to act on those feelings, either. He'd had plenty of crushes on people before and done nothing about it. Adan thought back to when he first started to crush on Bo and almost laughed. That felt like an entire lifetime ago. And Adan could break things off with Garun now if he needed to. It would hurt both of them in the short term, but it might make things easier down the road.

But Adan wouldn't do that. If he'd wanted to take the easy road, he would've turned Rune in back at the DFTC and been done with it. And that had never been a question for him. No, he would just have to watch out for Garun, Bo, and Jenra. They would be his responsibility to protect for as long as he was with them. And also Rune. And Dr. Kitola, too. It wouldn't be easy, but Adan could do it. He would just have to do better than he did that day.

Sleep must've come for Adan soon after that because the next thing he remembered was Garun untangling himself from Adan's arms and getting up.

"Sorry," Garun whispered when he realized Adan was awake. "I've really got to piss."

Adan smiled and nodded. "No worries."

Garun smiled back, then crawled out of the tent. Warm, rosy light filtered through the tent material, so it must've been morning. Adan stretched to loosen up his stiff muscles. Even wearing the harness all night, he'd slept well enough. He'd have to take it off to change and wash up, but he planned on keeping it close at all times until he knew everyone was safe.

"Is anyone on their way to attack us, Besi?"

"I detect no signs of possible attack within my sensor radius."

"How far is that?"

"My active sensors can reach up to two kilometers under the appropriate conditions."

That wouldn't be a lot of warning, but it was better than nothing. And, out in Tepani, Adan could see much farther than that anyway. "It's too bad they can't reach farther."

"I would require a satellite uplink to access the Neskan orbital sensor grid."

Adan suddenly sat upright. "Are there any satellites in orbit right now?"

"Unknown. It is unlikely given the amount of time since they were placed there. But I have been disconnected from the InfoNet for too long. And that is too far for me to detect."

Adan almost asked what the InfoNet was but realized he already knew. He'd read about it in the First Explorer's book.

To connect Besi to the InfoNet and possibly a satellite, he would need a node and an uplink. "Where is the nearest node?"

"I do not have that information."

Interesting. Usually, Besi was full of answers. Maybe Davi would know something. Adan pulled the sleeping bag off and crawled out of the tent. The chill in the morning air was refreshing after sleeping in all his clothes and boots. The sky had a lovely pink hue to it. When he looked east at the Osbaks, he could see the first hints of Pamu about to climb over the mountain tops.

"Adan!"

He turned to see Dr. Kitola approach him from the truck. She must've slept in the cab. Adan waved. "Good morning. Davi. I was just going to come look for you."

"Really? What about?"

Adan laughed. "But you were looking for me, right?"

Davi nodded. "I was, but I'm curious now."

"I was going to ask you about InfoNet nodes and if you knew where one was?"

Davi smiled and shook her head. "I have to say, you never fail to surprise me, Adan Testa. The fact that you even know about the InfoNet is impressive."

Adan shrugged. "I read about it. The DFTC Library has a copy of the First Explorers' official logs from landfall."

Davi nodded. "Ah, of course. I'm just impressed you bothered to read it. It feels like most people aren't interested in that anymore."

"Do you know where any InfoNet nodes are, Doctor?"

Davi shook her head. "Officially? No. But I can think of one place where we might find one that still works. And

420

that tablet Besi had you give me is full of the most amazing things!" She looked at the rest of the camp, then back at Adan. "Let's get everyone up and give them some tea. Then we can talk about where we need to go next."

"And where's that?"

Davi smiled. "Get the others." Then she hurried off.

Adan huffed with frustration. Then, after visiting the designated toilet area, he gathered everyone around the fire pit. The fire had gone out, so Rune used his camp stove to boil water for tea. Adan tore into a ration bar while he waited for Davi to finally share her discovery. He'd finished most of it and most of his tea when she finally said she was ready.

"Here's what we're facing," Davi began. "Adan can activate and use Old Tech, which no one else has been able to do for hundreds of years. The Union, and especially Commander Sala, want to use Adan to figure out how they can use Old Tech, too. But they don't have the equipment for that. And neither do we."

"We know all that," Rune countered. "So, what have you found?"

"One of the First Explorers from the Jennix bridge crew was convinced that he'd found the location of the missing Jennix lander. He even led an expedition to retrieve it. But that expedition never returned."

"That's right!" Adan exclaimed. "Sander Varis led that expedition. Everyone assumed they'd all died."

Davi nodded. "It's likely that they did. And many others have looked for it since then, but none have been successful."

Rune scoffed. "Of course not. That's like trying to find a barge in the middle of the ocean. It would take pure luck."

"Or," Davi suggested, "it would take someone who can

operate Old Tech and follow the original trail."

Everyone sat in silence for a few moments while they considered what Davi was implying. It seemed foolish to Adan. How could they possibly succeed where even the First Explorers had failed? But the more he thought about it, the more he warmed up to the idea.

"So, where should we start?" Adan asked.

Then Davi flashed Adan her mysterious smile. "The same place they did, of course. Broken Valley."

Map of Neska

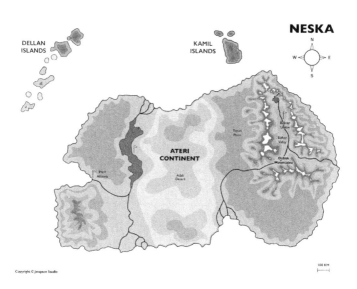

Copyright © Jenspace Studio

100 KM

Bo & Adan

Acknowledgment

I can hardly believe that what started as an idea while walking with my partner is now a published book! Thanks to Robert, José, Eric, Ryan, and Jetspace Studio for their invaluable aid in getting this work off the ground and onto the page. Thanks also to the early reviewers for their kind words and helpful feedback.

About the Author

Owen Lach (he/him) is a queer artist, gamer, and best-selling author who lives in the PNW. He loves to write queer stories. Especially YA fiction and science-fiction, that's also queer. When he's not writing, Owen enjoys reading books from queer, femme, trans, and POC authors, watching anime, or playing video games.

You can connect with Owen at:
🌐 https://lachwrites.com

Printed in Great Britain
by Amazon

40775669R00245